Anne Melville is  novels including *The House* ... *The Lorimer Line*, *The Lorimer Legacy* and *Lorimer Loyalties* amongst them). The daughter of the author and lecturer Bernard Newman, she was born and brought up in Harrow. She was a scholar of St Hugh's, Oxford, where she read Modern History, and after graduating taught and travelled in the Middle East. She and her husband now live in Oxford.

By the same author

The Lorimer Line
The Lorimer Legacy
Lorimers at War
Lorimers in Love
The Last of the Lorimers
Lorimer Loyalties
The House of Hardie

ANNE MELVILLE

Grace Hardie

This edition published 1993 by
Diamond Books
77-85 Fulham Palace Road
Hammersmith, London W6 8JB

Copyright © Margaret Potter 1988

Set in Times
Printed and bound in Great Britain by
BPCC Paperbacks Ltd
Member of BPCC Ltd

CONTENTS

CONTENTS

PART ONE

A House for Grace Hardie
1898–1900

1

On a day of Indian summer in 1898 Richard Beverley, Marquess of Ross, travelled to Oxford to see his great-grandchildren for the first and last time.

As the carriage approached Magdalen Bridge he knocked with his stick to indicate that the coachman should bring the horses to a halt. He had given no notice of the visit, and an unexpected guest was under no obligation to be punctual. After the footman had lowered the step and helped him down, he stood for a moment on the pavement without moving, leaning heavily on his stick until he was sure that his balance was steady.

Even so early in the evening a mist was rising from the river, stroking Magdalen's tower with wispy white fingers. The wandering scholars of the Middle Ages who came to rest in Oxford chose for the home of their new university a place surrounded by water, dank and unhealthy, an area of swamps and fevers. The marquess, who as a young man in the eighteen-thirties had spent four riotous years at Christ Church, remembered his undergraduate days as a period of golden sunshine; but he was old enough to recognize that such memories were created by youthful high spirits and energy, not by climate.

Now he could feel the dampness of the air attacking his bones, and see its chill turning his breath into plumes of mist. It would not do for him to remain long in the city. To a man in his eighty-sixth year, danger came in many disguises.

At a good steady pace he stomped across the bridge, the tapping of his stick echoed by the hooves of the carriage horses just behind him. He walked past Magdalen and past Queen's before halting to stare across the High at a row of three shops. A tailor, a wine merchant, a tobacconist. As an undergraduate he had been in debt to them all, and had for forty years or more afterwards continued to patronize their London establishments.

One year he had given up tobacco for Lent and, finding himself the better for it, had never placed another order. More recently, taking note that he had more than enough clothes to last him for the rest of his life, he had also ceased to call at Savile Row.

Wine was a different matter. Although he himself drank little but brandy these days, he regarded it as an obligation to buy the best of the new vintages each year and lay them down for his sons. But no longer from The House of Hardie. It was The House of Hardie which had robbed him of his heart's delight.

'Pretentious rubbish!' he muttered to himself, studying the mock-gothic letters above the unrevealing dark green glass of double bow windows. The House of Hardie, indeed! A shop that had been in business since 1710 was still, in 1898, only a shop.

A family of tradesmen might hand down expertise and commercial good sense through six generations. They might become prosperous, and well-respected within their own social circles. But they remained where they had begun – in trade. When a girl of good family, a Beverley, eloped with the son of her grandfather's wine merchant, society was right to be scandalized. The girl's brother was justified in refusing to allow her any share of the estate left by their parents. And the girl's grandfather was in honour bound to close his account with The House of Hardie.

It was less easy, though, to rule off affection. Ten years had passed since he last saw Lucy, and he had never in word or deed recognized the existence of any of her children. But silence and neglect could not kill his love. A few days earlier, giving orders for the planting of a new chestnut avenue at Castlemere, he had been startled by a new thought. For eighty-five years he had enjoyed almost unbroken good health. It was, nevertheless, possible that he would not live for ever. He wanted to see Lucy again before he died.

In his youth the marquess had fathered three sons – blond babies who grew up to be wild boys before maturing imperceptibly into sober middle age and grey-haired dignity; the future marquess, a general, and a dean. Sons to be proud of, if he had ever thought to consider the matter. But it was his daughter Rachel who had been his darling for all the twenty-three years of her life.

He had allowed her to marry one of her brother's fellow-officers for love, making a handsome settlement so that she could continue to travel and dance and hunt and look beautiful in the style to which she was accustomed. And when, only three years after the wedding, she died giving birth to her second child, the pain of his loss stunned him, so that for many months he could hardly bear to mix with anyone who was happy.

But the baby, Lucy, survived to be his only granddaughter. As golden-haired as her mother, impulsive and extravagantly generous in her love, she warmed his heart into life again. The two motherless children were brought up at Castlemere while their father continued his military career, and they remained there after his death. It was at Castlemere that the trouble had begun.

The marquess recognized his own contribution to the disastrous events of 1887. He had summoned his wine merchant, John Hardie, to inspect the cellar books and advise on new purchases. The two men had known each other for twenty years. It did not seem an impertinence when Hardie's son, attending with his father to note what was decided, enquired whether he might be permitted afterwards to inspect the herb garden for which Castlemere was famous. The young man, it appeared, although destined one day to inherit his father's business, had a passionate interest in botany.

From that moment on, everything had happened at breakneck speed. It was not surprising that young Gordon Hardie, catching sight of Lucy as she painted in the herb garden, should have thought her the most beautiful girl in the world, because this was undoubtedly the case. But neither the marquess nor his grandson Archie, Lucy's brother, ever discovered exactly how the two young people had contrived to further their acquaintance. In no time at all, it seemed, Lucy was demanding that she should be allowed to marry Gordon Hardie.

Naturally, permission was refused. The marriage was unsuitable on all counts. Besides, she was proposing to accompany this headstrong young man on a journey of exploration to Central Asia to look for new seeds and plants, or some such rubbish. It was a preposterous plan for a young woman brought up with every comfort wealth could buy. Archie, as his sister's guardian, laid down a decisive veto, making it clear that if she were to defy him she need never expect to see her family again, nor to receive a penny piece from them as long as she lived. He appealed for his grandfather's support in this declaration and was given it.

The marquess did not expect, as he nodded in agreement, that he was pledging himself never to see his favourite grandchild again. He assumed that when she found the two men she most respected to be united in their disapproval, she would see sense and abandon her fantasies in favour of a London season.

Five weeks later Lucy ran away from home. The marquess had not seen her since. The letter in which she informed him of her marriage was posted in Shanghai. A later letter, announcing the birth of her son, had been written with pride when she should have been ashamed and apologetic, and her grandfather had been too hurt and angry to answer.

Other babies followed: a second son, twin boys, a girl. He reminded himself that The House of Hardie was a thriving business; and on the death of John Hardie in his fifties, his only son had become its proprietor. Nevertheless, it was difficult to dismiss from the imagination a picture of a harassed young woman with five children tugging at her skirts. Her brother, it was certain, would never speak to her again. But an old man might be excused his moment of sentimentality. The Marquess of Ross had come to Oxford to forgive Lucy for the pain she had caused him. And perhaps to say goodbye.

Half an hour later, standing with his legs apart in front of the drawing room fire, the marquess stared at his grand-daughter with an intentness which made her flush. Like all the Beverley women she was golden-haired and very tall. She had been a beautiful girl who should by now have matured into an elegant woman; but instead her appearance was dishevelled. He had to remind himself that she had not expected a visitor; and it appeared that she had been playing with her sons when the doorbell rang.

'When do you expect your husband home?' he asked, after the first startled and awkwardly restrained moments of reunion were over. He had no wish for a meeting with Gordon Hardie.

'In five or six months.' Lucy laughed to see that her grandfather had not expected such an answer. 'He's gone back to China. Our expedition together was a great success, you know. One of the lilies he found was awarded a

13

gold medal. And his work on the propagation of new rhododendron species has been much praised. He was invited to return and explore the higher valleys, and to bring back an even greater variety of rhododendron seeds.'

'So that's what all your dreams of excitement have come to!' growled the marquess. 'Your husband has all the adventures while you sit at home alone.'

'With five young children –' began Lucy, but her grandfather interrupted her.

'Oh yes, yes, of course. You can't go gadding about any longer: no need to explain that. But anyone could have told you that's what would happen. You wouldn't listen, though, would you?'

'If I had stayed at Castlemere,' said Lucy, her voice quietened by self-restraint. 'If I had then married the son of some suitable duke, I might still be the mother of five children today – living more luxuriously, perhaps, but still bound by all the restraints of society. And then I should never have had those two years in the mountains. Travelling so far; experiencing so much. What I saw and learned during that expedition with Gordon is something that I have in my memory for the rest of my life, something I could never have found in England or Europe – something that no one will ever be able to take away.'

She stood up and took a turn up and down the room before facing her grandfather again. 'I'm sure that you and Archie were sincerely trying to protect me when you forbade me to marry Gordon,' she said. 'And I understand that you were hurt as well as angered by my disobedience. I was sorry to lose your love as well as Archie's, Granda, because I hoped perhaps . . . but then, I know that the family is more important than any single member of it. What I'm trying to say –' She needed to struggle with the words before looking him full in the face. 'You and Archie had the right to be angry with me, and unforgiving. I shall never complain about that. But you are not to be *sorry* for me, because I have a husband whom I love and who loves me. And five dear, loving children. And now that I've seen my darling Granda again, I'm the happiest woman in the world.'

The marquess studied her flushed face in silence. He didn't believe her claim to be happy, but he approved of the courage with which she made it. She had chosen her own life, and it was right that she should hold her head high in defending her choice. He held out a hand and at once she was in his arms.

They were interrupted by the arrival of her four sons in the drawing room. Their sleekly brushed hair, scrubbed and polished cheeks and identically neat sailor suits made it clear that the past half hour had been a busy one on the nursery floor. Like a monarch inspecting his troops the marquess passed along the line, acknowledging introductions.

'This is Frank.' The eldest boy, seven years old, was the only one of the four to have inherited the thick golden hair with which most Beverley children were born. He was a sturdy, pleasant-faced lad, who put out his hand to be shaken with an almost military precision.

'Philip.' Philip was dreamier, staring at his great-grandfather with a slightly anxious intensity, as though trying to calculate what the importance of this unexpected visit might be. Perhaps he had not known of the marquess's existence until that evening.

'Kenneth and David.' The four-year-old twins were not identical. Kenneth, brown-haired and freckled, fidgeted restlessly, looking down at the carpet, whilst David stared steadily at the visitor with dark, intelligent eyes. His hair was very dark as well: almost black. Hardie hair, Hardie eyes.

The marquess grunted his acknowledgement of the

15

introductions, asking each of the four no more than a polite ration of questions. He had no great interest in small boys and nothing he wished to say to them. It was a relief when their mother told them that they could go.

'There's another one,' he said when he and Lucy were alone together once more. 'A girl.'

'Grace. Yes. She's in bed. Not very well. Would you like to see her?'

'Might as well, while I'm here.' He followed his granddaughter up two flights of stairs, pausing at the first landing window to catch his breath while pretending to study the view. The grounds of the house, he saw, sloped down to the river – it must be the River Cherwell here, rather than the Thames. No wonder the place smelt damp and musty. But Lucy had paused to wait for him. He hauled himself up the narrower stairs which led to the children's floor.

A fire was burning in the nursery. The nurse who had been sitting beside it rose with a rustle of skirts as Lucy opened the door and led the way across the room.

The marquess looked down at his sixteen-month-old great-granddaughter. A pair of round black eyes looked back at him. They were bright, lively eyes – their darkness emphasized by the pallor of her face.

Even if he had not been able to see her ill-health, he could hear it, for she was fighting for each breath, gasping to gulp in the air before wheezing it out again. Seeing a stranger, she tried to sit up in her cot, but was imprisoned by the tightly-tucked blankets. The effort made her cough and her little hands pushed at the bedclothes as she tried to free herself. But she was smiling at him even through her struggles.

'Lie still, there's a good little girl,' said the nurse; but the marquess shook his head, disapproving of the instruction.

'She'd be more comfortable sitting up. Pillows behind her, that's what she needs.' He loosened the blankets

16

himself, and reached out with the intention only of raising the child into a sitting position. But Grace, seeing his hands stretched towards her, held out her own arms, smiling. Much to his own surprise, the marquess picked the little girl up and held her.

Now, so close, he could hear the bubbling and wheezing with which each breath fought its way through her chest. He lifted her higher, to lie over his shoulder, so that her head hung down and her arms dangled towards the ground. With one hand he held her legs, while the other stroked her back, pressing it gently but firmly.

For a moment or two her coughing increased and she panted even faster for breath. But within moments she was calm again. The marquess was conscious of her small body relaxing into confidence and contentment. Yet even in the rigidity of her struggle for breath, he realized, she had not been frightened. She was a fighter; too young to understand that there were moments when it was better not to struggle but to lie back and wait for easier times.

The nurse, although disapproving, had piled up pillows in accordance with his instructions. Stiffness made it hard for him to bend easily, but the marquess did his best to be gentle as he set the little girl back in her cot and covered her warmly but loosely with the blankets.

Lucy, he noticed, had tactfully turned her back and was holding the nurse in conversation, as though guessing that he might not wish to be discovered in a gesture of sentimentality. Leaning over, he kissed his great-granddaughter on the forehead. Then, with a nod to the nurse, he made his way down to the drawing room again.

'Didn't like the sound of that chest,' he said to Lucy. 'Had the doctor, I suppose?'

'Yes. He doesn't seem able to do anything. We should try mountain air, he said last time he came. When Gordon gets home again –'

17

'He should be home now. What does he think he's doing, leaving you with all the responsibility of a sick child?'

'He doesn't know.' Lucy's chin tilted upwards with the firmness which he remembered from her youth as she turned to look straight at him. 'He left England seven months before Grace was born.'

'Didn't you tell him of your condition?'

'I was hardly sure myself. And this expedition meant so much to him. It would all have been spoilt if he'd had to ask himself whether he should still go, or how long he should stay. He needs to remain in his collecting area for several seasons, so that he can find plants when they're in flower and return later to collect the seeds. The journey itself is so long and difficult. Reaching Shanghai is only the beginning. The western areas of China, near the border with Tibet, are almost inaccessible, but that's where he has to travel. And then he must establish a base and organize his various expeditions – to go for anything less than two years would be useless. It's best, really, for him to be away for almost three. I understood that from the moment we first discussed it.'

'But when your circumstances changed . . . By now, surely, he must know that he has another child.'

Lucy's eyes remained steady, refusing to accept any criticism either of her own behaviour or of her husband's. 'By now he may perhaps know,' she agreed. 'But I didn't make any mention of the baby until Grace was six months old. Even then I could only write to the agent in Shanghai and hope that he has a forwarding address. I made it clear in my letters that I wanted Gordon to finish his programme. To make the important seed collections this autumn. I told him that everything was going well here.'

'That was hardly the truth.'

'What good would it do to worry him, at such a distance?'

18

cried Lucy. 'And even if he were at home . . . We can't just pack up and go off to Switzerland, not all of us; and Grace is too young to send anywhere on her own.'

'There must be something in between. This house is damp. I can feel it in my bones. The whole city is damp. A few hundred feet could make all the difference. Higher air, a different aspect. Seems to me, Lucy, if you stay here, you're going to lose her.'

Lucy knew that already. He could see her eyes mist with tears that she would not allow herself to shed in front of him. Turning away, pretending not to notice, he called back into his memory that first glimpse of the child in her cot. It was possible, he supposed, that the brightness of her dark eyes was an indication of fever rather than of a lively intelligence, but there had been an outgoing cheerfulness in her look which impressed him.

She was not, admittedly, a beautiful child. Her black hair had framed a pale complexion, bearing no resemblance to the blonde, rosy beauty of her mother and grandmother in their infancies. But the feel of her small warm body on his shoulder, rigid at first before relaxing into confidence and sleepiness – even the smell of her reminded him of the two little girls he had loved earlier in his life. In appearance she might be a Hardie, but a few drops of Beverley blood must flow in her veins. And it would be enough if he could banish the anxiety from her mother's eyes.

He laughed without explanation as he turned to face Lucy again. Years ago his father had said to him, 'In every generation there's one Beverley who goes off the rails.' Lucy, without doubt, had been the member of her generation to show a lack of good sense. The marquess had never expected that he himself would act irrationally, but the thought growing in his mind was not one of which any other member of the family would approve.

He had promised never to make any present to Lucy.

He regretted the promise, but did not intend to break it. Still, there would be no breach of honour if he were to help one of her children. The boys, as far as he could tell, were intelligent and healthy; they could look after themselves. Little Grace Hardie, small and vulnerable, was the one at risk.

What would become of her, if she lived? It had seemed easy enough to foretell a future for his daughter and granddaughter when they were in their cradles. They were destined to marry men of good breeding and then, as the wives of aristocrats, to become the mothers of aristocrats. On such sure foundations did the stability of society rest.

Yet both his certainties had crumbled into misfortune. Rachel had died young and Lucy had eloped. Her daughter was a tradesman's daughter, without expectations. If she was to make anything of her life, she would have to do it for herself, and it was hard to imagine how she would set about it in the future. But one thing was certain. If she were to be brought up in Oxford's mists and miasmas, she was unlikely to have any future at all.

'Get her out of here,' he said abruptly. 'Out of this swamp of a city. Find yourself a piece of land on a hill. Fast. While she and I are still alive. No need to worry about money. You'll be hearing from my lawyers. Build her a house.'

2

Four months after the death of the Marquess of Ross, two weeks after Gordon Hardie's return to England and less than an hour after the end of term, Midge Hardie hurried to catch the Oxford train at Paddington. Her pupils would have been startled to see the athletic speed with which she moved, for within the school which she ruled as headmistress, Miss Hardie was regarded with awe.

Whether taking morning assembly, presiding over a staff meeting or pressing her views upon the board of governors, Miss Hardie's appearance when on the school premises was severe. Her petite figure and lack of inches – for she was only just over five feet tall – in no way detracted from her dignity. The dark hair strained off her face was plaited into neat coils; her tightly-fitted jackets and long skirts were invariably black in the winter and grey in the summer, worn with a high-necked white blouse. The girls could not imagine her dressed in any other style; nor could they believe that she had ever been young.

Yet in 1899, six years after being appointed to her present post, Miss Hardie was only thirty-four years old. Each evening, when her day's work was over, the gown into which she changed was likely to be as bright in colour as it was fashionable in style: greens and reds were her favourites, and she never wore black out of school. She accepted invitations to dances as readily as to dinners. When invited to stay with friends, she took her skates or tennis racquet with her, according to the season; and when, in each school holiday, she returned to her old home in Oxford to spend a week with her brother's family, it was not as a disciplinarian but as the laughing Aunt Midge who was determined to spoil her niece and nephews and to beg for their company on bicycle rides.

Her welcome in the summer of 1899 was as boisterous as ever. All five children were waiting to greet her, for little Grace was as lively as her brothers now, and beginning to chatter. A good deal of hugging and kissing and the distribution of small presents took place before at last Midge turned half apologetically to her sister-in-law.

'Would Gordon mind, do you think – would *you* mind – if I were to call at the shop? It's been such a long time. Three years. To wait another four hours to see him seems unbearable.'

'He'll be delighted,' Lucy assured her. 'Would you like to take the pony cart?'

'Gracious, no. I'll go by bicycle and be back for tea. It's just to say hello. I shan't expect him to tell me the complete story of his adventures.'

She set off at once on the machine that was stored at Oxford for her and oiled in readiness for each visit. The streets of the university city always made her feel young again. As a twenty-year-old student she had walked this way, along Longwall Street, every Monday morning in term – prepared for a history coaching but dreaming of the young man whom she might, if she were lucky, meet again outside her tutor's door. Archie Yates was Lucy's brother, and often when Midge remembered with shame what had happened in his rooms in Magdalen, she found herself glad that he had refused to speak to his sister since her elopement with Gordon Hardie. The stone walls of the college might remind Midge of those salad days, but she would never have to endure the embarrassment of facing Archie again.

A different encounter awaited her, however, before she could greet her brother. As she turned into the High

Street, kicked a pedal down to steady her bicycle against the kerb and opened the door of The House of Hardie, Will Witney rose to greet her, a grin of pleasure on his freckled face. Will had been in love with her for thirteen years.

'How well you look!' Midge exclaimed as she shook hands. During Gordon's long absence it was Will, as manager, who had taken charge of the Hardies' family business, and the hard work and responsibility had given him an anxious appearance. But it seemed that his employer's return had restored his cheerful spirits. Beneath a shock of bristly red hair, his face was flushed with good health. He had the strong body of an athlete: only when he moved did his limp betray a leg crushed in boyhood.

Whilst well aware of his feelings, Midge saw no reason to let them spoil a friendship. She had told him long ago that she would have to choose between marriage and a teaching career, and the governors who appointed her to her present post had made it clear that a married headmistress would be unacceptable. But in all honesty she had to admit to herself that the choice had not been too difficult. She had liked Will from the moment of their first meeting, enjoying his conversation and his company. But she had never felt for him the kind of overwhelming love which might have tempted her to waste her education and abandon her ambition. Occasionally she wished that he would find someone else to marry, so that she need not feel guilty at depriving him of a family life. At other times she delighted in the warmth of his greeting, and her eyes sparkled with as much pleasure as his own.

'Mr Hardie has an outside appointment,' Will told her. He would not use his employer's Christian name in the presence of the counter clerks. 'But he may not have left yet. I'll send someone out to see.'

Midge sat down to wait as the messenger set off at a run

23

for the warehouse. Within only a few moments her brother burst through the door. 'Midge!'

'I couldn't wait,' she told him. 'It's so good to see you safely back after such a long time. But I won't keep you if you have a meeting arranged.'

'The appointment is with an architect. I hope to persuade him to design a house for us. We're due to meet at the site.' Gordon looked at her bicycling clothes and sturdy footwear with approval. 'I propose to go there by bicycle for the exercise. Ever since I returned home I've been sitting at a desk. Would you care to come too?'

'Certainly I would.' They set off together across Magdalen Bridge and took the old road leading towards London. Although Midge was fit, the steepness of the hill which led up towards Shotover proved too much for her. Gordon dismounted to walk at her side.

'Did Lucy tell you about the land?' he asked.

'Lucy had no time to tell me anything. I came straight to see you.'

'It's a gift from the old marquess. That's to say, he gave the money to buy it.'

'Lucy told me that they'd been reconciled before he died, and that he'd been very generous.'

'His generosity was actually directed at Grace. Don't know why. The old man set up a trust fund. All the money has to be spent within three years on buying or building a house which will become Grace's sole property on her twenty-first birthday. Lucy and I and the boys will be graciously allowed to live in it until then!'

His tone of voice was light enough, but Midge could guess that he found it humiliating to have been excluded from managing his daughter's affairs.

'So you'll have to shoulder all the running costs?'

'There's no problem there,' said Gordon. 'The House of Hardie can afford to keep the family in greater style than any of us has ever bothered about. The only thing that annoyed me was that Lucy wasn't allowed to wait for my return before buying the land. Her grandfather sent his land agent to help her choose, but I'm not sure, all the same, that she's got it right. We'll have to see what the architect says.'

By now they had left behind them the stone walls and cottages of Headington Quarry, and arrived in unspoiled country. The old road continued up to the summit of Shotover Hill, but Gordon indicated that they should turn right along a rough track.

'This first stretch of woodland belongs to one of the colleges,' he said. 'But the bridlepath is a public right of way, and leads us to our boundary here.' He leaned his bicycle against a stone wall, next to a five-barred gate.

Midge followed his example and studied the land in front of them with interest. A wide swathe of neglected woodland clothed the lower slope of the hill. So thick was the undergrowth and so rampant the brambles and ivies which clung to every tree that it was impossible to see more than a few yards in that direction. On the other side, looking up the hill, the view was more open. The ground near the gate was overgrown with scrub, but as it rose higher it opened into rough grassland. She had no time, though, to consider the site more carefully, for at that moment she saw someone walking down the hill towards them: a tall, fair-haired man of about thirty, wearing a green tweed knickerbocker suit.

'Ah, good; you've been having a look round already!' exclaimed Gordon. 'Midge, this is Mr Patrick Faraday. Mr Faraday, my sister, Miss Hardie. We'll go up to the top.' He opened the gate and strode ahead through a spinney, over the rough scrub and up the slope of the hill. Midge, who could not match his long stride, was unable to keep up, and grateful for Mr Faraday's politeness in remaining at her side.

'My brother has only lately returned from an expedition to the Himalayas,' she explained. 'After surviving landslides and earthquakes, it's not to be expected that he should be held up by mere nettles or brambles. And he's accustomed to lead a caravan of sure-footed mules rather than a townswoman like myself.'

'This may be tame by Himalayan standards,' commented the architect. 'But as a site for a house and gardens it must be considered very rough. And steep. There will be problems.'

As though it had occurred to Gordon at the same moment that the unkempt state of the land might give a wrong impression, he came to a halt and waited for the other two to catch up before making an announcement. 'My wife,' he said to Mr Faraday, 'is a granddaughter of the late Marquess of Ross. She expects the best.'

Midge, glancing at her companion, saw his eyes flicker with surprise, and was able to read his thoughts. Presumably he already had some idea for the kind of house which would be suitable for a vintner in a prosperous way of business. But a family connection of a marquess . . .! Any architect would be familiar with at least the outside appearance of the great house at Castlemere. No doubt Mr Faraday's head was now swimming with visions of a masterpiece on a palatial scale. A Palladian villa, a Jacobean manor house, a French château? Terraces, double staircases rising from marble entrance halls, libraries and ballrooms and dining rooms to seat fifty guests. His unconscious sigh gave all his hopes away.

Gordon was as quick as his sister to realize the effect of what he had said. 'Within reason, of course,' he added.

'Of course.' Mr Faraday took any disappointment like a man. 'The slope has a south-west aspect. You'll want to build well below the brow of the hill, I imagine, to give the house protection from northerly winds.'

Gordon shook his head. 'Come just a little higher,' he said.

Midge and the architect joined him at a point from which it was possible to survey the whole generous parcel of land. Seen from above, the grassy slope which they had just climbed gave the impression that it had once been terraced, but that over several hundred years the contours of the flat strips had been blunted by rain and wind. For the first time, too, she could see the movement of water running along the valley at the foot of the woodlands. 'Is the stream yours?' she asked.

'Yes. And the flatter area on its further side, towards the city. Now then.' Gordon turned towards the architect and pointed down towards a place where the ground appeared to have been scooped away, creating an area of grassland flat enough to suggest that it had provided the base for some earlier habitation, perhaps many centuries ago.

'I've no doubt you see that as the ideal position for the house,' he said. 'And so it would be – for any house except the one which is to be built for the benefit of my daughter's health. She is to live not less than three hundred feet above sea level. The terms of the trust are specific on this. So we must build here, above this beech tree.'

'Are there any other special requirements?' The architect was careful not to sound critical.

'I suggest that a design to enclose three sides of a courtyard would be particularly suitable. We have five children, and there may be more. They could have a wing to themselves, instead of merely a nursery floor. The little girl, Grace, must have a room of her own facing as nearly south as possible. The entertaining rooms could face west, to catch the evening sun, whilst a north aspect would keep the kitchen quarters cool and provide the best light for a studio. My wife is a talented painter.'

'And for yourself, Gordon?' asked Midge, knowing that he devoted all his free time to experiments in plant propagation.

'I shall require a glasshouse – separate from the ones to be used by the gardeners – and a plant room and study next to it. None of that needs to be part of the main house. They could be lower down the hill.'

'To keep you away from the hurly-burly!' laughed Midge. Spending all her life surrounded by children, she was well aware of the noise they made. She and her brother watched as the architect studied the sun and the land, seeming almost to sniff the air as he tried to get the feel of the atmosphere before taking out his notebook. He looked up for a moment, indicating that he would like to make one point clear before considering the matter further.

'It's my preference, wherever possible, to use whatever building material is locally available,' he said. 'In this case it would be the grey stone from Headington Quarry. The choice of material, of course, affects the nature of the design.'

'Agreed!' Gordon was a businessman, accustomed to taking prompt decisions. 'I'll put a point to you in return. Money. I'll tell you the situation straight, Mr Faraday, and then you must decide whether it suits you. I don't want you coming to me in a year's time and saying that you thought this and you didn't realize that. I like people to know where they stand – and where *I* stand.'

He paused; and the architect nodded his head to indicate that he was waiting.

'I've got a fixed sum available for this enterprise,' Gordon continued. 'Twenty-six thousand pounds. Quite enough for a fine house, with the land already purchased.

If you undertake the commission, the whole sum will be at your disposal. But not a penny more than that. Everything's to come out of the twenty-six thousand – clearing the land and landscaping and planting it; building the house and decorating it; your own fees, and the cost of putting right all the things that go wrong. I've had good reports of you as someone who works to an estimate. But this may be larger than anything you've set your hand to before. If you think you can't handle it, this is the time to say so. And if you know for a fact that every new house costs ten per cent more than its owner expected, then allow for that before you start.'

Mr Faraday looked first at Midge and then at his client. 'When a house turns out to cost more than the owner intended or the architect promised,' he said, 'it's always for the same reason. Because the owner has had a change of mind.'

'There's a second half to that reason, I'll be bound. The owner changes his mind and the architect doesn't warn him that the changes will be expensive. I know as well as you do, Faraday, that it's the easiest thing in the world to sell a gentleman something he can't afford, because he doesn't choose to enquire the price – and even if he did, he wouldn't know or care whether he has the money to hand. But you and I, who are in the business of knowing the costs of other people's whims, must understand each other from the beginning.'

For a few seconds, in the silence as the two men stared at each other, Midge held her breath. It was none of her business, but she felt an intense wish for Mr Faraday to accept the commission. He was a stranger, and yet she felt in him an unusual quality of sympathy. Not in the sense of compassion, but of understanding. If he agreed to design the house he would in some way, she felt sure, make himself a part of the family, realizing what was needed and

29

looking at his own plans from inside rather than outside. It was not a notion which she felt able to express clearly in words – but Mr Faraday himself came near to doing it for her.

'I would be glad of the opportunity to meet the other members of your family, Mr Hardie,' he said. 'The little girl whose health is to be considered. And in particular, of course, I ought to discuss the needs of the household with your wife. To learn the number of servants she expects to employ, the rooms she requires for special purposes.'

Midge was tempted to clap her hands in delight at the request. It hardly seemed conceivable that Gordon had proposed to commission a house – to be paid for with money from his wife's family – without inviting Lucy to discuss her requirements in detail. Yet the startled expression on his face suggested that he had expected all the decisions to be his own. The grin which Midge was unable to conceal was so easy to interpret that for a moment Mr Faraday's eyes glinted with a shared amusement. But he was quick to bring it under control.

'Those are small matters, though,' he said. 'On the main point . . . Twenty-six thousand. It's a handsome enough sum. Yes, Mr Hardie, I can build you a house. And we shall both be proud of it.'

The two men shook hands on the commission. Midge moved away as they discussed practical arrangements. Then she walked down the hill at her brother's side to reclaim their bicycles, leaving Mr Faraday to explore the land more thoroughly.

'Lucky little Grace,' she said. 'I have the feeling that she's going to be given something magnificent.'

Gordon stopped dead and looked at her thoughtfully.

'Perhaps I was unwise to be so frank with you,' he said. 'Grace is only one of our children. Such a gift would be hard to explain to the boys. It will be best, I think, if the terms of the trust are never mentioned again. It's certainly true that the house will belong to Grace one day. But for the next nineteen years there's no necessity for her to know that.'

'I believe in telling the truth to children,' said Midge.

'And I believe in not telling them lies. Grace is only two years old. She couldn't possibly understand the situation.'

Midge would have liked to continue the argument. Throughout their childhood she and Gordon had debated vigorously on every possible subject, and each had enjoyed the clash of opinions. But the ownership of this property was none of her business; she had no right to interfere between a father and his children. She shrugged her shoulders, giving in with a smile.

'Lucky little Grace,' she said again.

3

Excitement sparkled in the October air like frost in sunshine. Three-year-old Grace Hardie was accustomed to a life of routine. There were days when she was ill and days when she was well; nothing else caused her regular timetable to vary. Today, though, was full of surprises. There was a sense of importance about each event which imprinted itself on the little girl's mind and memory. Many years later, when she was an old woman, this would be the first day in her life that she could clearly recall.

'Be still, child,' said Nanny Crocker every few minutes. But Nanny was waiting for something as well – listening for the sound of carriage wheels and doors opening; and sending Milly, the nursery maid, on unnecessary errands to the kitchen.

Not until two o'clock, though, did the first out-of-the-ordinary event take place. Nanny dressed Grace warmly for her walk as usual, tying on her bonnet and buttoning her boots. But then, instead of putting on her own hat and cloak, she gave Grace a final inspection and said, 'Your father's taking you for your walk today. Be a good girl, now.'

Papa! Papa never took her for walks. Grace hardly knew her father. He had been travelling abroad for the first two years of her life. Although it was more than a year since his return, he went off to work early each morning and was never home in time for the hour which Grace spent with her mother in the drawing room after tea. As she was led downstairs, she felt as shy as though she were meeting a stranger.

Mr Hardie was infected with the same excitement as everyone else. He held out his arms to Grace as if he had been waiting all his life for the pleasure of taking her on an afternoon walk. His curly black hair was bouncing off his head instead of being flattened down with macassar oil, and in place of the formal dark clothes of his office days he was wearing tweeds and high boots, as though he were just about to explore a jungle full of snakes.

'I've got something very special to show you,' he said as soon as Grace appeared. 'Where are those boys? Right, come along, then.'

That was another surprise, that the boys were coming too. Usually they were taken out by Miss Sefton, the governess. The schoolroom walk was different from the nursery walk. It was longer, and was supposed to be educational, with flowers and birds and trees and animals to be noted and named – the boys were even expected to keep a diary of everything they saw, although only Philip took this duty seriously. The nursery walk, on the other hand, was short, so that Grace would not tire.

There was to be yet a third treat. The pony cart was waiting in front of the house and they were told to climb in, though it was hardly big enough to take them all. Grace sat on Philip's lap, whilst her father flicked the reins to start Prince on his steady way.

'We'll go to the bottom and walk up,' said Mr Hardie. 'Can't expect poor old Prince to haul five and a half great hulking people up to the top.'

'The top of what?' asked Frank – but all Mr Hardie would say was, 'Aha! I've got a surprise. What do you think it is?'

'I like Ahas,' said Philip. Grace felt his arms tightening around her waist with pleasure. She tried to think what the surprise could be.

'I guess you've bought a motor car,' suggested Frank. It

was probably not so much a guess as a hope, but Mr Hardie shook his head, laughing.

'Noisy, smelly things. No thank you.'

There was a moment's silence. Everyone wanted to be the first to make the right guess.

'School,' said Philip suddenly. 'You're going to send Frank to school, and you're taking us to look at it.'

This time their father looked startled. 'School's something we have to think about, I'll grant you that. But not today.' He looked enquiringly at David and Kenneth, waiting for their contribution. As usual, the six-year-old twins discussed their answer together under their breaths before they spoke.

'We're going to buy a horse,' said Kenneth. 'Or a dog,' suggested David.

Again their father shook his head. 'No. You tell them, Grace.'

Grace didn't know; couldn't even guess. On nursery walks Nanny often promised marvellous surprises just round the corner if only she would hurry up, but there was never anything there. There might not be anything today, either.

Mr Hardie began to whistle with pleasure that no one had guessed his surprise, and Prince, cheered by the sound, broke into a trot. Before very long they had arrived, although none of them knew where. 'All out,' said Mr Hardie. He lifted Grace down and tied the reins loosely to a tree so that Prince could graze on a grass verge.

'Are we trespassing?' asked Frank as he and the other children followed their father across a field and towards a wood. Frank was not frightened of anything at all, but he liked to be clear about a situation so that if – as might happen today – someone appeared carrying a gun or shouting furiously, he would know whether he ought to retreat or apologize or say that he had a perfect right to be there.

34

'All this land,' said Mr Hardie, 'belongs to us. You boys can have ten minutes to explore the wood if you like. You're in charge, Frank. Don't let anyone fall into the stream. And run up the hill as soon as you hear me call.'

With whoops and yells the four boys rushed into the wood, their footsteps crashing through over fallen branches and the crisp, dead leaves of many winters. Rooks cawed indignantly at the intrusion and rabbits scuttled for cover, their white tails bobbing in alarm. 'Wait for me!' called Grace, but her brothers were already out of sight.

'I want you to stay with me, Grace,' said Mr Hardie. 'There are some very special surprises waiting for you today. One here and one at home – and perhaps even a second one at home, but I'm not promising that until I've had a word with Mama. The first surprise needs to be seen from nearer to the top of the hill. Give me your scarf so that I can blindfold your eyes.'

Grace stood still while he tied the scarf round her head. How was she expected to walk up the hill if she couldn't see where she was going? But her father solved the problem by lifting her to ride pick-a-back on his shoulders. He started off at a canter, jolting Grace up and down, but slowed to a walk as the hill became steeper. Grace, holding tightly round his neck, had no free hands with which to tug at the blindfold. She squinted down her nose, but all she could see was her father's head jutting forward as it always did when he was in a hurry, and his long legs striding over the grass.

At last he set her down and undid the scarf. 'Well then, what do you think of *that*?'

Grace's eyes opened wide as she stared at the biggest house she had ever seen. It looked like one of the pictures in her book of fairy tales, with a tower in one corner from which a princess could let down her golden hair. 'Is it a palace?' she asked.

35

'Indeed it is. A palace for Princess Grace. It's called Greystones. Shall we all come to live here?'

Grace stared up at him, not certain whether he was joking. Greystones. It sounded almost as though the house was named after her. 'But I'm not really a princess,' she reminded him.

'You're *my* princess,' said Mr Hardie. 'Would you like to live here?'

Grace nodded.

'And if you could choose, which room would you like for your own?'

Without hesitation, Grace pointed towards the tower.

'Then let's see what we can do about it.' Mr Hardie gripped her hand and ran with her towards the house. Taking a bunch of keys from his pocket he unlocked a door and led her along a corridor and up two flights of stairs. 'Can you read yet?' he asked, pausing before he opened a wooden door.

Grace was just about to shake her head, but instead laughed with surprise and delight. She could read her own name, although nothing else, and there it was, painted on china and screwed to the door. 'Grace!' she told him triumphantly.

'Then this must be Grace's bedroom.' He led her into a round room with three large windows. 'On a very hot day you can open all the windows and the wind will blow through. And on a very cold day, the sun will move round from one window to another and keep the room warm.'

'*Really* mine, Papa?'

'Really yours. Let's open a window and call the boys.'

'But they can't come here unless I ask them? My tower?' It was important to be clear on the point. Of course she *would* ask them, but she would expect a return for her invitations. For his ninth birthday Frank had been given a toy castle with a turret at each corner and lead soldiers in

36

red coats to defend it with cannons which fired matchsticks. Grace longed to play with the castle, but had been told that fighting battles was only for boys. She hoped that she would be a boy as well when she was older; but perhaps now she wouldn't be made to wait.

'Not the whole tower,' her father told her, leaning out of a window to make an extraordinary yodelling sound. 'Nanny Crocker will be in the room just below, with any new babies that we may happen to have in the family.'

'But my tower *room*. Can I sleep here tonight?'

'We'll just wait until Mama is well enough to move. In three weeks or so.'

Grace saw little of her mother and didn't know that she had been ill; but there was no time to think about that, because she could see her brothers rushing up the hill and into the tower, and she was anxious to hold her territory against any challenge. She enjoyed the envy in their eyes as they stared from each of her windows in turn; but, in a businesslike fashion, Frank staked out a different claim on behalf of the boys as soon as they were told that this was to be the family's new home.

'May we have the wood to play in, Papa? There's nothing there to spoil.'

'We could dam the stream and make a pond and have newts and tadpoles in it.' Philip was quick to support his elder brother. 'It would be good for our nature study.'

'You mean you want to run wild in it,' said Mr Hardie, laughing.

Even Grace knew that such a comment was not fair. It was true enough that Frank would play at battles all day if he were allowed to; and the twins, like any six-year-olds, liked to rush about without much purpose. But Philip was genuinely interested in the natural world. He was the only one of the boys who without being asked offered to help his father with fiddly jobs like pollinating the plants in the greenhouse. But there was no need to argue, for Mr Hardie was nodding.

'We've got plenty of land. There should be room for everybody,' he agreed. 'Yes, you can have the wood. Subject to my inspection once a month. I don't want you flooding the valley or making a pond that someone might drown in. Come along, and I'll show you your bedrooms.'

He led them off on a tour of the new house; but Grace stayed where she was, almost too happy to breathe. She had never seen a round room before, nor such a sunny room. But the best thing about it was its newness. It had never belonged to anyone else. It was her very own.

4

By the time the Hardie children, excited but tired, returned to their home in Oxford, Mrs Hardie had produced the second surprise of the day. Grace, settled into a low chair, was allowed to hold the new baby on her lap.

'His name is John Archibald Yates Hardie,' said Mr Hardie, while Nanny Crocker watched to see that Grace did not clutch the woolly bundle either too tightly or too loosely. 'But we shall call him Jay.'

'Why does he have so many names?'

'He's named after my father and Mama's brother. Your grandfather and uncle.'

Grace knew that she possessed an aunt, Aunt Midge; but Aunt Midge was not married and no one had ever mentioned an uncle before. It was curious that Mama's brother should never have come visiting – but Grace was not greatly interested in him. More important was the fact that she was no longer the youngest in the family. The other boys might claim that she was too young to join in their games, but this brother would do what she told him. She was pleased. 'When will he be big enough to play with me?' she asked.

'Not for a while yet.' Mr Hardie nodded at Nanny Crocker to take the baby away. 'But I've got one more surprise for you. A different kind of playmate. Stay where you are and shut your eyes tight.'

Something small and furry was placed in her hands. She opened her eyes and gasped with delight. A tower room and a kitten on the same day! Her pleasure was almost too great to bear. The kitten wriggled, struggling to escape, as

39

her grip tightened. Grace could feel its heart racing in alarm. She relaxed her fingers, cupping her hands instead round her new treasure to keep it on her lap.

It was a tabby kitten, with bright blue eyes which seemed too big for its tiny body. The black markings which framed those eyes and pointed down on each side of its nose gave it the fierce expression of a tiger, incongruous in an animal so small and soft. Trying to escape, it began to climb up her dress, its claws catching in the smocking in a way which would not please Nanny Crocker. Then it fell back on to her lap and for a few moments tramped round and round in a small circle until it found a comfortable place to sit. Grace stroked it gently. 'For me?' she asked. 'Mine?'

Her father nodded. 'Do you like him?'

Grace loved him. Happiness snatched her breath away. She bent over the kitten, burying her face in its fur. The fur tickled her nose, making her sneeze several times. Alarmed, the kitten jumped from her lap to hide under the chair, while her father produced a handkerchief.

'If your kitten's going to make you sneeze like that,' he suggested, 'we shall have to call him Pepper!'

Grace liked the name Pepper. 'But it wasn't Pepper who made me sneeze,' she said anxiously, afraid that if her new pet were blamed he would be taken away again.

For the same reason, she did her best not to let her father see that she was needing to gasp for breath. This kind of gasping was often followed by the wheezing and gurgling and whistling noises in her chest and throat which Grace herself didn't mind too much but which always made Nanny frown and send for the doctor.

Luckily everyone was more interested in Mama and the new baby today than in Grace. She was left alone to catch and play with her kitten. For the first time in her life, too, she was expected to go to sleep by herself when it was bedtime. Nanny tucked her up as usual, and Milly popped her head into the nursery every few minutes to see if she was still awake. But neither of them, it seemed, had been told about Pepper, who had hidden under the bed while all the washing and undressing went on but was now tucked up under the blankets – at first fidgety, but soon confidingly asleep.

Next morning Grace was ill. Even if she had wanted to conceal the fact that she was wheezing more noisily than ever before, she would not have known how to do it. Every breath was painful: she gulped for air, but there was never enough. The doctor, called in after he had visited Mrs Hardie and the new baby, took her temperature and murmured about autumn mists. Half an hour later Nanny Crocker bustled into the nursery to announce a treat.

'Baby Jay's got a nurse of his own for his first month,' she said. 'So we're going off to the new house today, just you and me. Milly'll bring us up our meals, but we'll have the whole place to ourselves. You'll like that, won't you?'

'Can Pepper come too?' Grace needed to gasp for breath between every word.

'Who's Pepper?'

'My kitten.'

'So *that's* where that puddle in the corner came from. I should have been told.' But Nanny did not seem cross as she told Milly to give the kitten some milk and put it into a carrying basket. Grace herself was given a dose of medicine. It made her so sleepy that she was hardly aware either of the journey to the new house or of her first night there. But the next morning she awoke breathing as easily as if she had never been ill.

'Where's Pepper?'

'Let's get you dressed first; then we'll see. How d'you like your new room, then?'

'It's lovely.' Grace climbed on to a chair to look out of a window. From her high vantage point she could see into a walled garden, although nothing was yet growing there. Nearer to the house the earth had been dug and raked level, ready for lawns and flower beds; an avenue of small trees had been planted along a newly gravelled drive which wound down the hill towards a lodge cottage and gateway. So high was the tower that she could look right over the garden area and see the wood, with the grassy slope just above it. It was a lot of space. 'Pepper will get lost,' she said anxiously.

'We'll put some butter on his paws.'

'Why?'

'Come here and let me dress you. Well, we butter his paws and leave him to explore the rooms that are to be his home. Then he licks his paws – all little kittens do that, to clean themselves – and he tastes the dust which has stuck to the butter. That teaches him where he lives. After that, he'll never go too far away, and he'll always find his way back.'

To Grace, who was expected to wash her hands before touching any food, it seemed a dirty way of learning a lesson, but she held Pepper still, gently stroking the black and white stripes of his stomach, whilst Nanny applied the butter.

'Now you stay here with him. I've other things to see to. Keep the door closed. He's not to be let out for at least an hour. After that, we'll give him another dab of butter and let him down the stairs to find his way in and out. All right?'

Grace nodded, pleased to be given the responsibility. She watched as Pepper explored, sniffing curiously at all the smells of new wood and paint and linoleum, and chasing with enthusiasm a ball which his mistress made for him out of crumpled paper. Then, as Nanny had promised, he sat down on the floor with one leg pointing upwards, and began to lick and clean himself.

Later that day, after a meal which was a kind of picnic, brought up from her old home in a wicker basket, Grace was put back to bed for an afternoon rest, because she had been so ill the day before. But after tea she was allowed to explore the whole of the new house. Leaving Pepper asleep in a basket lined with pieces of old blanket, she held Nanny Crocker's hand as they walked along wide corridors and opened heavy doors, making guesses about what they would find inside.

Each of the rooms intended for the boys had a name painted on the outside, so that there should be no disputes. Beneath that row of bedrooms were three long, bright rooms which Nanny knew were to be the schoolroom, the day nursery and the children's dining room. Grace thought of the battered furniture and scuffed walls in their old house and wondered how long the new rooms would continue to look so clean.

Round a corner they came to two large rooms flooded with the late afternoon sun. One was already furnished as a dining room. The other, Nanny told her, was waiting for the drawing room furniture to arrive from their old house. Already there were long curtains hanging at the windows and a new carpet on the floor, giving a feeling of warmth and homeliness.

But in the third side of the house was a room which was bare. It was twice as tall as any other, and the only windows were high up along one wall, so that no one could possibly see out of them. Grace, overawed by the size and height of the room, tried to imagine what could possibly go inside it. Ordinary furniture would look quite wrong. There would have to be something very tall – something which had a winding feeling to it, like a creeper twining round a tree. She could almost see the shape in her mind.

'It's a studio,' said Nanny Crocker. 'Your mama will

43

come here to paint her pictures. Now then, can you show me the way back to your tower room?'

Grace tried and failed, ending up on the staircase which led from the kitchen to the servants' quarters. The house was too big for her to remember all its turnings. It was a worry, for Nanny might not always be there to help. Later that evening, after she had been tucked up and had pretended to be asleep, Grace cautiously opened her eyes to check by the flame of the night candle that she and Pepper were alone. She slid out of bed and dabbed butter on Pepper's paws once more, to make certain that he would never run away. Then, biting her lower lip with concentration, she smeared the rest of the butter on the soles of her own feet and began to walk round the room, her fingers outstretched to run along the surface of the wall.

Round and round the green linoleum she went, marking out a magic circle. Pepper padded silently behind her, occasionally darting forward to tap at her heels with a soft paw. Licking the bottoms of her feet proved difficult, but she managed to suck her big toes; perhaps that would be enough. By the time she climbed back into her new big bed she was shivering with satisfaction as well as with cold. Now she was safe in her new house. She would never get lost in it: would never run away.

PART TWO

Death at Greystones
1903

1

Where were the boys? Six-year-old Grace wandered disconsolately through the grounds, calling her brothers. It was the first day of the holidays and she had been looking forward to it for weeks. The twins had joined Frank and Philip at school just before their ninth birthdays, so that with Jay still in the nursery, Grace now had all her lessons alone with her governess. Even Miss Sefton, who was often bad-tempered and too particular about small mistakes, had understood how much Grace wanted to share the first day of their freedom with her elder brothers. She was allowed to leave the schoolroom as soon as she had written her daily spelling list and repeated her five times table without a mistake. But what good did it do to have a free morning if there was no one to play with?

She pushed open the door of the walled garden. After breakfast the boys had dashed off to search for their bows and arrows. If they were going to play Robin Hood, they would need their only sister to be Maid Marian. But perhaps they had decided to go hunting instead.

Frith, the head gardener, lived in a perpetual state of war with rabbits, squirrels, mice, pigeons, crows, blackbirds, tits – indeed, almost anything which could be suspected of making a meal from his lettuces or peas or fruit. In the Easter holiday he had offered a farthing for any corpse which could be strung from a pole as a warning. Grace had earned one of the farthings, although the dead mouse she took to him had really been killed by Pepper, not by herself; and Frank, who had been given a gun for his twelfth birthday, killed two squirrels and a rabbit.

47

Perhaps the offer had been repeated for the summer.

The furry and feathered thieves would not be in much danger today. Frank was only allowed to use his gun in his father's company, and with bow and arrow neither he nor his three brothers had ever managed to hit anything which moved. They would be useful only as bird-scarers.

The walled garden was peaceful; the only sound that of the purposeful humming of bees. Frith was earthing up the celery, but he straightened himself and tipped his hat, leaning on his spade as Grace told him her trouble.

'Lost your brothers, have you? Your father's looking for them as well. Sent young Andy off to see where they'd got to. If you hold on here, Andy will be back to say where he tracked them down. I could spare a raspberry or two while you're waiting. The red ones, not the yellow. Look out for the wasps as you pick them.'

It was quite a long time before Andy, the gardener's son, returned – time enough for Grace to have stained her mouth with raspberries and her fingers with strawberries and to be sitting down with a lapful of pea pods. When he came at last he was panting.

'They were in the wood,' he reported to his father. 'When I told Mr Hardie, he said I was to take the little 'un down and tell Master Frank to look after him while Nanny Crocker and Milly was wanted somewhere else. So then I had to go down to the wood again, and back up.'

Andy was a sturdy, wide-cheeked boy with curly red hair and freckles all over his face and arms. Although almost exactly the same age as David and Kenneth, he had nothing in common with them, being neither clever like David, nor impulsive like Kenneth. Mostly he took things slowly – but when, in the Easter holidays, Frank had suggested – in words conveying an order rather than an invitation – that he should come down to the lower meadow to give them batting practice, Andy had accepted his

48

father's nod of permission and proved to be a useful fast bowler.

As a rule, though, he spent his holidays helping in the garden. Frith had an under-gardener, two journeymen and a boy to help him with the fruit and vegetables and the pleasure gardens, but was glad to accept his nine-year-old son as a temporary apprentice. It was taken for granted that Andy would become one of his father's assistants as soon as he was old enough to leave school. Jay, who liked to pretend that everyone was somebody else, had nicknamed him Jack-and-the-beanstalk because of his habit of producing seeds from his pocket and sowing them in unlikely places. A giant sunflower, to everyone's surprise except Andy's, was at this moment in full bloom outside the schoolroom; and three runner bean plants had climbed the wisteria and were groping with curious fingers through the open nursery window.

'Miss Grace has been wondering where her brothers have got to,' his father said now. 'Take her down and see if you can find them again for her.'

Grace popped the last podful of peas into her mouth and followed Andy out of the walled garden. She liked him, because he was kind and patient, never running so fast that she could not keep up. As her elder brothers in turn started school, they had become secretive, refusing to talk to her about things which they claimed she would not understand. They didn't always invite her to share their games and, because they had become rough and noisy, she less often wanted to do so. But that was something which she only remembered after they had been at home for a few days. On this first morning of the holidays she was sure that they would enjoy each other's company.

Andy, unlike her brothers, was willing to share his secrets. 'Would you like to see my forest?' he asked.

Grace didn't know what he meant, but nodded all the

same. Instead of plunging into the wood, he helped her across a ditch and led her to a corner of the meadow where a small patch of turf had been cut away. Proudly he pointed to a miniature grove of seedlings, two or three inches tall.

'Those are oak trees,' he told her. 'And those are chestnuts. And over there I've got sycamores and beeches. I don't know what this one is, but I'll be able to tell when it gets some more leaves. And I planted an acorn near the tower as well. Specially for you.' Andy's freckled skin flushed, and he kept his eyes on the ground as he went on speaking. 'It'll grow real high, so you won't have to lean out of a window and make a ladder out of your long golden hair for people to climb up, like in the story.'

'I haven't got long golden hair.'

'Well, the princess in the story had. Rapunzel. Anyway, with an oak tree there, that can be the ladder.'

What was he talking about? There was no oak tree near to her tower. With a puzzled face she stared down at the seedlings which he had described as beeches. There was a beech tree just below the house, but it looked nothing like this. It was almost as tall as the roof and its leaves spread so thickly and widely that she and her brothers often used the space beneath as an outdoor playroom. 'They're not big enough,' she said.

'They'll grow. I planted just acorns and conkers and sycamore wings and beech nuts and they've grown already. Just like babies. Getting taller every year.'

'We're going to have another baby.' Grace was not much interested in the trees, but was proud that she had news to tell. None of the Hardie children had known in advance about Jay's arrival in the family, but this time they had been entrusted with the secret. 'It's coming in September.'

'Sooner than that,' said Andy, and Grace pouted a little because he did not seem surprised.

'No, September,' she repeated. 'Mama told me.'

50

'Reckon she got tired of waiting, then. I heard Mr Hardie talking in the stable yard when I went to tell him about your brothers. He was sending a message down to Dr Sidley's place. "Ask the doctor to come at once to deliver the baby," he said.'

Grace considered the message with interest. Ever since she had heard the news from her mother, she had wondered how the new baby was going to arrive. She had asked Nanny Crocker, who talked about gooseberry bushes; and she had asked Miss Sefton, who told a different story, something about a stork. She asked her father as well; but he would only say 'Aha!' – not the triumphant Aha with which he was accustomed to greet some new discovery or achievement, but a mysterious, secret-keeping Aha. As for her mother, she only smiled and would not say anything at all.

Grace had even asked Jay, who after all had been a baby himself more recently than anyone else in the family. But Jay was three years old by now and had forgotten how it felt to be born. He pretended to remember, acting out a vigorous demonstration of how he had bounced into the nursery like a ball before unwinding his head and arms and legs and fingers and toes one at a time, but Grace didn't believe him. Ever since Jay had learned to talk he had practised his new accomplishment non-stop, making no distinction between the true facts of everyday life and the more interesting products of his imagination. Grace enjoyed his pretendings; but had learned that it was not safe to believe them.

This new idea, though, made more sense. It was reasonable that the doctor should deliver new babies to his customers, just as the fishmonger delivered the weekly fish order. And that would explain why Mama had said that although she had ordered a girl baby this time, she could not be sure that she would get one. Grace knew that the fishmonger's basket quite often arrived at the kitchen door with a note on the top saying, 'Sorry no sole, have sent plaice instead', or something of that sort.

Everyone in the family took it for granted that Grace was hoping for a baby sister instead of another brother – and they were right, but not for the reason they thought. It wasn't that she wanted to play girls' games with a companion. Instead, she hoped that if there was another girl in the family, she herself would be allowed to become one of the boys. The new little girl could be the one to be dressed in frilly clothes and told to keep clean and forced to have her hair tied in rags to make ringlets. Grace felt sure that the reason why her brothers didn't play with her nowadays was only because they thought that a six-year-old was too young to join in their games. But she was growing older and bigger all the time. Soon she would be able to climb trees and catch balls as well as they could. Anyone who wanted to fuss over a girl could have the new baby instead.

For the moment, though, she decided to go back to the house. Watching the arrival of the new baby would be more exciting even than playing with her brothers. But as she scrambled to her feet she was frozen into stillness by a sound which she had never heard before.

It was a snarling, hissing, spitting sound: the sound of a wild animal preparing to defend itself by attack. There were other noises as well – the trampling of feet through the undergrowth of the wood. If one of the boys was coming this way, he might be in danger from whatever beast was lurking in the shadows. Grace knew that she ought to call and warn him; but instead she clutched Andy's hand, unable to move.

'No!' It was Frank's voice which shouted the single word, from a long way away. The sound of moving feet had already stopped, so that for a fraction of a second the wood was silent, as if everyone in it were holding his breath. Then the air was filled with a sound more terrible than anything Grace had ever heard in the six years of her life: a high-pitched wail of agony, followed by a growling, choking sound which seemed to go on for ever. Grace flung herself into Andy's arms with her hands pressed over her ears.

'What's happening?' she cried. But Andy didn't know, and by now the wood was silent again, offering no answers.

2

It was David who on the first day of the holidays had suggested that they should all search out their bows and arrows. David was the cleverest of the four elder Hardie boys, and had brought home the best set of examination marks on his school report. But he was not a fast runner like his twin brother, Kenneth; nor was he a good cricketer like Frank and Philip. He had had enough of racing and team games during the school term, and he wanted to play something at which he could be best.

'We ought to wait for Grace,' objected Philip as they lifted their bows off the rack in the carriage house.

'She's with Miss Sefton. We can play Robin Hood another day. Why don't we get some practice? Just shooting at a target, to see who hits it most.'

Accepting the idea, their eldest brother took charge. Frank was twelve years old: a carefully efficient boy. He insisted on inspecting each bow to make sure that there was no danger of any accidental snapping when it was drawn for the first time after a three-month gap. It was Frank, too, who decided that it would be a waste of time to make a proper archery target. Instead, they should go down to the wood, choose a tree, and see who – taking one step backwards after each attempt – could hit it from the furthest distance away.

The contest was interrupted by two messages brought from the house by Andy Frith, the gardener's son. Philip, who often helped in his father's plant experiments by pricking out seedlings or hand-pollinating flowers which were to be crossed with each other, was asked to go at once to the glasshouse to draw the shades. Frank was given a greater responsibility. He was to look after three-year-old Jay, who arrived bubbling with excitement at his unexpected release from the nursery to play with the big boys.

'I'm a Red Indian!' he announced, sticking a pigeon's feather into his fair hair; and the others agreed that they would be Red Indians as well, at least until Philip returned to continue the target competition. They set off in single file in search of cowboys to fight. It was perhaps because Jay was the smallest, with eyes nearest to the ground, that he was the first to see a quick movement in the undergrowth. 'It's a tiger, it's a tiger!' he shouted.

'Can't be,' said Kenneth scornfully. 'Expect it was a squirrel.'

'It might be a fox.' David moved forward cautiously with his bow at the ready.

'It was Pepper.' Frank was more realistic. But Jay was not to be talked out of one of his pretendings.

'It's a tiger,' he insisted. 'Going to *eat* Pepper. Or the baby rabbits.'

'It's more likely to eat *you*,' suggested David, and Jay shivered in delighted anxiety.

'Tiger hunt!' he demanded. 'Want a tiger hunt.'

'This way, then.' Kenneth set off in pursuit.

'Hold on.' Frank, as always, took charge. 'If you chase it, it will just run away. We have to make a circle and drive it into the centre. Kenneth, you go to the oak tree and work in from there. David, you start at the ditch.'

'What about me?' Jay did not intend to be left out. It was his tiger.

Frank considered how best to keep the three-year-old out of the way. 'You can be the bait,' he said. 'We'll tie you to a tree and then when the tiger comes to eat you up we'll be able to kill it.' He laughed at the anxiety on Jay's face. 'I'm only pretending, silly. It isn't a real tiger.' But he recognized that to his little brother a pretended tiger was as dangerous as a real one. 'All right. You can be the look-out.' He lifted Jay up to sit astride a strong branch of a tree. 'Tell us if you see the tiger coming this way.'

'Can tigers climb trees?'

'Not English tigers,' said Frank reassuringly, and went off to direct his twin brothers in the chase. Pepper – because of course it was Pepper – proved to be a co-operative participant in the game. Instead of running away he was ready to play, teasing the boys by first disappearing and then jumping out in front of them, climbing a young sapling with an agility which would have alarmed Jay if he had seen it, and breaking off from the role of quarry to stalk a field mouse with an intent quietness rivalling that of his hunters.

After a little while, however, he abandoned the mouse and turned in the direction of the house, threading his way in a leisurely manner between the trees.

'Tiger approaching oak tree!' called Frank. 'Kenneth, cut it off.'

Kenneth stepped forward, his bow at the ready. The cat hesitated and turned away, only to find his way blocked by David. Either alarmed or angry, he bolted away towards a more heavily wooded area. A squeak of horror revealed that he had climbed the very tree in which Jay was keeping watch.

'To the rescue!' shouted Frank, and the three brothers, from different directions, rushed forward without attempting to keep their footsteps quiet. The twins were the first to arrive. Pepper, realizing that there was one boy above in the tree as well as the two on the ground, froze into stillness with claws gripping the tree trunk.

Kenneth, carried away by the excitement of the hunt and intent on saving his little brother, was the first to fire his arrow. Even with an unmoving target his shot went wide, posing as much danger to Jay as to the cat. But Pepper seemed to recognize that the game had become dangerous. He turned his head and snarled at the two nine-year-olds, spitting at them with a ferocity that made him seem the wild animal which they had been pretending him to be. David was just as excited by the chase as his impulsive twin, but faced their quarry with more care, moving his feet until his balance was steady and biting his lip with concentration as he drew the bow and took aim.

'No!' shouted Frank, recognizing as he arrived on the scene that their game was out of hand. But he was too late. David's arrow had already left the bow, and he was too close to miss.

None of the four brothers ever forgot the sound of the agonized yowl with which Pepper fell to the ground. The wailing continued for a few seconds as he tried to free himself from the arrow lodged in his eye, but then gave way to a lower sound; a rattling growl which forced its way up from his stomach as his body jerked convulsively.

'Stop it!' pleaded Kenneth, unable to bear the sound of Pepper's agony. Frank was silent, aghast at what had happened, and Jay was crying. David, slowly lowering his bow, was only just making the transition from pride at hitting his target to a realization of what he had done. But to Kenneth every jerk and groan of the wounded cat went straight to his heart until he could stand it no longer. He knew what ought to be done, because he had often heard his father describe how it had been necessary on one of his expeditions in China to shoot a mule badly injured in a landslide. 'Stop it!' he cried again – and then, because Pepper continued to writhe on the ground, he picked up a log of wood and hit the cat three times hard on the head.

The silence as the wailing came to an end was absolute. No birds sang in the trees; no breeze stirred the leaves. Even Jay, wide-eyed with shock, had ceased to cry. When

Philip, who had heard Pepper's first squeal of pain from as far away as the glasshouse, came running to see what had happened, his footsteps were heard approaching through an emptiness so intense that the boys felt alone in the world.

'What's going on?' he asked, not immediately catching sight of Pepper's body; but nobody answered. Frank and David and Kenneth were facing the same appalling question, which they did not need to put into words: what were they going to say to Grace?

They were all tempted by the same thought. If they promised each other not to tell, Grace would never discover what had happened. She would assume that Pepper had got lost or had had some kind of accident.

But Frank's nature was too honest for him to consider any deceit for more than a few seconds; and the twins, knowing this, realized also that Jay was too little to keep a secret. They would have to confess.

There was no need to do so in words. Seeing Philip's eyes flicker with surprise, David and Kenneth turned and found that their sister had arrived on the scene herself. She was wearing the linen smock and black stockings which were her schoolroom uniform. Why had Miss Sefton chosen today to release her from lessons! And how long had she been there?

It was not a question which any of them could put to her, for their mouths were too dry to speak. Only Philip, innocent of guilt, was able to swallow the lump in his throat. 'I only just came,' he said.

Grace looked at her eldest brother, knowing that he would have been in charge of whatever had been going on; and Frank recognized his responsibility.

'It was an accident,' he said. 'We didn't mean – we're very sorry, all of us.'

Grace, still without speaking, looked down at Pepper's

58

body, and at the arrow. For a moment her eyes seemed to move in circles, as though the world had gone out of focus. Then she stared first at David's bow and afterwards at the bloodstained lump of wood which Kenneth was still holding. Her face was white, making her eyes look blacker than usual and, although she did not appear to be conscious of the fact, she had begun to gulp for breath in a way that often presaged one of her bouts of illness.

Frank realized that it was up to him to break the silence. There was nothing to be done for Pepper, but some kind of positive action might be helpful to Grace. He had noticed that Andy was standing a little way behind her, half hidden by the trees. 'Bring us a spade,' he ordered; and then announced to the others, 'We'll have a proper funeral.'

'Want to get down.' Jay, feeling himself forgotten in his tree, began to wail again until Frank lifted him to the ground. He ran across to his sister and tugged at her unresponsive hand. 'Pepper's only pretending,' he said – and then, seeing that she was not reassured, 'We were only pretending too.'

'Leave her alone, Jay,' said Frank. He took off his jacket and spread it on the ground, indicating to Grace that she should sit on it. But she shook her head, continuing to stand motionless as the funeral got under way.

Frank dug a hole himself, dismissing the gardener's son as soon as he had handed over the spade. Philip disappeared to pick wild flowers, and David looked for a piece of sacking in which Pepper's body could be wrapped. When the grave was ready, all five boys stood round it, singing a hymn and reciting the Lord's Prayer, but Grace could not be persuaded to join in. Only when Frank picked up Pepper's body, ready to put it into the grave, did she give a little moan and step forward to touch her pet for the last time. There was a moment in which she seemed to stop breathing. Then she turned away and ran through the wood in the direction of the house.

'D'you think she'll tell?' asked David anxiously. Their father did not beat them very often, but he hit hard if he thought the crime deserved it.

'Of course she'll tell,' said Frank resignedly. Grace was only six. 'You'd better run after her, Kenneth. Not to stop her. Just to make sure she's all right. And then go and find Nanny Crocker and tell her that Grace is having one of her wheezy chests. I heard it, just before she went.'

Kenneth nodded and set off in pursuit. Frank put Pepper's body into the hole he had dug, and each of the boys threw in a handful of earth before using the spade to shovel the ground level. Although Grace was no longer watching, they continued to behave with the formal gravity that they supposed she wanted. Their ceremonial was mixed with an uneasiness which they shared but could not have explained. Each of them, on any day in the year, was accustomed to carry the guilt of a variety of sins: food stolen from the garden, rules broken at school, truths suppressed to have the effect almost of lies, neglected duties, small disloyalties – all these offences were to some extent matters of deliberate choice. In committing a small crime they took into account not only the likelihood of punishment but the probable disturbance of conscience. It seemed unfair that something which they had never intended to happen should now overwhelm them with guilt. Frank had spoken sincerely when he claimed that the killing of Pepper was an accident. But they all knew that Grace could not be expected to believe that.

The ceremony was over. Philip arranged his armful of poppies and cornflowers above the disturbed earth. Frank picked up his jacket and took Jay's hand. The four boys walked together through the wood and up the hill to face the music.

3

Halfway up the hill Grace was forced to pause, gasping
for breath; but when she saw Kenneth emerge from the
wood she set off again, panting and crying at the same
time. Kenneth was a fast runner. If he did not catch her
up it was because he was not really trying; but she did not
look round again. He could say he was sorry as often as
he liked: she wasn't going to listen. She was never going
to speak to him again, nor to David. She was prepared to
believe that Philip had had no hand in the death of her
pet, and Jay was too young to have understood what the
others were doing. With more difficulty, she could accept
that Frank was horrified by what had happened. He never
told lies, and she had read the shock in his eyes. But David
with his arrow and Kenneth with his lump of wood had
hurt Pepper and made him dead. Grace vowed that she
would never forgive them.

She ran first to the nursery for comfort, but Nanny
Crocker, who was usually there, was not there today: nor
was there any sign of Milly, the nurserymaid. Disappointed, Grace pulled off her straw hat and threw it on
the nursery floor. Then she hesitated for a moment. She
was not supposed to bother her mother in the mornings,
and for the past two weeks Mama had been ill, so that all
the children had been restricted to a single short visit to
her bedroom just before their own bedtime. But she would
surely not mind being disturbed now, for such a special
reason.

There was a strange atmosphere of bustle outside Mrs
Hardie's room. Milly was carrying two jugs of hot water

along the corridor as Grace approached, and one of the housemaids was hurrying behind her with a pile of clean sheets. Grace tried to follow them in, but was stopped by Nanny Crocker. 'Not now, dear,' she said, and closed the door in Grace's face.

It was the third betrayal of a day in which no one was prepared to love her or be kind to her. Her tearfulness turned to an angry resentment; but then she remembered that there was another way into her mother's bedroom. She opened the dressing room door.

In the middle of the room stood the cradle which had once belonged to Grace herself, and more recently to Jay. A strange woman in a blue uniform and white belt was bending over it.

'Who are you?' asked Grace.

'I'm Nurse Bruton. I've come to look after your mother and your new baby brother for a little while. He's just this minute arrived. Would you like to blow him a kiss? But you mustn't touch him or come near him, because he's very new and small.'

'I want Mama,' said Grace.

'Not just now, dear. She's having a little sleep.'

'I want Mama.'

'Run along back to your classroom, there's a good girl.' Grace felt herself being pushed, kindly but very firmly, out of the room. Once again a door was closed, shutting her out.

Banished to the corridor, Grace stamped both feet in frustration. What right had a stranger to keep her away from her mother? She tried the door again and found that it was not locked, so for a second time she went into the dressing room. Nurse Bruton had disappeared, but the way to Mrs Hardie's bedroom was still barred, this time by Milly.

'I want . . . I want . . .' Grace struggled to force the

words out. But the wheezing in her chest, which had begun when she first saw Pepper's body lying on the ground and which had been made worse by her run up the hill, seemed no longer to be only inside her body, but to encircle it like an iron band which was being slowly tightened. She was unable to speak; almost unable to breathe. Milly's eyes widened in alarm.

'Stay just where you are, there's a good girl,' she said. 'I'll go and fetch the doctor to you. He's but this minute left your mother.'

The nurserymaid hurried away, leaving unguarded the connecting door to Mrs Hardie's room. Grace took two steps towards it but then was forced by a lack of breath to stop. Her wheezing was so loud and painful that perhaps it disturbed the new baby, who began to cry. The sound resembled the mewing of a kitten, reminding Grace how she had first held Pepper on her lap just after she had seen Jay for the first time in this same cradle. But Pepper was dead. She would never hold him again.

She looked down at the baby, whose red and wrinkled face screwed up as he cried. How could anyone want a baby as ugly as this? And why had Mama not insisted on having a girl, when that was what she had asked for and as good as promised? There were enough boys in this family already: horrid, rough, cruel, *hateful* boys. This new one should be sent back to wherever he had come from. Grace gave a petulant push at the cradle before forcing out another wheezing breath.

A crash was followed by a single cry. She had pushed harder than she realized, overturning the cradle and throwing the baby to the ground. A soft white shawl had been wrapped round his body and the top of his head, but he had fallen out sideways, banging his forehead on the ground. Had she killed him? It was not his fault that he had been sent by mistake. What should she do? Whom

63

should she tell? Guilt paralysed her, rooting her to the spot.

She heard a footstep behind her and felt someone brushing past. It was Kenneth. Following her, he must have seen what happened. He wasted no time in talking, but set the cradle upright again. Then, bending to the floor, he carefully picked up the baby. Grace put her fingers to her mouth and began to bite her nails without noticing what she was doing. The baby's head, unsupported by Kenneth's arm, hung downwards just as Pepper's had done when Frank was about to put him into the grave. There was no arrow and no blood; that was the only difference.

Now Kenneth was tugging at the shawl to make it look as though it had not been disarranged. Grace tried to help him; but, although most of her body was hot and sticky, her fingertips were as cold and clumsy as though she had just been making a snowman in December.

Kenneth looked at her across the cradle and the motionless baby. He was not interested in his new brother, any more than Grace was, as his anxious brown eyes appealed for understanding.

'Pepper was an accident too,' he said. 'We're all sorry.'

Grace was unable to answer. She had begun to cough, trying to expel the heavy weight which was clogging up her lungs, and in between the paroxysms her chest heaved with the desperate need to snatch a breath. She had to hold on to the edge of the cradle if she were not to collapse on to the floor, and was hardly aware of Dr Sibley striding into the room, nor of Milly picking her up and carrying her to bed. Too much had happened which she did not want to remember. It was a relief when at last the day slipped away into darkness and sleep.

4

For as long as Grace could remember, Sundays had been family days. As a family the Hardies walked down the hill to the church at Headington Quarry in the morning, and as a family they sat down to mid-day dinner when they returned. Even little Jay was allowed to leave the nursery for this one meal of the week. Grace had missed two Sundays while she was ill, and on this third one she was left at home whilst the others went to church. But she could get up for the meal, Nanny Crocker told her, and from then on could enjoy the holiday with her brothers as usual, as long as she was careful not to tire herself.

It felt odd to be wearing shoes and stockings again, and to hear her starched petticoat rustling as she walked. Even odder was the sight of her brothers. She had not seen them for three weeks, and looked at them now as though they were strangers. The four elder boys had been made to wear their best knickerbocker suits, although the day was hot. Their hair was sleeked down with water, and they sat stiffly at the table as though afraid of spoiling their unnatural cleanliness. Jay alone was his usual excited self, bouncing dangerously up and down in his high chair as he waited to be served.

The boys were not the only ones to appear restrained. Mrs Hardie looked pale and tired, whilst Mr Hardie silently concentrated on carving the meat instead of providing his usual lively comments on the morning's sermon. Only when he had said grace and nodded permission for them all to start did the grave expression on his face relax into a smile.

'We're all glad to see you down again, Grace. Are you feeling better?'

'Yes, thank you, Papa.' Grace looked down at her plate and discovered that she was not hungry. All morning, while the others were at church, she had wondered who would be the first person to mention the baby and to accuse her of hurting him. She ought to keep quiet, and wait to be told what had happened. But until she knew, she could not enjoy her meal or anything else. Fear made her sly: she approached the subject sideways. 'Papa, what name did you give to the new baby?'

Her parents looked at each other, and the pause before either of them spoke increased her anxiety.

'He was christened Felix,' said Mr Hardie. 'But –'

'I'm afraid he died, darling,' said Mrs Hardie. 'He arrived early, you see. He was very small. Too small to live.' Upset, she looked down at her plate.

So the nightmare had come true. Over and over again while she was ill, Grace had re-lived the moment in which she knocked the baby to the ground in a fit of temper, and those following moments when she had stared at him in the hope that some movement or cry would indicate that he was not too badly hurt. If he was dead, then it must mean that she had killed him. She could not pretend that it was someone else's fault, because Kenneth had seen her.

'I didn't mean,' she began slowly – but her father, speaking now with his usual briskness, interrupted her.

'We're not going to pull long faces about this, Grace. It was a sad moment when we had to say goodbye. But there are eight people left in this family to be happy together. Not to mention Pepper. Come to think, I haven't seen Pepper around while you were ill. Has he been sleeping in your room?'

Even until that moment, the big dining room had been much quieter than on an ordinary Sunday. But the silence which followed the simple question was of a quite different kind. It seemed that all the boys were holding their breath as they waited to learn what Grace was going to say.

She looked round at each of her brothers in turn. All of them had been brought up to sit straight-backed and tall, but Frank held his head higher and more firmly than the rest, as though taking it for granted that he was about to be punished, and determined to accept it like a man. David's chin was just as firm, and his black eyes just as steady, but there was a glint of defiance in them; he was not admitting to any shame. Philip's expression held a glint of resignation. He had had nothing to do with the killing of Pepper but no doubt recognized that he was likely to be tarred with the same brush as the others. Even Jay was still, waiting anxiously to be told by his elder brothers what he should say. Only Kenneth's eyes flickered uncertainly, and his mouth moved as though he were about to speak.

There was a moment in which Grace felt anger rising within her as though she were about to be sick. The boys deserved a beating for what they had done. But no beating could bring Pepper back to her. Had she been able to see her mother immediately after the funeral in the wood she would certainly have poured out the whole story, but now there seemed no point in involving the grown-ups. She would punish David and Kenneth herself, by never loving them again and leaving them out of her bedtime prayers.

'Nanny won't let Pepper sleep in my room because he makes me sneeze,' Grace said. 'I haven't seen him either. Perhaps he's lost. Or perhaps he's run away because he thought I'd forgotten about him.'

How odd it was that she could tell such lies and at the same time feel smugly virtuous – and even odder that her parents did not seem to recognize the lies. Until today she had always been sure that they could tell when she was not speaking the truth. But now they were sympathetic, hoping that Pepper might return, offering to arrange a search of the grounds and of any outhouses in which he might be accidentally imprisoned.

The boys, of course, knew that no search would be successful. They had all relaxed. Jay was busily chasing the food round his plate with a spoon and pusher. Philip was smiling in a friendly and relieved fashion whilst Frank gave an almost imperceptible nod of approval. David applied himself to his meal as though the disappearance of Pepper had nothing at all to do with him. Only Kenneth made her uneasy by catching her eye and winking. Did he think that she was trading with him, one silence for another? She had not meant it to be like that.

The wink disturbed her. Instead of congratulating herself on behaving well, she was made to feel guilty again. Kenneth knew what had happened in their mother's dressing room. What else did he know? Had her parents been telling lies in the same way as Grace herself? Had the baby really died just because he was too small?

That afternoon Grace broke her best china doll, the one she was only allowed to play with on Sundays. She was not as a general rule interested in dolls, preferring to play with her brothers' toys whenever they would let her. But since Pepper's death she had taken her rag doll to bed with her; and on this Sunday afternoon, when she was told to rest for an hour, she climbed up on a chair to fetch Princess Anna down from her shelf and quite deliberately dropped her on to the floor.

Nanny Crocker, unsuspecting, was sympathetic to Grace's distress. She spread glue over the broken edges of the doll's head and wound a bandage round and round to hold the pieces in place. 'Leave her for a day or two and she'll be as good as new.'

'*Really* as good as new, Nanny?'

'Well, very nearly. You'll see a brown line if you look very hard. And if you were to drop her again, she'd crack more easily. There'll always be a weakness. You'll have to look after her. But tuck her up in bed now and kiss her better and you won't need to worry any more.'

Grace did as she was told, but the expression on her face reflected her troubled conscience. 'Why did our new baby die, Nanny?'

'Poor little scrap, he was too small to live. No strength to take any food.'

'When did it happen?'

'I don't exactly know. Two days he was here, getting weaker and weaker. Then Dr Sibley sent him off to the hospital, and that special nurse went with him. Your mother wasn't strong enough to go too, but your father called in to take a look at him every evening on his way back from business. It must have been six or seven days later that we were told he'd slipped away in the middle of the night to be with Jesus.'

Six or seven days! A cloud lifted from Grace's head and heart. In her nightmares the baby had always been lying without sound or movement in his cradle after he had been picked up from the floor and tucked back in. She had been sure that he was dead already and that it was all her fault. But if Felix had still been alive when he was carried out of the house, and for a week after that, it meant that she had not killed him after all. Her father and Nanny Crocker must be telling the truth. The doctor had delivered a baby who was not as big or strong as he ought to be. It was Dr Sibley who was to blame. The relief was so great that Grace's own strength rushed back, flushing her cheeks and filling her body with energy. Her breathing was no longer laboured, but smooth and easy. When Philip put his head round the door to ask if he could take her for a walk to show her something special, she bounced hopefully up and down to show that she was better and accepted without argument all the special instructions about not tiring herself.

'What's the special thing?' she asked Philip, but he refused to tell her.

'Wait and see,' was all he would say.

She skipped happily across the garden and through the rose garden and past the walled vegetable garden. They walked down the hill, through the long grass of the meadow, and skirted round the side of the glasshouse and their father's plant room. Only when it became clear that they were making for the wood did Grace begin to falter and hang back. Philip took her hand. 'It's all right,' he said.

He was taking her to Pepper's grave. Grace realized that even before they arrived. But there had been a change since she last saw it as a rough piece of earth, hastily dug and filled. Someone had tidied it up. A neat frame of grey pebbles outlined what had become a garden bright with pansies.

'Andy got the flowers,' said Philip; and when Grace looked up she saw the gardener's son hovering amongst the trees, waiting to learn whether his contribution was approved. 'And I did the name.' He had used a hot poker to write PEPPER in uneven capitals on a piece of wood which had been placed at the foot of the grave. 'But now we've found a proper headstone. It's too hard for any of us to carve. But if you like it, we'll all pay to have it done properly.'

It was not really a headstone but a paving stone, which must have been left over from the time when the paths and terraces were laid near the house. It was too big – larger than the area of the grave. And too heavy: if it were to topple over it would crush Pepper beneath it. Except, of course, that Pepper was crushed already. Well, it would

70

break the flowers which Andy had planted. Grace shook her head silently. 'I don't want that there,' she said.

With help from Andy, Philip dragged the big stone away. That left the grave looking somehow empty. The boys had been right to think that there ought to be a headstone of some kind – it was just that they had chosen the wrong size. It must be a shape which had some connection with Pepper as he had looked when he was alive. Pepper lying on his back with his four legs in the air, waiting to be tickled. Or stretched to an unnatural length as he stalked a bird and froze for a moment before pouncing. Or alert, with his ears pricked up as he waited to discover what kind of game Grace would play with him.

That was it: the last one. The headstone ought to look like a pair of ears. Grace realized that her hands – as though they had a mind of their own – were tracing the shapes that would be right. Where could she find something like that? She frowned with concentration, and the answer presented itself like a picture in front of her mind. Leaning against the potting shed were some broken pieces of slate; just what she wanted.

As she set off towards the gardener's domain she met Frank running down. 'D'you want to play with us?' he asked. 'We're going to have a Zulu war. You can be the colonel of the regiment if you like. Or the Zulu chief.'

Grace understood what he was saying. This was to be her reward for not sneaking on her brothers about Pepper's death. She had observed the schoolboy's code of honour. So not only could she play with them, but she could play as though she were a boy, no longer confined to the role of a nurse or a maiden needing rescue.

For as long as she could remember – ever since she first became aware that she was a girl and somehow different

71

from the others – she had listened to her parents using the phrase 'Grace and the boys' and had longed to be one of the boys. Now she was being offered the opportunity, but she no longer wished to take it.

She didn't want to be rough and cruel, always looking for someone to hit or something to kill. She didn't want to be a boy and she didn't want to play with boys. She was content to be herself, Grace Hardie: not one of a group, but someone on her own. Her only wish at this moment was to find two pieces of slate which were exactly the right shape to show that it was Pepper who was buried in the woodland grave. She shook her head, not even bothering to thank her eldest brother for the invitation, and plodded on up the hill.

Andy, helping his father to pull carrots, heard the clinking of the slates as she sorted through them and came to see what was happening.

'I want another one just like this.' Grace showed him the broken piece she held in her hand. 'With a point at the top. But sloping the other way.' She wet her finger and drew the pointed cat's ear shape on one of the other pieces of slate.

'It's broken already,' said Andy. 'Don't suppose any-one'll mind . . .' He balanced the slate on the edge of a stone, put his foot on half of it and hit the protruding edge hard with a spade.

'It's *nearly* right,' said Grace, inspecting the result. 'A bit more round.' Never in her life before had she been so sure what she wanted. Andy had to break two more slates and chip away the corner of one of them before she was satisfied. 'Will you help me put them in?' she asked.

Half an hour later she stood back and looked at Pepper's finished grave. The pebbles and the pansies and the two ear-shaped stones all added up to something that was complete. Nothing could cure her grief, but with one last sigh she cleared her mind of rage.

'Thank you very much,' she said to Andy. 'It's exactly right.'

PART THREE
Aunt Midge
1908

1

Grace had always been sure that her aunt liked her best of all the family. In school time, no doubt, a headmistress had to be careful not to show any favouritism, but she relaxed this rule at Greystones.

In the August of 1908, for example, two months after Grace's eleventh birthday, Aunt Midge arrived – as she did in each school holiday – to spend a week with her brother's family. For each of the children she brought with her a gift from Switzerland, where she had spent the previous month. All the boys received chocolate – thick rich bars for the elder ones and a hollow cow for Jay. Grace's present was different.

It was a clock to hang on the wall of the tower bedroom. A clock in the shape of a Swiss chalet, with an overhanging wooden roof and four painted windows surrounded by brightly coloured flowers. From it a thin golden chain hung down, and pulling the shorter end was all that was necessary to rewind it. Once every hour the double doors of the chalet opened and a wide-mouthed cuckoo sprang out to call the time.

'Cuckoo, cuckoo, cuckoo,' it said as Grace was still staring in delight, for the unwrapping of the gift had been timed to take place just before three o'clock.

'Thank you, thank you!' Grace hugged her aunt in delight. 'It's the best present I've ever had.' The best present since Pepper, she might have said; but she never nowadays allowed herself to think about Pepper.

'We'll put it up after tea,' Aunt Midge suggested. 'Are you going to take me for a walk now?' It was part of the routine of every visit that after the greetings were over she should go outside to explore the grounds. 'To blow London away,' she would say, as though that mysterious city were swathed round her head like a scarf of smoke, to be dispersed by the first puff of wind.

Grace nodded happily, and Jay announced his intention of accompanying them. He was almost eight now, and in a few weeks' time would become a day boy at Lynam's, just as his twin brothers moved on from there to boarding school. In his usual wholehearted manner he had thrown himself into the new role of schoolboy already. He insisted on wearing his uniform, with its dragon badge, even during the holiday, and pestered his brothers for hints on what he must remember to do or refrain from doing.

Before joining his aunt and sister he hurried upstairs to change into sports kit, so that he could practise dribbling a football as he ran beside them. The jersey was a hand-me-down from his brothers, all of whom had started school at a slightly later age, so that the garment covered his hands and reached down to his knees. His thick fair hair had not yet been cut with the severity which the new regime would demand and he made a quaint, elf-like figure as he danced, rather than ran, through the meadow, chasing ahead to catch up with his football whenever it rolled too fast down the slope.

'He's very excited about school,' Grace told her aunt.

'I'm not surprised. In the houses around my school in London there are forty girls who must be feeling just the same excitement now. My next two classes of new girls.'

'Don't they ever feel frightened?'

'I hope not. Not for more than a day, anyway. Wouldn't you like to go to school, Grace? You're going to be the only one left in the schoolroom.'

'What would Miss Sefton do if I went to school?'

'She'd have to find another family. But she's been here for twelve years. That's a good run for a governess.'

'I don't think she'd want to go anywhere else,' said Grace. 'And I don't think I'd like playing football all the time.' She was watching Jay as he dribbled and kicked and missed and fell over.

Her aunt exploded with laughter. 'You wouldn't go to a *boys'* school. And girls don't spend nearly as much time playing games. They have more interesting lessons than boys as well. More French and less Latin. You're good at French, aren't you? And more history and less Greek. Proper history, I mean. None of your kings-and-queens-of-England business.'

Grace laughed at the mention of what was a regular tease. Her aunt had asked her on a previous visit what history she had learnt from Miss Sefton, and professed to be shocked by the boast that she could recite the kings and queens in order without a mistake, as well as remembering almost all their dates. Aunt Midge didn't seem to bother too much about dates, and liked to talk about the names in the history books as though they had been real people. 'But you silly goose, they *were*!' she exclaimed when Grace once expressed surprise.

She had even brought one of the kings and queens to life by describing how Ethelred the Unready had had a bad chest, just like Grace herself as a little girl, and how – like Grace again – he had moved from the marshy swamp of Oxford to live on the top of a hill – at Headington, only just across the valley from Greystones.

She often talked about Grace's own hill as well, describing how most of the land had been a royal hunting forest where deer and boar were chased and shot. And how, later, the road from Oxford to London had climbed over the summit so steeply that in the days when there were no railways, and certainly no motor cars, the passengers in

79

each stage coach were expected to get out and walk up Shotover Hill, and sometimes even to push the coach. They would all be very nervous, she said, because the top of a hill, when the horses were going so slowly, was a favourite place for highwaymen. Aunt Midge's descriptions of things that had happened once upon a time were just as exciting as anything Grace read in story books, and were always true.

She didn't on this walk say anything more about school – a subject which perhaps she preferred to put out of her mind during the holidays. But five days later, as the end of her visit approached, Kenneth came to sit beside his sister on the edge of the croquet lawn.

'Aunt Midge thinks you ought to be sent to school,' he said.

'How do you know?' But Grace could guess how he knew. Kenneth had the bad habit of listening at doors. It was a habit made tempting by the fact that their father disliked being in a closed room. Except in his glasshouse, where he was careful to guard against draughts and changes in temperature, Gordon Hardie tended to leave doors open behind him. This meant that any passing child who found an excuse to stray into the adults' part of the house and then lingered in a corridor might hope to pick up some interesting snippets of information. Kenneth, though, was the only one who deliberately courted such opportunities. His brothers and sister disapproved – but could not quite bring themselves to pretend a lack of interest in any news which concerned themselves. 'What did they say?'

'They were all talking last night. Aunt Midge thinks that girls should have as good an education as boys. Father said that they'd thought about sending you somewhere, but of course the village school was out of the question. Mother said that she'd been to visit Mrs Clancy's, and she didn't think the teachers there were any better than Miss Sefton. And Miss Sefton gives you individual attention.' Kenneth pronounced the words carefully, making it clear that he was giving a verbatim report. 'So then Aunt Midge said, what about the Oxford High?'

Aunt Midge herself was an Old Girl of the Oxford High School for Girls. She had had such good teachers there that she was able to pass examinations and study at the university. Lessons at the Oxford High School would be very different indeed from lessons in Miss Sefton's schoolroom. Grace waited to hear how her parents had answered.

'Father said No. Just like that. He said that the standards would be too high. That you weren't brilliant like Aunt Midge had been. But you'd want to do well and you'd try too hard and it would make you ill again. Out of the question, he said.'

Grace supposed it was true that she was not clever – although it was hard to know for sure, when she had no one with whom to compare herself. Except when Miss Sefton was in a bad temper, she said, 'Very good, Grace,' to every piece of work. Anyway, since it seemed that the subject of school had been dismissed, there was no point in wondering whether she would have enjoyed it.

'Let's play croquet,' she said. In the past few months she had started to shoot up in height, so that she was nearly as tall as Kenneth and could at last control the long-handled croquet mallets.

The game was interrupted by a message from one of the maids, summoning Grace to the drawing room, where her mother and aunt wished to speak to her.

'Your aunt has invited you to spend a few days with her in London, Grace. Would you like to do that?'

'Yes, please.' Grace's eyes brightened with excitement.

It would be the first time she had ever spent a night away from home by herself.

'I hoped you might.' Her aunt smiled in a friendly way. 'So you can travel with me when I leave tomorrow. I have a week before the new term begins. I could show you a little of London.'

'We'll ask Gordon when he's next going there,' Mrs Hardie said to her sister-in-law. The House of Hardie had an establishment in Pall Mall as well as in Oxford, and Grace's father divided his time between them. 'He can collect her from you and bring her home. Off you go then, Grace, and choose what you want to take.'

It was all arranged as easily as that, and everything about the visit was an adventure. Grace had travelled in a train before, because her mother took all the children to the seaside for a month each summer. But the bustle of the London terminus was bewildering – and were she to become separated from her aunt, she would have no idea where to go. Not wanting to seem babyish by holding hands, she kept as close as possible until they were safely inside a cab.

The roads were as crowded with vehicles as the railway station had been with passengers. Carriages and carts and horse buses and motor buses overtook each other and hooted at each other and turned in front of each other in what seemed a chaotic and dangerous manner. It was a relief when Aunt Midge leaned forward and told the cabbie to stop.

'Is this where you live?' asked Grace. They had come to a halt in front of an imposing double-fronted mansion, four storeys high.

'No. I live in a tiny stick of a house. Almost as tall as this, but very, very thin. I'll tell the cabbie to take our luggage on there, because you and I can walk from here.

This is my school. I thought you might like to have a look at it, since we were passing.'

'Does the school belong to you?' Aunt Midge used the phrase 'my school' frequently and Grace had never been quite sure what it meant.

'Alas, no. I'd have liked to own something like this. But to buy a building of this size, with the grounds which are necessary, and then to equip it and employ staff – I could never have found enough money. And the business side of it would have been a worry as well. So in the end I had to choose whether to have a small school of my own or to be in charge of a much larger one without owning it. I chose the large school because it has so much more to offer the girls – we can employ more teachers, better teachers, in a greater variety of subjects. And although I have to satisfy a board of governors I run the school very nearly as though it were my own property. There are a few rules which headmistresses have to obey, that's all. Just as there are rules for the girls.'

'What kind of rules?' asked Grace, climbing down to the pavement and waiting while the cab was set on its way again with their luggage.

'Not many. I have to be a member of the Church of England, and unmarried. To live within three miles of the school. And generally to be a respected member of the community.'

It wasn't clear to Grace what that implied, but by now her aunt was leading the way up the steps towards the front door.

'It looks like a house,' Grace commented.

'This part of it *was* a house to start with. This is where the school began – with only a few girls – and we still use the rooms in it for small classes of the older pupils. But so many girls wanted to come here that four years ago we put up a new building in the garden. That's where the new girls start off. Come and see.'

She unlocked the door and led the way through the old building and along a covered corridor which linked it to the new wing. Opening the first classroom door, she showed Grace into a large, bright room. Its windows were high – the pupils here would not be able to stare at the garden, as Grace so often did in her schoolroom at Greystones – but they ran the whole length of the wall. At the end of the room a blackboard and easel stood on one side of the fireplace, with the teacher's desk and chair on the other. Facing these were twenty desks arranged in rows. They still had a shiny new look to them – quite unlike the schoolroom table which four Hardie boys had stabbed with knives and pen nibs and on which they had inked their initials before Grace sat down at it for the first time. Each desk had a bench attached to it, a shelf beneath for the storage of books, and an inkpot and pen tray set into the top.

'It looks bare now,' said Aunt Midge. 'But as soon as the new term starts, the walls will be covered with charts and pictures and pieces of specially good work, and the orders.'

'What are the orders?'

'We have little tests every Monday morning, to make sure that everyone has worked hard and paid attention during the previous week. All the marks are added up as the term goes on, and the name of each girl in the class is put up in order. It's like a ladder – everyone starts in the same place, but someone who works hard can climb right to the top.'

'And someone else can fall off the bottom,' suggested Grace.

'Not fall off, exactly. Anyone who finds herself at the bottom will work harder next term, and do better.

Most of the lessons take place in these classrooms, but we have special rooms for art and music and exercise.' She led the way down a corridor, opening doors as she went.

'Climbing ropes!' Grace clapped her hands at the sight of some of the gymnasium apparatus. 'I can climb ropes. Mama said that it was a most unladylike activity, but Papa said that I might want to go to China one day, like a certain young lady he'd known once, so that the nearer I was to being a monkey, the better. Anyway, Frank built a tree house once, and that was the only way in.'

'I'm sure you can do almost everything that the other girls here can. You're probably very good at cricket, from practising with the boys. I don't expect you know how to play hockey, though. That's our winter game here. Would you like to try?' Aunt Midge opened a cupboard and pulled out a hard white ball and two battered hockey sticks. 'Come on,' she said, unbolting a door which led out on to a large area of grass. 'There's no one looking.'

Grace took off her straw hat and her gloves and her summer coat with its cape collar and ran out on to the field. Her aunt taught her how to bully off, and they practised, making satisfying clicks as their sticks banged together, until the first time that Grace was able to get the ball away. Then she was shown how to dribble it. She was a good runner and her hands and wrists were strong; she was quick to get the knack of the game, although she tended to hit too hard, sending the ball ahead of her. Her aunt, running even faster, demonstrated how easy it was to rob her of possession, dribbling the ball herself for a few strokes before allowing Grace to tackle her and get it back.

'You're very good at it, Aunt Midge!'

'I used to be once. When I was at school and university I played a lot. But I'm out of practice now – as well as out of breath! Dashing around a hockey field is thought undignified for a headmistress, I'm afraid.'

'Not being a respectable member of the community?' suggested Grace, laughing. She hit the ball as hard as she could manage away from the school building and then, biting her lip with concentration, dribbled it back again. 'I wish I could go to a school like this!' she exclaimed.

'Do you?' Just for a second, before bending to pick up the ball, her aunt gave her a considering look. 'Well, perhaps . . .' She didn't finish the sentence. 'You must be getting hungry,' she said briskly instead. 'And my housekeeper will be wondering what's become of us. Shall we walk home?'

The distance was not very far – not long enough, indeed, for Grace to sort out her thoughts. She had taken her aunt's invitation, when it was first issued, to offer exactly what it said: a brief holiday visit. But suppose there was more to it than that. Was the inspection of the classroom – and even the hockey lesson – all part of the argument which Kenneth had reported after his session of eavesdropping? Aunt Midge would not have wanted to press the matter of schooling unless she believed that her niece would enjoy it. Now she had heard Grace's own opinion. What was she going to do about it?

They had arrived at a house which had no front garden. Between it and the road one flight of steps led up to the front door and another, behind iron railings, went down to a basement area and a kitchen in which someone could be seen preparing a meal. Grace followed her aunt up the steps and waited while she unlocked the door.

Inside the hall, Aunt Midge held a hand out towards Grace in welcome. 'Here we are,' she said, smiling affectionately. 'Very small compared with Greystones, but I hope you'll be comfortable. Lots of stairs, I'm afraid. There's only a dining room on this floor. We have to go up to the drawing room and up again to the bed-rooms.'

Still holding her niece's hand, she turned towards the staircase and then gave a startled gasp as the figure of a man appeared on the half landing. Her grip tightened round Grace's fingers until it hurt.

'Patrick!' she exclaimed.

2

Grace was as startled as her aunt by the stranger's unexpected appearance – a little frightened even, since her first thought was that he must be a burglar. It was reassuring to find that her aunt appeared to know him by name – and the man himself was smiling and holding out both hands towards them in a friendly way.

'Welcome home!' he exclaimed – but he cut the words off oddly, as though he would have suppressed them altogether had he had time to think about it. There was a moment of silence – a curious silence, as though everyone was waiting for someone else to speak first. Puzzled, Grace looked from one adult to the other.

'Miss Hardie!' In the end it was the gentleman who took the initiative. 'I hope I didn't alarm you. Your housekeeper kindly allowed me to await your arrival here. Your luggage had just been delivered when I called, so that she was expecting your return at any moment.' He turned towards Grace, whom perhaps he presumed to be one of the headmistress's pupils. 'I had the good fortune to meet Miss Hardie while she was on holiday in Switzerland a few weeks ago,' he explained. 'She expressed interest in a modest sketch I was making. I've taken the liberty, Miss Hardie, of having the painting framed, in the hope that you'll accept it as a memento of your stay in Lugano.'

'How very kind, Mr Faraday. Grace, come and admire it with me.' Aunt Midge led the way briskly up the stairs and into the drawing room, where the water colour was propped up on an armchair. 'The view from the terrace.

The lake and the mountains. How delightful!' She was talking in a breathless manner quite unlike her usual voice. No doubt she was as excited about this unexpected gift as Grace herself had been when she unwrapped the cuckoo clock. 'Where do you think it should hang, Grace?' she asked.

This was the first time that Grace had been in her aunt's drawing room: she looked carefully around to find the best place. Between two tall windows which stretched almost from the floor to the ceiling hung a painting which seemed to her greatly to resemble the one on the chair. Both were water colours, mounted and framed in exactly the same way, and of the same size. The one on the wall was of a waterfall rather than of a lake, but each of the two pictures contained trees and areas of sky and cloud which were painted in a similar style.

'It would make a pair with that one,' she said, pointing. 'You could put one on either side of the fireplace.'

'You're quite right, Grace. And I haven't introduced you. Mr Faraday, this is my niece, Grace Hardie.'

'Grace Hardie of Greystones?' asked Mr Faraday, shaking hands.

Grace's eyes opened wide with astonishment. 'How did you know that, Mr Faraday?'

'Mr Faraday is an architect,' her aunt told her. 'It was he who designed Greystones.'

'Specially for you.' The remark was made with a smile, but it caused Aunt Midge to frown at him as though he had said something wrong.

'Well, for your family,' she told Grace. 'But with that very special room for you.'

'The tower, yes.' Mr Faraday accepted the correction. 'Because you were ill and needed a high room with a lot of sunshine. I hope you liked it.'

'It's lovely,' said Grace. 'It's still my bedroom now.'

'I'm glad it was a success. Well, Miss Hardie, you'll be wanting to rest after your journey. I'll be on my way.'

'You must come and take tea with us when the picture is hung. Until then, thank you very much indeed for a most generous gift.' Aunt Midge held out her hand and the architect bowed over it before withdrawing.

'Now I must show you where you'll be sleeping,' Aunt Midge said to Grace. 'More stairs, I'm afraid. And then Mrs Linacre will have luncheon ready for us.'

It was fun to explore the house and to sit down in a proper dining room, just as though she were grown up. Only after the meal, when they returned to the drawing room, did Grace once again look closely at the water colour.

'Mr Faraday's a very good painter, isn't he? Did he draw a picture of Greystones before he built it?'

'A lot of pictures,' her aunt told her. 'They're called plans when architects draw them. They don't have to be as pretty as a picture like this – just to show what the new building will look like. So he would have made four drawings of the outside – one from each side – and then added another set of plans to show how it would look inside.'

'How do you do that?' asked Grace. 'When I do painting with Miss Sefton she tells me to paint what I can see, but you can't see inside from outside.'

'I'll show you. Your father's got the plans for Greystones, of course. But Mr Faraday designed the new wing of my school as well, and I have some of his first sketches for it here.'

'That was curious,' commented Grace. 'I mean, Mr Faraday doing my house and then your school.'

'It was *because* he did your house so well that I suggested

90

his name to my governors when they were considering the extension.'

'But I thought he said he only met you a few weeks ago.'

'He met me in the sense of running into me again by accident.' Her aunt spoke now with a touch of irritation, as though she had had enough of this conversation. 'I'll go and look for the portfolio for you.'

She returned within a few minutes and spread out half a dozen large sheets of paper. Grace, who had spent those moments wondering whether there was some kind of mystery about Mr Faraday, banished the question from her mind as she studied the drawings and tried to work out what it was about the lines that made her feel as though she were indeed looking into one of the classrooms. Miss Sefton had never taught her anything about the rules of perspective.

'I'd like to be able to draw the insides of things like that,' she said wistfully. 'Are the girls at your school taught how to do it in that art room I saw?'

'Yes, that's one of the things they learn.'

Grace said nothing more then; and the next few days were busy with treats as she was taken to see some of the sights of London. Only as the end of the brief holiday approached did she ask the question which had been in her mind ever since the hockey lesson.

'I wish I could come to your school, Aunt Midge,' she said. 'Do you think, if I asked Father . . .'

She hardly dared to go on. The chance to become a pupil at the school was only half of what she was pleading for. It would only be possible if she could live in her aunt's house; and that was a tremendously large favour to ask. The only reason why she dared to hint at it was the feeling she had had when she first arrived in London – the impression that she was *expected* to ask, and had indeed been taken into the school building expressly to be shown what treats were on offer. But if she had been right about that, her aunt would at this moment be clapping her hands with the enthusiastic pleasure with which she usually greeted Grace's suggestions. Instead, she looked undecided, her forehead creased in doubt.

'I'd love to have you here, dear, if you think you could manage the work,' she said. 'Would you like me to set you a little test tomorrow? You wouldn't want to come to a school like this if you were always going to be bottom of the orders, of course. But if you felt you could do well and keep up with the other girls, I'd be happy to ask your parents whether you might stay with me during term time. Suppose you sit down now and write a list of all the lessons you do with Miss Sefton – and then tell me what the last thing is that you learned in each subject. Then I'll know what kind of questions to ask you. There's no point in my giving you a long division sum to do, for example, if you've never been shown how to solve it.'

Grace licked her lips nervously. She had not expected her request to be answered with an examination. Since the girls at school had tests every Monday morning as well as examinations at the end of each term, she could see that she would have to get used to doing them. But she was not good at sums, and she suspected that the kind of history and geography she had learned was not the kind that Midge would ask her to write down. Her French and German were quite good, she thought, because as well as her lessons with Miss Sefton she spent an hour in conversation with her mother in each language every week. In English, too, she knew her parts of speech and could do parsing. She wrote these three subjects at the top of her list before struggling to think of some rule of arithmetic that she could be sure of applying accurately.

That night, for the first time since her arrival in London,

Grace slept badly. As she brushed her hair in the morning, she could see in the glass that her eyes were ringed with black circles, making her face appear even paler than usual. 'Did you have a bad night, dear?' asked her aunt, concerned, as soon as she appeared for breakfast.

'My chest was a bit wheezy,' Grace confessed. 'It's all right now, though.'

'Your room wasn't damp, I hope. I asked Mrs Linacre most particularly . . . Your mother said she thought you'd grown out of these attacks. Does your wheezing start again every time you leave home?'

Grace had not had a bad attack since she was seven. Her holidays at the seaside had never affected her health. But if she were to confess this, it would put an end to her hopes of being invited to live in London. 'I'm quite all right,' she repeated. 'May I do the test straightaway?'

A paper with two questions on each subject was waiting for her on the bureau in the drawing room. Her aunt read the morning paper whilst Grace settled down to work. The French part of the test was easy, and she could manage the English as well. But the sums refused to come right. Grace scribbled figures and crossed them out and tried again. Tears of frustration and disappointment began to trickle down her cheeks. As long as she kept her back to her aunt, and neither sniffed nor dabbed with her handkerchief, perhaps no one would notice. But as she continued to struggle, a rasping noise made itself heard first in her throat and then in her chest. She had to fight for breath, and soon was unable to think of anything else.

'You must leave that and rest a little,' said her aunt, alarmed by the sound of her breathing. She came over to the bureau to take the paper away. 'Oh, Grace dear, it's not worth crying about. We shouldn't have spoiled your holiday with nasty things like tests.'

'I can't make the sums come right,' sobbed Grace. 'Miss Sefton tells me what to do, but I keep forgetting.'

Aunt Midge crumpled up the paper and tossed it into the empty grate. 'We're going to forget about all this,' she said. 'Off you go and put your hat and coat on. I'll take you to Kensington Gardens. You can sit down and rest in the sunshine until you feel better – and watch the children sailing their boats in the Round Pond. There's to be no more talk of lessons or tests.'

That promise was kept – but the holiday was in any case almost at an end, for it was later the same day that Grace's father arrived to take her home. This was the moment when the invitation might have been issued – that Grace should become a pupil at her aunt's school. But nothing was said, and she knew that nothing would ever be said.

She assumed that it was because she was not clever enough. It was only just as they were leaving that another possibility entered her head.

Her father was studying the new water colour, which had been hung in the place suggested by Grace herself. 'Pretty,' he said to his sister.

'Yes, isn't it?' That was her only comment. Nothing about the fact that she knew the artist. No mention even that that artist had designed Greystones and so was known to her brother. Although Grace was not good at sums, she could put two and two together in other ways. She was not supposed to have met Mr Faraday, and her aunt did not want her to meet him again. She would be in the way here: that was why she was being sent back to Greystones.

Well, Greystones was her home and everyone had taken it for granted that she would return there at the end of her visit. If it hadn't been for the hockey lesson, no other idea would have entered Grace's head. She ought not to be disappointed when she had had no reason to hope. Anyway, Greystones was where she liked to be.

'Thank you for having me, Aunt Midge,' she said politely.

PART FOUR

First Love
1913–1914

1

'Grace! Grace, come and tango with me.'

Jay was calling from the old schoolroom, which was a schoolroom no longer. On Grace's sixteenth birthday, two months earlier, her years with Miss Sefton had at last come to an end. The scuffed desks at which all the Hardie children had learned their letters and carved their initials had been pushed to the wall to clear a space on the green linoleum.

Grace smiled at the eagerness in her younger brother's voice. Of all the Hardie family, he was the quickest to pick up a new craze – and to drop it again. The year 1913 had come in to the sound of ragtime; but by now, in August, ragtime was old hat. Everyone who was anyone was dancing the tango. That, at least, was the report which he had brought with him from London, where he had just spent a month of his summer holiday with a schoolfriend.

At the age of thirteen Jay was not precisely sophisticated, but he possessed a talent for social adaptability. His schoolfriend's sister, an eighteen-year-old debutante, had been doing her season, and Grace listened in amazement as Jay described the timetable of visits to photographers and dressmakers and milliners, rides in Hyde Park and formal calls, soirées and parties, dinners and balls. What a contrast with her own uneventful life!

Her brother had been too young to act as an escort, but his aptitude for observation and mimicry enabled him to give a realistic impression of a young man about town. He had taught Grace the new dance as soon as he returned. Now, winding up the gramophone, he led her into the tango with self-possessed elegance, as though he were six feet tall and wearing white tie and tails.

One day, no doubt, he *would* be six feet tall, but for the moment Grace towered above him. Stronger as well as bigger than her younger brother, she found it hard to follow his lead with the swerving fluidity demanded by the rhythm. It was easier, when the record came to an end and Jay was rewinding the gramophone, to continue dancing by herself to imaginary music, dipping and pausing and turning with a swishing of skirts. Jay restarted the record – the only tango he possessed – and took her hint, touching just her fingertips as they danced side by side, together and yet separate.

Very soon now, Grace supposed, Jay would enter the clumsy stage through which all their brothers had passed, but for the moment he was a neat dancer, in perfect control of his body. There was a look in his eyes, dreamily intense, which she remembered from earlier enthusiasms. It meant that he had temporarily become someone else – Vernon Castle, perhaps, that most elegant of ballroom dancers, whose fame had crossed the Atlantic. She waited until the record ended for a second time before speaking.

'How's the poetry going?' she asked, picking up a gramophone needle and sharpening it.

'Oh, that.' Jay's pale cheeks flushed like a girl's. 'I've given that up.'

'I thought you'd decided you were a poet.'

Jay had spent the first days of the summer holiday sprawled in the shade of the beech tree while he composed verses addressed to a beautiful young woman – although at that time, as far as Grace knew, he was not acquainted with any girls of his own age at all. He was regularly ragged by the whole family for the wholeheartedness with which he threw himself into each new enthusiasm – a wholeheartedness matched only by the rapidity with which he abandoned one role in order to play another.

100

'I wasn't *being* a poet,' he mumbled. 'I was just pretending to be one.'

'What's the difference?'

'I can't explain. I just know, that's all.' He turned away with the suspicion of a pout on his face.

'But I want to understand.' Jay being honest about his previous pretensions was a more interesting person than Jay aggressively pretending. 'I mean, what you *are* is a schoolboy. But you won't stay that for ever. You don't want to. So I can see that you must be something else at the same time. Our futures – mine as well as yours – must be inside us now, if only we could recognize them. In July you thought you *did* recognize yours: you were going to be a poet. Now you say you were only pretending. How did you find out?'

'If you put a real thing and a pretending thing next to each other, you can see which is which.'

'So what's the real thing?' She tugged at his unwillingness to speak. 'Come on, Jay. Tell.'

'You'll laugh.'

'No, I won't. Honour bright.'

For a moment longer he hesitated, whilst Grace's eyes stared steadily into his. 'Well,' he said. 'In London, while the others were all at their parties and things, Barrington and I were allowed to do pretty well whatever we liked. We went to the theatre almost every night. I'd never been before. Have you?'

Grace shook her head. 'What did you see?'

'We saw Nijinsky. Of course, I'd never be able to dance like him. And we heard Chaliapin singing Boris Godunov, but I wouldn't be able to sing either. We went to the music hall lots of times as well. Gosh, performing like that – I mean, standing on a stage and being yourself and trying to make people laugh . . .' He gave a mock shudder. 'No. But as well as that we saw some plays. One of them was

101

frightfully boring. And some of them were rather silly. But that didn't seem to matter. It was just that while I was in the theatre, watching ordinary people pretending to be other people, I realized what I was. What I *am*. Really.'

'You mean that you want to write plays instead of poetry?'

'Oh no.' Jay was indignant at her mistake. 'I mean that I'm an actor.'

'You want to go on the stage!' With a struggle Grace managed to keep both laughter and astonishment out of her voice. 'Mother and Father will have a fit.'

'I don't know if that's what I want. It could be. But what I might want to do is different from what I *am*.' The sulky expression returned to his face. 'I knew you wouldn't understand. But you asked me what was inside me, and that's the answer.'

'You think that what you are and what you do are two different things?'

'Well, look at Father,' said Jay earnestly. 'He's an explorer. It's the only thing he cares about, really. Think of those books he reads! All the time he's fiddling around in his plant room, he's dreaming of making another trip some day, to look for new plants. He knows a lot about wine and he knows how to run a business, but being a wine merchant is just something he has to do to get money for the family. And even Mother . . . She's not interested in running the house and paying calls on people, not really. But when she's painting – haven't you noticed? If you go into the studio when she's painting, she'll look up but she won't see you properly for a moment. And then her face changes. As though she's coming out of a dream. I don't mean that she wants to be an artist; not to earn money for it. But she's a painter inside herself, I'm sure. Everything else is a kind of pretending.'

Grace considered this analysis with surprise and interest. Her youngest brother's aptitude for mimicking other people frequently led him to reveal – almost without intending it – an unexpected insight into their characters; but she couldn't recall that he'd ever before put it into words.

'Does everyone feel that, d'you think?' she asked, genuinely interested. 'All the boys?' Her elder brothers were young men now, but she still called them the boys. 'Frank?'

Frank, who was twenty-two, had gone into the business which one day he would own, bringing to The House of Hardie his considerable talent for organization. Whether or not he proved to be a knowledgeable vintner, he was certainly going to become a successful businessman.

'Frank likes running things and bossing people about.' Jay's summing up agreed with Grace's own opinion. 'The being and the doing may be the same thing for him. I don't know. Or if they aren't, he hasn't found out yet, like I have.'

'The road to Damascus!'

'You can laugh, but –'

'Don't be so touchy, Jay. I'm not laughing. Not really. You're saying something important. I'm just trying to think whether it's something general or just about you, that's all.'

'Well, take Andy Frith,' said Jay. 'Andy would know what I mean.'

Grace allowed her surprise to show. The nineteen-year-old gardener's son – who had been employed straight from school as assistant to his own father – was her favourite companion, but she couldn't imagine what he had in common with Jay. She said so.

'Andy is a grower,' said Jay earnestly. 'He's paid to grow things and growing things is what he'd want to do

103

even if he wasn't paid.' He laughed, pleased with himself. 'I shall call this the Hardie theory of happiness. You're happy when what you are is the same as what you do.'

'What am I?' asked Grace.

Jay looked surprised. 'You're a girl.'

'Is that everything? Under your theory, I mean? Doing as well as being?'

'You'll get married and have babies,' said Jay. 'That's what being a girl is.'

'Aunt Midge never married.'

'Perhaps no one asked her to.'

'She might like being a headmistress better than having babies.' But Grace could tell that her brother, who had little love for his own schoolmasters, was not convinced by the suggestion, and she hardly believed it herself.

'Anyway,' he assured her. 'You're different from Aunt Midge. *You*'ll get married.'

'I suppose so.' It was true. That was what would happen. Grace took it for granted. It was what she wanted, in a way. The only problem, if it was a problem, was that she could not quite imagine what it would be like. But probably everyone who was still living at home with parents had the same difficulty in seeing the way ahead. And certainly, unlike Jay, she had no alternative vision of something inside herself which would demand to be expressed in a different way.

'One more tango,' she said.

As they danced, she looked down at her brother. He was a strikingly good-looking boy, with thick fair hair which rose in waves from his forehead, and darker eyelashes, long and curling. To Grace it seemed unfair that a brother should have the attributes which would have been so much more useful to herself.

104

She knew that she was not pretty. She had inherited her father's strong features instead of her mother's blonde beauty; and the high forehead and wide eyebrows which looked distinguished on him were forbidding on a sixteen-year-old girl. She was tall for her age, and her hands were too large. The wide stretch of her fingers was useful for playing the piano, but at other times she felt self-conscious, wishing that she – like her brothers – had pockets in which to hide them. Her dark eyes might have been attractive in someone else's face, but contrasted too dramatically, she felt, with her pale complexion.

Often – unfairly, in her opinion – she was reproved by her mother for staring. Grace believed it only polite to look straight at anyone who was talking to her, and certainly she liked to study objects with a sustained scrutiny, as though by concentration she could see all sides – and even the centres – at once. She could not help it if her eyes seemed to focus more strongly than other people's. She was only looking. Presumably she had also inherited from her father the intense gaze with which he seemed magically able to deduce from the outside of some bulb or even seed what it would become one day.

'You're staring,' said Jay, as severely as if it were their mother speaking.

'Sorry. I was just thinking. About what you said. It was interesting. Rather like one of Father's lilies. Until it goes into the earth it's just a small brown object, rather ugly, with scales flaking off it. But the flower is inside all the time, waiting to emerge.'

'Not the same.' Jay gave an elaborate twirl and bow as the music came to an end. 'The lily can't be anything but a lily, and nobody can stop it. But we have choices. And if we choose wrong, we may never find out that we're lilies at heart. If you see what I mean,' he added, giggling at the ridiculous comparison.

Yes, Grace saw what he meant, and her understanding made her uneasy. 'I'm going down to the boulders,' she said. Jay would know what she meant.

2

Deep in thought, Grace made her way round to the side of the house and down the hill. To reach the wood and the stream she had first to pass her father's plant room and glasshouse, and as she approached it she saw Andy Frith emerging, closing the door carefully behind him. He looked excited, as though he had been given good news. Andy spent much of his time helping her father instead of his own, and it might be that one of the new hybrids had just flowered for the first time. She could see that he was longing to tell her something; but he hung back, not liking to speak first.

His appearance reminded her of the doubts which Jay had sown in her mind when he used the gardener's son as one of his examples. 'We have choices,' Jay had said, and that was undoubtedly true of himself and the other boys. But was it true for her? As her brother had pointed out, she was a girl, waiting to become a wife and mother. One day, perhaps, a young man would walk into her life as once upon a time her father had walked into a garden and fallen in love with the beautiful girl he saw there. But it would not be for Grace to choose whom she would marry. She must wait to be chosen – and who would ever want to love a tall, ungainly girl with fierce eyes and too large a nose? Grace stopped dead in her tracks and directed her gaze straight at the young gardener.

'Do you think I'm pretty, Andy?'

Even before the words were out of her mouth, she was appalled by her own question. It might have been just permissible to ask her mother or one of her brothers, but not anyone outside the family. And especially not one of the staff. She blushed – and the more she tried to control the blush, the more rapidly it spread, suffusing her neck as well as her face. Quickly she turned away, hoping that Andy would be tactful enough to pretend that he hadn't heard. But he was clearing his throat, determined to speak although apparently having difficulty in forcing the words out.

'I think you're beautiful, Miss Grace.'

Unable to believe her ears, Grace turned slowly back to face him. Had her emotions been under control, she might have laughed to see her own blush reflected in Andy's cheeks. Although his arms were so freckled as to be almost brown, his face had the fair complexion which went with his red hair. The wide-brimmed cloth hat which he always wore for outside work prevented his skin from being reddened by the sun. But no hat could save him from the flush which rose from within as uncontrollably as her own.

'I'm sorry,' Grace mumbled. Was she apologizing for her own forwardness or for Andy's embarrassment? Without waiting to think it out she ran away from him, through the wood and towards the stream.

Panting, she came to a halt by the boulders – and almost at once, as she allowed her fingers to stroke them, they performed their usual miracle by calming her spirit.

The two huge boulders which stood on the bank of the stream were immensely old – millions of years old, according to Andy. Unlike Grace's brothers, Andy had never learned any Latin or Greek at school, but he seemed to know more than the Hardies themselves about the land they owned. The boulders, he had told Grace, must have been moulded by a glacier during the Ice Age. Nothing else would explain their almost perfect roundness. Not quite perfect, because in each of them there was a small, scooped-out hollow about twelve inches across.

The boulders could be approached only through the densest, dampest, darkest part of the wood. They stood in a depression which in the wettest months of the year filled with rainwater to become a pool. Grace had first discovered them when she was six or seven years old. She had been angry about something – what it was, she no longer remembered – and so almost deliberately fought her way through the barrier of brambles which had discouraged exploration before. By the time she stepped into a clearing on the further side of the thorns her skirt was torn and her stockings bloodstained; but both the scratches and the punishment to come were forgotten in astonishment at what she had discovered. It was as though she had broken through a magic wall into a haven of calmness like a prince discovering his Sleeping Beauty.

At that time the hollows in the huge stones had seemed to her to be fingerholds, ready for a giant to pick up one boulder in each hand and hurl them away. Now that she was sixteen she no longer believed in giants, of course – and yet it was odd that the hollows should be so similar, when the stone was too hard to be chipped or carved. She still felt the boulders to be in some way supernatural, out of the ordinary. There was a spooky atmosphere about them.

Her mother would have said that Grace herself carried the atmosphere to the stones – and it was true that she most often visited them when her spirits were disturbed. They had a soothing quality. When she touched them she could feel them absorbing all her tensions, leaving her mind and body at peace.

Today she had no cause for unhappiness, and hardly understood her own mood as her fingers, like those of a blind woman, passed lightly over the stones. From a distance they appeared smooth, but her touch was sufficiently sensitive to register the thousands of tiny pitted circles which covered the surface – just as Andy's arms were covered with the overlapping circles of his freckles. For a moment it was as though it was the young gardener's arms, and not the boulders, that she was stroking. Guiltily she let her hands fall to her sides. She did not want to think about Andy now.

But she had no choice, for he had followed her down the hill and through the wood, and was standing motionless in the shadows. Grace had never before felt uneasy in his presence, but there was something different about him today – a change which could not simply be explained by her shameful behaviour of a few moments earlier. Just as Jay appeared to have left boyhood behind him during his visit to London, so Andy had abruptly matured from a youth to a man. What had happened to inspire the excitement he could not conceal? She did not speak, but her eyes gave him permission to step forward and explain.

'Mr Hardie sent for me this morning. I'm to be promoted. To take over all his own work while he's away. The plant room, the glasshouses, the seed beds, the records. Sole responsibility, he said. I'll still help in the garden with the time I've got left, but my father's to have another journeyman, so that I'll be at no one's beck and call. It's what I've always wanted. My own kingdom, you might say. Three years. There'll be time for me to try crosses of my own, as well as keeping to the plan Mr Hardie's leaving behind. I might surprise him with something.'

Never in his life before had Andy been heard to deliver such a long speech, but Grace was startled by far more than his sudden fluency. Her first reaction was one of relief that her childish question had already been forgotten, but this was quickly followed by a stab of indignation. If it was true that her father was going away for three years, she ought to have been told before a member of the staff.

What a selfish reaction! She should be happy for Andy,

whose whole body seemed to be glowing with pride in his new responsibilities. And indeed she *was* happy for him, instinctively stretching out her hands as she smiled her congratulations. 'I'm sure you'll do marvellously well, Andy.'

'Thank you, Miss Grace.' The words were what she expected. More startling was the movement with which he caught and gripped her hands. Grace realized that her gesture had been too impulsive – but Andy should have known better than to take advantage. Although he looked down at their clasped hands with as much surprise as she did, he did not relax his grip, but instead gave an odd kind of gasp. 'Oh, Miss Grace!' He pulled her close, enfolding her in his arms.

It was Grace's first kiss and took her by surprise, giving her no time to think how she should respond. It was wetter and rougher than the cool touch of her mother's lips on her cheek or forehead. At first she felt herself to be outside the embrace, observing and worrying about it. What was she supposed to do with her hands? Tentatively she moved them upwards until they rested on Andy's arms. How firm and strong they were compared with Jay's! Her fingers moved over the soft skin which covered the hard muscles rather as they had earlier explored the boulders, trying to feel through the texture of the surface the quality of what was inside.

And then, without warning, she could not remain outside the scene any longer. Andy had been holding her close enough already, but suddenly he flung himself at her, pressing her back against one of the boulders. The first long kiss was over. His mouth moved over her face and neck as if no inch of skin must be left untouched. Grace's hands no longer awaited instructions, but held him tightly, pulling him even nearer. Their closeness robbed her of breath and the beating of her heart was suspended by happiness. When at last he let her go, she staggered a little from faintness.

Andy, for his part, was gasping. He struggled to speak, but no words emerged. Then he turned and ran away through the wood. The child that Grace had been until an hour earlier would have felt disappointment, but the woman she was now was aware only of a glow of happiness. Andy thought she was beautiful. She had found someone who could love her.

3

It was to her aunt that Grace first confessed her feelings. Midge Hardie was as much a part of Christmas at Greystones as the family charades on Christmas Eve, the mince pies waiting for the wassailers and the frosty walk down the hill to Headington Quarry church on Christmas morning. No doubt she had to remain on her dignity all through the school term, so she made up for that by flinging herself wholeheartedly into all the fun of the festivities – playing silly games with her nephews and niece, as well as beating them at the pencil and paper games which required more thought.

Aunt Midge was expected to arrive on 23 December, and this year, Grace realized as she kneaded and plaited the dough for a special Christmas loaf, she would notice a difference. Grace's father was an all-or-nothing man, who balanced any neglect of his children during the working part of the year by the vigour with which he threw himself into the celebration of birthdays or Christmas. But the head of the household was absent. He had sailed for China two months earlier.

The boys had changed, too. Well, they were not boys any longer; perhaps that was the trouble. Only Jay, who at this moment was sitting on the edge of the kitchen table, swinging his legs and eating scraps of raw dough, was still a schoolboy. He certainly was as high-spirited as ever. But the twins had left school and gave themselves the airs of grown-ups, complaining when they were still treated as juniors. David was articled to a firm of solicitors, while Kenneth, unable to produce any suggestions of his own about a career, had been placed by his father in the family business as a trainee. He grumbled that Frank used him as an errand boy, and at home was apt to become tetchy.

Like Frank, the twins were expected by their superiors to stay at work until late on Christmas Eve, being allowed only Christmas Day and Boxing Day as holidays. That was another difference from the time when the family celebrations stretched over at least a week. Philip, who was working for a degree at London University, had arrived home a few days earlier, but even he claimed that he must spend all the vacation in study, and rarely emerged from his room. So Grace and Jay had already concluded that it was up to the two of them to turn this Christmas into a merry occasion. They were confident that their aunt would prove an ally.

She came to search for them in the kitchen, looking startled and amused at the sight of Grace's floury hands and apron, and at the anxious expression on the face of Mrs Charles, the cook, who busied herself in the larder whilst waiting to regain control of her kingdom.

'Have you become assistant cook?' Midge embraced her niece more cautiously than usual, lest her clothes should be marked with flour.

Grace shook her head laughingly. 'I'm just making one special thing. A Christmas loaf.'

'You make *bread*!'

'This is only the second time,' Grace explained. 'In the autumn one of Mother's friends asked if I could help her. She always makes the loaf for the church's harvest festival, but this year her hands were too rheumaticky and she couldn't manage the little fiddly bits. She told me what to do, and I did it. It was beautiful. We made a huge wheatsheaf, with every ear of corn showing and two little mice nibbling.'

114

'It was inedible.' Jay, as usual, was teasing. 'Hard as rock. Convict fare.'

'Nobody was expected to *eat* it. It was for looking at.' Grace had had this argument with Jay before and was not prepared to waste time on it again. 'I enjoyed doing it,' she told her aunt. 'So I thought I'd try making one by myself, for Christmas. Not a wheatsheaf, of course. It was meant to be finished before you arrived, so that I could be waiting with Mother to say hello; but everything took longer than I expected.' She glanced at the kitchen clock. 'It should be ready now.'

As she opened the oven door, Jay slipped down from the table, ready to help; and Mrs Charles also stood by. But Grace – taller and sturdier than either of them – was already thrusting in the paddle to slide the tray out. She set it down on the table and studied her handiwork with critical pride.

She had fashioned a holly wreath, weaving the stems into a plait. The leaves lay neatly in a circle, but eight sprays of berries curved slightly outwards to break the solidity of the shape, and a robin perched above to give it height. Except for the robin's dark raisin eyes and the sesame seeds decorating what had been made to look like a bow of ribbon, the surface had a smooth, honey-golden gloss.

Her aunt took a deep, appreciative breath. 'There is nothing, nothing in the world that smells quite as good as newly-baked bread.' She laughed as Grace glanced anxiously at her. 'Oh, don't worry, dear. I'm not going to start breaking pieces off.'

'Jay's right, really,' Grace admitted. 'It's too dense to taste nice. If I used ordinary rising dough, it wouldn't keep its shape. I had to make a tougher mixture, so that I could model it like clay.'

'Have you ever made anything out of clay?'

115

Grace shook her head. 'No. But I can imagine what it feels like, or nearly. When I was small I used to make mud pies down by the stream. And then squeeze the water out so that I could make little men and animals out of the mud. They always crumbled as soon as they were dry, though. Clay must have the same sort of feeling, but stickier and stronger. Well, that's finished.'

She pulled off her apron, leaving the clearing up to the cook. 'Shall we go for a walk?' she asked. It was always the first thing that her aunt wanted to do – to fill her lungs with country air. They separated only for a few minutes, to dress themselves warmly before setting out together.

The first snow of winter had not yet fallen, but the grass, stiffened by frost, crackled beneath their feet. Grace, tall and long-legged, set off with the athletic stride of someone used to walking in male company, but quickly adjusted to her aunt's pace.

'You walk like your father,' Midge told her. 'I suppose at this moment he's pressing through the Himalayan valleys, full of purposeful energy, sniffing out new plants. Have you heard from him since he left?'

'No. There's hardly been time. He wasn't going to write until he reached Shanghai. I expect the first letter's on its way now. I hope so. Mother's worried. She didn't want him to go. She thinks it's too dangerous.'

'Of course it's dangerous. But that didn't stop her from going with him when she was only a few months older than you are now.'

'It's worse now, she says. He first planned this expedition a few years ago, if you remember – just before the news came through about all the awful things that were happening in China.'

Midge nodded. 'That terrible Boxer Rising. Murders, massacres. Yes, I do remember how disappointed he was at having to abandon his plans.'

'Mother says that the area he wants to explore is un-friendly to foreigners even at the best of times. But when the agent wrote to say that the situation was calm again, I suppose she didn't like to argue.'

'I noticed as soon as I arrived that she wasn't sparkling in her usual way. I've always admired her, you know. She married your father because she wanted to share the excitements of his life, but ever since Frank was born she's had to stay at home and look after you all.'

It was a new thought to Grace that she was partly responsible for condemning her mother to a life of dullness. 'She never says –'

'Of course not. She's not a grumbler. And no doubt it happens to all of us. We have our time of adventure when we're young, and then we have to live on the memory for the rest of our lives. What's your adventure going to be, Grace?'

If there was any excitement in Grace's life it was to be found in Andy's kisses and her own daydreams. But she was not ready to confess to that. 'Nothing ever happens here,' she mumbled. 'Mother makes me go to dancing classes, but I hate them. I'm taller than any of the boys. I look stupid.'

Midge, walking briskly, made no comment on this and for a little while was silent. When she spoke again, it was with her usual decisiveness.

'When I was about your age, my father sent me to France for a year, to stay with the family of one of his suppliers. It would be easy for your mother to make the same kind of arrangement for you. Wouldn't you like that – to go and live in a château of one of the great wine-making families?'

'What for?' asked Grace. 'What would I do there?'

'You wouldn't need to *do* anything unless you chose to. It would simply be a very agreeable way of life. You could learn a good deal about wine if you wished. You could even ask to be given instruction in cookery. French cuisine is thought to be the best in the world.'

'I don't like cooking!' Grace was horrified by the idea.

'But that beautiful loaf —'

'That was different. A special occasion. And no one will eat it. I watch Mrs Charles sometimes, icing cakes or decorating fish in aspic – taking such trouble to make things look nice, and then it's all spoilt and eaten in a second. I couldn't bear that. Last year, when Mother and Father had a silver wedding party, I made a swan out of meringue for the centre of the table.'

Grace was silent for a moment, remembering how difficult it had been to make the mixture keep its shape, and how beautiful it had looked as it came out of the oven, baked slowly for just long enough to form a crust – and then how, by the end of the evening, there had been nothing left but a mess of sticky crumbs. 'I like to do things that will last. I'm giving Mother a cushion cover for Christmas – but you mustn't tell her, of course. I don't specially enjoy doing *gros point*, but now it's finished it will be there to be looked at for years; so I suppose it was worth it.'

'I wasn't suggesting that you should *become* a cook,' her aunt assured her. 'I'm sure you'll always have someone to do that for you. But it's useful to know what you can expect of your servants, to the highest standards. Well, even if that doesn't attract you, a stay in France would help you to perfect your French.'

Grace sighed. She had never wholly understood the point of education. Almost everything that Miss Sefton had ever taught her seemed to be useless. Her brothers, she was sure, felt much the same. Frank and Philip had spent years at school swotting up Latin and Greek. What Philip had really wanted to learn about was soil and air and water and plants, and the school had given him no lessons about that at all. Now that he was at university he could choose what he wanted to study and was content, but he called his schooldays a waste of time. As for Frank, he was never likely to open any of his texts again. What use would Caesar or Homer be in the running of The House of Hardie? 'I can speak French quite well already,' she said. 'But I never need to.'

Her aunt's voice betrayed a touch of irritation. 'You're – how old is it – sixteen? You ought to feel excited at the suggestion of a change. You don't want to stay here all your life, surely.'

Grace quickened her pace so that Midge, falling behind, should not be able to see her flush. 'I don't want to leave my friends,' she said. Even to herself that did not sound convincing. She had grumbled often enough to her aunt about the fact that she had so few chances to meet anyone of her own age.

'Your friends will leave *you*. People move away as they grow up. All your brothers have left home – even Jay is boarding now.'

'Not everyone goes. People from the village stay here all their lives. Most of them have never been even as far as London.'

'You surely don't wish to be like that.' Grace felt her aunt's hand gripping her own to hold her back. 'Is it one special friend that you don't want to leave?' Midge hardly paused for an answer before interpreting the blush that Grace was unable to control. 'Who is it?'

Grace looked down at her feet. 'Andy,' she mumbled.

'Who is Andy?'

'You know, Aunt Midge. Andy Frith.'

'The *gardener's* son! Grace, my dear – Does your mother know?'

'There's nothing to know.'

'You shouldn't have secrets from your mother, Grace dear.'

'Andy and I have been friends for the whole of my life. Mother doesn't need to be told that.'

'Friends as children, yes. But he isn't a child any longer. Nor are you.'

Then stop treating me like one, thought Grace; but she did not dare put her resentment into words. Instead, she looked her aunt straight in the eye. 'You're not going to sneak on me, are you, Aunt Midge?' It was a good many years since Grace had put her tomboy phase behind her and distanced herself from the roughness of her brothers; but she had absorbed their schoolboy code of honour in the nursery, and the resolution in her voice now checked even a headmistress. There was a moment's pause before Midge answered.

'I shall say to your mother what I have just said to you – that I think a year in France would be of great benefit. If she agrees with the suggestion, she'll ask what you think about it, and you'll have the chance to put your own point of view.'

'You don't understand. You don't know how it feels.'

'Oh yes, I do.' Midge's smile and eyes were sympathetic. 'Do you think I've never been in love, Grace? I know that first love is like an illness. Everyone suffers from it sooner or later. I did myself – and I wished afterwards that I'd confided in someone who could have helped me to avoid all the heartbreak. There's no protection against the infection, and it hits you without warning. It can cripple you for life if it's not properly managed – or it can serve a good purpose and give you a kind of immunity, like an inoculation, so that you're never swept off your feet in the same way again.'

'Why should I want to be immune?' cried Grace. 'I love

120

Andy, and he loves me. It's nothing like an illness. I don't want to be cured. I just want to be left alone.'

'You can't be expected to make good judgements at sixteen,' Midge said soothingly. 'You need more experience – a wider circle of acquaintances, so that you can make a choice and be certain what it is that you're choosing.'

'Mother was only seventeen when she fell in love with Father. She'd never loved anyone before and she's never loved anyone since in the same way. She told me so herself.'

Midge hesitated for a second. 'That doesn't mean that she might not have been wiser to wait,' she said. 'It's chilly, standing here. I think I'll get back to the house. Are you coming, dear?'

'Not yet.' Careless of whether she was being rude, Grace hurried away round the side of the hill. On a frosty day like this, when the ground was too hard to dig, Andy would be working in the plant room. Andy wouldn't treat her like a child. He would comfort her and tell her again that he loved her. But even as she ran, with her arms held out sideways to steady her balance on the slope and her breath freezing into white clouds, she knew that Andy would not be able to offer any protection. Her mother and her aunt between them were bound to get their own way. She would have to go to France.

4

For the first few days of what she regarded as her banishment from Greystones Grace was resentful and homesick; but within a week her own robust spirits and the companionship of the daughter of the house restored her to good humour. She knew very little about the wines which provided her family with its income and expected to be bored when her host promised that he would take her to watch the culture of the vines at each season of the year. But as he showed her round the vineyards which surrounded the château and the *caves* in which bottles of his champagne were racked and turned, she found herself genuinely interested in learning more about the complicated processes of viniculture.

She missed Andy, naturally, but was sensible enough to acknowledge that she was still too young to marry. Had she remained in England, the two of them would not have been permitted any private meetings. To be close at hand and yet kept apart might have proved more frustrating than the separation forced on them instead. Andy would remain loyal to her, and she took almost as much pleasure in re-living his kisses through daydreams as she had in his company. Time passed happily enough and in her letters home she made no complaint.

So it came as a surprise when, at the beginning of August, 1914 – only half-way through the twelve-month stay which had been arranged – her eldest brother called without warning at the château. If Frank was continuing his father's custom of calling on his most important suppliers each year, he had chosen an odd time for the visit.

In France, as in England, August was a holiday month.

'Did you come here meaning to do business?' she asked, after he had formally presented himself to her hosts and been left in private conversation with his sister.

'No. I've come to take you home.'

'You mean that my sentence of exile is over – that I've received a pardon?'

Frank failed to return her smile. 'Haven't you heard about the war?' he asked.

'There's been talk, yes. It's expected. But I've been told that England won't be involved.'

'Then you've been told wrong. The order to mobilize the army was issued yesterday, as I was leaving. We may already be at war by now. In any case, it isn't the situation in England which may affect you, but here. Germany has refused to respect Belgian neutrality. That's why we shall have to fight, to defend it. It means that the invasion of France is certain to come from the north-east. Go and pack your things whilst I talk to your hosts. They'll be glad not to have responsibility for you in a time of crisis.'

Grace had not wanted to come, but she was sad to leave and made a formal speech of thanks and real regret in her now fluent French. The regret, however, could not last long. Thanks to the German threat she would soon see Andy again.

Twenty-two hours later the Hardies' carriage made its way slowly up Shotover Hill. The day was hot and the journey had been exhausting. The ultimatum to Germany had expired an hour before midnight on the previous day and every train and Channel steamer was crowded with travellers returning hastily to their own country. In spite of her tiredness, though, Grace asked Frank to stop the carriage soon after it turned into the long drive of Greystones, so that she could approach the house on foot.

The moment of rounding the last bend and seeing her

home for the first time after an absence was always a satisfaction. 'A palace for a princess,' her father had said when he first removed the blindfold from her eyes, and at each new return Grace recaptured some of the pride she had felt then. When she tried to explain her feelings to Frank, who dismounted to walk beside her, he nodded understanding, but not agreement.

'Greystones isn't right really,' he said. 'Not right for us, I mean.'

'What are you talking about? It's perfect.' They could see it now, although still at a distance above them, standing proudly on the higher slope of the hill with its tower – Grace's tower – commanding attention. It was the tower which most of all she loved, but she would not accept criticism of anything about the house.

'Sometimes I think this is why Mother never seems to have many friends,' he said. 'You haven't either, have you? It doesn't matter so much for the rest of us. We've made friends at school, and now there are the people we work with. But – I mean, there are other families like ours in Oxford. If we lived in North Oxford, say, they'd pay calls on Mother and she'd call back. But when people of that kind look at Greystones, they think Mother must be too grand for them. Whilst the people who live in other big houses, the county families, aren't going to mix socially with trade.'

'That's ridiculous,' protested Grace.

'I know it's ridiculous, but it's the way things happen. People like to put other people into boxes. We do it ourselves in The House of Hardie. The amount of credit a customer can draw on isn't written down anywhere, and there are no rules to help us work out a figure. But we all know how far a duke's son can go, or a scholarship boy. And look what happened to Mother when she married outside her own class. Her family never spoke to her again.

124

They made her choose between their circle and Father's circle, because none of them was prepared to cross the line.'

Grace stopped walking and turned to face her brother. 'Are you still talking about Greystones?' she demanded.

'No,' admitted Frank. 'Mother told me about Andy. I'm talking about you and him. Well, perhaps I *am* still talking about houses. I suppose that if Andy takes over from his father as head gardener one day, we'd let him stay on in the cottage. Can you imagine yourself living there, Grace – able to see Greystones, but knowing that it wasn't your home any longer? Because that's what would happen. Andy wouldn't move up: you'd move down.'

'He doesn't have to stay a gardener all his life.'

'He doesn't *have* to – but I think he wants to.'

'Are you trying to tell me that you'd behave like Mother's family did to her? Cut me off?'

'Of course not.' Frank put an arm round his sister's waist and hugged her affectionately. 'I'm behind you whatever you choose to do – as long as you wait until you're old enough to understand the consequences of your choice. Sounds pompous: sorry. But while Father's away I have to speak on his behalf. He'd tell you that you're far too young to think seriously about Andy. Everyone falls in love when they're your age. You think it's going to last for ever – but then you discover that it was the falling in love that was important, not the person you thought you loved.'

'I *do* –'

But Frank, having embarked on his brotherly lecture, was not ready to be interrupted.

'Andy understands all that perfectly well,' he said. 'That's why he's joined up as well. So that you both have time to grow older.'

'Andy!' Grace's heart jumped in panic. 'Andy doesn't

125

want to be a soldier. You can't make him go into the army.'

'No one's making him do anything,' Frank said soothingly. 'Anyone of spirit knows that this is the time to defend his country. He's a good chap, Andy. He can see what his duty is, and he's going to do it.'

'Where is he?' Grace did not wait for an answer, but turned away from the house and ran as fast as she could towards the wood.

'Mother thinks it would be best –' Frank was calling after her, but Grace closed her ears to the words. She didn't care what her mother thought.

Andy was waiting for her by the boulders. She had known that he would be there when she was expected. He stood up as she approached and she flung herself into his arms. Happiness at seeing him again and terror of losing him mingled with the excitement of realizing that he still loved her. The fierceness of his embrace overwhelmed her so that she could hardly breathe. He had kissed her before, but never as passionately as this. When at last he released her, she found herself trembling with weakness.

Side by side they sat down on the ground, leaning back against one of the huge boulders. In the world outside the sun was shining brightly, but here it only pierced through the canopy of trees in narrow shafts, dappling her clothes with a pattern of leaves or illuminating circles of moss or water like spotlights. There was so much to talk about – all the thoughts and feelings saved up during their six-month separation – but Grace was able to voice only a single plea. 'You mustn't go. Don't do it.'

'It's done.' Andy's arm tightened round her waist. 'I went to the recruiting office yesterday. Got to report to Aldershot tomorrow. Reckon it's best, anyway. They're not going to let us meet. Might make it awkward for my father if I were to stay on here. He's only got the cottage for as long as he's employed at Greystones.'

'Mother wouldn't dismiss your father just because of us!' Grace was aghast at the thought, but Andy shrugged his shoulders.

'She won't need to. It's right for me to go. A job to be done. And time for me to make a life for myself. So's when I come back it won't be just as old Frith the gardener's son.' He checked himself, thinking over those last words. 'Not ashamed of that,' he said. 'But Andy Frith, me, separate; I have to show people.' He was not used to expressing his thoughts in words. 'Best I should go,' he repeated.

His hand rested on top of hers, gently stroking her fingers. Grace stared down at it, intent on memorizing the moment through the pattern of freckles on his skin and the colour of his fine, sandy hair.

'Will you write to me, Andy?'

'Not much of a hand at writing,' he confessed. 'But when they allow, yes. Reckon you'll soon forget about me, though.'

'No!' Grace would have protested at greater length, but at that moment she caught the sound of Frank's voice calling her name. She scrambled to her feet as he came nearer.

Andy, equally quick to stand, pulled her round to the far side of the boulder. It was quite large enough to conceal them both. For a second time he took her in his arms.

'Say it,' she pleaded. 'Please say it.'

'I love you.' He pressed her back against the stone with such force that her body seemed to take on the hardness of the rock and her lips bruised against her teeth. Then, as Frank's footsteps approached, Andy broke away and disappeared silently into the shadows of the wood.

Would she ever see him again? Grace stood for a moment without moving, her shoulders still pressed against

127

the boulder, her breath still trapped in her lungs. Then, with a sigh, she began to brush down her skirt and fasten her hat back into place.

When she was ready, she stepped out into the clearing and waited for Frank to appear. His expression was anxious, and at any normal time she would have laughed at the relief on his face when he saw that she was alone. But even her anger at the family's interference in her life was numbed by the suddenness of her meeting with Andy and their parting.

And Frank was going to war as well. He had told her that twenty-four hours earlier, but only now did she appreciate that there was to be another farewell. As she took his arm and walked on up the hill, she could think of nothing to say.

PART FIVE

Brothers in Arms
1914–1917

1

The disruption caused to the Hardie family's life by the war was immediate and far-reaching, but was not expected to be more than temporary. Before Christmas, without doubt, the army would march back from France in triumph and everything would return to normal. In the meantime Frank, one of the earliest volunteers to enlist, was also amongst the first to be commissioned.

Wearing his second lieutenant's uniform, he came to say goodbye before leaving for France. Jay borrowed his cap and cane and marched up and down in a parody of drill whilst Frank, entering into the game, barked orders. His delight in the prospect of going to war was plain for all the family to see. He had never given any indication of discontent with his work in The House of Hardie, yet his beaming smile revealed now that in joining the army he was not so much reacting to an emergency as fulfilling a vocation. To express that in words would have been too solemn. Instead he announced that he was off to give the Huns a good hiding. Grace had wept bitterly after Andy's departure, but it was impossible to say goodbye with anything but a smile to someone so proud to serve his country.

Patriotism affected Philip in an opposite manner, turning him away from the life he wanted to lead rather than towards it. From early boyhood he had been fascinated by his father's hobby of breeding new plants. He had planned to follow his years at university, which had just ended, with two years of field work in different parts of Europe, analysing the soil and noting the flora supported by it.

Looking ahead, he saw himself as a specialist in the nutrition of plants – in a university, a botanical garden or a commercial nursery. Had he been the eldest son, he would have been pressed to enter the family business. But Frank had taken up the appointed place there, leaving Philip free to pursue his own interests.

He was still free now. Enlistment in the army was a matter of choice, not of conscription. He had no reason to believe that he would enjoy being a soldier, nor that he would be of much use. Unlike Frank, who was a good shot and a fine horseman, Philip held the lives of animals in too much respect to kill them for pleasure. He would shoot for the pot and, for the sake of other animals, would occasionally take a gun to a fox; but he never hunted.

For all these reasons, he was slower to act than his brother. But he was young and fit and had no dependants. The finger of Lord Kitchener, he realized, was pointing at him, and he too crossed the Channel to France.

Kenneth and David, now aged twenty, resisted the wave of jingoism. David, serving his articles as a solicitor, thought it foolish to interrupt his studies until he had qualified. Kenneth, who had gone into the family firm without enthusiasm, might have welcomed a break had it not been for one thing. He was not prepared to kill.

The death of Pepper eleven years earlier had had as traumatic an effect on Kenneth as it had on Grace. He had put the cat out of its agony because he could not bear to hear its wails; but afterwards discovered that his sister's grief in bereavement was equally unbearable, leaving him uncertain whether he had made the right decision. When the death of a mere cat caused so much anguish, how could he bring himself to take the life of a man – even a German?

For the moment he felt himself to be useful in England. Business was brisk as the customers of The House of Hardie hurried to fill their cellars while stocks lasted. With

Frank away, Will Witney, the manager, was left with sole responsibility for running the firm. He worked mainly from Oxford and was glad to have a member of the family in London. Kenneth did his best to close his mind to the war. But as more and more of his generation changed into khaki he found it necessary to keep his eyes on the ground as he walked the streets of London, lest he should be challenged by a contemptuous glance or handed a white feather.

More surprising was the transformation of Grace's life. During the first few weeks of war it seemed enough that she should devote her time to the knitting of socks and jerseys and balaclava helmets, as well as joining in the communal activity of cutting and rolling bandages. It was her aunt, arriving earlier than usual for her regular Christmas stay, who produced a revolutionary suggestion.

'I called at the High on my way here,' she announced. To any member of the family 'the High' referred not to Oxford's main street but to The House of Hardie's bow-fronted establishment. 'Poor Will Witney's rushed off his feet. One of his cellarmen and both his clerks have left to join up and he can't find anyone to take their place. He has to have someone strong and able-bodied for the cellar, of course, but he's seriously thinking that he'll have to consider young women for the office and the counter. It's a problem, though – the first girl he tried couldn't pronounce the names of any of the wines or understand what people were asking for. With all the Christmas business rushing in she simply became flustered and burst into tears. Will's trying to deal with it all himself, but it's far too much for him.'

'Poor Will,' said Lucy, but Midge was not content with such an ineffectual murmur of sympathy.

'I wondered whether Grace couldn't lend a hand,' she said.

Grace was startled. 'I don't know anything about selling wine.'

'You know more than most girls. Granted, you may not be able to recommend a particular vintage, as Will can. But you know the names of the châteaux and whether they produce claret or burgundy; the basic things. And you must have picked up some information about champagne while you were in France. Your French is good, so you could help with correspondence. Even keeping accounts is a simple enough matter if you're shown exactly what to do.'

By now Grace was alarmed, for she had never been good at figures. Her mother too looked doubtful, although for a different reason.

'For someone like Grace to take employment –' she began; but her sister-in-law interrupted briskly.

'There's no shame in that for a young woman these days. I've been employed ever since I left university, and no one thinks the less of me for that. Quite the opposite, I hope.'

'To be a headmistress is rather different from serving in a shop.'

'Grace needn't think of it as being a shop assistant. There'd be no need for her to accept wages if she chose not to. She should see it simply as helping out her own family in an emergency. After all, what happens to your income if The House of Hardie runs into difficulties?'

Such frank speaking was startling to Grace, who had been brought up to think any discussion of money matters to be vulgar. But her mother, surprisingly, was looking thoughtful.

'It's true that when Gordon returns – whenever that may be – he'll expect us to have taken all possible care of the business. Why not go down for an hour this afternoon, Grace? Just to watch and see what needs to be done. Then you could decide yourself whether you wanted to go again.'

'I'll come too.' Jay, on holiday from school, had come into the room in the middle of the conversation. 'I'll do the adding up, Grace. You're hopeless at that. You can smile sweetly at the customers so that they buy twice as much as they intended.'

Jay's high spirits were always infectious. With him beside her, the ordeal would be transformed into a game. After a few days, no doubt, the pretence of being an accounts clerk or sales assistant would begin to bore him. But he would make a reassuring companion whilst she made up her mind whether she was capable of conducting business with strangers.

The need for her assistance was obvious as soon as she and Jay stepped through the door that afternoon. The House of Hardie did not as a general rule serve many customers over the counter. It was more usual for wines to be tasted or selected from the list, ordered by the case, charged to account and delivered. Under this system there was no pressure for haste and no need for many wines to be placed on display. The cases were loaded directly from the cellar on to the dray. But the approach of Christmas attracted a different kind of customer. He might wish to buy only a single bottle of wine for a gift or a special celebration; he had little idea of what he wanted; and he would pay cash and take the bottle away. If Mr Witney had to give advice and supervise the till, he was left with no time to deal with the larger orders. There was relief in his smile as he learned why Grace and Jay had come.

It was surprisingly easy to be businesslike, Grace discovered. Mr Witney was available to give advice; but for straightforward transactions she sent Jay down to the cellars to collect whatever was required whilst she made out a bill and copied the details on to a sheet of paper. Someone else could add up the totals and alter the stock-sheets later.

135

Jay, for his part, was quick to improve on the system of making frequent journeys to collect single bottles. He carried up a whole case at a time, setting out the unsold bottles on a table behind the counter. It was quickly discovered that these sold themselves, since customers unused to buying wine found it easier to point than to make a pretence of understanding the list. Within the space of only an hour the two young Hardies transformed a high-class vintner's establishment into an ordinary retail shop. If Mr Witney found the change disconcerting, he did not say so, but at the end of the day thanked them sincerely and hoped they would come again.

As Grace expected, her younger brother's enthusiasm was short-lived, ending on Christmas Eve. The House of Hardie's reopening after the two-day Christmas holiday coincided with the first snowfall of the year, and Jay decided that tobogganing was more fun than acting as an errand boy.

But Grace – to her own surprise – was enjoying the experience of work. She had expected to feel shy, but instead was flattered by the courtesy with which she was treated. Mr Witney made a point of addressing her as Miss Hardie in front of the customers to make it clear that they were being served by a member of the proprietor's family. Her aunt had been right to suggest that even such a small talent as being able to pronounce the names of wines correctly would breed confidence; and her willingness to undertake the front-of-shop duties meant that the manager was able to hire an accounts clerk without any knowledge of wine, so that no bookkeeping was required of her.

The feeling that she was being useful and appreciated gave her such pleasure that Grace volunteered to attend regularly until the war was over or her father returned from China. It had not occurred to her before that life at Greystones was lonely or boring, but now she looked back almost with wonder to those days when she met no one except her family and the servants and it was an effort to pass the time.

The first day of the university term was exceptionally busy. Every undergraduate must have emptied every bottle in his rooms before returning home for Christmas and now, in January, needed to replenish his store. When would closing time come and give her a chance to sit down?

At the very last moment – indeed, it was later than the last moment, for the new accounts clerk had already left and Grace herself was fastening her cloak – a young man arrived at a run to knock at the door. Had he been dressed in civilian clothes, Grace would not have admitted him, but through the green glass of the window she could see by the street light that he was in uniform. A man who was fighting for his country must not be inconvenienced by closing hours. She opened the door.

'I know I'm too late.' The young officer was breathless from his dash. 'But it's practically a matter of life and death. I mean, I'm leaving for France tomorrow. Tonight is my last chance to say goodbye to my friends. Think of me as expiring of thirst in the middle of a desert and you as the only oasis.'

'What is it you'd like?'

'A case of champagne. You're an angel.'

As Grace opened the door more widely to let the stranger come in she was conscious that Mr Witney, working late in his office, had stepped quietly out to make sure that all was well. The rules of chaperonage seemed to have been abandoned with the outbreak of war, but Mrs Hardie had only been prepared to let her seventeen-year-old daughter help out in The House of Hardie on condition that she was never left alone on the premises.

The lieutenant took off his cap as he stepped inside,

revealing dark wavy hair above a fresh complexion. His eyes were bright with the success of his dash to beat the clock and the prospect of his party. 'Well,' he said, 'ten bottles would do, to save trouble.' He had noticed that on the counter stood an opened case from which two bottles of champagne had already been sold. 'The college porter's on his way with a trolley. I didn't want to risk hearing you say that you couldn't deliver in time.'

The porter arrived at that moment.

'Take them to Mr Jordan's set,' the lieutenant instructed him. Then he turned back to Grace. 'I've got an account with you, of course, but I want to settle it now. There's four terms' steady drinking down to it already, and I shan't be coming back into residence. Well, that's probably obvious. And if there should prove to be a bullet with my name on it, I wouldn't want my last thought to be that I owe The House of Hardie for a lakeful of champagne.'

'We can't deal with that now, I'm afraid, Mr Jordan.'

'Bailey,' he said. 'Christopher Bailey. Mr Jordan is the friend who'll be acting as host for my farewell, though he doesn't know it yet. I've already given up my rooms. No, of course, I've kept you late already. I can't expect you to stay on just for the sake of my conscience.'

'Could you come back tomorrow?' she asked.

'Bleary and hung-over; but yes, if you'll promise to attend to me yourself. I'll report at noon. Did I mention before that you're an angel? Six happy gentlemen will bless your name tonight.'

Grace tried not to laugh as she bade him goodnight, but that evening she found herself smiling as she recalled the brief conversation – and next morning it was the first thing she mentioned to Mr Witney.

The manager opened the book in which personal accounts were detailed. During his four terms at Oxford Mr

Christopher Bailey had been a regular customer without, however, taking advantage of the amount of credit required by some of the bloods.

'Tell him not to trouble himself,' he instructed Grace. 'When the war's over we'll talk about it again.'

'He's anxious to settle his affairs. In case – in case he should be killed.'

'All credit to him. But we won't put his anxiety to the test.' Mr Witney gave the sudden grin which invariably made Grace smile in sympathy. Anyone who met the manager of The House of Hardie in the street would be impressed by his gravity. He was a tall, broad-shouldered man who wore his formal business suit of frock coat and dark trousers with dignity. But when he came indoors and took off his high hat, the thick bristle of red hair which stood straight up from his head made him appear years younger. His face was as freckled as Andy's and his eyes were as bright and alert as those of Grace's father. He had been employed by The House of Hardie ever since he fell through a carelessly-opened trapdoor outside their premises at the age of twelve, laming himself for life, and his loyal hard work had made him almost one of the family. His forehead wrinkled now with earnestness as he explained.

'It was one of the first things that your grandfather taught me when I came to work here in Oxford,' he said. 'When it comes to choosing which tradesmen to patronize, the aristocracy – and other gentlemen as well – will always be most loyal to those they owe the most to. Give a young gentleman generous credit for three or four years while he's at university, and he'll be a faithful customer for the rest of his life.'

Grace considered this dictum doubtfully. She had no money of her own to handle; nor did she take any part in the spending of the household budget – she had, in fact, no idea of the cost of anything except, now, wine. But the idea that bills need not be paid was as instinctively displeasing to her as obviously it was to Mr Bailey.

In this case, however, there was a different consideration. It did seem right and proper that a young hero who had pledged his life to defend his king and country should be excused payment of his debts. It would give her pleasure to tell him so, with the manager's authority. She waited eagerly for Mr Bailey's return.

He came half an hour before his promised time – not bleary-eyed at all, but as full of energy as on the previous day. Mr Witney, calling Grace to attend to him, used her name, as was his custom, and the young officer remarked on it at once.

'The daughter of the house? I didn't realize yesterday that I was so privileged. We drank to you last night, of course – but because I didn't know your name, the toast had to be to "the angel in the High".'

Grace did her best to conceal her pleasure under a pretence of businesslike efficiency as she explained that he had no need to settle his account.

'You mean that if I'm lucky enough to survive the war, I shall be rewarded by realizing that I'm still in debt?' He sounded doubtful whether to accept the arrangement, but then smiled cheerfully. 'Oh well, thanks. There's no doubt that trying to settle everything at once imposes rather a strain on the exchequer. And my father's on your books at Pall Mall, so I shan't disappear into thin air.'

He held out his hand and Grace, after a moment's surprise, took it in her own. 'Good luck,' she said.

'That's something I have.' He was still smiling, but his eyes were serious. 'Some people are born lucky. I'm one of them. Everything always turns out well for me in the end. You must have noticed. Even when I arrive at a shop after closing hours, there proves to be someone at hand to open the door. I shall be all right. So I hope we shall meet again.'

2

The excitement and movement of the first few months of the war did not endure for long. When the German army ceased to retreat and instead dug itself into trenches guarded by barbed wire, the British casualty lists printed in the newspapers became daily longer and more alarming. But even before Grace and her mother became aware how short was the expectation of life of a young officer in the trenches, another anxiety grew. Why was there no news from China?

Gordon Hardie had left on his latest plant-hunting expedition in the autumn of 1913. He had written once to announce his safe arrival in China; and six months later a second letter, sent by runner from the Tibetan frontier to his agent in Shanghai and forwarded from there, had been safely delivered. After that, there had been only silence.

Although he was not due to return until July 1916, Lucy had written to him as soon as the war began and Frank left home, suggesting that he was needed back in England at once. She knew that it would take many months for the letter to reach him in the wild area of the Himalayan valleys which he was once again exploring, and more months after that for him to return to England: the end of 1915 was probably the earliest time at which he could be expected to arrive. But why were no letters reaching Greystones?

Because she had once accompanied her husband to China, she knew all about the difficulties of communication. For the same reason she was well aware of the dangers which would be surrounding him now. To those which she had experienced herself, the war had added another. For whilst many families in England hung a map of Europe on their walls, marking the hard-fought advances or retreats of the opposing armies with flags or pins, the Hardies referred more frequently to the large globe which stood in the schoolroom. They noted with alarm the passage of Admiral von Spee's squadron through Chinese waters and the attacks of the *Emden* on British shipping in the Indian Ocean. The voyage home might well prove as hazardous as the exploration itself.

Grace did her best to provide reassurance by reminding her mother how many ships had been requisitioned by the Navy. Overseas mail services were bound to be disrupted – and it was more than likely that some of the letters so eagerly awaited were at the bottom of the ocean, victims of U-boat attacks.

In spite of these attempts at comfort, Grace shared her mother's growing unease. And she had her own reasons for sympathizing with the daily hope and disappointment with which each delivery of post was greeted, for she too waited hopefully for letters. The conditions of war made it impossible for Andy to write regularly, and letter-writing did not come easily to him. To his own mother and father he sent as a rule only the army issue of printed postcards which assured them that he was well. But he had written Grace the first two love letters of her life, and she longed for more.

The second, written during the Christmas truce, reached her early in 1915. After that there was no further news. Grace waited patiently for some weeks and then could be patient no longer. Doing her best to pretend that the question was a casual one, she approached the head gardener as he pricked out seedlings in the potting shed.

'Do you hear regularly from Andy?' she asked, when

they had exchanged comments on the weather and the likely effect of a late frost on the fruit trees.

'Not for more nor three months. Can't be expecting to, neither.'

'What's happened? Is he hurt?' Fear tightened Grace's throat, so that her voice hardly seemed recognizable as her own.

'Wounded, yes.' The gardener set down the trowel with which he was mixing a compost. 'End of January. His officer wrote a letter.'

'But why didn't you tell us?'

'Reckoned the mistress had enough to worry about on her own account, with Master Frank and Master Philip both being away at the war. Didn't want to bother her with our troubles.'

'Is it serious? What happened?'

'A shell on the billet. There were six of them, in some kind of farmhouse barn behind the line. Sent there for a night's rest, but they might have been safer in the trench. Three of them killed. Two hit by shrapnel but able to get away. Andy couldn't walk, though. The Frenchy farmer's wife said she'd do what she could until a stretcher could come for him.'

'And did she? Was he all right?'

'Well, now.' His father gave a sigh. 'Bit of time must have passed. The shell that hit him was part of an offensive. A new German push. A lot of noise and confusion, I don't doubt, and other casualties to be brought in. By the time they sent to look for Andy, the Germans had advanced and the farm was behind their lines.'

'So where is he now? D'you mean that he's a prisoner?'

'Don't rightly know. Not on any lists yet.'

'You mean – you mean he might even be dead!'

'The officer didn't think so, and so no more do I. Can't manage to persuade the wife that she doesn't need to cry.

144

According to his mates, though, his legs were in a bad way but that was the beginning and end of it. Likeliest is that he's a prisoner of war. It takes a bit of time, I'm told, for the names to come through.'

Close to tears, Grace needed to be alone, but managed to remain calm enough to ask one more question. 'I'm so sorry,' she said. 'You must be terribly worried. You will let me know, won't you, when you hear anything? Anything at all.'

The gardener tipped his hat in acknowledgement of the request and returned to his work. Grace, for her part, should have hurried off to Oxford. Now that the days had become lighter she rode to The House of Hardie on her bicycle every day instead of waiting for the light delivery trap to come and pick her up. But she needed to recover from her feeling of giddiness before she could feel safe on the machine. Pushing it slowly down the long drive, she brought herself under control at last. It was inconceivable that Andy should die – and so, because she could not conceive of the possibility, she brought herself to believe that it could not happen.

From that time onwards Grace made a point of calling every month at the lodge where the Friths lived. Her visits were ostensibly to offer sympathy to Andy's mother, but actually to enquire whether there was any news. The wait was a long one and, on the day when she found Mrs Frith in tears, she naturally feared the worst. But they proved to be tears of joy, and there was no need for Grace to ask her usual question.

'He's alive, Miss Grace. In hospital and not able to walk yet, but alive.'

'I'm so glad, Mrs Frith. Where has he been? How was it that he couldn't write?'

'He was in that farmhouse all the time. The one with the barn, where he was wounded. They kept him hidden there, the farmer's family, even when the whole place was swarming with Germans. And now our boys have got the village back again, so he's been able to come out.'

'But in hospital, you said?'

'One of his legs isn't right, like. He was on his feet, in a manner of speaking, but limping. They've broken the bone again and reset it, or some such thing. Still, with proper doctors and nurses, he'll be coming along a treat now. Not that – what's her name?' Mrs Frith fetched her son's letter from a drawer and found the place, running her fingers along the words as with some difficulty she spelled them out. 'Madame – I don't know how to say this. Funny sort of word.'

'May I see?' Grace leaned over, almost as excited by the sight of Andy's handwriting as she would have been by his presence in the room. 'Madame and Mademoiselle Delavigne.'

'That's right. They did their very best for him, he says, and it's not their fault that his leg didn't heal up right.'

Grace was still looking at the letter. The address was a number, which presumably identified the hospital. Memorizing it, she said goodbye so that she could write it down quickly before it slipped from her mind.

It was natural that Andy should first of all reassure his parents; but with that accomplished, he would certainly write next to her. Grace sent off her own message of relief and happiness and waited for a reply, watching for the postman's arrival as eagerly as she had done six months earlier. Letters from France did indeed arrive, but they were from Frank or Philip, and were addressed to their mother.

Grace was glad to learn that all was well with her brothers, but disappointment was mixed with relief. When would there be a letter addressed to her?

3

The day came at last when a letter with the familiar markings of a Field Post Office bore Grace's name on the envelope; but it was delivered to The House of Hardie, not to Greystones.

'For you,' said Mr Witney. He had set it aside from all the business correspondence on seeing that it was marked 'Personal'.

'Thank you.' Grace's first joyful reaction was that Andy must have chosen not to write to her at home lest her mother should disapprove. But her excitement faded as she studied the envelope, for the handwriting and the writer's name were unfamiliar to her. Who was Christopher Bailey? She was still struggling with her regret that the letter was not from Andy as she read the words with which Mr Bailey re-introduced himself.

Dear Miss Hardie,

You won't remember who I am, since I expect you have to deal with dozens of customers like me every day of the year. But perhaps not all of them impose on your good nature by keeping you at work after closing time. I haven't been able to forget you so easily, because my conversation with you was the last civilized thing that happened to me.

There seems to be a kind of rule out here that people at home should never be told exactly what life in the trenches is like, so I can only say that for the past seven months I've done my best to put each day out of my memory as soon as it's over. That leaves me with an unclouded recollection of Oxford and your smile and your voice.

You'll be thinking that it's a frightful cheek on my part to write to you when you hardly know me. I can only say that it seems

147

desperately important to be able to feel that ordinary life is still going on. I imagine you walking down the High at the end of every day; perhaps pausing to look down on the river as you pass over Magdalen Bridge. Your garden, I like to think, is full of roses. Of course, it's not really your garden that interests me, but the thought of you sitting in it in the sunshine. In my mind, the sun is always shining in Oxford.

I didn't mean to write in such a tone. But to ask, in a business-like manner, whether I may visit you one day. I'm overdue for leave – it's been cancelled twice in the past month, but it can't be long in coming now. May I call on you? Well, you won't be able to stop me calling, but please don't turn me away. I want so much to see you again.

Your most indebted and humble servant,
Christopher Bailey

Astonished by the letter, Grace read it through for a second time before pushing it into her pocket. That evening she showed it to her mother, who raised her eyebrows in surprise. 'You didn't tell me –'

'There was nothing to tell,' Grace assured her. 'He came into the shop to pay his bill. That was all we talked about. It was months ago – I'd forgotten all about it.' But even as she said this, she wondered whether it was true. During the course of the year there had been similar conversations with other undergraduates who were anxious to settle their affairs. Every time she repeated what Mr Witney had told her to say, she remembered the handsome young man to whom she had first spoken the words.

In earlier days Grace's mother would certainly have hesitated before encouraging a visit from a young man whose own family she did not know, and to whom none of the Hardies had been introduced. But the war had relaxed social conventions. It was generally felt that young men who were enduring so much in the trenches deserved to have their every wish – or nearly their every wish – fulfilled when they came on leave. Any mother in England was prepared to treat a stranger in uniform exactly as she hoped other people would treat her own son if for some reason he could not reach his home. The fact that young Mr Bailey and his father had accounts with The House of Hardie was also a consideration. It offered some reassurance that his background was respectable.

'Well, of course,' she said. 'If your admirer arrives on the doorstep, he must certainly be made welcome.'

'He's not an admirer.' Her mother's choice of words made Grace flush.

'You don't think so? Well, your customer then, if that's how you prefer to think of him. But you'll have admirers now, you know, Grace. You must notice when a young man begins to find you interesting, and not be taken by surprise.'

Her tone of voice was encouraging, but it increased Grace's embarrassment. She did not want to find herself surrounded by admirers. All she wanted was Andy safe home again.

Her hunger for his presence, or at the very least for news, drove her to call again at the lodge on her way home from work the next day. The first thing she saw when she was invited in was a letter from Andy flattened out on the table. But his parents, instead of looking pleased to have heard from him, seemed gloomy and at first disinclined to talk. Only when Grace asked a direct question did Mrs Frith find her voice.

'Yes, we had a letter today, and no pleasure in it, I can tell you. These Frenchies! Andy was always a good boy. He'd never have got into this sort of trouble if she'd been a decent sort of girl.'

'Who?'

'The maddymoselle or whatever she calls herself.'

'She saved him from being taken prisoner,' Mr Frith reminded his wife, trying to calm her down without disagreeing.

149

'And now she's making him pay for it. Imposing on his good nature, I call it. He should have stopped to think about us. He must have known that we couldn't be doing with a foreigner in the family.'

'In the family? What's happened? What has he done?'

'He's gone and married the Frenchy girl,' said Mr Frith. 'Because he had to. It's done, and that's the end of it. No good getting ourselves into a stew about it now.'

'What do you mean by saying that he *had* to marry her?'

There was an awkward silence. It was impossible for Grace to tell whether the subject was considered unfit for her ears or merely too discreditable to Andy.

'Because she's going to have a baby,' Mrs Frith said at last. 'Andy's baby. That's what. I know it's a terrible thing for an unmarried girl to have a baby, but she should have thought of that earlier, shouldn't she? She's had her mother and grandmother and the priest and the schoolteacher and heaven knows who else all telling her she's got to marry the father or else she'll go to hell. What else could Andy do? He's not happy about it – we can tell that from his letter. But he's made his bed and he'll have to lie on it.'

Grace was unable to speak. What else was there to be said? At any other time her silent departure might have led the Friths to suspect the truth, but on this occasion she could feel sure that they were too deeply upset on their own account. Forgetting the bicycle which she had leaned against the cottage wall, she ran across the meadow and into the wood, where nobody could see her cry.

But the wood was full of Andy. Here as a boy he had planted seeds to grow a miniature forest. Here he had held her hand to comfort her on the day when Pepper was killed. Here, beside the boulders, he had kissed her. Grace had been sure that he would love her for ever, as she would love him. And perhaps he did still love her – but what was the use of that, if he was married to someone else? Angry and hurt and miserable, she paced up and down beside the stream until all her tears had been shed.

Only when at last she felt that she could behave normally did she walk stiffly up to Greystones, keeping her eyes away from the young oak tree which Andy had planted as an acorn to reach to her tower window. Was there nowhere she could go without being reminded of him?

Her mother came out into the hall to greet her.

'There's a letter for you, Grace.'

It was the letter which she had been awaiting for months. Her mother would know who had written it because the writer's name could be read on the top of the envelope, under the censor's stamp.

Grace stared down at the silver tray on which it lay, but did not touch it. 'I'll look at it later,' she said with an indifference which a few hours earlier would have been a pretence. There were questions to be asked, but she must wait for a moment when her mother would be receptive. Meanwhile, she rehearsed in her mind what she wanted to be told. Later that evening, not knowing how to lead up to it, she broached the subject abruptly.

'I'd like to know about babies,' she said. 'How do they come?' Her pale cheeks reddened with the embarrassment of a forbidden topic.

Her mother did not meet her eyes, but bent her head over the khaki sock she was knitting for Philip.

'When you're ready to get married –' she began. But Grace, not usually irritable, was barely in control of her emotions and determined to be given an answer.

'Why do you treat me like a child? I'm almost eighteen. I ought to know these things.'

Mrs Hardie raised her head and considered the question.

'You're quite right,' she said at last. 'When I married your father, I didn't know what to expect. That was my own fault, of course, because I ran away from home before anyone had thought that it was time to talk to me. I remember, when our first baby was on the way . . .' She paused, and it was Grace who broke the silence.

'Frank, you mean?'

'No, before Frank. While we were still in China. I had a little girl. Rachel, we called her.'

'You've never told any of us about that.'

'She died,' Mrs Hardie said. 'She gave one little cry, and died. She was born too soon: that was the reason. I'd had an accident, travelling through the mountains. I've never liked to talk about it. It upsets me. But if I'd been told more about babies, I might have been able to keep her alive. I didn't know then how long it took for a baby to come. I didn't know *anything*. So you're right. I ought to tell you. The trouble is that when it's put into words it sounds frightening. What makes it all right is when you love your husband.'

'Does it have to be a husband?'

'It *must* be a husband. You mustn't ever –'

'But does it *have* to be?'

'No,' said Mrs Hardie. 'Any man and any woman can make a baby together.' She put down her knitting and told Grace how.

'Thank you, Mother,' said Grace quietly when she had finished. 'I'm going up to bed now. Goodnight.'

Mrs Hardie stood up to hold her back.

'You mustn't think of it as disgusting,' she said. 'It's an expression of love; if you feel the love, it will bring you joy. Now will you answer a question for me? Why should young Andy Frith be writing to you?'

Grace ran out of the room without replying. On her way to the tower she picked up the letter from the hall table. Andy had loved the French mademoiselle, she told herself as she rushed upstairs. He had forgotten all about the

152

kisses in the wood, forgotten all about Grace. If he had written merely to say that he had fallen in love with another girl, she might have waited for him to come back to her, but he had loved the girl in a different way. He had given her a baby and married her and there was no point in thinking about him ever again. No doubt his letter contained an apology, but what was the use of that?

Turning on her heel, she went back downstairs to the drawing room to answer the question she had been asked.

'I've no idea why Andy should write,' she said. 'I shan't even bother to read the letter.' She tore the unopened envelope into little pieces and threw them into the waste paper basket before kissing her mother goodnight.

4

When at last he was granted leave Christopher Bailey did not, as he had threatened, arrive at Greystones unannounced. Instead he earned Mrs Hardie's approval by writing to ask formally for permission to call, and she responded with an invitation to luncheon.

Only five days had passed since the news of Andy's marriage reached England. Grace's sense of betrayal displayed itself as indifference to the proposed visit. Mrs Hardie, not knowing the real reason for her daughter's unhappiness, ascribed it to anxiety caused by their late-night conversation.

'I hope I didn't alarm you by what I said the other day, dearest. No gentleman, if he *is* a gentleman, will force his attentions on a young woman who makes it plain that she doesn't wish for them. That's why it's so important never to let a young man take liberties. Some gesture – a mere touch of the hand, or a kiss – which you might believe to be trivial, could be seen by the man as an invitation to go further. And what so many girls don't realize is that once a man – even a gentleman – feels himself encouraged to express his love, it's not easy for him to check himself. You have to look ahead and decide where you want to go before you take the first step. But Mr Bailey, I'm sure, will understand that. You needn't be afraid –'

'Of course I'm not afraid,' Grace interrupted impatiently. 'I've met Mr Bailey twice, altogether for about half an hour. I hardly imagine –' But her protest faltered as she remembered his letter. Her mother's remarks and her own reaction would both in normal circumstances have

154

been sensible. But circumstances were not normal. A young man who faced death daily might well have a different approach to life from the one which Lucy Hardie took for granted.

'When I was a girl, of course –' Mrs Hardie was reading her daughter's thoughts – 'the rules of chaperonage were very strict. How they fretted me! I remember how bold and independent I felt when I ran away with your father.' She sighed and laughed at the same time. 'You know, Mr Witney promised me that you would never be left alone on the premises of The House of Hardie. But two years ago the idea that an unmarried man could be a suitable protector for an unmarried girl would have been thought ridiculous!'

'Is Mr Witney in love with Aunt Midge?' asked Grace, to turn the conversation away from herself.

'What makes you ask that?'

'He brings her name into conversations as if it gives him pleasure just to speak it. I wondered if that was why he was still unmarried – because he has a hopeless passion for her.'

'Hopeless passion! What *have* you been reading!' But although Mrs Hardie was laughing, she answered the question seriously enough. 'I'm sure, yes, that Mr Witney admires your aunt greatly. And when they were younger . . . well, I don't know what may have passed between them. But it's a rule of your aunt's profession, you see. Should she ever marry, she'd have to resign her post.'

'Why? I should have thought that a married woman, perhaps with children of her own, might have a greater understanding of her pupils than a spinster.'

Mrs Hardie shrugged her shoulders. 'I don't pretend to see the reason for it. A poor woman in need of money may work all day in a factory and come home to work half the night in her house, and no one will protect her from herself. But if the woman is talented and educated enough to make her way in a profession, it's assumed that she can't have the energy to be a home-maker as well – or that if she has, her profession will suffer. And yet such a woman would have servants and assistants in both aspects of her life. It could only be her concentration which might be affected.'

'How many professions are there in which a *gentleman* is forbidden the distraction of a wife and children?' asked Grace, laughing.

'That's not a question that anyone asks. It's possible that Mr Witney may once have made an offer of marriage to your aunt, in spite of their difference of upbringing. But even when she was your age, she was determined to become a headmistress one day. She would have had to turn him down for that reason alone. Of course, if the governors of her school were to change their rules –'

'I don't think she'd marry him anyway.'

'Why not?'

Grace flushed with the knowledge that she had been indiscreet. She had seen Aunt Midge chatting pleasantly to Mr Witney and enjoying his company. But she had also once seen her aunt in London, standing close beside Mr Faraday, the architect, as they looked at a painting together. The fingers of the two adults, although not quite touching, appeared to be linked by some powerful energy in the air. At the age of eleven, Grace had not understood what it was that so charged the atmosphere. Now that she had been in love herself, she could make sense of the memory. If Aunt Midge were allowed to marry, it would be Mr Faraday she chose, not Mr Witney. But that fact, discovered by accident, must be regarded as a secret.

'Oh, it's just that she likes teaching so much,' she said vaguely. 'Do you ever wish that you had followed a profession?'

'I wasn't brought up to look for employment. My education wouldn't have qualified me for anything and my family would have regarded it as demeaning. What I would have liked . . .' She paused, sighing. 'I wish that I could have accompanied your father on all his expeditions, and not only the first.' Her face clouded, and Grace knew that she was not only regretting her own house-bound existence but was once more overcome by fears for her husband's safety. It was time to change the subject again.

'How shall we entertain Mr Bailey when he comes?' she asked.

This was not a matter which need have caused them anxiety. The young lieutenant made it clear as soon as he arrived that the greatest treat he could be offered was a day of normal family life.

'I need memories,' he said to Grace after luncheon, asking her to show him round the grounds. 'Sitting in a trench and waiting to be shelled, or running towards a machine-gun, or tearing through barbed wire, you can't help wondering what the point of it all is. Well, there *isn't* a point. So the only thing that makes it tolerable is the hope that there'll be something to come home to in the end. An unchanged way of life. Married men have their own dreams, I suppose, but the rest of us stare out of shell craters and picture girls in white dresses walking over green lawns or picking roses.'

'I'm sorry not to have dressed for the part,' laughed Grace. Even in summer she rarely wore white, which did not suit her pale complexion. Her dress was of a flowery blue and green muslin. 'But roses – yes, I can offer you roses.'

'That's the least important thing. What I want . . . Last time we met, Miss Hardie, you gave me permission to write to you. If you knew how many letters I'd drafted in my head, or scribbled on scraps of paper, without daring to post more than one or two stilted efforts . . . What I want to ask now is whether *you* will write to *me*. To tell me about your daily doings. Little things. Just enough to keep a picture of normal life in my mind. But *your* life in particular.'

'I work in a shop,' said Grace bluntly. 'Compared with your experiences, mine are safe and easy, but they have little to do with the gracious way of life in your daydreams.'

'You're a beautiful girl living in a beautiful house on the edge of a beautiful city,' said Christopher. 'It would hardly matter what events you might choose to describe. You would be thinking of me as you wrote the letters – that's all I'd care about.'

Once before in her life Grace had been told that she was beautiful and had been warmed by the compliment although she knew it not to be true. But the speaker had abandoned her, making it hard to offer affection again in case it should again be rejected.

'Our acquaintance is very slight, Mr Bailey,' she said.

'And how are we to change that – if you wish to change it, that is? If things were normal my mother would write to yours. There could be visits, social occasions. But as it is . . . It's because I want to improve our acquaintance that I dare to suggest a correspondence. I'm not likely to write to you about gas gangrene and trench fever. I'd like to describe my home, my family, my horses, so that you begin to know a little more about me as I learn more of you. I'm not asking for anything more than your letters, your thoughts.'

There could be no doubt of the sincerity in his voice, yet Grace still hesitated for a moment. Might this – not a kiss or a touch of the hand, but a promise – be the first gesture to which her mother's warning had referred? Ought she to consider more closely before she started how she wanted this new friendship to continue? Yes, she ought; but she did not. It was the duty of every patriotic girl to offer what comfort she could to a man who was fighting to defend his country.

Less worthy thoughts also sneaked into her mind. She was not going to have Andy feeling sorry for her and imagining that she was pining away for love of him. He had treated her disgracefully, but she must show him that she didn't care, and how better to do that than to have another admirer? 'Yes,' she said. 'I'll write. As long as you don't expect –'

'I expect nothing,' Christopher assured her. After the brief spell of seriousness his grin reminded her of the light-hearted undergraduate who had burst into The House of Hardie. 'I don't even expect any regularity in our correspondence. In fact, I'll specially ask you to be erratic. Letters addressed to the front are bound to be delayed and bunched. If I start expecting an envelope addressed in your handwriting every Wednesday, or anything like that, I shall be in constant anguish at its non-appearance. As long as I know for certain that you will write within a few days, I can wait patiently for ever. I can't tell you how happy you've made me, Miss Hardie. May I call you Grace? Will you call me Christopher? How old are you? When is your birthday? I shall leave a gift with my mother, for her to send at the right time.'

'She'll have a long time to wait. I shan't be nineteen until next June.' Grace felt that she was being rushed, and was not sorry, when they turned back to the house, to discover that Jay was carrying out the croquet mallets for a game.

Christopher partnered Grace against Jay and Mrs Hardie and sent the opposition balls flying in all directions so that the rest of the afternoon passed in laughter. Over a strawberry tea Jay teased his sister's new friend and treated him as a good sport, and Mrs Hardie asked questions about his home and family.

Grace found the interrogation embarrassing, but listened to the answers with interest. Christopher's father owned a large country estate in Leicestershire on which he bred hunters. His only son shared his enthusiasm for horses. Grace made a mental note to mention that she did not like to ride, since contact with horses made her ill. Yet this fact could not be of the slightest importance unless there was a possibility that she might marry Christopher, and of course nothing was further from her mind than that! So she did not say anything after all.

The Baileys, it was clear, were of a higher social status than the Hardies, but this did not seem to bother Christopher. Grace remembered Frank's comment that Greystones was a large house for a mere vintner to own. Although Christopher came of a county family, his home might be no grander than hers. But she was sure that he was not a snob.

Only as he was leaving at the end of the day did he mention her father. 'I didn't like to ask the question in front of your mother, for fear of upsetting her,' he said quietly. 'But I couldn't help noticing the lack of any reference to Mr Hardie. He's not, I hope . . .'

'He's abroad,' Grace explained. She described her father's enthusiasm for plant-hunting and the nature of his present expedition. 'It's so long since we had any news that my mother becomes distraught when she thinks of what may have happened. We try to persuade her that the problem must only be one of communication, and that he'll return next year as he planned. But . . .'

Christopher tutted with annoyance at the tactlessness of his question. 'Now I've upset you, and I want you to remember every moment of our day together as being full of happiness and laughter.' He set himself to bring the sparkle back to her eyes before he said goodbye. She could tell that he wanted to kiss her, but was pleased that he did not.

So it was with a feeling of satisfaction that she turned back into the house. But later, as she lay in bed in the tower room and re-lived the events of the day, all her happiness was suddenly banished by the memory of Christopher's question.

What, indeed, had happened to her father?

5

Left, right, left, right. Gordon Hardie was marching on the spot, lifting each knee in turn high so that his full weight would shift from one leg to the other. A systematic programme of exercise was essential if he were ever to get away from this remote eyrie in the Himalayas, for the size of the cell in which he was confined did not permit him to take more than two paces in any direction.

It was a monastic cell, not a prison cell, but the difference was only one of words; he saw no hope of escape from it. The lamas had brought him back from death's door, but they were not going to let him pass through their own.

Every morning, as he awoke to a new day of confinement, Gordon cursed the impulse which had carried him so far into Tibet. The temptation had been irresistible for, at the time of his earlier expeditions, Tibet had been a closed country and Lhasa a forbidden city. Any foreigner found trespassing was thrown into the nearest river. More to the point – because it meant that no guides could be procured – any Tibetan who gave help to a foreigner in those days was beheaded.

But between his last trip and the present one, much had changed. A British expeditionary force had reached Lhasa and negotiated a treaty after defeating an army of Tibetans who believed that a mantra written on a scrap of paper would render each of them invulnerable. Had Gordon been a map-maker or mountain-measurer he could almost certainly have obtained permission to enter the country through Sikkim. But he was a plant-hunter, and travelled first to China because he had been successful before in that country's mountainous western region.

The frontier was unmarked on the land and differently drawn on every map he possessed. Only several days after crossing it did he realize that he must have strayed on to Tibetan territory. Almost without thinking he allowed one high pass to lead him to another. A new treasure appeared round every corner – a gentian, a primula, a lily, a rhododendron and, on one never-to-be-forgotten day, a brilliant blue poppy, unlike anything ever seen in Europe. He was climbing to higher altitudes than any botanist before him, hoping to make new studies of plants which could survive such conditions.

His Tibetan guides conferred anxiously when he announced his intention of travelling further into the country, but he had taught himself enough of their language to understand that they were anxious lest the spirits of the mountains should be disturbed. A promise that he would not kill any living creature was sufficient to resolve that difficulty, although it confined the party to a monotonous diet of boiled barley flour. Onward and upward they pressed, until the day of the disaster.

Trouble might have come from any direction, for the hazards of travel were many. Mountain rivers, fierce and icy, could be crossed only by low bridges which were liable to be swept away in floods, or on insecure contraptions of rope and bamboo slung across the tops of steep gorges. Mountain paths, hacked from the precipitous cliffs, were so narrow that an unexpected encounter with another mule train could lead to hours of delay and argument before one party at last agreed to retreat to some passing place. Rocks tumbled in avalanches from above. Sections of the track crumbled and fell away down the cliff.

But it was none of these natural hazards which brought his expedition to an end. He had known before leaving

England of the Chinese expulsion from Lhasa, which they had occupied by force three years earlier. As reported in the columns of *The Times*, the country seemed to be settled when the Dalai Lama returned from exile, but the real situation was different. The Tibetans were intent on preventing any new invasion, while the Chinese marauders who for centuries had raided villages near the frontier saw no reason to change their habits.

It was with one of these gangs that Gordon's mule train came face to face. His shooting guns were stowed away, and the muleteers carried only knives. In the brief skirmish which followed Gordon was hurled off the path and down the mountainside because he was in the company of Tibetans. But when the men of the nearest Tibetan village came rushing to the scene, he was left where he lay because he was a foreigner. Only after many hours of pain and cold was he rescued by two of his own guides. Finding him unconscious, they strapped him between two poles and took him to a remote monastery with a reputation for healing.

At least a year had passed since then, and his broken bones had somehow knitted together. To the Tibetans, time was of no importance. They had no clocks, and no wireless to make contact with the outside world. As for a calendar – at the monastery's high altitude the year was divided by the June monsoon between a four-month season of extreme cold and an eight-month season which was even colder. Gordon could only guess how long he had lain delirious. Keeping track of the days since his return to full consciousness, he reckoned it must now be about August 1915.

The year – if it was a year – brought him close to despair. The monks gave him a bed on which to lie and food to keep him alive, but only the most rudimentary medical treatment. The toughness of his mind and body pulled him

164

through. He was still alive – but to what purpose? No locks and bars were needed to hold him, for the murderous terrain served as his chains. Without guides and the means of making a fire he could not hope to survive in the open. This tiny cell which, like everything else in the monastery, smelt of the rancid butter which the Tibetans used for food, drink and body-cleansing, incarcerated him as securely as any prison.

At their only meeting the chief lama refused to accept the explanation that a foreigner had come only to look for new plants, and took it for granted that he was a spy. A request for instructions on how to deal with him had been sent to Lhasa, but none had arrived; and Gordon's repeated demands that his presence should be notified to the senior British official there had apparently been ignored.

So there was nothing for it but to make and keep his body fit, ready to snatch at any opportunity for escape which came his way. Painfully he had brought his legs back into use and spent three hours a day doing exercises to strengthen them. Even when divided into twenty-minute sessions, this was as much as he could manage, for the monastery stood fifteen thousand feet above sea level and every exertion left him panting for breath.

At first, as he rested between exercises, he allowed himself one luxury: that of recalling his home and family. But as time passed, memories of those he loved brought only anguish. He could imagine Lucy's anxiety turning to fear as days and months went by without news. Had she by now given up hope, believing herself to be a widow? No, she would still be praying for his safety, and making enquiries about his last known movements. But her search would be in China. Even if she were to extend it to Tibet she would be given no information.

He could think of her only as weeping, and so tried not

to think of her at all. He ought never to have left her. He had abandoned his business, deserted his children, behaved disgracefully from every point of view. If he ever returned to England . . . but he had almost ceased to believe that such a day would come. The only way to keep himself sane was to continue the regular stretching of his muscles. Left, right, left, right, left, right.

A monk appeared at the door of the cell with a bowl of yak butter tea. Two years earlier such a sour and greasy drink would have brought a grimace of disgust to Gordon's face, but now he accepted its warmth gratefully. The bearer was one of the younger monks, a cheerful fellow who enjoyed correcting the foreigner's mistakes in conversation and acting out explanations of his own words. It had not occurred to any of the monks that Gordon was deliberately improving his own grasp of their language in the hope of escaping one day and making his way across country.

Today there was startling news. He was to be moved to a disused storehouse at the bottom of the building. The monastery was constructed vertically on a mountainside, with staircases instead of corridors linking the rooms. This did not sound a change for the better – indeed, it carried a hint of the oubliette in a castle. It was apparently necessary for him to be kept out of sight whilst some kind of official visitation took place. It was in his own interests to hide, he was assured; but he saw the situation differently. Had his opportunity come at last? 'Take me to see the head lama!' he demanded.

He anticipated a battle of wills, but found himself being led to the great room.

Awaiting him, the head lama sat on a raised platform, flanked by six senior lamas at a lower level. Two younger men in the corners behind him turned the huge prayer wheels which were believed to send millions of invocations up to heaven with each rotation. This was to be a kind of trial, Gordon realized uneasily.

He was accused, not for the first time, of spying. What other purpose could a foreigner have for coming into the country? The lamas ought to have turned him away when he was carried in. But it was against their religion to kill. Gordon understood the unspoken words – they had expected him to die without their help.

By surviving, he presented them with a problem. For the first time he learned for a fact what he had always suspected. No one in Lhasa, whether Tibetan or British, had been told of his existence. He was a shameful secret, and now they feared exposure. They were not hard men, and by living as their guest Gordon had established a claim on their continued hospitality. They ought to cast him out to die. But if he would promise to remain hidden during the imminent visit of a special messenger from the Dalai Lama, they would receive him back in their midst when the visitor left.

Gordon felt his head – his whole body – swelling like a balloon about to burst with a mixture of hope and panic. This was his chance, and probably his last chance. Keeping his body still and his language unemphatic, because to show emotion would be to invite contempt, he began to speak with words as correct and formal as he could manage.

He was grateful for the care that had saved his life, he told his judges, and grateful too for the hospitality which had induced in him such a favourable view of their religion. He would not wish them to be blamed for sheltering a foreigner. He was not a spy, as he had often assured them, and his only wish was to leave the country which he had entered by accident, due to the error of his guides. To hide in a building which might be searched by the Dalai Lama's emissary would be to invite retribution on the whole community.

167

With the greatest respect, therefore, he requested that he should be provided with a guide to escort him to the Chinese border. In return he would promise never to re-enter Tibet and never to reveal where he had spent the last year.

A hand waved. Gordon felt himself being pulled backwards out of the room. He was taken back to his cell and noticed that for the first time one of the monks was stationed outside it as a guard. The night which followed was one of the longest of his life – but not in hours. For long before it was light next morning two young monks entered his cell. When he saw what they were holding, his excitement was so great that he felt sick and light-headed. One of them held out a travelling coat and boots, and the other was carrying a heavy pack. He was free!

For fourteen days the three men travelled together eastward through the mountain passes. Although Gordon had worked so hard to strengthen his muscles, the fractured bones in his legs, imperfectly mended, made his gait awkward and the balance of his body insecure. More than once he was saved from a fall only by the rope which his companions tied around his waist for safety. So there was uncertainty as well as elation in his spirits when at noon on the fifteenth day he was told that he had reached the boundary of Tibetan territory and must continue now on his own. Three days' walking would bring him to the nearest Chinese village.

Could he manage it alone without falling? How would he be greeted by the Chinese, who hated foreigners and showed their distrust with a fierce cruelty? Well, only time would tell. There had been moments in the past fourteen days when he had wondered whether his escorts had secret instructions to push him to his death. But instead they had held him steady and saved his life. It must mean that his luck had changed at last.

He listened carefully as they indicated the general direction in which he must travel and pointed out the pass for which he should aim – for there was still one more spine of bleak mountains blocking any signs of habitation from his view. They checked that his pack contained sufficient rations, the flint and steel to start a fire, and a tiny tent of skins for protection against the worst of the weather. Then, putting out their tongues in a last gesture of friendliness, they turned back, leaving him alone.

That night, down in the first valley, he settled himself to sleep in the posture he had learned from the Tibetans – a crawling position, so that only his elbows and knees touched the icy ground. A blanket thrown completely over him warmed him with his own trapped breath. How Lucy and he had laughed when, on their honeymoon trip, they first noticed their guides sleeping in such a ridiculous posture, like a flock of grazing sheep. It was a mark of Gordon's relief that he could allow himself to think of Lucy once more. His lovely wife, whom he would never leave again.

The children, too. Jay would be still a schoolboy, but Grace, released from the schoolroom, must have grown into a young woman. Eighteen years old: old enough to start thinking of marriage. Once again Gordon shook his head in shame that he had abandoned his family so irresponsibly. A young woman needed a father to guard her.

About the business he felt less guilty. Frank was a steady, hard-working young man with an orderly mind. One day he would own The House of Hardie, and it could do him nothing but good to experience responsibility. Philip too would not have suffered from his father's absence. By now he would have taken his degree and found employment suited to his academic achievements. But the twins – yes, he should have been on hand to help the twins

169

as they made the difficult transition from boyhood to adult life.

How old would they be now? If this was 1915, as he thought, Kenneth and David would at about this time be celebrating their twenty-first birthdays. They would have hoped at least for a message from their father. His silence would surely have convinced the family even more strongly that he must be dead.

During his months in Tibet, Gordon had studied the extraordinary way in which the people of that country used their mental powers to control their bodies. After days of incessant rain in which no dry wood could be found, he had once watched one of his guides stuff his clothes with damp kindling. Using the art of *thumo reskiang* the man had by extreme concentration raised his body temperature so high that within three hours the grass and twigs were dry. Anything is possible when the mind is directed clearly on a single object, he had explained gravely.

The lesson had not been forgotten. Crouched on hands and knees and shrouded in a blanket on the remote boundary of China, Gordon Hardie concentrated his mind on one thought, willing his message to travel thousands of miles around the world to Greystones.

'Happy birthday, Kenneth. Happy birthday, David.'

6

'Oh, we don't want to lose you, but we think you ought to go.'

On the stage of the music hall a young woman wearing male evening dress twirled her cane before pointing it – sometimes like a gun and sometimes as a telescope – at any man in the audience who was not in uniform. A dozen pretty girls in flounced skirts swayed and twirled and swung their legs as they shouted the chorus. 'For your King and your Country need you so.' Throwing out their arms, they invited the audience to join in. Soon the auditorium reverberated with the sound of singing, kept in time by stamping feet and clapping hands.

Kenneth Hardie shifted uneasily in his seat. This was intended to be a merry occasion, part of an exciting week. On Sunday the twins had celebrated their twenty-first birthdays at Greystones. David had learned of success in the last of his law examinations on Monday, and was to be married in London tomorrow. A stag party of the old sort had proved impossible to arrange, since so many of their friends were in France, so the two brothers were content to share a slap-up meal and a visit to Collins Music Hall.

Until this moment the evening had gone well. But now the chorus girls were streaming off the stage and moving round the audience while the orchestra continued to play the same emotionally stirring music. The girls kissed every man in uniform and flirted with all the male civilians, sitting on their laps as they wheedled promises of immediate visits to the recruiting office out of them. Two rows in front of the Hardie brothers a middle-aged man rose to his feet, his arms stretched upwards as an earnest of his intention to enlist. As his wife, frantic with worry, tried to pull him back into his seat, the audience roared approval.

'Let's get out of here,' said Kenneth. They made their way into the street and found it filled with running people. Faintly in the distance could be heard the sound of anti-aircraft guns, and the noise increased as the two young men, pausing, stared up at the sky. Over the rooftops of Islington a Zeppelin appeared, looking so much like a huge silver cigar case floating in the sky that it would have seemed ridiculous had the sound of exploding bombs not proved it to be lethal.

It was perhaps because the music hall's recruiting song had touched raw nerves that Kenneth and David did not join those who were running to take shelter. Instead they stood their ground to show that they were not alarmed; but their comments revealed different attitudes to the war.

'How can the gunners miss?' asked David incredulously. 'Something so large and moving so slowly. If the range of the guns is inadequate, surely it can be improved.'

'But if they hit!' Kenneth shivered at the picture conjured up by his imagination. 'Just think of all the men up there falling to earth in flames.'

'If they came to kill, they deserve to be killed,' David replied briskly. 'You should keep your sympathy for the English men and women who are lying dead or injured now.'

'Well, I feel that as well, naturally. But the Germans are human beings too. The gunners must have in their minds a picture of men burning all the time they're firing.'

'Their picture is of their own families, innocent targets. In any case, they're not likely ever to *see* their victims.'

'But they must know . . . David, do women ever give you white feathers?'

172

'No. I've noticed, it's only men who look half ashamed of themselves who get them. If you walk confidently, like someone who knows that he's making his own contribution to the war, you don't get pestered.'

'And *do* you feel that?' asked Kenneth. 'That you're contributing?'

'If the war ever ends, this country will need qualified professional men to manage it. It's my opinion that our generals are incompetents. They appeal for more men without having the least idea what use to make of them – except to replace other men who have been unnecessarily killed. I don't care to see myself as cannon fodder. It would have been foolish to enlist in the middle of my training, and even now that I've finished with examinations, I need practical experience. I consider that I'm more use to the country as a qualified solicitor than as an incompetent second-lieutenant.'

The explosion of another bomb, nearer than the last, made the building around them shudder and checked their conversation for a moment. As they walked briskly westward towards David's lodgings, Kenneth continued to nag at the subject of enlistment.

'Three white feathers I was given today,' he said. 'The pleasure these women take . . . I'm determined not to go. But it seems likely that there will be conscription sooner or later. Ever since we all had to register, people have been talking. I had a letter from a recruiting officer this week, David. "I am only waiting the word to call up every man of eligible age and, as you see, I have you on my list." There was a lot more about how much worse it would be for me if I waited to be fetched instead of enlisting voluntarily.'

'He had no legal authority to write such a letter,' said David bluntly. 'If you don't want to join the army, then my advice to you would be to get married. You're right to believe that conscription must come. But the government has pledged that no married man will be forced to enlist until the whole pool of unmarried men has been absorbed.'

Kenneth was tempted to reply that he was too young to marry, that he could not afford to keep a wife, and that he had not yet met any girl with whom he would want to spend his life. But instead, he looked aghast at his brother.

'David! That's not why you're marrying Sheila!'

'Of course not.' David had known his fiancée for two years and, as the daughter of the senior partner in his law firm, she was an eminently suitable match for an ambitious man. 'Although,' he added more honestly, 'since we were already engaged it seemed a good reason for not delaying the wedding. In normal circumstances I suppose we might have waited until I was older. So as from tomorrow I shall have a wife dependent on me, as well as a mother and a family business.'

'Mother! You can hardly claim –'

'Can I not?' David spoke with unusual vigour as he turned to face his twin. 'Father has gone off and left her unprotected. After so long a silence, we must begin to fear that he may be dead. Certainly he's not at hand to manage affairs. He expected Frank to take his place as head of the family. Frank and Philip have the noblest of reasons for leaving home; but the effect is that she's left with all the responsibility of running Greystones without the support of either her husband or her eldest sons. There must be one member of the family ready to give advice and practical help.'

Kenneth, though not convinced by this argument, was impressed by his brother's confidence. His own certainty that conscription must come soon filled him with alarm.

'They can't make a man fight against his will,' he said, talking more to himself than to his brother. 'There will

174

have to be some kind of alternative service. I could become a medical orderly, perhaps, or a stretcher bearer.'

David failed to offer the reassurance for which he hoped. 'I'd have thought you'd enjoy the adventure of fighting, Kenneth. You don't give the impression of finding your work of much interest.'

'That's true enough. But – do you remember Pepper, David?'

'Pepper?'

'Grace's cat.'

David frowned with the effort to remember. 'A sort of tabby, was it?'

The appearance of the cat was the least important thing about it. 'You shot it in the eye with an arrow,' Kenneth reminded him.

'Oh yes.' David, recalling the incident, shrugged it away as unimportant. 'That was a long time ago. What's that got to do with the war?'

Kenneth had been about to explain, but sensed that his brother would not understand. They had never experienced the intense sympathy and wish to share that people seemed to take for granted in twins. Perhaps it was because they were not identical. He felt no closer to David than to any of his other brothers – and yet, perversely, he looked to David for an empathy which he would not have expected from anyone else.

'Nothing,' he said untruthfully. But even as he brushed the subject away he recognized that the time might come when he would have to explain himself more coherently and to an even less sympathetic audience.

175

7

Even before his name was called, Kenneth knew that his appearance before the tribunal in the summer of 1916 would be a waste of time. Conscription had come and was being enforced with little sympathy for individual cases. Each man who went before him into the village hall was absent for only a few minutes – a contemptuously short time to decide a matter of life and death. And each, when he reappeared, was pale-faced with anger or despair as he was marched away under military escort. Kenneth's heart sank as his turn approached.

'Mr Kenneth Hardie.'

He stood up. He was wearing his usual business clothes, and the high, stiff collar choked him as he tried to swallow the lump in his throat. Not since the day he was summoned to his headmaster's study for a beating had he felt like this, for he had never before needed to submit himself to an interview of any kind.

The hostility as he walked the length of the hall was unmistakable. The four members of the tribunal – three in civilian clothes and one in uniform – were seated behind a table on a low platform, looking down on him in a manner which reinforced that old memory of the headmaster's study. Their chairman and spokesman was a retired colonel and a magistrate. It was a trial he was conducting now, with the verdict almost a foregone conclusion.

'Your name?'

'Kenneth Hardie.'

'Age?'

'Twenty-one.'

'Married?'

'No, sir.'

'Dependants?'

'I have a mother and a young brother and sister.'

'Father?'

'Missing, believed dead.' Kenneth used the military phrase deliberately. Although misleading, it was the truth.

'In what sense is your mother dependent on you? Do you provide her sole source of income?'

'Her income derives from a family business. With my father missing and my two elder brothers both serving at the front, it's my responsibility to keep the business going.' This second misleading statement was further from the truth than the first. It was Will Witney on whom The House of Hardie depended.

'An older man, or a disabled one, could do that.' The military representative was entering the interrogation. 'So you've got two brothers doing the decent thing, eh? What do they think of someone who stays at home while they're risking their lives?'

Kenneth paused before answering. It was true that Frank – although careful not to spoil his home leaves by quarrelling about it – found it hard to understand why his twin brothers did not join up. But he believed that an unwilling soldier was a bad soldier, and had never attempted to press them into a change of mind.

Philip, by contrast, was disgusted with the war. He wished he had never volunteered, and lived for the day when he could return to civilian life. He regarded his younger brothers as showing greater sense than himself in keeping their distance from the army for as long as possible.

'They are glad to feel that our mother can rely on my support,' said Kenneth firmly.

The military man, a major, looked disbelieving, whilst the chairman resumed his questioning.

'Are you a Socialist?'

'No, sir.'

'Religion?'

'Church of England.' Kenneth knew that this answer would do him no good. In the church which he attended whenever he spent a weekend at Greystones, every sermon was a recruiting speech. Only a man who could prove that he had been a Quaker since before the beginning of the war could call on his faith to support his stance.

'On what grounds, precisely, are you claiming exemption from military service?'

'On the grounds that I'm incapable of killing anyone.'

'I don't understand you,' said one of the other members of the tribunal; a tall man, cadaverously thin, who had the look of a retired schoolmaster. Less aggressive than the two who had taken the lead in asking questions, he gave the impression of wanting to understand the answers. 'You mean that you are a pacifist, holding all life sacred?'

Kenneth wondered whether it would be sensible to accept the suggestion which had been offered, but chose to repeat the truth. 'I mean that I'm not able to take life. If I attempted it, my hands would not obey me.'

'Now come, really.' The chairman was back in action again. 'If a mosquito landed on your skin, you'd squash it before it bit you.'

'No, sir. I would brush it away, but not kill it.'

'And suppose you saw this mother who depends on you, or your young sister, about to be ravished by some filthy Hun – and it will happen, mark my words, unless we all close ranks to keep the invader at bay – what would you do then? You can't "brush away" a Hun.'

'I would do my best to defend them, naturally, by wrestling with him and giving them time to get away.'

'Where could they run to, if the country was swarming with Jerries?'

'If the country was swarming with Germans, then killing one of them would have little effect.' He knew as soon as the words were out of his mouth that it was a mistake to argue.

'You're assuming that every other Englishman would behave like you. Other women would have protectors who wouldn't shirk the task, and we'd soon have the Hun on the run. We're fortunate that at the moment the enemy isn't on British soil. But the principle's the same. We're fighting to defend our wives and daughters and mothers and sisters. Other men are fighting for you. Give me one good reason why you shouldn't take your place beside them.'

'They would find me an unreliable companion. Even if I came face to face with an enemy and recognized that he was dangerous – even if I forced myself to hate him – I still couldn't kill him.'

'It would be his life or yours.'

'That might be the easiest situation. What you're asking me to consider is the possibility of it being his life or that of my comrade-in-arms. But it wouldn't make any difference. If I was asked to stick a bayonet into his body' – for a second Kenneth closed his eyes, made faint merely by the thought – 'I couldn't do it.'

'You may think that now,' said the thin man. Once again his voice conveyed a hint of sympathy. 'You've had a soft upbringing, no doubt. But in the heat of battle –'

'If I were talking of some rational decision, sir, I'd agree that in a confused and dangerous situation I might behave irrationally. But I'm talking about instinct, not will. I'm not saying that I refuse to kill, but that I'm incapable of killing.'

'Never heard such nonsense in my life,' exclaimed the

179

chairman. 'Part of the natural order of things. All living creatures kill. Cats kill mice, foxes kill hens, men kill their enemies. What d'you know about it, anyway?'

'Twelve years ago,' began Kenneth – but he was not allowed to finish the sentence.

'Twelve years ago you were only a boy. You're living in a man's world now. If you've nothing more to say . . .' He looked to his left and his right and received a nod of support from the thin man and another from the third civilian member of the tribunal, who had not opened his mouth. 'Exemption refused.'

Kenneth set his dismay to one side of his mind while he made the all-important request. 'In that case I would like to apply for non-combatant duties.'

'You're in no position to ask favours.' The major had been given his man and spoke contemptuously. 'If you'd done the decent thing and volunteered you'd have been allowed to express a preference. But now –'

'I understand that there are forms of alternative service open to conscientious objectors.'

'You're not recognized as a conscientious objector. Your objection has been over-ruled. From now on you'll go where you're sent and obey the orders you're given. And let me tell you this, young man. You'll be sent to France as soon as you're trained, and if you disobey an order once you're across the Channel, the penalty is death. Just think about that. Right, corporal, take him away.'

For a moment Kenneth was unable to move. What a fool he had been to tell the truth! And how much more foolish he would have sounded if he had come out with the whole truth and said: 'Sir, twelve years ago I killed my sister's cat because it was in pain. I smashed in its head. Its blood and brains spattered over my boot. I looked at my sister, and it's because of the horror and grief I saw in

180

her eyes then that I shall never again be able to take life and bring such anguish to a living person.'

Even to himself it didn't make sense that a small incident so far in his past should have had such an effect. How then could he ever have hoped to convince those hostile interrogators?

Was the major right? Would fear, extreme fear, break down the inhibitions grounded in boyhood? Certainly, as he was escorted past the men who were still waiting for their own fate to be decided, Kenneth was afraid. From now on he would be surrounded by enemies; and not all of them would be German.

8

In July 1916 the world seemed to come to a standstill. It was as though the earth had stopped spinning. No clouds moved; no breeze blew. Thunder gathered itself together in the air without ever quite coming to a head. In the oppressive atmosphere people walked slowly and spoke almost in whispers, but their apparent lethargy was caused by more than the heat of the glaring sun. Everyone was waiting for the news from France.

A massive offensive had been opened. The communiqué had been printed in the newspapers and the brief details were at once augmented by word of mouth. The sound of artillery was said to have been heard as far inland as London. At other times such a claim might have been dismissed as fanciful, but now it was accepted without question. According to rumour, casualties were so heavy that the newspapers had been asked to print only short sections of the lists of dead and wounded. Since what they did print covered many columns in the smallest type, this suggestion added to the prevailing horror. There was hardly anyone in England without a loved one at the Front, and every breakfast table became a place of silent anxiety as the casualty lists were scrutinized.

Mrs Hardie was as anxious a reader as any. Kenneth's forcible conscription had taken place only three weeks earlier, so he would still be at a training camp in England; but she had two other sons at risk. Grace, waiting for the sigh of relief which would, if all were well, mark the end of a second reading, knew that her mother would look out for Christopher Bailey's name as well as those of Frank and Philip. It was less certain that her eyes would be alert for mention of Andy Frith. But if anything terrible were to happen to him, they would learn of it from his parents.

On this Saturday morning all was well. Mrs Hardie was able to smile as Grace kissed her goodbye before cycling off to work.

The tension which had gripped the whole country was as strong in Oxford as anywhere else. The city was stiflingly hot and there was less activity than usual in the High now that the university term had ended. The bow windows of The House of Hardie did not open, and even when the doors to the rear yard were left ajar there was no breeze to cool Grace as she waited for customers who did not come.

It was frustrating to waste time in the city when she could have been enjoying the fresh air of the garden on the hill. Fortunately, though, her duties ended at one o'clock on Saturdays, and she hurried home with as much energy as the heat allowed.

Her mother surprised her with a piece of news. 'Your aunt has come for the weekend.'

'In term time?' Although the university year was over, schools were still hard at work and it was unusual for Aunt Midge to visit Greystones before the holidays began.

'She said she was feeling tired and needed a rest. She went straight upstairs. Asked me to tell you that she'll see you at breakfast tomorrow.'

Grace wondered what could be wrong. She had never seen her aunt anything but brisk and cheerful. But it would be inconsiderate to disturb her rest. She put the puzzle of the unexpected arrival out of her mind as she sat in the rose garden, enjoying its perfumes while knitting yet another khaki sock.

Next morning, awakening in the energetic mood which the prospect of a day at leisure always induced, she looked

183

forward to her aunt's company for a walk before church. Midge, however, did not appear for breakfast.

'I'll see if she'd like a tray in her room.' Grace ran upstairs and tapped lightly on the door. When there was no answer she hesitated for a moment, not wishing to disturb her aunt if perhaps she had only just fallen asleep after a bad night. But uneasiness prevailed. Quietly she opened the door.

Midge was sitting on a chair, looking out of the window. She wore one of the dark costumes which she was accustomed to describe laughingly as her school uniform and which she never as a rule brought to Greystones. Her hair was plaited and coiled into its usual severe style and her back was as straight as ever. Yet beneath the rigidity of her body, Grace was immediately aware of a despair of spirit. 'What is it, Aunt Midge?'

Without turning towards her, Midge shook her head.

'Please tell me.' Grace hurried across the room and went down on her knees beside her aunt's feet.

'Can't talk without crying.' Midge's voice was unnaturally thick and abrupt, and she still would not allow Grace to see her face. 'Well, that's why I've come here. To cry. With no one looking. Just let me alone. I'll be all right directly.' But even as she spoke she broke down, burying her head in her hands and gasping for breath as she attempted to control her sobs. 'Go away, dear.'

'Not till you've told me what's wrong. There must be something I can do.'

'No, nothing. Nothing to do, nothing to say. When someone dies, that's final. There's no comfort anywhere.'

'Well, talk about it, please. Who is it who's died?'

There was a long silence before Midge slowly turned her head. There would have been no need for her to say in words that she had come to Greystones to cry; her face, red and swollen with tears, spoke for her.

She made no other movement, and yet Grace recognized that by an effort of will she was bringing her emotions under control, as though the headmistress in her was telling the snivelling schoolgirl which for a moment she had become to pull herself together. Giving a single deep sigh, she spoke with a voice which was almost recognizable as her own.

'No one you know. Although, as a matter of fact, he knew about you, in a way. He was the architect who designed Greystones.'

'Mr Faraday?'

Astonishment flashed light into Midge's dead eyes. 'How –?'

'I met him at your house once. Don't you remember?'

Grace had never forgotten. It was because of Mr Faraday that she had been forced to do all her lessons with Miss Sefton in the schoolroom instead of being invited to stay in London and enjoy the excitements and companionship of school life. She had never quite forgiven him for appearing to remind her aunt that a headmistress's secret life must remain secret. But this was not a time to express resentment.

'You told me who he was,' she said, 'and afterwards you showed me some of his plans.'

'Yes, I remember now.' Again she fell silent, and Grace did not know what questions to ask.

'It was here that we first met,' Midge said at last. 'On the land here, before the house was built. We liked each other at that first meeting. He looked me up in London. He'd let me know when he was coming to Oxford for discussions with your father, or to supervise the building work, and I would try to plan my visits for the same time. Just as though I were a moonstruck seventeen-year-old. Then, later on, when it was decided to extend the school, I managed to get him chosen as the architect. He's – he was – a very good architect. He always believed in spending a lot of time with his clients, to find out exactly what was wanted. The governors dealt with the money, of course, but I was the one who could tell him all the small things – how much space there should be between the desks, how wide a corridor needs to be, what kind of windows are best. There were so many details to discuss.'

'Didn't anyone ever suspect?'

'There was nothing to suspect then, except that we took pleasure in each other's company. After the extension was finished, that was when it became difficult. We had to make rules. Never to meet in term time.'

'But you went on holiday together.' Grace remembered how Patrick Faraday had painted a picture from the terrace of her aunt's hotel.

'Not together. But to the same place.'

'Did you want to marry him?'

'It was never possible. He was married already. Not that it was much of a marriage. His wife ran off with another man and took the children with her.' Midge stood up and began to walk restlessly about the room, leaving Grace seated on the floor. 'The other man died, or else abandoned her, I don't remember which. Patrick would have taken her back for the sake of the one child who was his own. But she went to live with her family in Ireland.'

'Couldn't he have divorced her if she ran away from him?'

'I don't know about these things,' said Midge. 'The only cases I ever heard about, it was always the gentleman who pretended to be at fault, even when the wife was really to blame. But we didn't even talk about it. I could never have married a divorced man. In fact, I couldn't marry anyone at all if I wanted to go on teaching. I've always known that. When I wasn't much older than you are now, someone asked me to marry him. I said no. I was already sure what

186

I wanted to do with my life, and I knew that marriage would be an obstacle. I didn't love Will enough to make that worth while. I *liked* him, but that was all.'

The idea that Will Witney had once been in love with her aunt was not new to Grace, who made no comment. Midge, for her part, seemed to be considering what she had just said. She sat down again by the window.

'Perhaps that means that I didn't love Patrick enough either,' she said. 'But it felt . . .' Her voice trailed away for a moment before recovering some of its more usual firmness.

'I'll tell you what really hurts, Grace,' she said. 'I have no right to mourn him. All over London – all over England – bereaved women are weeping over the loss of their husbands and sons and fathers, and society weeps with them. Patrick leaves a widow who hasn't spoken to him for ten years and a son to whom he's a stranger. *They* can dress in black and expect consolation. But I . . . That's why I came here. So that I could be sad for a while in secret. And angry, as well. He was forty-four. Too old to be a soldier. No one expected, there was no need – it was such a waste. Oh!' Rage and grief and frustration shuddered out of her body through the single syllable and left her trembling but calm.

Grace stood up quietly. 'Let's go out,' she said. 'I'll take you to the boulders.'

Midge emptied her jug of cold water into the washbasin and pressed a wet cloth against her swollen eyes. 'What are the boulders?' she asked.

'I'll show you.' Grace waited until her aunt was ready and then led the way downstairs, out of the house, through the gardens and down the hill.

As they plunged into the wood Midge looked curiously around her. She must often have walked beside the stream where it splashed and sparkled along its rocky bed; but

187

here it ran silently into a deep pool, falling away from it at a lower level without disturbing the surface. The crowns of tall trees touched overhead to give a dappled shade in which no birds chose to sing. There had always been something eerie about the silence of this spot. Grace came to a halt in front of the two huge stones and kept very quiet, wondering whether her aunt would prove sensitive to the atmosphere.

'I've never been here,' said Midge. 'And yet I've been for so many walks through the grounds.'

'No one ever comes here except me. Well, Andy used to as well. The boys played all over the wood when they were younger, so they must have seen the boulders; but they never seemed to notice anything special about them. Can you feel it, Aunt Midge?'

'I'm not sure. What is it that's so special?'

For a moment Grace felt almost hurt. The soothing effect of this place on her own spirits, whenever they were troubled, was so intense that she thought of it as being almost magical.

'It's their shape,' she said. 'The bigness and the roundness.' Put like that, it sounded babyish. 'You need to touch them.'

Midge stretched out first one hand and then the other. They moved downwards, feeling the texture which she would find to be rough and yet smooth at the same time. Her shoulders tensed as she pressed firmly, passionately, against the hard surface – as though she were giving her lover a last embrace. She cried out once and then dropped her head, leaning her forehead against the grey stones.

'I'll leave you to find your own way back,' Grace said. Instead of returning directly to the house herself, she walked along the edge of the stream until she came to the place where Pepper had been buried. Covered with fallen leaves, it was marked only by two pointed ears of slate:

sharp-edged, spiky stones, not comforting like the boulders, but disturbing.

That had been her own first bereavement, and her last. When she thought about her father, she felt anxious in case he was dead, but that was not the same as the terrible certainty of knowing that she would never see him again.

The effect of Pepper's murder on Grace had been quite the opposite to the effect of Mr Faraday's on Aunt Midge. She could remember how rage and misery had left her unable to speak or cry or even breathe. She had hated her brothers at that moment, and something of the hatred lingered in the air above the grave. Men called themselves hunters and soldiers, but they were murderers at heart. Patrick Faraday had been murdered by Germans; while Frank and Philip and Andy and Christopher were doing their best to murder Germans, and all for no reason that Grace could understand.

Turning away, she emerged from the wood to find her aunt staring up the hill at Greystones.

'It's his memorial,' Midge said. 'This house, and all the other buildings he designed. It means that he won't just disappear. I remember something you said once, dear. About not liking to cook because you couldn't bear your work to vanish. You wanted to make things that would last. Patrick did that.'

'I never have.' They walked slowly up the hill together. 'Was it worth it, Aunt Midge? The choice you had to make. Do you wish that you'd chosen differently and married?'

'If I'd lost a husband now, and not a friend, I should be left with nothing at all. But –' She seemed to be weighing the words she was about to speak, as though to test whether they were true. 'But I don't think there was ever really a choice. I believe that each of us was put into the world for a purpose. As soon as we know what that purpose is, we have to follow it. Whether it calls us to be a nun, or the mother of twelve children – or a teacher.'

'But suppose you never feel that call?' asked Grace. 'There's something inside me, I'm sure, waiting to burst out. But I don't know what it is. How do I find the key?'

'Perhaps "purpose" is the wrong word. I tell my girls at school that each one of them has a talent; a gift. It's part of what the staff and I must do, to search out those talents and develop them. That's what *my* gift is, I suppose – for helping them. Not everyone can have great abilities and great ambitions. The talent of most girls is for loving – for bringing up children in a happy home. That may prove to be your talent as well.'

'I remember Jay saying something like that once,' commented Grace. 'A long time ago.'

But it couldn't really have been so very long ago. It was just that everything that had happened before the war seemed to belong to a different chapter of history.

'He was talking about happiness,' she explained. 'You're happy if what you do is the expression of what you are, he said. It's odd, really, that someone like Jay should think that, because *he's* only happy when he's pretending to be someone else. But I know what he means.'

For a moment they walked on in silence, but Grace was still considering Jay's theory.

'You know, Aunt Midge, Frank loves being a soldier. When he joined up, it was as though he'd been waiting all his life for the war to happen. Last time he came on leave, he was terribly tired, and unhappy because so many of his men had been killed. But within only a day or two he seemed to become excited. Packing as much as he could into a couple of weeks, but then almost longing to get back again. Being a soldier was what he always wanted to be.

Whilst Philip hates it. He doesn't say, but I can tell. When *he* has a leave, he just wants Greystones and the family to swallow him up.'

'Philip's a very clever young man,' said Midge. 'It's a waste, a terrible waste.' It was easy to tell that she was still thinking about Patrick Faraday. 'Grace, dear, will you tell your mother what I've told you? If I try to say the words myself, I shall start to cry again. Tell her that I'm all right again now, but I don't want to talk about it. I'll join you for luncheon. And then I must take the train back to London. The girls will expect to see their headmistress standing on the platform as usual tomorrow for morning assembly; and I shall be there.'

She made a brave attempt at a smile, and Grace smiled back, admiring her aunt's courage. They were approaching the house now, making their way towards the front door; but the sight of a boy on a red bicycle brought them both abruptly to a halt, clutching each other's hands.

There had once been a time when the appearance of a cheerfully whistling telegraph boy had been a welcome sight, bringing news of a visit, or the time of a train by which the master of the house would return. But since the beginning of the war telegraph boys had ceased to whistle, knowing that too often they carried tragic news.

The boy, brisk and smart in his navy-blue uniform, leaned the bicycle against the steps, opened the pouch which hung from his belt and took out a small orange envelope. He handed it to the maid who answered the door and waited while it was carried inside. Within a few moments the girl returned, shaking her head. There was no answer.

'Oh God!' Midge's voice was hoarse with sympathy even before she knew what the telegram contained. 'A Blighty wound. Pray hard that it's a Blighty one, Grace.'

They ran up the hill and arrived breathlessly at the front door. News these days was never good, but how bad would this be? And would it be of Frank or Philip?

9

Five weeks after the news of Frank's death reached Greystones, Grace returned home from her duties in The House of Hardie one Saturday to find the household in turmoil. One of the maids met her at the front door and began to chatter in agitation even before she had had time to take off her hat. The words made no sense. Grace held up a hand to check the flow.

'Start again,' she said. 'What's happened?'

'It's the mistress, Miss Grace. She's been crying and screaming and groaning, but she won't let any of us in to see to her. We've tried asking through the door if she's ill, but all she'll say is "Go away." Thank goodness you're here, Miss Grace. We didn't know what to do.'

'You should have sent down for me at once. Or for the doctor.' But there was no point in being angry with a foolish girl. What could have caused her mother to collapse? The most likely answer was that something terrible had happened to Philip. She hardly dared to ask her next question. 'Was there a telegram?'

'No, Miss Grace. But there was a parcel. I took it in myself. It was about ten minutes after that that we heard her scream. Cook and I went running; but she just said, "I don't need you. Leave me alone." Later on we went again, because there were noises and we was worried. I looked from outside the window and Mrs Hardie was crying; but when she saw me she came rushing over and hit on the glass as though she was mad, like, and shouted, "I told you to go away." So after that we didn't like to bother her any more.'

'Where is she?'

'She was in the conservatory when I took the parcel in. I asked if she wanted scissors and she said she could use her gardening ones. She'd gone into the drawing room by the time we ran to her.'

'All right,' said Grace. 'I'll ring if I want you. Have a kettle boiling ready to make tea.'

Outside the drawing room she stood still, listening, but could hear no sound. 'Mother,' she called, and at the same time tried the handle. The door was locked. 'Mother, it's Grace. Will you let me in?'

There was no interruption of the silence. Not even the sound of breathing was audible through the heavy mahogany door. She lingered for only a moment before hurrying along the corridor. It was impossible to lock the double doors between the dining room and the drawing room – had the maids not thought of that? Crossing the dining room with a quick but quiet step, she opened both doors at the same time before standing still with her arms outstretched, one hand on each handle.

Her mother was lying face down on the carpet, so still that for one terrible moment Grace feared that she was dead. But no; the slightest of movements revealed that she was breathing.

'Mother!' Grace knelt down beside her and took one hand in her own. Lucy Hardie's blue eyes opened and stared blankly at her daughter. Then they closed again, as though she wished to see nothing of the world.

'Come on to the day bed.' With her arms beneath her mother's shoulders, she lifted her off the floor and supported her across the room. Panting from the exertion, she pulled a chair close and looked down at the reclining figure whose eyes remained firmly closed.

In the few hours since seven o'clock that morning, Mrs Hardie seemed to have aged by several years. Her long corn-coloured hair had been torn from the smooth chignon in which she usually wore it, to hang untidily round her shoulders. Her skin, which had retained the pink and white delicacy of a young girl's complexion, was blotched and puffy with weeping.

Although she had never been extravagant in her wardrobe, finding no need in a quiet country life for elaborate balldresses or fashionable city outfits, her tall slender figure was always dressed neatly, even for such everyday activities as gardening or painting. Within the last few hours, however, it seemed that she had torn at her own clothes, ripping off the buttons which fastened her bodice. Her habitually straight-backed and graceful posture was in a state of total uncaring collapse.

Grace took her hand and held it gently. 'Tell me what has happened, Mother.'

Mrs Hardie shook her head as though even an attempt to speak was too much.

'There was a parcel, Hetty told me. Where is it?'

Mrs Hardie's eyes opened at last; and her lips made the effort to move. 'Conservatory.'

Unable to imagine what had caused such a reaction, Grace stood up and walked slowly into the conservatory. It was in chaos. All the pots and plants so lovingly tended throughout the year had been swept off their shelves and stacks. The floor was covered with a mixture of earth and sand, compost and pea gravel, pieces of smashed china and scattered red petals. At first she mistook the geranium petals for drops of blood, and it was a moment or two before she raised her eyes and saw the contents of the parcel laid out on a table. Captain Frank Hardie's personal effects had been returned to his next of kin.

Her mother had set the first items out in a neat row. Here were the binoculars which had been a twenty-first birthday present from his father. An electric torch was next to them, and a battered tinder box. A compass in a metal case stood on top of a map pouch. Two leather wallets, filled with money and photographs, lay beside a cigarette case. There was a muddy copy of the New Testament, and a large brown envelope stuffed full of letters. A toilet bag revealed the familiar items which members of the family had sent him at Christmas – the silver-framed shaving mirror from his mother, the tortoise-shell soap case from Jay, the beaver shaving brush with his initials carved into the ivory handle which had been Grace's own gift.

Her fingers moved over the contents of the bag, fingering each object in turn as though in doing so she could make some kind of last contact with Frank, who must also have touched them on the last morning of his life. But his possessions were as dead as he was. A great heaviness descended on her spirits as she turned away from these small, intimate articles to the pile of clothes behind them.

Her sadness deepened as she looked down at what Frank had once kept as his 'best' uniform. How proud he had been when he first appeared to display it to his family; and how he had smiled, eighteen months later, as he waited for them to notice the third pip which signified his pro-motion to captain. Now the cloth was stained with damp and smelt musty. How odd it was that everyday objects like this could, simply by being neglected, make it so clear that their owner had disappeared from the world. Tears streamed silently down her cheeks. It was no wonder if this had caused her mother to collapse. There had been no hope even before, but this gesture with which the army closed its books on a dead officer held a terrible finality.

It was only as she turned back towards the drawing room that the emotional bomb contained in the parcel exploded in her face. Lying on the floor, where presumably her mother had thrown it, was another uniform – the one which Frank had been wearing when he was killed. It was not scattered in individual items, but was stuck and pressed into a single cube by mud and congealed blood. Hardly liking to touch, Grace bent down and turned it over. Then, at last, she understood.

The letter which Frank's colonel had written to his family had described the manner of his death. A sniper's shot straight through the head, they had been told; he would have felt no pain. But here was a bloody refutation of the kindly-meant lie.

From the condition of Frank's jacket it was possible to deduce the manner of his death. He had been hit in the chest by something large and jagged. He must have collapsed face downwards and lain for some time in his own blood before a nurse's scissors cut through the fabric in order to pull it away from his body. He must still have been alive then, for a field hospital would not have wasted its care on the dead.

For how many hours or days had he endured that agony, knowing that he was dying? What pain had he suffered? What had been his thoughts as all his hopes for the future slipped away? Grace heard herself groaning aloud and, as her mouth filled with a bitter bile, had to turn quickly towards the conservatory's deep earthenware sink to avoid being sick over her brother's effects.

As she retched and gasped for breath, she became conscious of a movement behind her.

'I've never been hysterical in my life before,' said her mother apologetically. 'But the sight of this took me by surprise. And the lies made me angry. A quick death, they said! Get rid of it for me, Grace, please. Burn it, bury it – I don't want to know what you do. I don't want to think of Frank like that. He was such . . . such . . .' For a moment she broke down again and the two women clung to each other, weeping as though they would never stop.

'I'll do it at once,' Grace promised, drying her eyes. But first she helped her mother up to bed. Then, changing into her oldest clothes and heaviest walking boots, she collected up all the pieces of her brother's uniforms.

Frith and the boy who was now his only assistant had finished their work for the week by the time she reached the garden tool room. She pulled out a barrow and loaded it with the clothes and a spade and fork before setting out down the hill. Her destination was the wood. This was partly because anything buried there would be safe from accidental disturbance, but there was another reason as well.

The wood had been Frank's special territory. He had claimed it as his battleground in the first moment of his arrival at Greystones, and through all the years of Grace's childhood took command of his brothers and sister whenever they went to play there. Whether the game was cowboys and Indians, Roundheads and Cavaliers, Robin Hood or any of his special inventions, it was always Frank who laid down the rules and chose the sides and told them what to do.

It came as a new thought to Grace that the wood had been more to Frank than only a playground. It was his training place for life. Here, as a boy, he had discovered and enjoyed the talent which as a man he was able to develop only through the accident of war.

Perhaps it was the memory of Frank as a boy which now caused Grace to carry the spade to a spot near Pepper's grave. Frank had been in command on the day of that death, and it was an occasion when his discipline had slipped. It was not his fault, but he had accepted responsibility and organized the solemn burial.

She dug a hole, throwing in the clothes and covering them with earth. Driven by anger that Frank was dead, and almost equally angry that he should so willingly have

198

played his part in that world of killing and being killed, she did not pause when the ground was level, but continued to pile on earth, scraping aside the top layer of decayed leaves from the surrounding area in order to find soft soil. She made a hump and battered its side with the back of the spade until it was transformed into a pyramid. Cutting off the pointed top, she built up the earth to resemble a tower on a triangular pediment. Then she tossed the spade away and went down on hands and knees, moulding the tower with her hands; squeezing it in, building it up, only half aware that she was trying to form the shape of a man.

The soil was too soft and too dry. In a few seconds the shape would disintegrate into trickling grains of earth, but before it had time to collapse of its own accord, she expressed her own need to destroy by punching it in the heart with her fist. Again and again. No doubt it was the same kind of gesture on her mother's part which had brought chaos to the conservatory.

Once her frenzy had spent itself Grace stood up, looking with surprise at her filthy hands and sleeves. The fallen earth had spread itself over the cat's grave. Well, the grave itself could not be distinguished, but the two triangles of slate which Grace had placed as a headstone were still in place. She bent down to brush them clear. How carefully, as a six-year-old, she had chosen the shapes by which she would remember her pet – the shapes of Pepper's pointed ears.

I must make a memorial to Frank too, Grace told herself. Perhaps it would never be known where he was buried, but at least he could have a headstone here. Except that it would not be a stone. At the back of her mind was an impression of something which would be more suitable, but she needed a few minutes' concentration before she could identify what she was remembering and where she had seen it. Loading up the barrow again with the tools, she left it there while she ran to the bank of the stream.

Yes, there it still lay; the fallen branch of a tree which the boys had used as a bridge. Grace herself had always been too unsure of her balance to follow them, preferring to use the stepping stone further along. She tugged the branch towards her and stared at the sturdy piece of wood which forked into two arms, their fingers jagged where they had broken in the original fall. With some effort, not caring if her dirty clothes became even grimier, she stood it upright, leaning it against a tree and stepping backwards to stare.

The proportions were right. The shape that she wanted for the memorial was already indicated by the present outline of the wood. A figure lifting its hands to heaven – in terror or agony or exultation? It didn't matter which: the line would be the same. But through the heart she would cut a jagged hole, just as a fragment of a shell had cut through Frank's chest.

The figure would not look like Frank, because she lacked the skill to carve a portrait; and indeed, she came to realize, it must not look like a man at all. Yet it would somehow express Frank's spirit, Frank's courage and her own anger. As though she were cutting through the piece of wood with her eyes, she understood how it ought to appear. Whether she would be able to find the right tools and learn to use them was another matter.

Common sense told her that she ought to try out knives and saws and chisels on some small block of wood, leaving this substantial branch to be carried nearer to the house – perhaps into her mother's studio – when the gardeners returned to work on Monday. But she was seized with a frenzy, and too impatient to be sensible. Running up the hill to the house, she searched for suitable implements.

There was a box of carpenter's tools in the cubbyhole which had once been used as a store by the handyman, and Frith had a variety of saws for lopping and pruning trees, although he would not be pleased to have them borrowed. Best of all, Grace remembered that Kenneth had once been given a set of woodcarving tools by a godfather, and managed to find it in his room. Her eyes were bright with excitement as she carried her booty back to the stream.

For a second time she stared hard at the branch. Her mother had taught her to draw, but she felt no need to make a design of what she hoped to produce. The design was there already. A long time passed in motionless study before she stepped forward, chose the tool she needed, and stretched up her hand.

Her first touch was too delicate, as though she were gripping only a pencil: it made no impression. Starting again, she pressed on to the narrow gouger and pulled it downwards with sufficient force to make a narrow groove. This was the line, and already she knew how deeply it would have to be cut away and how the curve should roll from front to back and from side to side.

For more than three hours she worked, stopping only when her mother appeared silently in the wood. Mrs Hardie, pale but calm, had washed her face and put up her hair again and dressed herself neatly. She stood amongst the trees without moving, careful not to disturb whatever it was that her daughter was doing.

Grace, noticing her at last, looked up and smiled, acknowledging that she was tired. For a moment longer she stared at her handiwork. There was little to show for her effort, but she was not discouraged. The next day was Sunday. She would miss church for once. The whole day would be free. For her and Frank.

'I'll come now,' she said to her mother, and bent to pick up the tools. There was nothing in her face to reveal that her life had been changed. How often in the past she had wondered what the future held for her, trying to envisage a husband, children, a home. These had all become of no importance. In this place where once Frank had shown by his boyish pleasures what kind of man he most wanted to be, Grace too had found her vocation.

10

Grace had started to work for The House of Hardie as an emergency measure, not expecting her help to be more than temporary. But just as the war was not, after all, over by that first Christmas, so too the shortage of men of working age continued. Her assistance, from being merely useful, became essential. She still refused to undertake any but the most simple accounts, claiming that the effort of balancing columns of money made her head spin, but she allowed herself to be educated in other aspects of the business.

Mr Witney held none of the usual prejudices about female inability to judge wine. He remembered the generosity with which Grace's grandfather had educated his own palate when he was not long removed from being an illiterate guttersnipe. The reason why so few women were capable of recognizing the difference between a good and a great wine, he told his new pupil, was that no one taught them what to appreciate.

Grace was already familiar with the names which appeared on the firm's list, and the general suitability of different wines for particular foods or occasions. Now, by tasting and making notes, she was encouraged to form more particular opinions so that she could advise her customers.

This was all the more necessary after Kenneth's conscription, when Mr Witney had to spend most of his time in London. Business was slack in Oxford. The young men who would normally have come straight from school to university were going into the armed forces instead. Most undergraduates were either medically unfit to join the army or had been invalided out of it, and there were few of the wild parties which had once been a feature of college life.

Grace would not allow herself to be called a manageress. But she was a Hardie. It was inevitable that other members of the staff should ask her opinions and, in spite of her youth and inexperience, defer to them. She had not been brought up to take such responsibility, and the strain often seemed hard to bear.

That was one reason why she liked to walk slowly up the hill towards Greystones at the end of each working day. Even in the darkest days of winter, when the old man who was The House of Hardie's only remaining driver brought her home in the trap, she chose to be left at the gates so that she could approach the house on foot, feeling the day's anxieties dissolve in the peace of being at home again. In summer, when her journey was made by bicycle, she dismounted at the same spot and pushed the machine up the long drive.

In July of 1917, however, on the first anniversary of Frank's death, she leaned the bicycle against a tree just inside the gates and made her way towards the memorial she had carved for him, now erected in a clearing of the wood which he had loved as a boy.

She was pleased with her work. The original shape of the branch seemed to give it an inner power, and in many hours of patient application she had smoothed the surface which represented her brother in life and created a central jaggedness round a hole which stood for his death. Merely to look at the work made her feel strong in the way that Frank had been strong, for as well as honouring the memory of her eldest brother it was the realization of an unknown and unexpected talent of her own.

In the past months she had made other wood carvings,

working on a smaller scale. These were less successful, and she knew why. Her first piece had been inspired by the certainty that the finished carving somehow existed inside the wood already, needing only to be revealed. She had not felt the same confidence again.

Nevertheless, these smaller works had provided useful exercises, teaching her how to produce particular effects. And Aunt Midge, noticing the pleasure which her niece took in this activity, had brought for Christmas a large pack of potter's clay, together with the special tools to work it and a book of instructions. Now Grace could build up the shape of whatever subject she had in mind and then cut into it again as though it were another piece of wood, using her tools either to change the shape or to detail and decorate its surface.

This new occupation filled her leisure hours to such an extent that she could not imagine how she had passed the time before. But Frank's memorial remained the only achievement which brought her real satisfaction.

Today, she noticed, her mother had been to the wood before her, plaiting an anniversary wreath of red and white roses round the wooden foot of the carving. Perhaps she had only just left, for the atmosphere prickled with life. As though someone were watching her, Grace felt. She turned her head with an abruptness intended to catch any spy unawares; but there was no one there.

Or so it seemed at first. But when, with her moments of mourning completed, she began to walk back towards the bicycle, she experienced for a second time the feeling of not being alone. Someone was moving behind her, with a sound heavier and stealthier than that of an animal. Someone who came to a halt whenever she herself paused.

For a moment she was uneasy. Even in July the wood was dark with shadows, and there would be no one within earshot if she needed to shout for help. But why should she be frightened? The intruder was probably a poacher, hoping to catch a rabbit. He would not want to reveal himself by attacking her. Shrugging her shoulders, she walked on towards open ground.

Twigs cracked under the weight of footsteps. The sound followed her and came nearer. Grace turned back to search the wood with her eyes. 'Who's there?'

'It's only me.'

The husky voice was unfamiliar and she was still unable to pick out its owner from the shadows. Could it be Andy, home on leave, ashamed to confront her yet unwilling to return to France without some kind of encounter?

'Don't be frightened, Grace. It's Kenneth.'

Grace let out the breath she had been holding and gazed at the dark figure now emerging from behind a tree. Had he not called his name she would indeed have been frightened, for this man, filthy and unshaven and with a dark scar across his forehead and eyebrow, was almost unrecognizable as her brother.

'You did startle me,' she confessed. 'Why were you hiding in the wood, Kenneth? What have you been doing? You look like an escaped prisoner.'

'That's just what I am. I need somewhere to hide, Grace, and something to eat.'

'Well, come up to the house and have a bath and a meal. You didn't need to wait for me. Mother's at home.' She and her brothers had never formed the habit of kissing, but she put her arms round Kenneth to welcome him home with a hug.

He shook his head. 'You don't understand. They'll be looking for me here. Probably they've been to the house already. They may have tried to persuade Mother that it's in my own best interests that she should give me up. The servants will have been told to report me to the military police if I show my face here.'

206

'What are you talking about? Who are "they"?'

'Grace, I must have something to eat. And no one must know about it.'

'The plant room,' she said, postponing any attempt to understand what he was talking about. Andy and Philip had looked after Mr Hardie's plant-breeding experiments when he left for China, but when they both joined up Mrs Hardie had instructed Frith to plant out all the seedlings and cuttings which might survive. The plant room and the glasshouse next to it had been closed. No one had been there for months. Taking care to keep out of sight of the house, Grace led the way there.

The wooden shutters were already bolted across the windows; it was safe to light a lantern. Now Grace could see more clearly the truth of her brother's claim to be hungry, for his body was emaciated and his face gaunt. In the year since she last saw him he appeared to have aged by a decade.

'I'll get some food,' she promised. 'And I won't say it's for you. Wait here.'

It was not easy to raid the kitchen undetected. The cook would be preparing the evening meal, and even if she left the room empty for a moment would know exactly what she had in store and be quick to notice any theft. A confident lie had the best chance of success.

'Mrs Charles, have you anything you could spare for a poor family? A jug of milk for the children, and some bread and cheese. And perhaps a cut off the cold mutton if there's enough.'

'Shouldn't be any poor families nowadays,' grumbled the cook, although the comment did not prevent her from opening the bread bin. 'Plenty of work for everyone.'

'The father has been wounded. He's lost an arm. I suppose it will be a little while before he finds what he can do with only one hand. I saw him looking for work in

207

Headington Quarry, but with no success; so I told them to come this way.'

Whether or not Mrs Charles believed the story, she cut the meat and the loaf generously, pressing together two thick slices loaded with pickles and adding others with cheese. For good measure she found a jam pasty for the children and tied the offering in a cloth.

'Sarah will take it down to the gate,' she said. The kitchen maid was already standing beside her, holding the can of milk.

'Thank you, but I promised to return myself. I'll wait while they drink the milk, so that I can bring the can back.'

She hurried off before any other help could be offered, wondering whether her lies had been convincing. It would have been unwise to ask whether the servants had already been questioned about Kenneth and impossible to be sure that they would help to hide him.

The plant room was in darkness again when she returned; but when she called his name Kenneth stepped forward from a corner, eager to see what she had brought. For a second time she lit the lantern and saw his eyes glistening with an unnatural brightness as he broke off mouthfuls of the bread and cheese and began to devour them.

'You should save something for breakfast tomorrow,' suggested Grace. Seeing that he was too ravenous, she pushed the jam pasty out of sight. 'And drink the milk first.'

Kenneth swallowed it as though it were a yard of ale, to be taken in a single gulp as a sconce. He handed the can back to her and returned his attention to the victuals.

'I must leave you now,' Grace told him. 'Mother will be expecting me for dinner. But I'll come back later, after she's gone to bed.'

'Don't tell her, Grace.' Kenneth interrupted his eating

208

for long enough to stand up and put a hand on his sister's arm. 'I've deserted, you see. This is more than a game of hide and seek. If anyone gives me away . . .'

'Your own mother! You surely don't think –'

'You must keep quiet unless she says something first, to let you know how she feels. Wait for her to speak. You mustn't know anything until she tells you, d'you see? When we were children, I didn't sneak on you, either, remember? The day you hit the baby.'

For a moment Grace failed to realize what he was talking about. Then, as she remembered, her face flushed with anger rather than shame.

'You didn't need to say that. I don't have to be black-mailed into behaving decently.'

'No.' Kenneth's arm dropped to his side. 'You've never been a tell-tale. I'm sorry, Grace. I'm frightened, that's what it is. These past five days – I've felt like a fox with the hunt after me. So many of them, all faster and stronger than I am. And all the time not knowing whether I'd find my lair earthed up when I tried to go to ground.'

'I'll be careful,' she promised. 'And I'll come back. However late it is.' She practised the rhythm of the knock by which she would identify herself and then, with a troubled face, left him in the darkened room.

11

If Mrs Hardie noticed that her daughter arrived home later than usual, she made no comment on the fact. Grace for her part waited to learn whether her mother had anything to say about Kenneth. So dinner that evening was a silent meal. Only over dessert, when for the first time there was no servant in the room, did Mrs Hardie abruptly come out with the words which must have been on her mind all day.

'Two military policemen called here this morning. They told me that Kenneth has deserted.'

'Deserted? Kenneth?' Grace put astonishment into her voice. 'How can he be said to desert when he has made it clear from the start that he doesn't wish to fight?'

'Wishes are not respected in time of war. He was refused exemption and so was deemed to have enlisted like any other fighting man. I understand from what my visitors told me today that even before his desertion he'd embarked on a course of disobedience. Well, there are minor punishments for that kind of thing, I suppose. But desertion is a different matter. The penalty is death.'

Grace half stood up in her chair and then slowly sat down again, hardly able to believe what she heard.

'Death? The army wouldn't shoot its own men. There must be other punishments.'

'I suppose that the punishment for running away has to be greater than the risks involved in remaining on duty. Men in danger must often be tempted to run away. And so –' Mrs Hardie looked down at the tablecloth, her eyes full of tears – 'I dare say it seems necessary from time to time to make an example, to show what will happen to anyone who fails to stick it out.'

For a moment both women were silent. Then Mrs Hardie, looking up, spoke more firmly.

'My father was an army officer who died for his country,' she said. 'My eldest son has been killed in action. I still have one son at the front, in danger of death every day, and I'm as proud of him as of Frank. I can't be proud to feel that I'm the mother of a coward as well. All the same, Kenneth is my son, and I love him. I'm not prepared to see his life sacrificed in such a stupid way. I'd give him shelter if I thought that was a sensible thing to do. But it would be foolish; dangerously foolish. Wherever he tries to hide, it ought not to be here.'

'I'm sure he must realize that this is the first place the military police would look for him.' Then Grace hesitated, not knowing what to say next. Was her mother's last remark a plea for the chance of a meeting with Kenneth? 'But if he were to appear one day –?'

There was a long silence. When at last Mrs Hardie spoke, it was with her head bowed so low over the table that Grace had to strain to hear the words.

'It would be best if I didn't know,' she muttered. 'It's not that I would send for the police; of course not. And if someone else saw him and reported his presence I would deny any knowledge of it. But I might feel angry at being forced to lie. And it would be hard for me to conceal the fact that I'm ashamed of him. To part in bitterness would spoil what might be our last meeting. It would be better that it should never take place.' She stood up. 'I'm tired, Grace. I think I'll go straight up to my room and read for a little in bed.'

She was giving her daughter the chance to spend the rest of the evening as she liked, and Grace took immediate advantage of it. The plant room was dark, and locked from the inside, but the door opened at once to her knock.

'I took some cheese and fruit from the table,' she said, setting it down in front of him. 'But it's difficult – there always seems to be one of the servants watching. I'd never noticed before. Kenneth, you were right about the military police. They've been at Greystones today. Mother told me.'

'You didn't let on –'

'No. She expects them to come back again. You were wise to warn me. If she tried to lie to them, they'd probably guess. Kenneth, how did you get into this? What made you run away?'

'I've been an idiot. I realize that now. Telling them the truth, that was my mistake. I ought to have gone along with the system and obeyed all their stupid orders until the time when it really mattered. In the heat of battle, I don't suppose anyone would have noticed whether or not I pointed my rifle at a man's body or into the air. But – do you know how the army punishes those of us who aren't heroes, Grace?'

'No.'

'The order that I disobeyed was to do bayonet practice. "Imagine that the sack is the body of a Jerry," the sergeant said. "Drive your bayonet into his guts and twist it." Well, I could do the imagining bit well enough. And because I imagined it, I couldn't stab it. Not wouldn't, but *couldn't*. For that I was sentenced to two years' hard labour. You'd think that they'd prefer to be quit of someone who was never going to be of any use to them, instead of wasting money and men on guarding people like me.'

He sighed with the absurdity of it all and for a moment was silent.

'There were four hundred men in the prison camp,' he told her. 'Sixteen to a bell tent, with barbed wire all round. It was January when I arrived there. There was snow on the ground. They took away all the clothes of the new arrivals. Sixteen of us were forced to take a cold bath in the open – all using the same water and the same wet towel. We were never given our woollen underclothes back again; only a thin prison uniform. We were put on to a ration of eight ounces of dry bread, morning and evening, with water to drink. The next day they started us on shot drill.'

'Shot drill?'

'You stand with a bag of sand between your feet. The bag is supposed to weigh twenty-eight pounds. There are detailed rules about these things, you see. But in the snow or rain it soon becomes far heavier. There's a warder in front of the line blowing a whistle, and at each blast you have to make a sharp movement. One, pick up the bag of sand and balance it on the palms of the hands. Two, take three quick steps forward. Three, place the bag down between the feet and stand up straight again. Four, bend down to pick it up – and on and on until your body can hardly stand it any longer and your mind is almost mad with the uselessness of the exercise. So in the end, after days or weeks or months, either you can't go on or else you refuse to go on. That's expected, I suppose, because the next punishment is ready and waiting.'

He paused, as though even to describe it was too much to bear, and then began to speak again.

'We called it crucifixion. The army call it Number One Field Punishment. They put you with your back to a post or tent pole or gun carriage. Your wrists are handcuffed high behind you. There are straps round your chest and knees and ankles. And there you stand in the cold and rain while anyone who's passing takes a swipe at you. When they release you at last, you can't move; can't even stand. After I'd had three days of that, they thought I'd give in, so they sent me back to the drill ground. But I was

213

so angry by then that I wouldn't obey orders even if I could.'

'What did they do to you then?'

'Put me on another charge for disobedience. I wasn't allowed a lawyer. There was an officer supposed to speak for me, but he was on *their* side. I was sentenced to death. They left me to think about that overnight, and then said it had been reduced to ten years' imprisonment.'

'That's cruel!' gasped Grace.

'A little game they like to play. In the past, I was told afterwards, they'd go as far as to take a prisoner out in front of a firing squad. But one man died of fright when they did that, using blanks, and there were questions asked in Parliament. So now they can't take the joke quite as far.'

'So they put you in prison?'

'I was in a prison camp already,' he reminded her. 'There were some pits dug at one end of it. I'd been told about them before. They lowered me into one of those. It was ten feet deep and not more than two feet across. I had to stand up all the time, with water above my ankles. Could hardly even turn round. Almost dark, because it was so deep. Nothing but mud in front of my nose. It wouldn't have taken long to go mad in a place like that.'

'How did you get out?'

'One of the sergeants chucked a couple of live rats down when he was passing. To keep me company, he said. Well, they drowned fast enough. But one of the guards, an ordinary Tommy, thought that was the last straw. He didn't join the army to see Englishmen treated in such a way, he said. He threw down some bits of wood so that I could climb out of the pit, and told me a place where I could get under the wire. Asked me not to make a break until after he went off duty, that was all. Just one decent chap!'

Kenneth buried his head in his hands, and for a moment Grace thought he was crying; but when he looked at her again she saw not tears but hatred in his eyes.

'The pleasure it gave them, Grace! The officers ordered those punishments, but the NCOs *enjoyed* them. And I thought, is this why we're at war – to give pleasure to bullies, sadists? If I get through this, I shall get out of England and never come back. I hate it, hate it. I don't hate the Germans, poor sods. Don't suppose they like fighting any more than I do. But the bloody British army – oh, I hate that, all right.'

Grace was horrified at what she heard and shocked by his language. None of her brothers had ever sworn in her presence before. She was aghast, too, at his bitterness. 'What can you do?' she asked.

Kenneth's fingers combed nervously through his short-cropped hair. 'I don't know. I don't know where to go. I can't stay here, I realize that, nor try to work again for The House of Hardie. But what else is there? No one will employ a stranger, a man of military age, without asking questions that I can't answer.'

'David will help you if he can.' But even as she spoke, Grace wondered how much he could do for his twin. David himself, when he realized that even marriage and a claim to be short-sighted were not likely to protect him from conscription much longer, had managed to arrange that he should be commissioned into the army to work in the legal department of the War Office, safely in London.

'I tried to telephone him. A clerk told me what he's doing these days. Drafting death warrants for people like me, it seems. And with a wife and baby, I can't expect him to harbour a criminal.'

'I know so little of the world outside Oxford,' Grace confessed. There was a long silence whilst each of them considered the problem. When she spoke again, it was with the tentative voice of someone who knows that a suggestion will be unwelcome.

'It seems to me that the safest place for you would be in the army. Under another name, of course. That's the one place where the military police would never dream of looking for you. Could you consider such a plan? If you were to offer your services as a volunteer – perhaps with some story of being medically unfit until recently – you might be allowed some choice of sphere, like David. To serve as a stretcher bearer, perhaps.'

Kenneth's expression showed his distaste for the idea. 'I think my only hope is to find work on a foreign ship. Once I'm out of England, I shall be all right. Until then –'

'I brought you some money,' Grace told him. 'It's all I have in the house. But I'm sure you'd be safe here for another day or two. I could take some more money from the shop.'

'I wouldn't want you to steal for me, Grace.'

She couldn't help laughing. 'An escaped convict like you, shocked that I might put my hand in the till! I work without wages because it's a family business, and because it's a family business it can surely be used to support a member of the family. I'll come again at this time tomorrow. And bring you clean clothes from your room as well. What else?'

'Soap. And a haversack. Grace, can you understand? Could *you* kill a man?'

'No. But it's not expected –'

'Why not? Is there such a difference between men and women? We're all taught as children to hold life sacred. If as adults we grow up to hold differing views, it can only be because boys and girls are educated differently. But suppose that part of our education is deficient in some way. Then it can hardly be our own fault if we see life through eyes unlike our brothers'. A girl who asks for a

216

gun and kills with it is thought unwomanly; a boy who refuses to shoot is derided as unmanly. But we're not talking about crimes or sins; merely about conventions.' His fists clenched with anger. 'Well, I mustn't burden you with my difficulties. Thank you for your help. And you'll come back tomorrow?'

'Yes, of course.'

As Grace hurried through the darkness to the house she intended not only to keep her promise but to think of some way in which Kenneth could start a new life. So it came as an unpleasant shock when, returning laden to the plant room twenty-four hours later, she found it empty.

'Kenneth!' she called quietly, first in the room and then outside it. There was no answer; no sound except for the rustling of the wind in the trees. Setting down the bundle of clothes and the pack full of food, she sat in the darkness for an hour, but he did not come. Had something happened to frighten him away – or, worse, had the military police watched her on the previous day and followed her to their quarry?

Grace took the money from her purse and pushed it into a pocket of the suit which Kenneth had worn as a young businessman. Then, unhappily, she returned to her room in the tower and went to bed. Very early next morning she ran down to the plant room. The clothes, the food and the money had gone. Kenneth had not trusted her; it was as simple as that.

Hurt and worried, she joined her mother at the breakfast table. 'You've been crying,' she said, recognizing an unhappiness that matched her own.

'I found it hard to sleep last night. It frightens me, the way the family is breaking up. Such a short time ago, your father and I and you and the boys . . . So happy together. I knew that it couldn't always be like that, of course. Still, I thought that even when you all married and had children

of your own, you'd keep coming back here. But now –
Frank is dead. And your father – I find it harder each day
to hope . . .'

She stopped, as though ashamed to break the convention
by which every member of the family professed to be
certain that Gordon Hardie's long silence was due only to
a severed line of communication.

'Every time I say goodbye to Philip, I'm terrified that I
may never see him again,' she went on. 'And now Kenneth.
I say to myself that he can't simply disappear – but he can!
I may have seen him for the last time. Without saying a
proper goodbye; without knowing.' She dabbed with a
handkerchief at the tears which were trickling down her
cheeks, and then looked up. 'Has he been here?'

Grace nodded.

'And gone?'

'Yes. He didn't say goodbye to me, either. But he'll
come back, Mother. When the war is over, Greystones
will pull them all back. Just by being here. It's our home.'

Even as she spoke, she knew that her words could carry
little reassurance. Frank would never come home again.
And her mother's fears for Philip were well justified. It
was all too easy to believe that he might never return to
their house on the hill.

12

Private Philip Hardie's life in the trenches was ruled by ritual. In this he was no different from his comrades, each of whom had private superstitions to be observed, talismans to be touched, runes to be repeated. It was the only way to cling to sanity and courage.

Every morning at the moment of sunrise he passed the same thought deliberately through his mind: that he was lucky to be alive. Lucky in that he had survived another night; lucky because almost all the other volunteers who had travelled to France on the same troop train as himself had been killed many months ago. On the day he forgot to recognize his good fortune and give conscious thanks for life, he would place himself at risk. Until then he was safe. That was his superstition.

His talisman rested in a breast pocket. Like many others he had faith that the slim New Testament supplied by a Bible charity would deflect any bullet from his heart. To be doubly sure, he kept inside its covers a photograph of his mother and sister on the terrace of Greystones. They were what he was fighting for – if the war had ever had any other purpose, he had lost sight of it by now. In Philip's world at school and university and in the army there had been no room for women. He was twenty-five years old, but had not yet fallen in love. The family was the rock to which he clung.

His most secret ritual was a legacy of his botanical training. Passchendaele in October 1917 was a lake of mud. For four months rain had been falling on the once-fertile countryside of Flanders, its drainage channels already shattered by the shellfire of the opposing armies. The water had settled, and the ground beneath was pulverized by continuing bombardments; trenches became streams and no-man's-land was a sea of slime, pock-marked by craters in which it was easy for a weak or wounded man to drown. Long before the first frost signalled the beginning of an autumnal fall of leaves the trees were bare, their shattered trunks pointing accusing fingers up towards heaven.

In this mud-saturated environment Philip searched silently for traces of green. Each day he tried to find a trampled or floating root of grass which he could rescue and press into some less heavily trodden patch of earth, as though giving new life to a blade of grass could increase his own hope of survival.

There was no grass within sight on the night of 23 October. As darkness fell, he was sitting halfway up a hill in a pillbox captured from the enemy. Its concrete walls were more than three feet thick, so that its present occupants could listen with less anxiety than usual to the artillery bombardment which seemed set to continue throughout the night. But almost certainly the shelling meant that the Germans were planning a counter-attack at dawn. On their way to the British line they would have to pass the pillbox and, because they had built it themselves, there was no protection facing the direction from which they would come; only an open entrance. The men who were stretched on the floor, taking it in turns to attempt sleep, knew that dawn would spell danger.

So loud and so continuous was the bombardment that it might have seemed impossible to catch the sound of any new element in the pattern of shrieking flight and explosive blast. But Philip was not the only one who suddenly raised his head to listen more intently, holding his breath as though amidst the thunder of the guns a faint inhalation would prove a barrier to hearing. Yes, there it was again; a thinner scream in flight, a duller thud on landing. A newcomer might have interpreted the sound as that of a mercifully unexploded shell, but an old hand knew better.

'Gas!' he said quietly. There was a scuffling as his companions, like himself, made sure that their respirators were at hand. They would wait until the last moment before putting them on.

Without distracting the sentries who were watching for any movement of an approaching army, Philip went outside and, flattening himself against the wall of the pillbox, moved quietly round until he was looking down on his own lines. He lifted his head, feeling for the wind, and found that it was almost still. If the gas shells had burst behind the trenches, the heavy poison might linger in the dip instead of climbing the side of the hill towards them. But even as he prepared to report this conclusion, a new salvo of heavy artillery shells exploded below, their blast pushing the cloud of gas towards the pillbox.

For a second or two he waited and watched as new explosions revealed the tendrils of mist, unnaturally tinted to the colour of a Clouded Yellow butterfly, creeping up the hill. By the time he made his way back into cover a look-out in the trench below was beating an urgent warning on the empty shell case which served as an alarm gong. Already the air was tainted with a smell stronger than that of the corpses putrefying in the mud.

Time had taught Philip to control his fear of bullets and shell splinters, but imprisonment in a gas mask always brought him near to panic. The men who were his friends, the men who trusted him and on whom he in turn must rely, were transformed within seconds into unrecognizable, identical, goggle-eyed toads. The nose clip which forced him to breathe through his mouth made him feel as though he could not breathe at all, and the air so painfully pulled through the filter was not like real air. It brought no strength, and every breath felt as though it might be the last, so great was the effort needed to fill his lungs. Still, there was no other protection on offer, and wearing the respirator would make the difference between life and death. He was as quick as the others to pull it on.

The use of gas confirmed what the bombardment had already suggested: that a counter-attack was imminent. The enemy was expected to sweep down the hill to the southern end of the newly-established British line in an attempt to re-occupy the hundred yards of land which they had lost a few days earlier. The occupants of the pillbox, reinforced by a detachment from the trenches further north, would emerge from behind the Germans and chase them until they were forced to turn and fight on two sides. It was not a plan in which Philip placed much faith; nor did he see any great benefit to be gained even from success. But the whole strategy of the war was incomprehensible to someone who was a mere cog in the fighting machine.

That was partly his own fault. As an educated man, a graduate, he had twice been offered and on a third occasion had been pressed hard to take the training which would earn him a commission. But unlike Frank, who was recognized as officer material on the day he volunteered, Philip had no wish to give the orders which would send men to their deaths. An unendurable life could best be endured in the ranks. He had refused all promotion.

The sound of the German artillery underwent a subtle change. Although still as fierce as ever, the range had altered. Every man in the pillbox was an expert on trajectories and blasts and could interpret the slightest grace-note in an orchestral score which was played fortissimo throughout. The attack had begun. They waited in the darkness while lines of low-stooping Germans, as though operating to the British plan, ran past them down the hill. What

222

could the occupants of a few pillboxes hope to achieve by attacking from the rear? Nevertheless, the men obeyed instructions, grouping themselves ready for the downhill dash as they watched for the Very light which would signal them to move.

The Germans were expecting them. The bullet which had Philip's name on it hit him in the throat while he was zig-zagging between huge mud-filled craters. Its force spun him round before he fell dizzily forward on to his hands and knees. He could no longer breathe through his mouth, as the respirator forced him to do, and he tore the mask off to free his nose, not caring that the muddy ground was carpeted by the heavy gas. His lungs were bursting; he must breathe something, anything.

There was a moment in which he was aware of every separate part of his body as though it belonged to someone else: his head, thick with pain and incomprehension; his throat, bubbling as it spewed out blood; his lungs, on fire; his legs, inexplicably devoid of strength, as if they were made of melted wax. With a single deep sigh he brought all these pains together and abandoned himself to them. There was just time for him to realize with relief that he was escaping from hell at last.

13

Christmas was approaching before Grace and her mother, after weeks of anxiety, were able to visit Philip in a Berkshire hospital; for so great were his injuries that he had not for many weeks been judged fit to endure the cross-Channel journey. Their first glimpse did little to reassure them. He was alive, certainly, but that was all that could be said. Propped by pillows into a sitting position, he remained motionless, his eyes closed and his face pale and strained. To breathe was painful and not to breathe was death. Grace recognized the signs of mental strain as well as physical suffering.

But what caused her to gasp with horror was the tube protruding from his throat. At the sound he opened his eyes. Unable to speak or even to smile, he did at least manage to move a hand so that his mother could take it. The two visitors sat down at the side of his bed and talked of their happiness at seeing him alive and their love and hopes for him – dividing the conversation between themselves since it was clear that Philip could not contribute to it. They told him all the family news of the past few weeks before the nurse appeared again to clear the tube and tell them that the patient must not be tired by too long a visit.

Outside the ward, the two women clung to each other in a dismay that they had done their best to conceal in front of Philip. Then Grace sat down to wait while Mrs Hardie went to speak to the doctor in charge.

The hospital was a converted country house, and on this raw December day those patients who were convalescent were taking exercise by walking round and round the great hall or up and down the double staircase. Some, their empty trouser legs pinned up, needed the support of crutches, whilst others, to judge by their ungainly movements, were attempting to come to terms with newly-fitted artificial limbs. One-armed men led blind men up and down; men with bandaged heads pushed other men in wheelchairs. A few, wearing hospital blue like the rest, but revealing no visible wounds, were talking to each other with a curious whistling sound. Grace followed these with her eyes, wondering whether this would be Philip's fate for the rest of his life.

Her mother, pale-faced, came to sit beside her.

'What did the doctor say?' Grace asked.

'The throat wound may heal. He won't die of it, in any case, after surviving as long as this. But –' her voice broke and she looked down at her lap, crumpling her gloves between her fingers.

'But?'

Mrs Hardie sighed before speaking with a briskness perhaps copied from the doctor.

'His lungs have been almost destroyed by gas. Burnt in some way. There's nothing that can be done about that. For the rest of his life he must be careful never to move too fast or work too hard or become too anxious. Just force himself to go on taking regular shallow breaths. Think of it, Grace! He's twenty-five, only twenty-five. He's lost three years of his youth already, and now he's never going to be able to live as a young man again. Never run or play games or – oh!' She was forced to pause, gripping Grace's hand to restore her courage.

'And there's another thing,' she continued, almost in a whisper. 'A kind of mental collapse. No one understands it or knows what to do about it, the doctor said, but it affects men who've been under shellfire for a long time. A kind of withdrawal from life. Sometimes they're frightened of any sudden noise; sometimes they don't appear to

hear it at all because they cut themselves off from whatever's happening all round them. No one will be able to
tell whether Philip is suffering in this way until he can talk
again, if he wants to. But they seem to be afraid –'

'That won't last, surely,' said Grace. 'When he's home
again at Greystones, safe, with nothing to be frightened
of, whatever it is will cure itself.'

'Let's hope so.' Mrs Hardie stood up and did her best
to smile. 'Yes, we must hope so. We must talk to him
about home. Remind him of all the things he loves. Grace,
when we were in there with him, why didn't you tell him
about Christopher?'

'There's nothing to tell.' But Grace's pale face flushed,
for she knew this was not true. As they were driven in a
cab from the hospital to the railway station, she used
thoughts of Christopher to banish from her mind the
tragedy of Philip's wounds.

In the three years since her first meeting with Christopher Bailey their friendship had developed by correspondence. At first he had written about the war,
describing his life in the trenches or in rest billets behind
the lines. The battle of the Somme altered all that. Perhaps
it was one of Grace's own letters which forced a change
of subject, for her description of Frank's death and its
aftermath could have left him in no doubt how deeply she
was upset. More probably, though, he was silenced by the
terrible nature of his own experiences.

So he began to write instead about England; describing
his childhood, his home, his family, until Grace felt as
though she knew them well. In return, he asked her to
describe the minutiae of her own life. Her duties and
customers in The House of Hardie were one source of
material for her letters, but mostly she liked to describe
the changing face of the woods and meadows and gardens
as the seasons passed. The need to paint an accurate

picture in words sharpened her observation. She carried a small note pad on her walks and the care with which she noted every detail for her next letter intensified the possessive love she felt for her family home.

The pleasure she took in putting most of her experiences into words made it all the more strange that she should never have mentioned to Christopher the memorial she had made to Frank, nor any of the carving or clay modelling with which she now filled her free time. Was it because she expected him to disapprove? Certainly this was not one of the accepted occupations for a young lady. Water colouring and embroidery and playing the piano were all approved pastimes, but it was a different matter to embark on an undertaking which dirtied clothes and roughened hands.

From time to time, indeed, when she first began to carve, Grace had cut herself with some tool which slipped out of control. Her fingers were no longer those of a gentlewoman, soft and smooth, for no amount of soaking in lemon juice and glycerine could soothe away all the blisters and splinters and scars.

Well, it was wartime, when many unusual activities could be excused. Only a few years earlier it would have been unthinkable for someone like Grace to work in a shop, even if it did belong to her own family. It was not shame which led her to conceal her new hobby, but a fierce determination to preserve it as something private to herself. In a household such as Greystones, of course, it was impossible to conceal what she was doing, and she made no attempt to do so. Whether she worked at one end of her mother's studio or out in the open, it could be no secret from the servants and family. What they did not know was the depth of feeling which she brought to the task. That was too private to share even with Christopher.

So Grace kept the greatest pleasure of her life to herself

227

with as much care as Christopher censored all the details of war. The word pictures which she sent him instead had a curious effect – for Christopher began to write poems. Even someone who had acquired little literary taste during her years in the schoolroom recognized that the verses were not great poetry, but she was flattered to find herself always the central character.

At first he wrote of her as he remembered her, and as he pictured her daily life. Later he tried to imagine her childhood. By the end of the year his viewpoint had changed again. No longer did he picture her wandering through the grounds of Greystones on her own; he provided her with a companion and a new home. The change of style was so gradual that it was some time before Grace realized that his poems were love letters.

The discovery should have made her proud and happy, but instead it disturbed her. Did he love her as she really was, or had he created a different girl in his imagination and fallen in love with her? He wrote of her as beautiful, but Grace knew that she was nothing of the sort. It was not that she was ugly: but a portrait of her own mother as a young woman had convinced her that beauty was to be found in softly-waving corn-coloured hair, a rosebud complexion and a slender, graceful body. Grace had inherited none of these.

It was for this reason that she brushed aside every attempt on her mother's part to suggest that Christopher saw her as a future wife. She was not prepared to discuss the subject now. In any case, she was too deeply affected by the sight of her brother to tear her thoughts away from him for long. As the train rattled towards Oxford, her heart swelled with the desire to express Philip's fate in some visible form. She could create something like the memorial to Frank – although in this case, thank goodness, the subject would still be alive.

How should it look? She felt herself withdrawing from all awareness of her surroundings, grateful that her mother was in no mood to talk. There was in her mind a sense of swirling which must be allowed to move until it settled its own form. Perhaps it was the swirling of the gas which had so nearly killed her brother; or perhaps it represented the invisible barrier which he had created to cut himself off from the world.

Could such a feeling be expressed in a hard material? She envisaged a central figure which would stand for Philip's endurance, surrounded by circles or spirals. But the technical difficulties would be very great. She had not yet thought how they might be solved when they arrived at Greystones.

Letters which had arrived in the course of the day were laid out in the hall. There was one from Christopher. Grace smiled as she opened it, putting Philip for a moment out of her mind. Then her smile faded as she read its contents.

PART SIX

Christopher
1917–1919

1

Christopher's letter began by acknowledging the receipt of two parcels. He thanked Grace for the contents of one of them and promised that the other would, as she had commanded, be kept for opening on Christmas Day.

Suddenly, in the middle of a page, his tone – and even his handwriting – changed. Words sprawled over the paper to express a frenzy of emotion.

'But shall I still be alive on Christmas Day to receive your gifts?' he asked rhetorically. 'I have to answer that yes, of course I shall, because often and often I've noticed in recent months that death comes to those who half expect it, that it's the fierceness of a man's determination to survive which ensures survival. Yet how is it possible to maintain such determination when one is permanently tired and tense, battered by noise and rain and constantly under fire?

'There's only one answer, dearest Grace – at least, only one as far as I'm concerned. I must have something – a way of life, a special person – on whom I can centre my hopes and dreams of the future. I need to know that there's someone who is praying for me and whose happiness is bound up in thoughts of my return one day, just as my own hopes of happiness rest on a life shared with her.

'Dearest girl, tell me that you'll marry me. On my next leave or after the war is over – I don't mind which as long as you promise me that the time will come, certain sure, when you'll be mine for ever. Write to me now, my darling.

Tell me what I want to hear. Nothing in the parcel you've sent me can give me half as much Christmas joy as a letter from you to say that you'll be my wife.'

Grace read the letter three times: first of all standing in the hall; then walking round the house; and at last in her bedroom. Not until later that evening, as she sat at dinner, did she reveal its contents to her mother.

'Darling!' Some of the distress which had aged Lucy Hardie's face during the hospital visit was smoothed away by her smile. 'I'm so happy for you! Dear Christopher! I was beginning to think that nothing good was ever going to happen again, but at last . . .'

'You think I should accept his proposal then?'

'Surely that's what you want to do? He's made it clear enough how much he loves you, and you love him too, don't you?'

'I don't know,' said Grace honestly. 'I hadn't thought that way. I feel – I hardly know him.'

'Don't be ridiculous, Grace. You've known him for three years. Far longer than the acquaintance of most girls with their future husbands.'

'But in that time we've only spent a few days together.'

'I knew your father even less when I ran away from home to marry him, yet no one could have been happier than ourselves until . . . until . . .' Mrs Hardie finished the sentence bravely. 'Until he left on his travels again. For a marriage to succeed, Grace, there must be an initial attraction – and you both felt that, didn't you?'

'I suppose so. Yes, I did.'

'Well, from then on, the process of learning to like everything about each other may continue for the rest of your lives. You've made a good start, by exchanging so many letters: all you need now is goodwill on both sides. The only thing required for a happy marriage between two people is a mutual wish to love, and the love will come.

In Christopher's case it's there already. I thought it was with you as well.'

'The man I write letters to – yes, I think I am in love with him.'

Had it not been for Andy, she would have spoken more positively. But she could still recall the feelings which overwhelmed her when the gardener's son kissed her for the first time. Never with Christopher had she experienced the same passionate need to be close. Was it just that anyone's first kiss, simply by being the first, aroused emotions which could never be repeated?

Or perhaps it was Christopher's own restraint which made her answer in turn restrained. He had always behaved as Mrs Hardie had promised that a gentleman would, never pulling her into his arms. But once they were engaged, there would be no need for him to hold back. Would she then experience the same joy in his embrace that she had once felt in Andy's? She must believe so.

'But is the man I write to really Christopher Bailey?' she asked.

The question no doubt sounded foolish. But it seemed to her that she had reason to feel uncertain. Her most vivid memory was still of the light-hearted young man who had arrived at The House of Hardie to plead for her sympathy. That boyishness had been killed by the hardships of war. His letters and poems suggested that he had become serious, and she was glad of this; but when the war came to an end he might change again. She knew little enough about Christopher as he was now and nothing at all about Christopher as he might be for the rest of his life. That didn't necessarily mean that she would dislike what she found, but it did give her cause to hesitate.

Her mother had no patience with such doubts. 'You can't say No, Grace. Just think what the effect of a refusal

235

would be. He's spelled it out to you in this letter. If he loses hope . . . You can accept his suggestion of waiting until the war is over before you marry. That would be perfectly reasonable. But he's asked for something to look forward to, and you can't let a fighting man down.'

'No. No, of course not.' How odd it was that she should need a reason for doing the expected thing. Grace was twenty years old. Most girls of her age were already wives and some were already widows. David and Jay regularly teased her with the prospect of becoming an old maid. She had nothing against marriage. It was what was expected of her, and it would be unwise to turn down a good offer. None of the young men she knew, apart from Christopher, had shown the kind of interest which might lead to marriage. Except, of course, Andy, and he had married someone else.

'There's no one else, is there, Grace?'

It almost seemed that her mother was reading her thoughts. The question startled her into a decision.

'No. You're quite right. I do love Christopher.' What other explanation could there be for her shyness whenever he arrived for one of his rare visits, or her feeling of desolation when he said goodbye. 'I'll write tomorrow. We'll be married as soon as the war is over.'

She accepted her mother's hugging and congratulations with a sudden lightheartedness. This was how a young woman's life should run, and she was glad to be ordinary. That night she lay in bed repeating to herself 'Mrs Christopher Bailey'. At first the words made her smile happily. Only as she was on the point of falling asleep did her uncertainties return. What sort of a life would Mrs Christopher Bailey be expected to lead? Where would she live? She was unable to answer those questions, but by morning had forgotten them.

Over breakfast next morning Mrs Hardie decreed that

it would soon be time to make contact with Christopher's parents.

'We'll allow long enough for your letter to reach him and for him to tell his parents of the engagement. Early in the new year I'll invite them here to meet you.'

Grace made a face at the thought of the coming ordeal, but had little time to think about it, for she was kept busy both at The House of Hardie and with the Christmas preparations at Greystones.

For Mrs Hardie, Christmas had become a time for regret rather than rejoicing. David and his wife were expected, and Midge would spend a week with them as usual. In addition, Will Witney was always invited to Christmas dinner, because he had no family of his own. Yet it was hard not to compare the tiny gathering with the lively pre-war days when her husband and daughter and five sons were all assembled for the festivities.

So Grace set herself the task of decorating the house as lavishly as in the old days, bringing in holly and mistletoe by the armful. She made birds out of paper, colouring them as brightly as parrots before suspending them from the ceilings; and when Jay arrived home from school he helped her to dress a tree as large as any in the past with tinsel and candles and the coloured glass globes which were stored in nests of tissue paper for eleven months of each year. Had Gordon Hardie walked into the house on Christmas Eve he would have seen nothing to suggest any lack of a festive spirit.

There was to be no hospital visiting on Christmas Day, they had been told by the sister in charge of Philip's ward. It made for unhappiness for any patients who found themselves alone. The doctors and nurses undertook instead to make the day a special one. So Grace and her mother, with Jay accompanying them for the first time, carried their gifts to the hospital on the day before.

They found Philip looking better in one way, because the tube had been removed from his throat. But there was no change in the deadness of his eyes, and he still lacked either the strength or the will to move. He attempted to smile as the parcels were piled beside his bed, but made no effort to touch them. His only movement, in fact, was caused by the unexpected bursting of a balloon brought in by the small son of another patient. This made him draw up his knees sharply and cover his face with his hands. It was half an hour before he ceased to tremble and managed to regain the state of immobility which alarmed his family as much as the trembling. When Mrs Hardie, at the end of the afternoon, emerged from the doctor's office, she looked more worried than ever.

'They're sending him away for convalescence,' she reported. 'There's nothing more they can do for him here, and he needs a period of quiet.'

'You mean he can come home to Greystones?'

'That was what I hoped. But the doctor . . .' Mrs Hardie's expression showed how much the interview had upset her. 'They suggest that he should live for a while in a community that they know about. They've sent patients to it before. There's nursing care available if it's needed, but the main advantage is apparently its peaceful atmosphere.'

'What kind of community? Do you mean a monastery?' Jay asked.

Mrs Hardie shook her head. 'Not exactly. It's run by an Anglican ex-chaplain, but it doesn't belong to any particular Order, as far as I can gather. It's been started for people who need to retreat from the world for a while. They work at whatever suits them, and leave when they feel ready to face ordinary life again. We should think of it as being – well, a convalescent home. There are a lot of men like Philip, the doctor said, who need rest of this special sort while they're coming to terms with their injuries.'

It still seemed to Grace that the right place for her brother was his own home, but it was difficult to argue with the doctor's opinion. She did her best to cheer her mother.

'He'll come home in the end. And he's alive – and safe. He'll never have to go back to the Front. That's all that matters.'

It was a thought which helped them all to be cheerful throughout Christmas Day – even at the moment when Will Witney rose to his feet at the end of dinner. Ever since Mr Hardie's departure four years earlier, Will had taken over the task of choosing a special selection of wines for the meal, and also of proposing the toast which would normally have been left to the head of the household.

'We remember our Absent Loved Ones,' he began. 'First of all Frank, who will always be present in our hearts. Gordon Hardie, for whose safety we all pray. Philip, who is thankfully on the way to recovery. And Kenneth, who still faces danger.' Kenneth's desertion was a secret which the Hardies had managed to keep to themselves, concealing it even from the manager.

The diners prepared to rise to their feet. Midge and Lucy, Grace and Jay, David and his wife Sheila, all gripped their glasses in readiness for the toast. But Will had not yet finished.

'And to these family names we must this year for the first time add that of Major Christopher Bailey. We hope that it won't be too long before he returns safely to England. In the meantime I ask you to drink to all those we love who cannot be with us today.'

Grace stood up at the same time as everyone else, lifted her glass to her lips, murmured with the others the names of her father and brothers, but then lingered tenderly on the words 'Major Christopher Bailey'. Yes, he must come back safely. He was the guardian of her future life, and she could not live without him. How could she have doubted her feelings even for a moment? Of course she was in love with Christopher.

2

It was towards the end of January 1918 that Mr and Mrs Bailey arrived at Greystones to inspect their future daughter-in-law, although the occasion was naturally not described in such terms. Grace as a rule gave little thought to what she should wear, but on the day of the visit her bedroom was littered with rejected garments by the time she went downstairs. How could she decide whether Christopher's parents would prefer someone who was neat and demure or someone smart and lively until she had met them?

The ordeal proved not to be as great as she had feared. Mr and Mrs Bailey were prepared to like Grace just because their son loved her. After the meal Mrs Bailey retired to the drawing room with her hostess while Mr Bailey asked to be shown the grounds, in spite of the cold. Grace took him first to the top of the hill. From there she could point out the view of Oxford and the boundaries of the Greystones estate.

'Hunt, do you?' enquired Mr Bailey.

'I don't myself.' Grace saw no reason to add that she never went near the family's horses, since they had so often brought on one of her bouts of wheezing.

'Good country for it, I can see. Christopher's a fine rider. Well, you know that. It's why he joined the cavalry – and now he finds himself sitting in one of these tank things! He's a first-class shot as well. Plenty of pheasant you've got here, I should say.'

'Yes.' Grace tried to disguise her lack of enthusiasm for the idea that they should be killed. Her father, on his expeditions abroad, shot for the pot and believed that every boy should be able to do the same. Each of her four elder brothers had been taught to use a gun, but only Frank had taken pleasure in it.

Kenneth had always refused point blank to kill even vermin. His twin was by now a Londoner, with no time for country sports. As for Philip, he – like his sister – took more pleasure in watching the handsome birds and their bustling mates than in killing them. Grace, who put out food for the pheasants in harsh weather, would have thought it a betrayal of trust to let anyone shoot them.

There was no need to feel shame about concealing her feelings. Mr Bailey might have hoped to acquire a hunting daughter-in-law; he was less likely to expect a woman to shoot. But his question made her uneasy. She remembered how Frank had once suggested that Greystones, because it was designed on such a grand scale, gave a false impression of the family's place in society. Was she unwittingly deceiving Mr Bailey, not by anything she said but by the simple fact of living in a spacious mansion with extensive grounds?

What a ridiculous question! Mr Bailey knew as well as his son that the Hardies were in trade, and the pleasantness of his manner suggested that this did not trouble him. So many wartime marriages were arranged quickly that dowries and settlements had lost much of their importance, and lavish wedding ceremonies attended by all members of both families were almost impossible to arrange. The parents of the bride and groom had to be content if the match appeared 'suitable'; and Greystones was probably helping the Hardies to pass this test.

There were, naturally, other tests. On her return to the drawing room she was invited to entertain the visitors on the piano, and did so willingly enough. Nor did she raise any objection when the visitors' attention was drawn to a watercolour which she had painted, hanging on the wall.

'Which is your favourite occupation?' asked Mrs Bailey, praising the painting. 'What would you be doing at this moment if we were not here?'

Would it be wise to tell the truth? But Mrs Bailey was smiling as she awaited an answer.

'I'll show you. If we may go into the studio, Mother?'

'Of course, dear.'

The large, high room in the north wing of the house had been specially designed for her mother's use. But after the Christmas when her aunt gave her a present of clay, the carpenter had been summoned to fit a wide, strong workbench across one end. On a table beside it was a potter's wheel, a birthday present which arrived six months after the first gift. Some of the pots which Grace had made stood on shelves above the workbench; but instead of pointing to these, she indicated a piece only recently begun.

Her first visit to Philip had put the idea into her head and dictated its shape. For a while it was forgotten in the excitement of Christopher's proposal and the bustle of Christmas. But it remained in the back of her mind and, by the time the family group dispersed, the problem of supporting the wispy, swirling spiral of gas around the central figure had solved itself.

Wood was not the right material. Stone would have been perfect, had she known how to carve out the spaces from a single piece. But she had no idea how to set about such a task, and was too impatient to wait until she had learned new skills when she had another material to hand.

Clay could be formed to the shape she had in mind, but needed a framework to bear what might prove to be a heavy weight. This must hold one part away from another, allowing the light which came through the spaces to be part of the design. She had raided outbuildings which

243

contained tools and materials needed for general repairs, and now her workbench was littered with wirecutters and saws and thick fencing wire and palings of split chestnut. Round one of the palings, gripped in a carpenter's vice, she had constructed an armature of twisted wire; on this she could build up the clay. She thought of the wire construction as being a skeleton, but of course it was not the skeleton of any recognizable shape. It was not surprising that the Baileys stared at it in a puzzled fashion.

What a stupid thing to do, to show them something so incomplete. Hastily she drew their attention to the row of pots and chattered about her experiments with glazes.

To judge from Mrs Bailey's doubtful expression, even the making of elegant vases did not represent a suitable occupation for gentlewomen. Well-brought-up girls were not expected to get their hands dirty. But that was the only moment to cloud what was otherwise a successful day. In the course of the next week Mrs Bailey wrote not only a formal letter of thanks to Mrs Hardie, but also an affectionate note to Grace herself. Nothing, it seemed, was to ruffle the course of true love.

So it was with no apprehension of bad news that Grace opened a second letter from Mrs Bailey six weeks after the first. Indeed, her eyes sparkled with hope: was Christopher expected home on leave? Her excitement at the possibility made all the greater the shock of what she read.

The first paragraph of the letter repeated Mrs Bailey's appreciation of the visit to Greystones. The sting came in the second:

Christopher has asked me to write to you, to suggest that it might after all be unwise for the two of you to consider yourselves formally engaged to be married in the present uncertain circumstances. So much could happen before the war ends and it becomes possible to look forward to any kind of settled life. Although we must all pray that the successes gained by the

244

Germans in their recent attack will eventually be reversed, there seems little hope of seeing a satisfactory end to hostilities for a long time yet. It would be wrong, he feels, for you to regard yourself as bound to someone who is unable to offer you companionship now or security for the future.

He wants me to make it clear that his affection for you is unchanged, but wishes you to regard yourself as free, released from a promise which he had no right to ask of you.

With a gasp which combined shock and anger and distress, Grace stood up from the breakfast table so abruptly that her heavy chair fell backwards to the floor.

'Grace, what's happened? Is it bad news?' So many letters these days contained tidings of death or injury that Mrs Hardie's question was a natural one.

Grace shook her head. Hardly able to speak, she forced herself to say the words once, so that she need never repeat them. 'Christopher has had time to repent of his proposal of marriage. He's broken the engagement.'

'Darling, but why?'

'I don't know and I don't care. I don't want to speak of it – or of him – again.' Seeing that her mother was hurrying to comfort her, Grace rushed out of the room. She went straight to her tower bedroom and walked round and round it, trying without success to calm herself. How could he do this to her? Without warning; without even a hint?

Sitting down at her bureau, she looked for his most recent letter. It had been delivered three weeks ago and was dated a fortnight earlier than that. Although this was the longest gap in their correspondence during the past twelve months, the wait had not worried her. She had been anxious for his safety, of course; she was always anxious about that. But she knew that it was not easy for him to write. Sometimes batches of letters were lost and on other occasions, when an attack was imminent, they were deliberately held up by the censors. The ferocity of the recent

245

German offensive had seemed explanation enough of the delay.

Now she re-read the letter with new eyes, searching for any sign that the writer was beginning to change his mind; but there was no hint of any craving to feel free.

The room was too small to contain her restlessness. Pushing the letter into her pocket, she ran down the stairs of the tower, across the garden and down the hill. The boulders had comforted her in times of earlier distress. Would they be able to soothe this greatest hurt of all?

A blustery March wind lifted the dead leaves as she ran through the wood, sending them flying around her ankles. As she came nearer to the two huge stones, however, she moved more slowly. The sense of awe which they induced seemed to enforce a silent approach. This gave time for her mind to become receptive to the atmosphere. Even before the boulders came into sight she was conscious that there was someone beside them already.

From the shelter of the trees she observed the figure of a soldier leaning against one of the boulders with his forehead pressed against it and his back to herself. Unmoving, she tried to decide who it could be. Had Kenneth secretly returned home? But no; the man turned and she saw that it was Andy.

It was here that Andy had kissed her for the last time before leaving to join the army. She had not seen him since. He had been granted leaves during the past two and a half years, but she knew from his father that he had chosen to spend them with his wife and baby in France instead of returning to Greystones.

How long had he been back? The size and weight of the pack which he now swung on to his shoulders suggested that this must be the beginning or end of his leave. Was he, like Grace, remembering their last parting? Was he hoping to see her again, or did he realize that they could have nothing to say to each other? She watched as he settled the pack into position. Then, as he made his way between the trees, she followed at a distance.

At the edge of the wood she stood still, in case he should turn his head. He walked down the long drive, past his parents' cottage and straight out of the gates, striding down the hill towards the city. It was the end of his leave, then. He must have been home for several days, but he had not shown himself at the house, and nobody had told her.

Well, why should they? The head gardener and his wife had never known that there was anything to tell, and Andy himself would have been ashamed to show his face. Grace watched until he was out of sight and a great desolation overwhelmed her. She had been rejected not once but twice. Andy had said that he loved her, but had married someone else. Christopher had said that he loved her, but would rather be free than married. What was it about her that made them both turn away?

There was more than unhappiness in her mood as she walked slowly back to the house. She felt disturbed, unable to understand where her inadequacy lay, and uncertain whether to be more angry with herself or with the two men who had let her down. Letting herself in, she went straight to the studio, ringing for a maid as she passed through the hall.

'Send a message down to the shop,' she ordered when the girl appeared. 'Say that I'm unwell and shan't be able to come in today.'

It was the first time that she had used such an excuse. She justified it with the thought that she was not a paid assistant. She had helped out in the family business for long enough. As the daughter of the house she should be free to attend or not as she chose. But her indignation came near to making the excuse a true one, for she could feel her chest tightening in a manner which was often the first warning of a wheezing bout.

This time, determined not to give in to illness, she forced herself to breathe steadily as she pulled on her working smock. Instead of continuing to work on the complicated spiral which she was gradually building up, with the risk of spoiling it through frustration, she slit open a new pack of clay. Before the material could be used, it was always necessary to beat it into a malleable form, slapping it down on the workbench over and over again until no bubbles of air remained. The heavy work suited her mood. A little at a time she worked out some of her unhappiness – but not all of it, because a despairing bleakness remained whenever she thought about the future.

If nobody wanted her, what was she going to do with her life? She slapped and banged with increasing vigour, but no answer came.

3

It was Midge, arriving for a half-term visit, who dragged Grace out of her despair. No doubt, as a headmistress, she had for years been telling schoolgirls to stop sulking or snivelling. She had enough respect for the feelings of someone who was no longer a child to make a more tactful approach to her niece, but there was a no-nonsense briskness below the surface.

She was waiting at the gates when Grace was driven home from The House of Hardie on Friday evening, so that the two of them could walk up the drive together.

'Your mother gave me the news of your disappointment,' she said after the first greetings were over. 'I was so sorry to hear it.' Her voice was full of sympathy; yet Grace sensed a hesitation in it – as though she wished to make a further comment, but feared that it might increase the hurt.

'I'm not disappointed. I don't care.'

'Oh, but that can't be true! If you're not disappointed by the ending of your engagement, it must mean that you felt no true joy earlier at the prospect of the marriage.'

With a sigh Grace indicated her reluctance to discuss the subject. 'Very well then. I was disappointed when I first received the letter, but *now* I don't care.'

Midge made no pretence of believing her. For a second time she seemed to hesitate. 'I find this difficult,' she confessed. 'There's something that I would really like to say to every young woman. But for an old maid who can't possibly know what she's talking about to speak her mind on such a subject is likely to be regarded as interference –

not by the young woman herself, perhaps, but certainly by her mother.'

Made curious by her aunt's apologetic tone of voice, Grace waited to find out what this was all about.

'All girls are brought up in the expectation that they'll become wives.' Midge spoke more briskly. 'This is in spite of the fact that there have never been enough husbands to go round, even in time of peace. Now, unfortunately, a great many girls who in normal times would have married and made good wives will be unable to do so. What I would really like to say to those girls – and the others – is that they may in the end be all the happier for being left with the power to rule their own lives.'

'But surely –'

Midge allowed no interruption. 'Marriage is only one way of life. It's curious that girls should be brought up to think of it as almost their sole ambition. When a man marries, he continues to be what he was before – a soldier, a clergyman, a shopkeeper, anything. He isn't simply a husband. Yet when a woman marries, she becomes merely a wife.'

'Probably she wasn't anything before,' suggested Grace.

'That's exactly my point. All she was before was someone waiting to get married. It's not good enough, Grace. Girls have minds as good as men's. They have the same strength of character, the same courage. They can look after themselves and be independent when circumstances force them to. How much better it would be if they were to learn independence as a matter of course! So that if they did eventually marry it would be because they genuinely chose to, and not merely because they feel there's no choice.'

'By the time they've acquired this independence, they'll be so old that no one will want to marry them anyway.'

'By the time they're independent, they may never wish

to change their status. Well, you can imagine how the mothers of my pupils would come down on me if I started preaching that kind of message in morning assembly! I can say it to you only because you're not a child any more.'

'But a happy marriage must be —'

'Yes, yes.' Midge's interruption implied agreement. 'For a woman whose happiness lies in being a support to someone else, a successful marriage is the perfect life. But not all marriages remain happy for ever. And some women are strong.'

'I'm not one of them.' In the past three days, as she cried herself to sleep, strength was the last quality with which Grace would have credited herself.

'You haven't had the chance to find out about yourself yet. You've lived here as a dutiful daughter and you've always assumed that you'll become someone's dutiful wife one day. But this is a good moment for you to take a clear look at yourself and decide what you want to do with your life. Not what you're expected to do, but what you *choose* to do.'

'It's all very well for you to talk like this, Aunt Midge,' Grace complained. 'You knew when you were my age that you wanted to be a teacher, and you knew what you had to do to qualify yourself. I haven't got any such ambition or talent. What use would independence be to me when I don't know what to do with it?'

'You say that because you've never given the matter thought. I'll ask you a question in turn. You're the daughter of a family which owns a business. Mr Witney has been managing the business with total devotion, but he won't be there for ever. Who is going to run The House of Hardie after him? Frank is dead. Kenneth has disappeared. Jay is too young at the moment, and gives no sign of being businesslike. From what your mother tells me, it may be a long time before Philip is well enough to undertake responsibilities which would put him under strain.'

'There's David.'

'Certainly David could be asked to take charge. But he might be reluctant to abandon his profession. Whereas you have nothing to give up – and unlike David, you're familiar with the firm's affairs.'

'But not from any position of responsibility!' Grace was aghast at the suggestion. 'I find the keeping of even the simplest accounts a difficulty. To understand a balance sheet and attempt to keep a business profitable – Aunt Midge, it's an impossible idea!'

'Only because it's a new idea. But you can hire qualified bookkeepers. As headmistress, I'm responsible for everything that goes on in my school, but I wouldn't be capable of doing the work of every individual member of my staff. My responsibility is to choose efficient helpers.'

'In a girls' school it's expected that the head should be a woman. But in a business –'

'Don't ever think of yourself as "only a woman", Grace. You're a Hardie, and inside The House of Hardie that's a qualification that no outsider can better. You'd only need to drop the slightest of hints to Mr Witney and he'd be delighted to discuss wider aspects of the business with you and give you the chance to share in decisions. That wouldn't commit you to anything. But it would give you confidence – and that's all you need.'

'You've taken my breath away! No more revolutionary suggestions for the moment, please.' They continued their walk in silence.

'Have you been doing any more modelling?' asked Midge as they entered the house.

The sparkle of enthusiasm returned to Grace's eyes. She put her aunt's extraordinary proposition out of her mind and led the way into the studio to show off the huge piece of work which Philip's gassing had inspired. It was six feet tall, but so delicate were the circles which surrounded the central stem that there was no feeling of bulk.

Midge gasped at the sight. 'I didn't realize you were so ambitious in your projects!'

'Too ambitious, I'm afraid. When I made pots on the wheel, I could use one of the sculleries for mixing glazes and one of the kitchen ovens for firing the pieces. But this is too large for any oven. I ought really to have made it out of stone.'

'Why didn't you then?'

'I don't know anything about choosing or carving stone, and I haven't got the right tools. But Headington Quarry began its life as a settlement of quarrymen and stone-masons. The tradition must still be alive there. As soon as the evenings are lighter I shall look for someone to instruct me – if Mother will allow it.'

She paused, surprising herself by what she was about to say. 'You know, Aunt Midge, if I *did* want to become an independent person, as you were suggesting, this is what I'd want to do all the time. Learning how to make shapes in different ways out of different materials. Modelling or carving – I don't know which I like best. I'd much rather spend my life in the studio here than in The House of Hardie.'

Her aunt looked disconcerted, as though that was not precisely what she'd had in mind while preaching her sermon on independence; but she was able to see the amusing side of it.

'You're a quick learner, Grace. You've understood what I was suggesting and you're independent enough to reject my suggestion. Well, why not? The important thing is that whatever you do should bring you satisfaction. And you may soon feel that you're better off being free of someone who could write to you so cruelly.'

'He didn't even write himself.' Grace was not ashamed to reveal how much she had been hurt. 'I learned of his change of mind through his mother.'

'Didn't write himself! But surely . . . Grace, dear, you wouldn't let me see the letter, I suppose.'

Grace pulled the letter out of the pocket of her working smock.

'I never met Christopher,' said Midge after she had read it. 'But when you described him I had the impression of a young man who was brave, not cowardly, and considerate of other people's feelings.'

'I thought so too. But it isn't his fault that he can't speak to me face to face. For an officer serving at the front, a letter –'

'But a letter that he didn't write himself! Have you given no thought to the reason for that? Only the most shameful coward would ask his mother to free him of some entanglement merely because he regretted it. There could be other reasons which would reflect more credit on him. Suppose he's sick or wounded. He might have spoken to his mother – or even sent a message through a friend – while in delirium. He might not even be aware now of what has happened. I wouldn't want to raise your hopes when I don't know the true state of affairs. But it seems to me that you have been very quick to take this letter at its face value.'

'I was humiliated,' said Grace. 'And upset. But in a way I'd expected this to happen, that he'd realize I wasn't good enough for him.'

'Rubbish!' said her aunt brusquely. 'Judging by this, he isn't good enough for you. But I do think you should give him the benefit of the doubt. I'm sure your mother would be willing to accompany you to his home, so that you can have a frank talk with his parents.'

'I could do better than that,' said Grace slowly. Mr

254

Bailey had mentioned in the course of his visit that he was a telephone subscriber. There was no line to Greystones, but the shop had a receiver. Tomorrow morning, as soon as she arrived at work, she would make a call to Mrs Bailey and discover the truth of the matter.

4

The maid who answered Grace's telephone call at half past eight the next morning was unused to the instrument, treating it as though it were a speaking tube to be moved between mouth and ear. Each urgent question was followed by a long silence before the answer came faintly over the line. No, Mr and Mrs Bailey were not at home and no one knew when they would return. They were staying in London to be near the hospital.

'Who is in hospital?' Grace asked, knowing what the answer must be.

'Mr Christopher.'

'What –?' But no; the nature of his injury was not something to enquire from a servant. Grace waited impatiently for details of the hospital to be fetched and dictated.

'I have to go to London,' she said, bursting into Mr Witney's office. 'I'm sorry to let you down. But a friend – no, my fiancé . . .' Emotion made her incoherent. The manager stood up and took her by the shoulders.

'Steady,' he said. 'Steady. Is Major Bailey wounded?'

Grace nodded. 'Will you send a message to my mother, please? I don't know when I shall return. But I shall be with Mrs Bailey. And may I take some money from the till?'

Within a few moments she had caught a tram and within half an hour was sitting in a railway carriage. Paddington Station was noisy and smoky and confusing, but there were cabs waiting for passengers and she was quickly on her way to the military hospital.

256

The bustle here was as confusing as at the station, for porters were pushing patients on trolleys through a maze of corridors, while beneath the painted board which listed the wards was a haphazard collection of pencilled arrows to more makeshift arrangements. Grace eventually found the ward whose name the maid had given her, but was stopped by a VAD.

'It's too early for visiting, I'm afraid. The doctors are doing their rounds.'

'But I've come all the way from Oxford. I've only just heard . . . I must see him.'

'Who?'

'Major Christopher Bailey.'

The young nurse gave a comforting smile. 'Major Bailey is out of danger. Nothing terrible will happen before visiting time. I'll show you where you can sit.'

The wait seemed interminable, but at last other people began to arrive in good time for the official visiting hour. Amongst them were Mr and Mrs Bailey, who looked startled as Grace rose to her feet, but then embraced her warmly.

'How did you know?' asked Mrs Bailey.

'Your maid told me. I telephoned. That letter – I couldn't believe it.'

'He dictated it and made me promise to send it,' said Mrs Bailey, as the two women sat down on the bench to wait. 'I didn't want to – but I didn't want to upset him by refusing, either. I understand how he felt, but I'm so glad you've come, dear. Even if, later on, you want to do as he suggests and be free again, he'll be stronger by then and better able to accept it. It can do nothing but good for him to have your support now. He's bound to find the next few months hard.'

'What's happened?' asked Grace. 'I don't know any details, except that he's here.'

'His tank was hit,' Mr Bailey told her. 'Buckled up so that they could only get out one at a time. Christopher was the last to leave. He's badly burned; very badly. All up one side of his body and face. Since it didn't kill him within the first few days, it won't kill him now, they say, although he'll be scarred. But besides that . . .'

'It's his eyes, you see,' Mrs Bailey explained. 'There's a piece of metal. A bit of shell, or of the tank itself. He's had one operation already. It didn't do any good. They're going to try again when he's stronger. But they're afraid he may never recover his sight.'

It was one of those occasions when a group of people who have been chattering amongst themselves fall silent at exactly the same moment, so that Mrs Bailey's last words were heard by everyone in the waiting room. A dozen pairs of sympathetic eyes rested on Grace as she trembled with the shock of the statement. A bell rang and she looked at Christopher's mother. 'May I?'

'Of course, dear. Tell him that we're here, but we won't come till you've had some time to yourselves. You'll find that he can talk quite normally. He's in the fifth bed on the right.'

As if I wouldn't recognize him, thought Grace as she walked up the centre of the ward. It was only when she came close to his bed that she understood the warning which Mrs Bailey had been trying to give her.

The man in the bed was almost completely covered with bandages. They encircled the top of his head, as far down as the middle of the nose, and passed beneath the chin in order to cover one ear and cheek, leaving only his mouth and a small area of the other cheek exposed. He was propped by pillows into a half-sitting position, with both arms on top of the sheet in front of him. One arm was also covered in bandages but the other, nearer to Grace, was undamaged. Its smooth skin seemed to be that of a young

258

man to whom nothing terrible had ever happened. Grace stretched out a finger and gently stroked that arm. The bandaged face turned towards her.

'Mother?'

'No. It's me. Grace.'

The sound which emerged from Christopher's lips was a mixture of a gasp and a sob, followed by a stammered protest that he had asked his mother to write a letter for him.

'And so she did.' Grace sat down at the side of the bed and took Christopher's good hand in her own. 'And very unhappy it made me. It was cruel not to let her explain the reason.'

'I was afraid you'd just be sorry for me.' Astonishingly, as he recovered from his shock, his voice was as light and cheerful as at their first meeting, although he hardly moved his lips as he spoke. 'Very reasonable, too. I'm sorry for myself. But then you might feel that you ought to hang on, and that *wouldn't* be reasonable. I'm not the same man as the one who asked you to marry him.'

'Then the new man had better ask me again – or else the old one may find himself being sued for breach of promise.' Grace tried to keep her voice as light as his.

'But seriously –'

'Don't let's be serious in that sort of way. Your parents will be along in a moment. I need the time to tell you how much I love you while nobody's listening.'

'Oh Grace! Darling Grace! All the same, seriously though. When these bandages come off they're going to reveal something like Frankenstein's monster. Maybe you could get used to that; I don't know. But a blind man – that's a different matter. Someone who's going to be dependent on other people for the rest of his life.'

'Nonsense,' said Grace.

'No, not nonsense at all. I don't know whether I shall

ever be able to earn a living. And I don't know how long I can go on pretending to be cheerful about it. When I look at the future, I don't like it much. As long as the war goes on, people will be sympathetic to all the chaps who've lost arms or legs or eyes. But as time passes everyone will forget the reasons for the wounds. We shall just be cripples or blind men – a bit of a nuisance to have around.'

'All the more reason for you to make a life for yourself in a safe home, surrounded by people who love you.'

'But even that may not be much fun, not when it's all there's ever going to be. Sooner or later, I suspect, one's temper will crack. Frustration will be taken out on the people nearest to hand. I don't want to involve you in that. All the same, I'm very sorry that I hurt you. I didn't consider properly what you might think.'

'What I thought was that you'd realized for the first time how plain and dull I was.'

'Don't be ridiculous! There's nothing I want more . . . But . . . oh, damn it all! I didn't have the courage to hear you say that you wanted to call it off. That's why I had to say it myself. And it was the right thing to do, though it was a mistake not to give the reason. I'm not prepared to let you tie yourself to a blind man by a promise you once made to someone quite different.'

'You talk as though it's certain that you won't be able to see,' said Grace. 'But your father said there was a chance –'

'He thinks it will cheer me up to hear that. But hope is something I can't cope with. I tell myself that I'm blind. I haven't come to terms with it in a practical way yet, but I'm beginning to accept it as a fact. If I start hanging on to the idea that there may be a happy ending after all and then there isn't – well, I don't think I could take the disappointment.'

He was silent for a moment and then spoke again.

'It's having to be passive that makes it hard. If I run a race and do my best and come second, that's disappointing in a way; but hoping that a doctor will perform a miracle and then finding that he can't – that's a harder sort of disappointment. Can you understand that?'

Grace nodded, and then remembered that he could not see the gesture. 'Yes. But it's different for me.'

'I don't think it is. Whether you realize it or not, you're going to be hoping for that happy ending. We must go back to where we were before I asked you to marry me. I want you to know that I love you. I want to feel that you still care for me. But for the rest, we must see what the future holds before we decide how to come to terms with it.' His hand turned to grip hers firmly and to raise it to his lips. 'We're not engaged to be married any longer, Grace. But I do love you – more than ever now. Don't be in any doubt about that.'

Mr and Mrs Bailey were walking down the ward, conversing to give warning of their approach. Christopher turned his bandaged head towards them.

'I've ordered Grace not to regard herself as engaged to me,' he said after they sat down at the bedside. 'You can't imagine how frustrating it is for an officer who's spent three years giving commands to everyone in sight to find himself suddenly being bullied by every doctor and nurse who passes by. Grace is all that's left of my private army and she's jolly well got to do what she's told.'

Mrs Bailey gave an understanding smile. Grace, for her part, hesitated, still wishing to argue but realizing that she could not win the debate. This was not how she had expected the conversation to go – and yet, she told herself, they were only talking about forms of words. In love as well as in health Christopher was afraid to hope. But he still loved her and still wanted her to love him. She had

261

only to wait, and for her at least there would be a happy ending.

On the journey home it occurred to her how much she would disappoint Aunt Midge by turning her back on independence. But she had no wish to take charge of The House of Hardie. Nothing would please her better than to live as Mrs Christopher Bailey.

5

Christopher's convalescence extended over many months. His burns healed only slowly and, as the bandages were a little at a time removed from all but his head, they revealed a body which had become alarmingly thin. It was decided that before there could be any further operation on his eyes, he must build up his strength. So in the summer of 1918 he was transferred from London to the south coast.

'Does hospital blue suit me?' he asked Grace cheerfully when she visited him in the convalescent hospital for the first time. 'I feel a terrible fraud. This place was a hotel before the army commandeered it, and it still feels like one. My medical treatment consists of eating healthy meals and breathing healthy air and sleeping on a comfortable bed and generally being fattened up.'

'That's good. Means that the doctors have plans for you.' In Philip's case, the damage to his lungs had been so great that nothing a surgeon could do would ever restore them to normal, and this was the reason for his early discharge. As long as Christopher was kept within the army's medical system, it must mean that there was hope for his sight.

In the meantime, as they walked together along the promenade with his hand resting on her arm, she learned how to indicate unobtrusively when they were approaching a step or obstacle. Although she could not be glad that he needed her help, she was pleased to be able to give it.

They never discussed the future. How could he plan the rest of his life until he knew whether he would live it in darkness? Their conversation, when she was not reading to him, was little more than badinage; and as autumn approached this became more and more difficult to sustain. Christopher, beneath the jokes, was anxious; and Grace was tired.

On top of her full-time work in the shop and the long journeys needed for each Sunday visit, she had volunteered to help in the garden. By this stage of the war food was short. The Hardies were lucky in having enough land to grow their own vegetables and fruit; but one by one the under-gardeners and journeymen had left to fight, leaving the indispensable Frith to manage the extensive acreage with only a succession of boys just out of school.

Grace, glad to spend some time each evening in the open air, willingly helped to thin vegetables or gather fruit, but at the end of every long day she went to bed exhausted. Her twenty-first birthday passed without celebration except for some family presents. With the war going so badly no one, least of all Grace herself, was in the mood for parties. She waited as anxiously as Christopher for the moment when he would be moved back to the London hospital for surgery.

That time came in September and was followed by a month of suspense. Tests were done. There was an exploratory operation, a period of rest, and then the major operation on which everything would depend.

At the time of Grace's first visit after that his eyes were still bandaged and the result not yet known. He was under orders to lie without moving his head. As she sat down, resting her hand on his, she could feel the tension he was under – and yet he could still speak in his familiar light-hearted way.

'I've learned a way of talking without moving my muscles,' he told her, hardly opening his lips. 'Terribly hard. Like a ventriloquist. *You* just try talking without moving your eyebrows or cheeks. If you make me laugh, you'll be evicted at once. And I'm prepared to bet anything you like that there isn't a looking glass in the room. If the first thing I see when they take off the bandage is my own face, my screams of terror will probably tear apart whatever they've sewn up.'

'You've got a good side and a bad side,' Grace said honestly. 'Like an actor. Jay says every actor knows which side he likes to be photographed from.' Jay had just left school and, while awaiting his call-up papers, had joined a concert party which gave performances in convalescent hospitals and leave camps. 'And even the bad side is far better now.'

Although the burned skin was still puckered and scarred, it had lost some of its first unpleasant shiny redness. In time, no doubt, the thick wavy hair which had been shaved for the operation would be allowed to grow and partly conceal his damaged ear; whilst the eye for which there had never been any hope could be covered by a patch. 'I'm looking at the bad side at this moment,' she said, 'and *I*'m not screaming.'

'But women are braver than men; everyone knows that. Oh dear, I nearly smiled then, and I mustn't. Grace, they're taking the bandages off on Wednesday. The room has to stay dark for a time after that. But by next weekend we should have some idea . . . My parents will be here on Saturday. Will you come on Sunday again?'

'Of course I will.' Grace's hand tightened on his as she looked down in a pity which there was no need to conceal. She understood how terrifying this week of waiting must be, and was overwhelmed by a desire to care for him. 'And Christopher, whatever happens, I shall be with you. To be your eyes if you need me.'

Christopher's lips moved no more than they had earlier, so that it came as a shock to hear the sudden bitterness which he managed to project in his voice.

'Can you be my eyes when I take my hunter over a hedge? Or point my gun when the grouse come over?' He made an effort to soften the effect of his questions by producing a laugh from the back of his throat. 'But we've promised, haven't we, that we're not going to talk about that. I'll look forward to seeing you on Sunday. I'll look forward to *seeing* you.'

'Yes, of course.' She was as frightened as he was when she said goodbye, and spent sleepless hours that week trying to see into the future. Her heart was in her mouth when, the next Sunday, she asked the ward sister how Major Bailey was.

'Coming along nicely. We'll have him out of solitary confinement and back in the ward tomorrow.'

'Coming along nicely!' But they said that, or something like that, every time. Cheerful news was part of the treatment rather than a statement of the truth. Grace opened Christopher's door.

Last time, whilst he was still bandaged, the room had been flooded with autumn sunshine. Today the window was curtained and dim. Grace stepped forward and Christopher turned his head slowly towards her. The silence seemed to last for ever. Then he smiled.

'I spy, with my one little eye, Miss Grace Hardie,' he said. 'Wearing, if I'm not mistaken, a most becoming grey dress with a white collar.'

Grace found herself sobbing with relief. 'Christopher, is it really all right!'

'Only half all right. I've had a chance to look at myself for the first time.'

'That's not important. Not important at all.'

'If you really mean that, then I have advance permission from Sister to let myself be kissed. Very gently, because I'm still fragile.'

She kissed first his good cheek and then his scarred one.

266

It had been the truth when she said that his appearance was unimportant. For a little while she felt too emotional to talk coherently, but listened instead while Christopher outlined his plans.

'Two more weeks here,' he said. 'Then the doctors reckon they can get rid of me at last. My parents came yesterday to discuss what we should do. We're all going up to Scotland to stay with my grandparents. Good air and good food up there, they say. I'm expected to go for long walks to get my muscles into shape after all these months of lying around. And I want to find out whether a one-eyed man can still shoot straight. We shall stay there for Christmas and then come home for the new year. My mother will be writing to ask you to stay as soon as we get back. We mean to have a New Year's Eve party, and I thought it would be nice if I could use the occasion to announce my engagement.'

'I seem to remember that you broke off your engagement.' Grace spoke primly, but her eyes were sparkling. 'Before you start making announcements, you'll have to find someone to propose marriage to again, won't you?'

'I suppose you're right. I think I could slot it in at about eleven o'clock on New Year's Eve. Would you be kind enough to keep that hour free, Miss Hardie, and meet me in the conservatory as the clock strikes eleven?'

'I'll enter it in my diary,' Grace agreed solemnly, and then burst out laughing. 'Oh Christopher, I'm so happy! How shall I ever be able to wait for the year to be over?'

6

The end of hostilities in November 1918 was celebrated in London with bonfires and dancing and inebriation, but at Greystones only with tears of relief and exhaustion. The past four years had cost the Hardies dear, ending Frank's life and wrecking Philip's and Kenneth's. But at least the Armistice had come in time to save Jay from conscription; while David had no further fear of being snatched from his desk in the War Office as medical standards were lowered.

The coming of peace did nothing to resolve one uncertainty. Since the war started there had been no news of the head of the household. Grace could understand how reluctant her mother must be to give up hope. It came as a shock, all the same, when in the middle of the Christmas celebrations Lucy made an announcement.

'I'm going to China.'

For a moment they were all silenced by amazement. Midge had only time to venture a mild 'Lucy, dear . . .' before David sprang to his feet.

'You can't be serious, Mother. It's impossible.'

'Not impossible at all. You forget that I've made the journey once already.'

'But so many years ago! And you had Father as a companion then. For a woman to travel thousands of miles into a barbarous country, without even knowing where to look –'

'I don't propose to travel alone. That's to say, I shall make the voyage to Shanghai unaccompanied; but on a British ship, where I shall be perfectly safe. I shall ask

268

Kenneth to meet me at Shanghai. The ship he's working on at the moment is in Far Eastern waters, and he only signs on for one voyage at a time. I'm sure he'll escort me on the overland journey.'

This statement caused a different kind of surprise. Except for Grace's secret glimpse of him at Greystones, the younger members of the family had had no contact with their brother since his desertion from the army. They had assumed that he must have escaped abroad, but this was the first intimation that he had been in touch with their mother. Grace and Jay began to ask questions about him, but were waved aside as David pressed his objections.

'Even with Kenneth to help you, how can you hope to trace Father after so long, and in such a huge country?'

'Anyone who has seen him will remember him. I know where he planned to start. If he changed his mind, he would have told his agent, whose advice I shall take. You won't be able to dissuade me, David dear. I realize perfectly well that I can't hope –' For the first time her voice faltered, and she needed a moment in which to compose herself. 'I've written so many letters, and had so many disappointing answers. I can't just sit at home, don't you see, not knowing what has happened and doing nothing to find out.'

She smiled round the table with a firmness which made it clear that there should be no further discussion of her plans. Only later that night, when she found herself alone with Grace, did she make one further comment.

'It will take a little time to confirm my plans with Kenneth, so I shan't leave England before March. We can arrange for you to have your wedding before I go.'

Grace flushed. After receiving a written invitation from Mrs Bailey to spend a week at their house in Leicestershire, she had confided to her mother that she expected

Christopher to renew his proposal of marriage then. But it seemed forward to take this for granted.

'Won't that be too soon?'

'In view of the fact that you've been engaged – or at least had an understanding – for a year already, I don't see why you should delay. Say a month after he asks you again, to give me time to order your trousseau and make plans for a reception and invite the guests.'

Grace felt hustled, but reminded herself that the month had not yet started to run. A more immediate problem was that of choosing clothes for her stay with the Baileys. Would there be only members of the family present, or might there be a house party at the weekend? The New Year's Eve party which Christopher had mentioned might prove to be a dance, or even a ball. At the time when Christopher first suggested the visit, there had been no sign that the war would ever end, and so no thought of frivolous behaviour. Even now she did not feel frivolous, but it was to be expected that social life would quickly return to normal. The problem was that Grace had been too young before the war to know what was normal.

Christopher came to collect her for the visit. His sight was good enough for him to drive himself down in a new motor car, with the chauffeur sitting beside him, ready to take over on the journey back. Grace found herself shy of holding hands with someone who seemed almost a stranger. For the past three months, while they were apart, she had remembered him as he was in hospital, lying in bed or walking cautiously. But his stay in Scotland had restored his health and energy. His hair had grown again and he had devised for himself something that was more than a patch although less than a bandage. It covered not just his blind eye but also the most severely damaged skin below and the top of the ear which the surgeons were unable to save.

270

'It comes in four colours,' he announced cheerfully when he noticed her studying it. 'Black for business or dramatic effect. Lovat green for shooting. A sort of beige flesh colour for loafing around at home. And pink for hunting, just for a joke. We're hunting tomorrow. The meet's at our house.'

'You know I don't ride?'

'Don't ride? Everybody rides!'

'I did tell you, right at the beginning. The time you came to Greystones.' But perhaps it was his father she had told; she could no longer remember.

'Father breeds hunters, you know. He's got a steady mare waiting for you. No need for you to ride to hounds if you don't feel up to it. Lots of people just follow the hunt at a distance, in a gentle kind of way.'

'No, I mean I don't ride at all. It's not that I'm frightened of jumping.' As a small girl, with a pony of her own, Grace had been as great a dare-devil as her brothers, giving the recreation up only when it was discovered to trigger her fits of breathlessness. 'It's just that horses seem to make me ill.'

'Bad luck. But you won't ask me to sit at home with you, will you? I don't think I could bear to hear the horn and watch them all canter away without me.'

'No, of course not.' There was only the fleetest of moments in which Grace wondered, as she had wondered in the past, exactly how she and Christopher would spend their lives after they were married.

On her arrival it was taken for granted that she would be tired after a long journey in an unfamiliar means of transport. Although Mr Bailey offered to show her round his stables as soon as she was rested, he did not seem put out when she shook her head.

Overnight she came to a decision. It would be impossible to stay in a house like this and become part of a family like this whilst cutting herself off from its chief preoccupation. She must surely by now have grown out of what was probably only a childish reaction to fur and feathers and horsehair. Perhaps, in spite of her denials, she had in truth been frightened of the animals which used to make her ill and had worked herself up into what Nanny Crocker called 'One of your states, Miss Grace.'

But no, that explanation was not sufficient. Even Pepper had caused her to sneeze and wheeze, and no one could have been frightened of a kitten. Her illnesses as a child were genuine enough – but she was not a child any longer. Surely by now she could keep her chest clear and her breathing steady by an effort of will.

The resolution did not tempt her to leap into the saddle of an unfamiliar hunter with muscles totally unprepared to control a powerful animal. But as the members of the hunt assembled in front of the house next morning she picked up one of the trays from the hall and walked out, smiling, to take Christopher his stirrup cup.

In saying that she was not frightened of horses she had spoken the truth; she made her way between them with no lack of confidence. It was only as she approached Christopher himself that she began to falter.

How large he seemed! Grace herself was tall for a girl and, when they walked together, was pleased that he was taller still. But he had been a thin young man when she first met him and, during the months since he was wounded, had appeared slight and fragile. Now, though, the period of recuperation in Scotland had built up his body. Seated on his chestnut hunter, he towered above her. His tight riding breeches stretched to show every muscle of his thighs, and the cut of his jacket made his shoulders appear even broader than usual.

Why should she feel frightened of him? His eyes sparkled with excitement as he bent to take the glass; but the only creature which had cause to fear him was the dog fox in the spinney whose habits had been the subject of discussion over dinner the previous evening. It didn't make sense that she should feel the same terror which in half an hour or so would strike the fox. Christopher and his father both claimed to believe that the hunted animal would enjoy the chase. Grace knew better; but that was not enough to explain why she should feel herself to be the quarry, waiting for Christopher to move in for the kill.

So confident and dominant did he appear that her chest tightened with panic. In a moment that breathlessness which had not attacked her for so long would overcome her again. She recognized the symptoms, but it was not these which frightened her. Very soon – in a matter of weeks – she would belong to Christopher. He would not have to hunt her down. She was standing still, waiting to be captured. What would he do with her then? She had had plenty of time to consider the question, but until this moment had continued to believe that he would want to be cared for: helped to come to terms with his wounds, and reassured of her love for him. That picture was out of date. He was the strong one now.

Wasn't that what she had hoped for? Why did she have to force herself to smile as she took back the empty glass and returned to the house?

Because she was ill: that was the answer. Her effort of will had failed, and she was struggling for breath long before the huntsman called his hounds together and led the way through the gates. Refusing to give in to the attack and retire to bed, she wrapped herself warmly and went out for a walk, counting each breath in and out as her feet moved at a steady pace. The sound of the hunt receded as she tried to come to terms with her future.

It would have been easier, no doubt, to have married at eighteen, moving without pause from being someone's daughter to becoming someone else's wife. Now she was twenty-one and had a life of her own. It was not the sort of life to impress Aunt Midge, who had tried to persuade her to make a career as a businesswoman. But Grace was happy in it.

Why should she have to leave Greystones, which she loved? She reminded herself that a change was bound to come one day. If her father was dead, her mother might well decide that the house and estate were too large for what was left of the family. That was only part of her anxiety, though. She didn't want to abandon her carving and pottery in order to run a household and bring up children.

Well, why should Christopher force her to do that? He loved her. He would want her to be happy. There was no reason why he should forbid her to continue a hobby which gave her so much satisfaction. Gradually she became calmer and breathed more easily.

When she heard the hunt returning it seemed sensible to go inside the house and wait while the grooms led away the family's horses. She stood in the hall, smiling, as Christopher strode in; but her recovery was short-lived. He smelt of horse and sweat – and even, it seemed, to Grace, of blood. She was overpowered by the mixture of scents as he pulled her into his arms and kissed her.

Not even a horse rearing above her could have made her feel so vulnerable. His excitement in the success of the chase revealed itself in a forcefulness which she had never experienced before. Even Andy, pressing her back against the boulders, had not bruised her lips so hard, nor encircled her with such firm muscles – whilst Christopher himself had always before been tentative, almost shy, in his endearments.

This self-confident man was a stranger. It was not only his closeness which was suffocating her. What robbed her

274

of breath was the appalling realization that in encouraging him to believe that she loved him, she had made a terrible mistake.

275

7

Lucy was tired and anxious as she returned to Greystones after a three-day absence early in January, 1919. There had been no difficulty in making a provisional reservation on a sailing to Shanghai. As soon as she heard from Kenneth it could be confirmed. But the visit to her bank manager to make arrangements about paying for the journey had upset her. He had expressed himself glad of the opportunity to mention some worries about her account, and had talked of an overdraft.

Lucy knew nothing about her financial affairs. She had no extravagant tastes and The House of Hardie had always been profitable enough to cover the costs of running the household. When Gordon was at home he paid all the bills. In his absence they were sent to the bank for payment, and this was the first suggestion of any problem. Fortunately her signature on a piece of paper had been enough to gain an assurance that her travelling expenses would be covered. But the worry remained, and was increased by the depression she always felt when she returned from Tilsden House.

If only she could take Grace or David with her on one of her quarterly visits – or even discuss the situation with them. Gordon had persuaded her many years ago that there were some things which were best kept secret from children. But Gordon was no longer at hand to share the secret, and what would happen if Lucy herself were to have some accident? The children were no longer children. Surely it could do no harm to tell one of them? Indecision aggravated the anxiety which nagged at her mind. She must write something down, that was the answer: just in case.

At least Greystones remained welcoming. Soon she would have to face the unpleasant task of telling the servants that they would be put on board wages during her absence. Perhaps, indeed, in view of her interview with the bank manager, she should reduce the staff before she left. But not yet. She would need them all for Grace's wedding reception.

'Will you have dinner in the dining room, ma'am?' enquired the parlourmaid as the cab driver carried in the luggage.

'Well, of course.'

'I only asked, ma'am, because Miss Grace has been wanting just a tray in the studio.'

'Miss Grace at home?' Lucy was astonished at the news. 'I wasn't expecting her until tomorrow.'

'She came home on New Year's Day, ma'am, poorly like. But she's picked up again now.'

'In the studio, did you say?' Lucy hurried straight there. Although it was four o'clock, and the light of the short winter day had already faded, Grace had not yet lit her lamps but was working almost in the dark. To judge from the repeated slapping sound, she was building up a clay model.

'Grace dearest, I didn't expect to find you here.'

'And I didn't expect to find you away. So we're both surprised.' There was an edge to her daughter's voice which Lucy did not recall hearing before, as though she had become more sure of herself than usual.

'I had to pay a visit. Are you ill? Hetty said –'

'I was unwell, yes, on New Year's Eve. And still wheezing when I returned home the next day.'

'You should have stayed in bed, rather than travelling. I'm sure Mrs Bailey –'

277

'Yes, I'm sure too. But it wasn't because I was ill that I came home. I've ended my engagement. Or rather, since it was formally ended some months ago, I've found that I don't after all wish to revive it.'

This revelation so startled Lucy that for a moment she could think of nothing to say. In the dim light she watched Grace, who had been bending over her work, straighten herself and lean back against the workbench.

'Tell me what's happened,' Lucy said.

'Do you remember, when Christopher first wrote to me, you said it was unthinkable to refuse a man who was serving at the front; and I agreed with that. But even then I found it hard to be sure what kind of a man I was agreeing to marry. Until this week, Mother, I'd never known him in his normal life. He wrote letters to me from places of great danger, he visited me on short leaves when he was light-headed with relief at being home, and he talked to me in hospitals when he was anxious about what was going to happen. I did feel that I was some comfort to him in all that time. But now he doesn't need comforting any more.'

'Well, of course not. He needs ordinary companionship and love. Why are we talking in the dark?'

There was no gaslight in the studio, which had been intended for use in daylight only. Lucy began to light the lamps which had been brought in when Grace first began to work there in the evenings; but as the first flame filled its mantle with light, her eye was caught by the piece on which her daughter had been working.

As had happened on other occasions when she was modelling with clay, Grace had first of all made a skeleton out of metal rods and wire. Even in its present unfinished state it was easy to see that the model represented a horse and rider at full gallop – and yet it was not a realistic representation; for the clay, still rough in some places, had

278

been smoothed in others to give the impression that man and horse were one.

Never before had she managed to fill her work with such power – especially in the knees and thighs of the rider as they gripped the horse. In the stretched head and legs of the animal, thrusting rather than controlling, there was a different sort of power. Looking at it as a married woman, Lucy could not help interpreting the feeling inspired by the model in a way which her daughter could surely not have intended.

'Grace, dearest,' she exclaimed. 'You're surely not *frightened* of Christopher!'

'Frightened? Yes, I think perhaps I am.' Grace was nothing if not honest. 'I stood beside him when he was in the saddle, and found that I could hardly breathe. I thought then that I must be frightened of the horse – that it might suddenly rear up and come down on me, smothering me. As of course it might have done. But then, later in the day, I had the same feeling with Christopher himself. He was only kissing me, but I felt suffocated. He's a hunter. I don't just mean that he goes hunting. He chases things down. Things like me.'

'You're speaking in metaphors. All men are hunters in that sense.'

'I don't think so. Frank was and David is. But not Kenneth or Jay or Philip; and not Andy.' There was a tremor in her voice as she spoke the last name. Lucy lifted her head in vexation. Surely that childish infatuation had faded long ago. But Grace was still talking. 'And not Father, surely.'

Lucy could not repress a wry smile when she remembered that it had been she who hunted her future husband down. But this was not a time for reminiscence. 'Most girls,' she said, 'are proud to feel that someone wants them enough to pursue them even if they pretend to run away.'

'And what happens to the girls when they're caught? They come under the domination of someone they hardly know.'

'Not domination, dear. It doesn't feel like that, not when you're in love.'

'Then perhaps it's best to think about it before you *do* fall in love. Why should I give up everything to share someone else's life when I don't even know what sort of life it's going to be? Why shouldn't I wait for someone to come and share *my* life?'

'Because you'll wait for ever, that's why.' Lucy's shock gave way to impatience. 'That's not the way the world works.'

'Why should I mind waiting for ever if I'm happy as I am?'

'You can't rely on everything going on unchanged. You'll grow older, for one thing. This week you may have felt that you had a choice, and that you could still change your choice. But in a year or two's time you won't be so young. And so many of the men who were of the right age to marry you are dead. Thousands of women who would have become wives in the normal course of events will find themselves condemned to live their whole lives as spinsters. You surely don't want to be one of those. You're lucky that someone who loves you is still alive. You can't simply turn your back on him.'

'That's just what I've done,' said Grace quietly.

'Then you're a silly little goose, and you'll be sorry. And have you thought how much you must have hurt Christopher?'

'Of course I have. But how much worse it would have been for both of us if I'd only found out that I didn't want to be married when it was too late.'

'You can't possibly know that you don't.' Lucy did her best to conceal her irritation and speak more sympathetically. 'All girls feel nervous as their wedding day approaches. Though I would have credited you with more courage, Grace. Well, it may not be too late. I'll do what I can to mend your bridges for you, if you want me to. I'm sure they'll understand that you were ill and not yourself. Think about it – and quickly, before Christopher discovers that there's no shortage of pretty girls waiting to console a hero.'

'That may have happened already.' Grace walked across the studio to fetch a chair for Lucy. 'When I told Christopher how I felt – I did it before he proposed again, so that he wouldn't have to hear me say no – to start with he didn't believe it. And then he was upset. And then he was angry.'

'As he had a perfect right to be.'

'Yes. Well, then I went to bed. I didn't want to join in the New Year's Eve celebrations, but I wasn't well enough to travel. I suspect that Christopher made a show of enjoying the party just to make it clear that nothing was wrong. And I also think that by pretending to enjoy it, he *really* enjoyed it.'

'I don't understand what you mean.'

'Next day, when I said goodbye, he didn't seem either angry or upset any longer. A little sad, perhaps. But I felt that I'd become just a part of his wartime life, and that he was almost glad to be putting all that behind him. If it hadn't been for the war, I don't believe he'd ever have been interested in a girl like me. Now he'll find one of his own kind and be much happier.'

'You're talking rubbish, Grace.'

'Am I? Well, I suppose I can only guess at Christopher's feelings. But I'm sure of my own. I shan't change my mind.'

'And I shan't change my arrangements.' Lucy allowed her annoyance to reveal itself in her voice, but it was

281

caused by her daughter's foolishness rather than by any threat to her plans. 'I shall stay here only as long as I originally intended, until after the date we'd settled for your wedding. If it doesn't take place you'll find yourself alone.'

'I shall like that,' said Grace softly. 'Just till you come home again, I mean.'

'Don't be ridiculous, Grace. You can't possibly manage –'

'Mother, if I were just about to marry, then in a few weeks' time I'd find myself engaging unknown servants and giving them instructions on how to run a strange house. I'd be expected to manage that. How much easier it will be to look after a house that I've always known. You don't need to worry about me. I'll be perfectly all right here.'

Her eyes were bright with satisfaction as she turned back to her work. Pressing a piece of clay on to the model, she smoothed it with a wetted wooden tool. She was blurring still further the distinction between man and beast, making a shape which gave an impression of strength and speed. The movement was loving, almost sensuous. Lucy bit her lips in exasperation. How could she make her daughter see sense?

There was no answer to that question. As Grace bent to stroke and pinch the clay, an absorbed smile played about her lips. She was happy, her mother realized in dismay; and happiness had closed her ears to reason.

PART SEVEN
Family Secrets
1920

1

In the spring of 1920 Grace received an unexpected letter from her aunt.

'I'm taking leave of absence for the summer term,' Midge wrote. 'May I spend a few weeks with you at Greystones? There's a special reason why I need to be near Oxford. I'll explain when I see you – it will make you laugh.'

Grace's first thought was that with her mother away, Midge wanted to keep an eye on her; but in this she was wrong.

'I need some coaching,' her aunt told her on the first day of the visit. 'I have the chance to take my degree at last.'

'I thought you'd done that long ago. Weren't you one of the very first women –?'

Midge shook her head. 'I was one of the first women allowed to take the same Final Examinations as the men. We *qualified* for degrees, but we were never in fact presented with them. The University of Oxford likes to move one step at a time, and only after prolonged thought. However, thirty years on, it's been decided that a second step might not destroy the whole fabric of academic society. So this autumn the degree-giving ceremony will be open to women for the first time.'

'Congratulations!'

'Well, it's not certain yet that I shall be able to attend. There's a snag. But I can tell you, it's going to be a very funny sight as women of every age up to my own mix with the twenty-one-year-olds who'll be graduating straight after their examinations. I should think every teacher in England who qualifies will be there.'

'You said there was a snag.'

'Yes indeed. You see, although I took Finals at the end of my studies, I didn't sit the intermediate exams which the men had to do. If I want to take my degree now, I've got to pass Divvers and Responsions first. That would have been hard enough work when I was eighteen, but at fifty-five . . .! I can work up Divinity well enough, and the Latin I need for Responsions won't be too bad. But Greek! So I've arranged to have special coaching here – and I'm hoping that my beloved niece will agree to put up with a poor wandering scholar while I struggle with it.'

'I shall love having you here.' As her aunt had expected, Grace was amused by the thought of dozens of head-mistresses preparing to sit down in an examination room again. She had not felt lonely since her mother's departure, nor found time hanging heavily on her hands. But it would be a delight to have company.

Had there been anything she could do to help, she would willingly have abandoned her work in the studio; but Midge rode off by bicycle at the beginning of every day and did not return until after tea. As well as her daily coaching, she needed a session in a library with a good lexicon in order to do the exercises she was set. In addition, she quickly made contact with two of her contemporaries who were in Oxford for the same reason. Over morning coffee or afternoon tea, or walking beside the river, the three headmistresses happily relived their student days.

Midge also regularly called in at The House of Hardie. At first these visits were to fill in time between other engagements; but within a week or so she began to ask for a regular sandwich packet so that she could stroll across the High to the Botanic Garden with Mr Witney and sit for half an hour on the bank of the Cherwell.

It was as a result of one of these lunch-hour interludes that she returned to Greystones in a more sombre mood than usual, and opened a conversation after dinner with a directness which was almost aggressive.

'I suggested to you a year ago that you might interest yourself in the affairs of the family firm,' she said. 'For your own profit and that of the business. Have you given that possibility any further thought?'

Grace shook her head. 'When you put the idea forward, it was because my engagement had just been broken, and it was the very next day that I discovered the reason for that.'

'But you're not engaged now. Perhaps you should consider the matter again.'

'It wouldn't be any use, Aunt Midge. I remember what you said about being independent and having my own interests and all that kind of thing. But I'm not suited to business. It isn't enough to be a Hardie, or even to have learned the difference between a claret and a burgundy. I couldn't possibly negotiate contracts, and I have no head for business. It would be foolish of me to meddle.'

'So you'll continue to leave everything to Mr Witney? Do you realize, Grace, what a burden it is? Since your father left – or, at least, since Frank died – there's been no one to share the responsibility.'

'I hadn't thought of it in that way,' said Grace. 'When you first raised the subject, I thought it was for my sake, not Mr Witney's.'

'And so it was then. But now for the sake of the business something must be done.'

'Perhaps David should be approached.'

'Mr Witney raised the subject with him last Christmas. Your brother made it clear enough that he has become a professional man and that any involvement in trade would be frowned on by his father-in-law. But the business can't just be left to drift. The problems created by the war have been enormous, and Mr Witney has been forced to solve them alone – to slave away on the family's behalf without being more than an employee himself.'

'Does he wish to be made a partner?' Although such a possibility had never previously occurred to Grace, she saw that it would be equitable for a share of the profits of the business to be offered to someone who served it so well.

'That question should have been asked years ago; when your father was planning to leave, if not before. It's too late now. If the business goes bankrupt, a partner would be liable for its debts; whereas an employee can't be asked to surrender more than his employment, his livelihood.'

'Bankrupt!' exclaimed Grace. 'Is there really a danger of such a thing happening?'

'He tells me that within the last few months the danger has become acute.'

'Then why has he said nothing? If there are steps which ought to be taken –'

'To whom should he speak? David has been discouraging, your mother is away, and you claim not to understand business. Besides, I suspect Mr Witney thinks that women should not be troubled with such matters, even when it's their own income which is at risk. I told him that I would see if you had changed your mind. If you're still unwilling to be more closely involved with The House of Hardie's affairs, what about Philip?'

'We oughtn't to worry him with such problems,' said Grace. In the course of her visits to the community in which her brother now lived she had come to understand that he had found peace and health only by cutting himself off from the world. It would be cruel as well as unprofitable to ask him to rescue an ailing business.

'Then David must be apprised of the new situation at

288

once and reminded of his responsibilities. There's no need for him to soil his hands by actually touching the wine if he's too good for us now. But his legal training should at least qualify him to understand the problems and perhaps see a solution. I should warn you, dear, that you may have to consider changes in your way of life. The servants' wages and tradesmen's bills are all paid out of the profits of The House of Hardie, and there may be no profits this year.'

'Ever since Mother went away it has seemed ridiculous that one person should be served by so many,' Grace admitted. 'But we have fewer servants than before the war, and the house is so large that they're all fully occupied, however many or few of the family are at home. Besides, except for the kitchenmaid, they've all been with us for years. It wouldn't seem right to send them away.'

'Rather than finding themselves put out of employment suddenly with no wages paid and nowhere to go, they might be glad of at least a warning –'

'As Mr Witney should have warned me!' There was indignation mixed with Grace's alarm. 'I don't know anything about the laws of bankruptcy, but if Greystones belongs to my father and The House of Hardie belongs to my father – or his heirs if he's presumed to be dead – then isn't there a danger that one could be sold by order to pay the debts of the other? Shouldn't I have known about that? It may be hard for a housemaid to find a new place at short notice, but where should I go if my home were to be snatched away? He ought, he most certainly ought –'

Midge put a hand reassuringly on her niece's arm. 'It won't be as bad as that,' she said. 'I may have exaggerated a little. I was indignant on Mr Witney's behalf, after I heard what he had to tell me. Part of the trouble lies in the uncertainty about whether your father is still alive. David will find a solution to that part of the problem, and then it ought to be possible to borrow money and set the

House of Hardie on its feet again. Certainly you'd be wise to reduce the costs of running the house as much as you can, but I'm sure there's no danger of losing it altogether.'

The soothing words came too late to soothe Grace's beating heart. She had refused to let marriage take her away from Greystones. Might an ailing business now force her to go?

2

What a serious young man David was! He had never been Grace's favourite brother and when, in 1915, he began to wear spectacles, she had unkindly assumed that he was pretending poor eyesight to evade military service. But he still wore them five years later, their thick rims giving his face a squareness further emphasized by the close trim of his hair. His expression was grave as he explained what he had discovered about the affairs of The House of Hardie during the past few weeks. Midge had by now taken her examinations and returned to London to await the results, so he and his sister were dining alone.

'Mr Witney should have brought the situation to our attention long before it reached its present serious state,' he complained.

'I understood that he *had* raised the subject with you last Christmas.'

'He didn't indicate that the problems were so serious. And he's always seemed competent enough to keep the firm running smoothly. But not, it seems, to deal with such an unusually difficult period.'

'What exactly has gone wrong?' asked Grace.

'A combination of misfortunes. The first one, of course, being Father's disappearance. He left a power of attorney behind him so that Mr Witney would have the necessary authority, but this has run out of time. Some contracts could be challenged in the courts. The first thing I must do is apply for a certificate of presumption of death.'

Grace frowned unhappily at the suggestion, and her

291

brother, understanding her feelings, gave what reassurance he could.

'It doesn't make any difference to the *fact* of whether he's dead or alive. It's just that we shall have more power to take action for the good of the business.'

'Yes, I suppose so. What sort of action?'

'Well, let me tell you some of the problems. One of them is peculiar to the Oxford branch. You must have proved a good saleswoman whilst you were helping out in the High, Grace. Bottles of wine went out of the shop in a most satisfactory manner. The only trouble is that the money to pay for them didn't roll in at quite the same speed.'

'It was the firm's policy, Mr Witney always said, not to press undergraduates for payment. It wasn't a new idea of his.'

'I'm sure it wasn't. However, he might have noticed that there was a new element in the situation. For five years the young men who had run up their debts in a traditional manner didn't go on to inherit their father's estates and become lifelong customers in the usual way. They got killed instead.'

'And all honour –'

'Oh, yes, yes,' interrupted David. 'There's no shame to anyone in this. I'm merely pointing out that for five years The House of Hardie has been supplying some of its Oxford customers as though it were a charitable organization. Eventually, of course, it will be rewarded by goodwill; but the immediate effect is a lack of funds to purchase new stocks.'

'Yes, I see.'

'And there are other factors,' he continued. 'Naturally the war affected supplies. Disruption of shipping, looting of some of our stocks being held in cask in France, destruction of vineyards. Because we were well stocked when the war started, Mr Witney could fill a high proportion of orders. But he continued to calculate the prices he should ask on the basis of what those stocks originally cost, without taking account of how much it would take to replace them. The cash reserve may have looked healthy for a time, but only because it was impossible to spend it at the normal rate. Now that the opportunity to buy has returned – and I'm told that the 1919 burgundies may prove to be the best vintage for half a century – he simply hasn't got the money with which to negotiate. You can never stand still in trade. How can you sell if you're unable to buy?'

'Surely Father had a reserve for emergencies.'

'I thought so. But he seems to have taken more than was wise to finance his expedition.'

'It was his own business. He was entitled to draw on it.'

'If that had been all, yes. But there was another withdrawal at the same time. A large amount, which appears to have been transferred into a trust. I haven't had time yet to find out about it. It may be that after Father has been presumed dead we shall be able to recover or use the money. But all these legal processes will take time, and The House of Hardie has no time to spare. We're living on credit. Fortunately, after two hundred years of honest trading our credit is good. But we can't extend it for ever. We need cash, and we need it quickly.'

'So what are you going to do?'

Until this moment neither Grace nor David had taken any notice of the parlourmaid who was serving the meal. They had grown up with the knowledge that everything they said at table would be overheard and, if interesting, repeated in the servants' hall. In any case, Grace had already made the first reductions in the staff, as her aunt had advised, so this conversation would merely confirm a

293

situation already known to the servants. But David now paused and then stood up.

'Shall we take coffee in the drawing room?' he said; and waited until the tray had been set down and the maid had left the room before answering his sister's question.

'I've been considering this carefully since Mr Witney approached me a few weeks ago,' he said. 'There's one very simple way of raising capital. We could take out a mortgage on Greystones.'

'What does that mean?'

'It means that we borrow a sum of money which we put to work in the business. We have to pay interest on the loan, but if the business is well run there'll be no difficulty in covering the interest and still making a good profit.'

'Where does Greystones come into it? If we can simply borrow money –'

'When a loan is secured on a property, the rate of interest is much lower. That's because there's no risk to the lender. If by any chance we were to default on the loan, he could take possession of the property and sell it. Most houses are bought in the first place with the benefit of such a mortgage. I was surprised when I looked into the matter and discovered that Greystones is free of any such encumbrance.'

'No!' exclaimed Grace. 'To risk losing the house –'

'There's no risk,' said David impatiently. 'The money will earn an immediate return. Even if it took a little time before the capital sum could be repaid, there could be no possible difficulty about meeting the interest payments, and that's all that matters.'

Grace struggled incoherently to express her doubts. 'But it isn't ours . . . We couldn't . . . What would Mother think when she returns and finds out?'

'If nothing is done, she'll return to find herself living in a large house without the income to support it.'

'All the same, it's too big a step to take without her approval.'

David sighed and continued his efforts to persuade her. 'Mother doesn't understand about business, Grace, any more than you do. When she comes back, she'll accept my advice – but by that time more than a year will have been lost. If you don't believe what I'm telling you, ask Mr Witney. He might consider it a presumption to suggest taking out a mortgage, but he'll certainly confirm the need for capital. You mustn't think that this doesn't concern you. If the trading profits continue to fall, or if they're absorbed by the interest payments on an unsecured loan, Greystones may have to be sold because it will be impossible for the business to pay all the expenses.'

Midge had made the same point when she first brought up the matter a few weeks earlier – but she had presented it as a warning. From David's lips it sounded more like a threat. He gave her a few seconds to consider this.

'Have you any idea how much it costs to run a property of this size?' he asked.

'I've been trying to find out, and to cut down. Mother used just to sign the tradesmen's books every week. She may have checked that they only charged for what they supplied, but I don't believe she bothered about how *much* they supplied. There's been a great deal of waste. Mrs Charles has told me that she likes to use only fresh ingredients, but I've said that this can't continue. Left-over food must be used up. Especially since I'm alone here, so that she's cooking mainly for the staff. And in the gardens, the cost of heating glasshouses just to produce out-of-season strawberries or vegetables is ridiculous. We shall make savings on coal there, and in the house as well. There's no need to keep so many rooms warm just for me.'

'That's not as simple as you think. If the building becomes damp –'

'We shall keep log fires burning low, using our own wood. It's only a short time since Aunt Midge first mentioned the problem to me. I intend to make every possible economy.' Grace spoke firmly to ward off the threat, but David was not to be gainsaid.

'About time too. But you still can't make real economies with a property which is far too large.'

'You didn't think it too large when you lived here yourself. You didn't complain that your meals were too lavish or your room too well-heated. You're talking as though all this is somehow my fault.'

'Of course it isn't. Calm down, Grace. The plan I'm putting forward is intended to let you and Mother go on living in Greystones in proper style. It's only if you refuse to co-operate that we should have to consider whether the business could continue to pay all your bills in the old way.'

The repeated threat made Grace angry rather than prepared to be helpful. 'I'm not prepared to put the ownership of Greystones at any kind of risk whilst Mother is away,' she said. That was an excuse. It was her own refusal to accept the risk of losing the house she loved so much which made her speak with such determination. Then she gave a rueful sigh. 'But I don't suppose anything I say is going to make any difference. As soon as you've done this business of presuming Father's death, you'll arrange everything the way you want it, won't you?'

'No. I need your agreement.'

'Why?'

There was a long silence. David seemed to be considering whether there was any alternative form of words he could use. At last, reluctantly, he answered her question, revealing something that no one had ever told her.

'I can do nothing without your consent,' he said. 'Greystones belongs to you.'

296

'Did you know?' Grace asked her aunt. David's reluctance to admit the truth about his sister's ownership of Greystones had led to a violent quarrel, and the matter had been on her mind ever since.

'Know what, dear?' Midge Hardie's attention was not on the conversation. With her examinations successfully passed she had returned to Oxford, dressed in the regulation black and white, to take her degree. As she awaited the start of the ceremony in which she would at last be presented to the Vice-Chancellor of the university, her dark eyes sparkled with excitement, searching for old friends amongst the animated crowd surrounding the Sheldonian Theatre.

'Did you know that Greystones belonged to me?'

'I knew that it would at some time or other. Not the details, though. When you came of age, I suppose.'

'I came of age in 1918. Why didn't anyone tell me?'

'I expect your father intended to; but then, of course, he wasn't here. Your mother may not have known the exact position any more than I do. It's not of any great consequence, is it? I mean to say, Greystones is your family's house.'

'But it isn't,' said Grace. 'It's *my* house. And that *is* of consequence, because David wants to mortgage it, and he can't unless I let him.'

She had lost her aunt's attention. 'Ah, the group of Home Students is assembling,' said Midge. 'Grace dear, I shan't be coming straight back with you after the ceremony. Mr Witney is going to open a bottle of champagne in the shop – just as he did on the day I finished taking my final examinations. We shall take luncheon together, and then he has suggested an afternoon on the river, since the weather is so mild. As though I were an undergraduate again.' Midge gave something which sounded very much like a giggle. 'Except that in those days I should have had to have a chaperone. I'll be at Greystones before dinner.'

She hurried away to join her group. Grace, taking her seat inside the Sheldonian, tried not to feel disappointed. It had been thoughtless of her to expect advice on a day when her aunt was excited about her own affairs.

There was a long time to wait. Only after all the male graduates had received their degrees was it the turn of the women – more than five hundred of them, so that Grace had to search for a sight of her aunt amongst the procession. Each curtsied to the Vice-Chancellor and was tapped lightly on the head with a Bible while a Latin formula was repeated.

After the last of them had left the building, Grace thought that the ceremony must be over. But in a dramatic gesture the great doors were flung open again. Standing in the entrance were the principals of the five women's colleges. Unlike Midge they had not been required to sit the examinations which they missed earlier in their lives, but had been given honorary MAs. Now, proudly wearing their scarlet hoods and long gowns for the first time, they led back into the theatre the procession of women in academic gowns.

The sight brought the audience of friends and relatives to its feet. Grace, joining in the applause, felt tears pricking her eyes. How pleased and happy her aunt must be!

By the time Midge was Grace's age she had completed her Oxford education. By that age, too, she had obtained her first employment as a teacher at Cheltenham Ladies' College. She must regard a young woman who was content to live at home as hopelessly unenterprising. Indeed, she had implied as much when pressing her niece to take a more active part in the family business. How could she understand the depth of Grace's feeling for Greystones? Were her advice to be asked again, she would probably recommend risk – the kind of risk that David was proposing – as a necessary step on the path to independence. Because Grace admired her aunt so greatly, there was a moment in which this seemed less unthinkable than before. Perhaps she should consider the matter again.

She intended to return to the subject after dinner that evening – but Midge had news of her own.

'You must be the first to know, Grace. Will and I are going to be married.'

'Married!' Grace stuttered for a moment in surprise. 'But – but you told me once that you weren't allowed to marry while you were a headmistress.'

'I'm not. So I shan't be a headmistress any longer.'

'You can give that up?'

'I've been teaching for more than thirty years; a head teacher for more than twenty. I shall be glad of a change.'

'You've always said that a woman fortunate enough to have a good education was under an obligation to put it to use.'

'True enough, but I've surely discharged that obligation by now. Anyway, I don't intend to sit at home and twiddle my thumbs. My first ambition when I was young was to have a school of my own, and I might start something of the sort in Oxford. On a small scale, perhaps – a tutorial college for older girls who wish to go to university. I thought you'd be happy for me, Grace, but you seem to be trying to persuade me to change my mind.'

'Oh no. I'm sorry if it seemed that way. I like Will immensely. It's just that you've always seemed to think that marriage was a bad thing for a woman.'

'I do think it's unfortunate that so many young women move from school to marriage without considering what other use they might be able to make of their lives. But I've had plenty of time to consider. A headmistress's life is a lonely one, you know, dear. Since Patrick died . . .' She gave a sigh before continuing briskly. 'There's no lack of society, but it's difficult to develop any intimacy with one's own staff or with the governors. There comes a time when you find yourself longing for companionship. Will's been a friend for very many years. It's taken me a long time to realize that a loving friendship lasts longer than a passionate love affair, and will bring more satisfaction in the end.'

'I'm so glad for you, Aunt Midge. Really I am. I'm sure you'll be marvellously happy.' Ashamed of her first ungracious reaction to the news, she embraced her aunt; and for the rest of the evening they discussed Midge's plans for her resignation and marriage.

Only after she had gone to bed that night did Grace acknowledge disappointment to herself. It was Midge's example which had encouraged her to believe that she could be happy without being married, and now it was Midge whose change of direction suggested that not even a successful professional career was sufficiently fulfilling. Earlier that day Grace had intended not only to ask for Midge's advice but to take it. Now she was not so sure. She must make up her own mind whether she was prepared to put Greystones at risk.

As clearly as though it were yesterday she remembered the first night she had spent in the house, in the very same round tower room which was still her bedroom. She was the first of her family to arrive, brought early because she was ill. Pepper had come with her: the tiny kitten which later had been shot by David.

Was it, she wondered, the memory of that death which

300

still, after so many years, prevented her from feeling friendly and co-operative towards the only one of her brothers who seemed capable of looking after the family affairs? She shrugged the question away, remembering instead how she had crept out of bed as a little girl to butter the soles of her feet, as Nanny had earlier buttered Pepper's paws. She had done it so that she would never find herself lost away from home. She had wanted to spend the whole of her life in Greystones, and that was what she still wanted.

Were it to be mortgaged, David could rob her of it at any time simply by failing to pay the interest and she didn't trust him not to be spiteful. Nor was she prepared to keep a watchful eye on the arrangement he proposed by going into the business. Buying and selling wine was not a woman's job.

So she must become businesslike at home instead. David would not be above carrying out his threat to cut off the flow of House of Hardie funds to the property. She must learn what was involved in running it. What precisely did its upkeep cost, and how could she make it pay for itself? No answer came immediately to mind, but in the security of the tower room she felt confident that somehow she would be able to manage.

Her confidence proved short-lived. It was shattered by a letter which arrived on the day after her aunt's return to London. Before Mrs Hardie left England it had been agreed that Grace should open correspondence addressed to either of her parents. What she read now was so unexpected that her breakfast cooled as she stared at the typewritten words, finding them at first incomprehensible and then alarming. What was Tilsden House? And why should its superintendent be regretting that its monthly charge must be increased and that a first instalment of the new sum was now due?

4

Tilsden House had an address near Bournemouth but no telephone number. Rather than rely on an exchange of letters to resolve the puzzle brought by the morning post, Grace decided to travel to the south coast next day, to see the place for herself and talk to the superintendent face to face.

A bus from the railway station carried her to the end of a long drive, leaving her to walk up to a large, secluded house which had the air of an institution.

'I came because I didn't understand your letter,' she confessed after she had been shown into the superintendent's office. 'You addressed it to my father, but he's abroad. Could you explain to me what the fees are for, and why they've been increased?'

'The increase has been caused by the need to transfer Mr Hardie – Mr Hardie junior – from our children's home to permanent quarters here. When I last saw your father, he explained that he'd set up a capital trust for Felix. The interest has covered all his expenses until now. Mr Hardie thought he would be back in England well before the time came to adjust the arrangement. But now that Felix is seventeen –'

Grace interrupted him. 'Who is Felix?'

The superintendent gave her a puzzled look. 'Surely, Miss Hardie, you know about Felix. Your brother.'

There was a long silence as Grace searched her memory. Yes, the name did seem familiar. Little by little she remembered the baby who had been born on the day that Pepper was killed, and what had happened to him. Her face and

302

neck flushed – was it with guilt or with horror? Silently she prayed that her first guess at an explanation might prove mistaken.

'I remember there was a baby,' she agreed. 'But he died. I was ill at the time, and only six, but I'm quite certain that he died. Because he was premature. Too small.'

'That was said, no doubt, to spare you grief. Small children are often alarmed when defects are found in other children, in case the same problems may occur in themselves. Your brother Felix didn't die, Miss Hardie. But it was suspected soon after his birth that there was an abnormality, and time proved this to be the case. He's seventeen now – a handsome, strong young man. But his mind is that of a child of three or four, and will always be so.'

'Why is that?'

'It's one of the dangers of a premature birth. The infant's lungs are immature, causing breathing difficulties. These in turn mean that the flow of oxygen to the brain is insufficient, inhibiting normal development. It was a wise decision on your parents' part to bring him to a children's home where his special needs would be understood and cared for. No one is to blame for such misfortunes in a family, but to keep such a child at home can prove disruptive.'

Grace was silenced again by shame. No one is to blame, the superintendent said, but she knew better. It was a six-year-old's fit of temper which had tipped the new-born baby on to the floor, banging his head. How vividly she remembered now!

'He's been very happy all these years,' she was told. 'The change of quarters is purely on account of his age. From now on he should live amongst adults. So you'll understand why a different scale of fees applies – and the

303

funds from your father's trust are unfortunately insufficient to meet these.'

That explained the withdrawal of capital from the family business which had puzzled David. But the solving of one mystery did nothing to resolve the immediate problem.

'Your request for an increase comes at an awkward time, because my mother is also abroad at the moment,' she said slowly. 'Until she returns, it may not be possible to vary the terms of the trust. But I'll discuss the matter with one of my other brothers to see what can be done immediately. If I could ask you to be patient –?'

'Oh, of course. The attention which Felix receives here isn't medical. He's provided with the attendance and care needed by a child. The most important consideration in his life is that he should remain in familiar surroundings. We've been bringing him over from the children's home every day for several months, to make him feel at ease here. Now that the move's completed, we wouldn't wish to upset him by altering the arrangements. As long as the matter is receiving your attention . . . And now I'm sure you'd like to visit your brother.'

Could she face that prospect? If she were to be confronted by some kind of gibbering idiot, whilst believing herself responsible for his condition, would she be brave enough to stand her ground?

'Did my mother come here?' she asked.

'Mrs Hardie has paid four visits every year until recently. I'm afraid she often found them distressing. Felix doesn't recognize her as his mother, you see. But he loves to have company. Even though he'll quickly forget that you've visited him, he'll be happy while you're here.'

'Then of course . . .' Grace rose to her feet and followed the superintendent out of the office and into a long, light room which had perhaps once been an orangery. She looked around while he exchanged a few words with the attendant in charge. The scene was not after all a frightening one. The twelve men in the room were neatly dressed. The only odd feature was that almost all of them were sitting without occupation. There was one exception. Felix Hardie was dipping a broad paintbrush into pots of poster paint.

She might have recognized him as a member of the family even at an unexpected meeting, so close was the resemblance to their father. He was broader in the shoulders and had not yet grown as tall; but his dark, curly hair and strong features, even to the aquiline nose, were those of Gordon Hardie.

There was even a moment, as he turned from his painting to see who had come into the room, when his black eyes seemed bright with the same alert intelligence which was typical of his father. But within a few seconds the light faded from his eyes, to be replaced by an expression of uncertainty in which she could recognize many elements: hope of some new excitement, worry at the sight of a stranger and doubt about what he was expected to do. Moving slowly, in order not to increase his anxiety, Grace approached her youngest brother.

'That's very pretty,' she said, looking at his painting – though 'pretty' was not the appropriate word, for the paper was covered with swirls of bright colour.

Felix nodded his head. 'Pretty,' he agreed. He set down the brush which he had been holding in his left hand and pointed. 'Red. Blue.' The words emerged with pride – a lesson well learned: but for a second time Grace was horrified that such a good-looking young man, strong and healthy, should spend the rest of his life imprisoned by the limitations of his mind.

The superintendent joined them. 'Felix, this is your sister.'

'Sister,' repeated Felix, smiling but uncomprehending.

'What do you say when someone comes to see you?'

Felix thought, and became anxious until he was prompted.

'Say "How do you do?"'

'How do you do?' His smile returned and there was triumph in his voice at the successful repetition. Slowly and shakily he held out his right hand to be shaken. There was something wrong with it. He had been painting boldly with his left hand, but this side of his body seemed to be not quite under his control. Grace was as uncertain as her brother what to do next. She longed to hug and kiss him, but feared that this would cause alarm. Instead, she watched without speaking as he took up his paintbrush again.

'Your sister is going now,' said the superintendent after only a short time. 'Say goodbye.'

'Goodbye.' He was still smiling as he repeated the word.

'You can see why your mother is always so distressed,' said the superintendent when they were outside the room. 'She comes to reassure herself that he's in good health and well cared for, but I have to remind her every time that it's for her own benefit only. It means very little to him. He'll have forgotten your visit already. And there was no point in your extending it, because he has no conception of how long you stayed.'

Grace nodded dumbly, near to tears.

'You mustn't upset yourself, Miss Hardie. Your brother is happier than most of us in the outside world can hope to be. He has no responsibilities, no fears. He's comfortable and secure. Think how painful it is for anyone to leave the safe world of childhood when the time comes to grow up into adulthood. Felix will never have to cross that barrier.'

'Yes, I understand. And I couldn't have understood without coming here. So thank you very much. I'm glad to know that he's well looked after. And I'll deal with the extra charge as soon as I can.'

Instead of asking how she could get a cab, she enquired whether there was a path along the cliff leading back into the town. She needed time to think, and fresh air in her lungs.

The sky was clear and cloudless above her but, when she reached the edge of the cliff and looked down, she could see that the October winds were whipping the waves up into huge rollers, which rose and curled and crashed on the shingle below. For a long time she stood without moving, watching and listening. There was something satisfying about the curve of the water just before it broke into spray – a curve which reminded her of the swirls of Felix's painting. Would it be possible to capture in stone that fleeting second in the movement of water? Yes, it would; and so vividly could she envisage the result that she seemed to feel at her fingertips its smooth hardness rising and turning and swooping downwards and inward.

She ought not to be thinking about her hobby now. Breathing deeply in the blustery air, she forced herself to accept that what she had been told about her brother Felix was the truth. He was happy. To feel guilt over her childish tantrum could spoil her own life without changing his. One of her other brothers, Kenneth, had killed a kitten out of pity for its agony and his inability to forgive himself had distorted the whole course of his life. The best thing she could do for Felix was to make sure that his bills were paid, so that he could stay where he was happy.

But she wasn't going to give in to David. It was odd that this new problem, which might have made her resolution falter, served to strengthen it. During the railway journey which carried her back to Oxford, she considered ways of finding money to look after Felix and preserve her own independence. No solution came immediately to mind, but she could not expect a miracle. A good deal of hard thinking and hard work was likely to be needed.

She had left her bicycle at Oxford station, and interrupted the ride home to call at the yard of the old mason who was giving her lessons in his craft. Since she first approached him for help he had shown her how to choose a piece of stone: how to recognize possible defects and to turn any variation of strata or graining to advantage. He provided tools and instructed her in their use, making her first of all practise on fragments, and then allowing her to assist him in carving a series of gargoyles. He did it for the pleasure of passing on his skill and would never accept payment. But he was glad of the fruit and vegetables which she usually brought him.

In recent months she had been tackling a piece of her own, finding it easier to work in the yard, with tools and advice at hand, than to make her own studio dirty with stone-dust. She had drawn a dragon encircled by flames from its own mouth, and cut it away as a relief. Now, pulling on a sacking apron, she studied the design with a critical eye, to see where improvements were needed.

'New vicar called by this morning,' said the mason, without interrupting his own work. 'Needs a good bit of repair on that old barn of his. That there dragon of yours caught his eye. Asked if it were for sale, he did.'

'It isn't finished,' said Grace. 'I've got to cut it away.' She had carved the relief from the front of a large block, and now would need to slice the panel off.

'He'd like it as it is. For me to put the whole block into the wall, where I'm making good. To frighten away the rats, he said, laughing like – but he was serious about having it.'

'How much would he pay?'

'Didn't say. Asked what you might be wanting for it.'

She stared at the dragon, wondering what to suggest. It

308

was the first stone carving she had completed unaided. She was pleased with the result and had intended to keep it. But what she had done once she could probably do again, and this, of all times, was when she needed money. Her mother would be horrified at the thought of a young lady selling her wares for cash; but what was the difference between that and an income derived from selling bottles of wine?

'How much should I give you for the stone?' she asked. She had not so far been charged for her materials, because she had taken nothing off the premises.

'Vicar'll be paying for that anyway, to fill his holes. Makes no difference to me if he has this block or another. Difference to him is in the decoration, and that's all yours.'

'I'll come back tomorrow and tell you,' said Grace. She took the apron off again without having done any work. There was too much to think about.

That night she lay for many hours awake in bed. The burden of guilt and anxiety was made heavier by her feeling of being alone, with no one to share or even discuss the problems. Her father must certainly be dead, and her mother's return could not be expected for many months. David would be no help unless she agreed to do what he wanted. Mr Witney would take the view that a mortgage was needed, to safeguard the business and his employment, and Aunt Midge must now be expected to support him.

How about Philip then? But no, Philip could not be asked for advice. To make him anxious would be unkind. Kenneth was unlikely ever to return to England. Frank was dead and Felix trapped in perpetual infancy.

That only left Jay. He was twenty years old and had been earning a living of sorts on the stage for three years already. But his income was precarious, and he seemed to live for the most part in lodgings or other people's flats. If he had an address of his own, Grace did not know what it was, but always had to wait until a light-hearted letter announced that he would be working in Oxford – or not working at all – and could be expected to stay for a week, or indefinitely. He could certainly not be asked for financial help; nor even for practical advice. She must make her own decisions.

Felix was the first consideration. The vicar's liking for her dragon provided a temporary solution to the problem of keeping him in a familiar place where he was happy. The difference between the new fees and the sum provided by the trust was not great, so the sale of her carving would give her a few months free from anxiety on this score.

Still thinking about the boy who would never take the step into adult life, she saw a parallel with herself. All these years she had been living as the child of the house, shielded from the outside world. But she was twenty-three years old. It was more than time she grew up!

Marriage was the event which carried most girls into the grown-up world – although not, even then, towards the kind of responsibilities which Grace would now face; for she was more determined than ever to preserve Greystones unencumbered. But in her case it was the discovery of so many secrets which had jolted her out of carefree girlhood.

Within a short time she had found that her family's business was near bankruptcy, that Greystones was her personal property, that Felix was still alive and that her aunt had not been as completely satisfied with a spinster's life as she had always pretended. Were there other discoveries still to come? She amused herself by considering each member of the family in turn, inventing revelations – but believing none of them. No: by now, surely, every secret must have been revealed.

5

Silently at first, Lucy Hardie wept. The tears ran down her cheeks to splash over the hard earth on which she knelt. Her head bowed lower and lower until it touched the ground, so that to the Chinese who watched curiously over the wall of the tiny Christian cemetery it must have seemed as though the foreign woman were kow-towing to a wooden headboard.

Five months had passed since she sailed into Shanghai and looked down from the upper deck of the ship to see Kenneth, bronzed and bearded, waiting to embrace her. Together they had first of all followed the route which she had originally taken with Gordon on their honeymoon; up the Yangtse River, whose cataracts were as terrifying in 1920 as they had been thirty-three years before.

After arriving in Chungking, though, she deviated from that earlier route, making not for the place where Gordon's first expedition had begun, but the point where it had ended. It was on the very last day of that exploration that he discovered the glorious white and golden lilies which were unknown in England at the time. She had always thought it likely that he would choose to begin his new trip in the mountainous frontier area, and the agent in Shanghai had confirmed this intention.

Before leaving Shanghai she marked on her map all the Christian missions near the frontier with Tibet. The Chinese would be unfriendly to strangers and unlikely to answer their questions honestly. British missionaries would offer safe lodging and sympathetic help in questioning both local people and travelling traders on her behalf.

311

Many weeks and visits passed before her quest came to an end, and certainty proved to be the confirmation of her fears, not of her hopes. In the little town of Kuan Hsien, to which Tibetan traders brought furs to trade for musk and tea, was a medical mission run by the Church Missionary Society. Here, on the morning after her arrival, she told her story and asked her questions for the twentieth time.

Instead of shaking his head, the Scottish doctor in charge of the mission revealed by the sympathy in his eyes that she had reached the end of the trail at last. He considered her questions in silence for a few moments, and asked some of his own to make sure that there was no mistake, before leading her and her son out to the little cemetery. Then he stepped back and stood beside Kenneth, leaving her to mourn alone.

The moment came when she could contain her grief no longer, but began to wail uncontrollably, gasping for breath and rocking her body so that her head banged against the ground.

'Mother!' Kenneth stepped forward to console her, but Lucy found just enough strength to wave him back. The anguish she felt had been fermenting in her breast for many years, and the need to expel it noisily could not be restrained. She had been brought up as a girl to control her emotions; but it was impossible to remain calm in the first moment of understanding that she was a widow.

Little by little her groans and shudders abated. She felt empty, hardly seeming to inhabit her own body – which, for all she cared, could remain on her husband's grave while her spirit slipped into the air. She was only half aware of Kenneth on one side and Dr Mackenzie on the other raising her to her feet and supporting her into the mission house.

Mrs Mackenzie brought tea and tucked blankets around

her on the couch. Kenneth knelt beside her, his bearded face expressing anxiety and a desire to reassure.

'You can't be sure, Mother. If no name was ever known . . .'

'The initials are enough.' The letters G.H. had been burned into the headboard, together with the date: 1915. 'And the fact that he was a European. Except for other missionaries, how many foreigners would pass through such hostile country in any year? It must be Gordon.'

'But you don't *know*.' Kenneth turned to their host. 'How was it that he didn't tell you his name?'

'He was only fitfully conscious when I first saw him, and was delirious for most of the three days he survived. A trading caravan from Tibet found him in a state of collapse near the frontier and brought him in on a litter. From the way he was dressed, they'd thought at first that he was a lama. When they realized he was European, they carried him here by night, afraid that they might be accused of harming him.'

'Do you think they had in fact robbed him?'

'No. He was suffering from extreme cold and hunger and exhaustion – quite enough to explain his condition. There was an injury to his head which might have been caused by a blow – but the dirt in the wound inclined me to the belief that he had fallen accidentally and injured himself. We did all we could for him, naturally, but it was too late.'

'So how did you know his initials?'

'After he died, I examined his clothes in the hope that they'd give a clue to his identity; but there was nothing. However, he was wearing a gold ring – another reason to believe that his condition was the result of accident, not robbery. I took it off before burying him, in case enquiries were made later.' Dr Mackenzie crossed the room and took a small packet out of a bureau. He unfolded a paper and handed the ring to Lucy. 'There's an inscription inside.'

Already sure what she would see, Lucy held it up to the light. 'L.H. to G.H. 1887.' That was the year she had run away from home to join Gordon on the first of his plant-hunting expeditions. She had had the ring engraved later with the date of their wedding. Had she held any doubts or hopes about the identity of the dead man, she must relinquish them now. For a second time she began to cry, but dabbed her eyes dry as Mrs Mackenzie bustled to her side to comfort her.

'I'm being foolish,' she said faintly. 'I've known for years that he must be dead. After all, what was the alternative? That he'd gone out of his mind and forgotten me? Or that he'd deliberately deserted me? Those were the only explanations for such a long silence. Perhaps there was a faint hope that he'd been imprisoned for some reason and that I might find him and arrange his release. But it was never more than a daydream. I knew, really, all the time. It's just that to accept the truth is harder than to guess at it.'

She sighed, and for a few moments no one spoke. 'When he was delirious,' she asked at last, 'did he mention my name?'

'There was a name.' It was Mrs Mackenzie who answered, but she stopped abruptly when she saw the frown of warning on her husband's face. Lucy easily interpreted the exchange of glances. The name had not been hers.

'Please tell me,' she said quietly.

'Grace,' said the missionary's wife. 'He called it over and over again. Grace.'

Lucy was bewildered by the news. It provided another proof, were any needed, that the dead man was indeed her husband; but that his last moments had been filled

314

with thoughts of Grace was surprising and hurtful. Gordon was fond of his daughter, certainly, but his children had taken third place in his enthusiasms; less important to him than Lucy herself and his efforts to find and breed new plants. Or so she had believed.

'I'm keeping you from your work,' she said, realizing that at this time of day Dr Mackenzie would expect to be in the mission hospital and his wife would have her own duties in the Christian compound. 'Kenneth will look after me.'

That was only a form of words. Kenneth could do nothing to console her. Their reunion in Shanghai after so long a parting had brought her joy, and as they travelled together she had been grateful for his protection and practical good sense. But for the moment she wanted only to withdraw into memory.

What she remembered was not the long period of her married life in England. The years of bringing up children in Greystones seemed dull and easily forgotten in comparison with the great adventure of her honeymoon. Those months were the high point of her life. Nothing before or since had aroused her emotions to such a pitch.

There had been the excitement of travel. There was sadness, for it was in this wild part of the world that her first baby was born: little Rachel, who had given one cry and then died. But most of all there was joy: the joy of loving Gordon and being loved by him.

'The lilies!' she exclaimed suddenly, startling Kenneth by the apparent irrelevance of the words. Her memory had reached the moment when Gordon – forced by the news of her pregnancy to divert from his intended route – had glimpsed a valley carpeted with lilies. Back in England he had named his discovery for Grace, the daughter who had not then been born.

'Perhaps your father came again to the valley where he

first saw the lilies,' she explained. 'Perhaps that was what put the thought of Grace into his mind when he was delirious.' Ashamed of herself for finding the idea comforting, she stood up, throwing off the rug with which Mrs Mackenzie had covered her. That night, alone in bed, she could weep once more for her husband, but now she must be brave. She walked across the compound to the low, whitewashed room which served as a hospital, to see if she could be of help.

Dr Mackenzie was giving the day's instructions to his two nurses, who had their backs to her. Lucy automatically looked first at their shoes. Both had large feet, which could never have been bound. So they were not converts but must have been brought up from babyhood in the Christian faith. As they moved away, Dr Mackenzie turned and smiled to see her.

'I suppose,' said Lucy, 'it's too much to expect that the nurse who cared for my husband is still here?'

'Oh, but she is. You'd like to talk to her, no doubt. I should have thought of that.' He raised his voice to call. 'Chung Ru Mai!'

The taller of the two nurses turned and came towards them. She was a big woman in her thirties, paler in complexion than most of the weather-beaten inhabitants of this district. Much of her hair was tied back in a white cloth, but a straight black fringe covered her forehead and partly obscured her dark eyes. She smiled and nodded as the doctor presumably asked her to describe the last days of her foreign patient.

Lucy was unable to listen to the translation. Something in the woman's appearance snatched at her heart, causing it to beat erratically. She could not bring herself to think what it was that upset her, until she heard Kenneth behind her laughing in surprise.

'She reminds me of Grace,' he said. 'A Chinese Grace.'

6

Wide-eyed and pale, Lucy turned to look at Kenneth. He had been joking, but the smile faded from his face as he saw that she was near to fainting. Dr Mackenzie, too, showed alarm at her condition; although the nurse, not understanding English, was merely puzzled.

With an effort Lucy took a grip on herself.

'I think this explains something,' she told the doctor. 'The reason why my husband called the name of our daughter, Grace. Your nurse – there's a resemblance. If he was delirious at the time, he might well have believed that it was Grace who was nursing him. Tell her from me, if you will, how grateful I am for her care.'

She listened to the exchange of words and watched intently as the woman smiled and bowed. Not until later that day did she ask Dr Mackenzie if she might have a private word with him.

'Your nurse,' she said. 'Chung Ru Mai. Is she Chinese? It seemed to me –'

'You noticed the round eyes? Yes, she must have European blood in her. That's one reason why she will always stay with us here – not only because she's a Christian, but because outside she'd be regarded as a freak. In the hospital, though, she's in her element. An excellent nurse. And married to our porter and odd-job man. A rice Christian he may be, and illiterate, but thoroughly reliable. We're lucky to have the two of them here.'

'What do you know about her past? Her upbringing?'

'She was brought up in the mission. Before that, I don't know. She was carried here as a baby. Before my time –

more than thirty years ago. As I understand it, she'd been found by a missionary from the China Inland Mission who was touring the country areas. You probably know, Mrs Hardie, of the cruel custom which obtains here, of exposing unwanted female babies outside the towns to die of cold.'

'I've heard about it, yes.'

'All of us in the missionary societies, whether or not we have medical training, keep our eyes open for such unfortunate infants. Dr Dennie left Chung Ru Mai here for what I believe he intended to be only a few weeks, whilst he was travelling and unable to care for a small baby. She was suffering from the jaundice of the new-born. It was his intention, I understand, to return and take her to his own mission, where his wife was a trained nurse. But he died in the uprising of '88. My predecessor in the hospital here was happy to bring the little girl up and – Mrs Hardie, you are unwell! Have I said something to upset you?'

'Dr Dennie, you said!' For a second time that day Lucy felt herself near to fainting, and for the second time she held herself in check. 'Can I speak in confidence, Dr Mackenzie? Until I've had time to think.'

'My dear Mrs Hardie, of course.'

'In 1888,' she said, doing her best to keep her voice unemotional, 'I gave birth to a baby girl in the village of Jinkouhe. There were no Europeans in the village at the time; not even my husband. The baby was born alive. I heard her cry. But by the time my husband joined me, we were told that she was dead and had already been buried. Later, when I was recovering, I stayed with Mrs Dennie at the China Inland Mission in Suifu. When I learned from her that her husband must have been travelling in the area at the time Rachel was born, it made me very upset – I felt that the baby might have been saved if I could have

318

called on his help at the time of the birth. But it never occurred to me to doubt that she did die.'

'And you're doubting it now? Are you saying that you believe –?'

'I believe that Chung Ru Mai is my daughter Rachel.' As she heard herself speak the words, Lucy felt suddenly calm. Yes, she did believe it. She was sure. 'There's a family resemblance to my other daughter. And the round eyes . . . How many Europeans, or concubines of Europeans, would have given birth in such a remote area at that time, and then abandoned the child? I believe that if it hadn't been for the disturbances of that year Dr Dennie would have returned safely to his wife and would at once have been told about the English visitors she had been entertaining, and the misfortune they'd suffered.'

The thought that a happy solution had been so close brought Lucy once again near to tears. She raised a handkerchief to her eyes.

'So what do you propose to do?'

'I need to think. That's why I must ask you to respect my confidence.' She stood up. It had been a harrowing day that had brought her the first sight of both her husband's grave and her lost child. 'I'm very tired. Goodnight, Dr Mackenzie.'

In spite of her exhaustion she was unable to sleep, tossing the night away on the hard, narrow bed. By morning she had made up her mind; but before speaking again to her host she went across to the little hospital and watched her daughter going about her duties. Not until the evening did she request another private conversation.

'Have you come to a conclusion about Chung Ru Mai?' asked the doctor.

'No. I'd like your advice. I so much want to take her in my arms and tell her that I'm her mother. That she was stolen from me when I was unable to move. That I would

319

never, never have abandoned her if I'd had the slightest idea that she wasn't buried, as they told me.'

Lucy could hear the pitch of her voice rising towards hysteria and did her best to control it. 'But that may not be in her best interest. What do you think? If I were to take her back with me to England –'

'You would have to take her husband as well. Theirs is a Christian marriage, and they love each other. They speak no English. They'd find themselves in a strange society with habits and values they wouldn't understand.' He threw up his hands in a gesture of helplessness. 'If you'd found her when she was still a child, needing care and wanting to understand that she was loved, that would be a different matter.'

'You're saying that it's too much to ask that she should uproot herself?'

'It's not a decision that I have any right to make. But a choice which would be comforting for you might not be kind to her. I've no doubt that in the past thirty-odd years you've thought many times about your dead baby, and always with sadness. But she can never have thought of you. She's happy here. Happy in her work and in her marriage.'

'And secure?' asked Lucy. 'I mean, the mission will remain?'

'For as long as it's God's will. Nothing in China is predictable, Mrs Hardie. But in these country areas it's change that meets most resistance. We're an accepted part of the community, although a foreign one. We're no longer called Child-eaters. Instead, children are brought to us to heal.'

'I saw one carried in today. By your porter. Her husband. They looked at each other – yes, you're right to say that there's love between them.'

For a long time she was silent. What Dr Mackenzie had

320

said was what she had expected to hear, although in her heart she had hoped that he might encourage a reunion between mother and daughter. She knew that he was right, but the knowledge was hard to bear.

'If I'm to leave her again, I suppose I shouldn't even tell her who I am.'

'I think that must follow. I realize how difficult it is for you, Mrs Hardie.'

'May I send her a little money from time to time? Not as her mother, but in thanks for her care for my husband. Just so that she may have some extra comforts.'

'I doubt whether the word comfort is part of her vocabulary,' Dr Mackenzie said. 'The mission provides all her needs – food, clothes, lodging – and it won't have occurred to her to want anything else. If you feel a need to give money, I'd suggest that it should be to the society. You could request that it should be used specifically for this mission. It would help to make sure that she remained in familiar surroundings.'

Lucy shook her head. 'I must have some more personal link than that. Certainly I'll give money to your society. But – I could ask her to care for my husband's grave. She won't think that an out-of-the-way request, since she nursed him and knows that I can't stay to look after it myself. I'd like to have a proper headstone made. I could ask her to plant flowers round the spot and then I could give her a present. It would comfort me to think of my daughter tending her father's grave, even though she'll never know.'

'She'll do it out of kindness if she realizes what it would mean to you. But of course you may make her a present if you wish. It's not for me to say what you should do.'

'May I stay here for a few days while the headstone is cut?'

321

'My dear Mrs Hardie, for as long as you like. Visitors from home are rare birds, and always welcome.'

Lucy's mind was set at rest by the definiteness of her decision. In the days which followed she spent much of her time unobtrusively sketching her daughter as she went about her hospital duties and also requested a formal sitting for a watercolour portrait.

The last painting she did during her stay was of Gordon's grave. She had drawn out a simple inscription for Kenneth to carve on the headboard, selecting for the man who had never wanted to be a vintner the description he would have chosen for himself:

GORDON JOHN HARDIE

explorer

1860 – 1915

While Kenneth, ready for departure, watched their luggage being loaded on to the horses he had hired, Lucy paid one final visit to the spot. Chung Ru Mai and her husband had already planted roses and azaleas and stood nearby, hoping for approval.

With a grateful smile she bowed to the hospital porter, her son-in-law. Unable to restrain herself, she took the nurse into her arms.

'I love you, Rachel,' she said, knowing that the words would not be understood. Then, sadly, she turned to leave. It was unlikely that she would ever return to China to re-visit her long-lost daughter. She could never see her husband again and before long must say goodbye to Kenneth, her wandering son. This journey had been a strange interlude, which now was coming to an end. Within six months or so she would be back in Greystones with her other daughter, picking up the threads of a familiar life in which nothing would have changed.

'Are you ready to go, Mother?' called Kenneth from the gate of the compound; and Lucy nodded her head.

7

There seemed to be few rules in the community to which
Philip had retreated after his discharge from hospital.
Nevertheless, his family had been made aware that visits
were best confined to certain dates. Boxing Day was one
of these, and Easter Monday another; whilst a whole week
in late summer was designated Community Week, when
personal visitors as well as local villagers were invited to
help themselves to fruit and vegetables grown on the
estate. Grace, making the journey without appointment
on a mild day in November 1920, had no idea whether she
would be allowed to see her brother or would be turned
away.

Cabs, like servants, were a luxury which she could no
longer afford. She left the railway station on foot, her long
legs striding out to cover the six miles as quickly as possible.
But she had walked less than a mile when a horse-drawn
cart turned out of a side lane and pulled up beside her, its
driver indicating that she should climb aboard.

He was one of the brothers. All the villagers called them
that, although the men themselves used only each other's
Christian names. Grace found the word appropriate.
Although they did not belong to any religious order, they
had discovered – as presumably had the earliest monks
and friars – that a habit was comfortable to wear in all
weathers and could be sewn by themselves from the wool
of their own sheep, spun and dyed and woven on their
own premises.

There was no rule enjoining silence, yet Philip was not
the only one of them who avoided speech. Knowing this,

324

Grace made no attempt at conversation, but merely smiled gratefully when they arrived at their destination. She made her way up the steps and under the portico of the Georgian house and sat down to wait on a bench in the hall. The driver of the cart would make her arrival known to someone; or else, sooner or later, she would be noticed.

Either Andrew or George would appear. They were the only ones who were able to converse in a normal way, without having to force themselves to speak. Had the community recognized any kind of ranking within itself, Andrew and George would have been the heads of staff.

Andrew, as far as Grace was aware, was the only ordained churchman in the group. He had spent his working life as a medical missionary, coming out of retirement to become the chaplain of a military hospital. It was there, in 1916, that he realized the need for a peaceful retreat in which men whose lives had been shattered could recuperate at their own pace.

Taking it for granted that the Lord would provide, he had perhaps not been surprised to receive, a few weeks later, a letter from an old friend. Colonel George Trafford, already a widower, had just received news of the death in action of the last of his four sons. With no remaining heir and no further interest in life, he was looking for a worthwhile charity to take over his house and estate while allowing him to live quietly in the lodge until his own death.

Bereavement was George's war wound, as debilitating as anything suffered by the men whom Andrew brought to live in his house and work his land; but he continued to administer the estate in the interests of the group, and this work had provided a speedier cure for him than for the others. The two elderly men together shouldered all the responsibilities for which the ex-servicemen did not yet feel ready – and that, today, included dealing with the young woman who was sitting in the hall with her head buried in her hands as though she were on the verge of tears.

It was Andrew, tall and bearded, who emerged from the office. He smiled and held out both hands in welcome. Grace jumped to her feet.

'I'm Philip's sister.'

'Yes, of course; I remember you, Miss Hardie.'

'I need him back at home. He has your company here, but I'm all alone.'

She paused, considering what she had just said. It was the truth, and yet not completely true. Any loneliness she might feel would only be temporary, for sooner or later her mother would return from China. And in fact she was not lonely in an ordinary sense. She would have been content with her own company had she not been confronted with the problem of maintaining Greystones. It was not simply companionship that she was hoping for, but support. Was that too much to expect?

She looked up at Andrew. 'Will you let him go?' she asked.

Andrew looked at her gravely. 'We've never held him. He's always been as free to leave as he is today. Tell him your problem and he'll make his own decision.'

'Yes, but –' Why was she about to argue against her own interests? It must have been something in Andrew's calm, sympathetic character which made her wonder whether she was being selfish. 'I don't want to say anything that will upset him. I mean, if he feels an obligation to come and yet knows that he isn't well enough, or ready –'

Andrew's eyes approved of her qualms before considering them. 'He's well enough to be asked,' was the verdict. 'And well enough to judge for himself whether he could cope with any demands you'd be making of him. I wouldn't like to guess what he'd decide. But this may be the right moment for him to consider whether he should take up his own life again. I ought to add that in my opinion he will always want quietness. A lack of stress. Good air. A country life.'

'He'd have all that at home.'

'Then let's go and find him. I'll show you where he's working and leave you to talk.' But outside the house Andrew hesitated for a moment. 'There's something I'd like to show you first of all,' he said.

He led the way round the side of the square house. The original garden area had been formally laid out in terraces and parterres; roses and herbs were still growing in the elaborate patterns which had been outlined by gravel paths two hundred years earlier. But Grace could see that within recent years the new residents had been allowed to make private gardens for themselves in the pleasure grounds. It was to one of these that Andrew now took her.

'Philip designed this, and dug it out, and planted it,' he said.

'Is he strong enough to dig?' She was surprised.

'His muscles are strong. He can do anything that doesn't need sudden spurts of energy. He's learned how to take things steadily and regulate his breathing to keep pace with the effort. But I didn't bring you here to make that particular point.'

He waited silently as she studied Philip's garden and considered the implications of what she saw. The design was an extraordinary one. A wide stretch of grass gradually narrowed as it led further and further into what appeared at first sight to be a maze of flower beds. But it was not a true maze, for there was only the one path which circled and doubled back on itself and spiralled inwards before ending at last in a circle of lawn. Around this had been planted young yew trees which would eventually grow into a high wall.

Grace might have found the place disturbing, but instead felt comforted, even relieved.

'After Philip was gassed,' she said, 'I made a sort of – of object. It was exactly this kind of shape – although quite different, of course, going upwards instead of on the ground.'

She paused, checking what seemed to be an incoherent rambling. 'What I mean is that when I saw Philip in hospital for the first time I knew what he was feeling. I could understand the hurt that had been done to his mind as well as his body. I still understand that. If he comes home with me, I shan't badger him with questions. I shall tell him my worries, because that's what I need, someone to talk to; but I shan't expect him to solve them. He can make a garden for himself at Greystones as well. I know that his wound is deep inside. I'll never ask more of him than he's able to give.'

'Good. Tell him that. And tell him, as well, that he can come back here whenever he likes, for as long as he likes. Let's go this way.'

They retraced their steps to the edge of the grassy spiral and then moved towards a walled garden even larger than the one at Greystones.

'Philip has invented a new fruit,' Andrew told her as they walked. 'A cross between a blackberry and a raspberry, with no thorns. Last year there was only the first trial crop, but this year he picked enough to experiment in making jam and wine. He's just planting out cuttings to increase the stock. He seems to have an instinct for what can and can't be done in the garden. Here he is. Come back to the house afterwards and tell me what has been decided.' He left her to go through the arched entrance of the walled garden alone.

Philip was on his knees, using his fingers to press the cuttings into the ground and tuck the earth around them.

He looked up as she approached. There was a peacefulness about his smile of welcome which dispelled Grace's misgivings. At some point in the past two years he had come to terms with himself. 'Can I help with anything?' she asked.

Without speaking, Philip produced a small garden trowel from the pocket of his habit and indicated a line parallel to his own where more cuttings should be planted. Grace set to work; and as she worked, she talked. Without asking any questions, without pausing for any comment, she told him all she had recently learned, starting with the parlous state of The House of Hardie and David's plans to mortgage Greystones.

Philip showed surprise when she spoke of Felix, straightening himself to look questioningly at his sister. She told him about her visit but was not ready – perhaps she would never be ready – to confess her own responsibility in the matter.

'I've been worried about it all,' she said at last. 'Wondering whether I'm being selfish – whether I owe a duty to the business, and what the right thing to do is. But now I've stopped worrying, because I've made up my mind. I'm going to make Greystones earn its keep, so that I needn't ever ask David for money. And if he won't take over the bills for Felix, then I shall earn enough for that as well. Even if I have to go out to work. I'm an experienced shop assistant after all! But I think the land will provide enough.'

Giving a slight nod, Philip began to tread down the earth beside his row of cuttings. With everything said that she had come to say, Grace watched without speaking for a few moments.

'I need company,' she admitted at last. 'Someone to talk to. Someone to stop me becoming the sort of old maid who chatters to canaries. Besides, Mother's going to get a terrible shock when she comes home and finds the servants gone and no money for quite ordinary things. I'd like to feel that I have your support.' She laughed. 'There's a vacancy for an unpaid market gardener, too. Will you come home, Philip? To do whatever you like, but just to be there. Please.'

So long was the silence that she could hardly endure it. But the request was not a trivial one; she had known that he would have to consider it very carefully. When at last he looked up, the sound of his voice, which she had not heard since he was wounded, amazed her by being unchanged, except for the effort needed to control his breathing.

'Three days,' he said. 'Will you allow me three days?'

'Oh, Philip!' She had been so determined to pursue her choice of life alone if necessary that only now did she recognize how devastating a refusal on her brother's part would have been. She flung herself into his arms, half crying – but almost at once began to laugh, so incongruous did it seem to embrace a man who looked like a monk.

Philip's eyes were laughing as well, although he said nothing more. It came as a second relief to understand that she could help him almost as much as he would help her. He had always been her favourite brother: the quietest and kindest of the boys. They would live separately and yet together in the house which each of them loved. Everything would be all right.

PART EIGHT

Mistress of Greystones

1927

1

On the morning of her thirtieth birthday, in June 1927, Grace Hardie rose early. Splashing her face with cold water, she pulled on a pair of khaki socks which had once belonged to one of her brothers, and then dressed quickly in the dark blue workman's overalls which could be called her gardening clothes or her working clothes or simply her everyday clothes. Although it was a Sunday, there would be no time for morning service today.

In a few hours there was to be a family luncheon party. Jay, still unmarried, would make the journey from London alone, but David would be bringing his wife and children. Midge and Will had only a short distance to travel from their house in North Oxford. Before they all arrived at noon Grace would dress herself as befitted a hostess, but the day must start with its ordinary working routine. There was no need to be tidy yet.

Her tower bedroom contained no mirror. As she ran a comb through her hair, she walked from window to window looking out; inspecting her domain.

'Lovely day.'

She made the comment aloud without being aware of it. Had she realized how often she talked to herself, it would not have worried her. Other people did the same, surely. For different reasons the three inhabitants of Greystones – Grace and her mother and brother – rarely indulged in social conversation. Grace used her own voice to break the silence and thought nothing of it.

Carrying her flat house shoes in her hand, she went to the garden room which had once been the schoolroom.

Her wellingtons perched upside down on the handles of the croquet mallets which stood, chipped and peeling, in their rack. Until a few months earlier she had always left the boots where they fell after she kicked them off. But one morning, as she worked her feet into the tight, clammy rubber, her heel shot down with such force that it squashed dead a nesting mouse.

Disposal of the corpse had brought on one of the asthmatic attacks from which nowadays she suffered only rarely. She remembered them as recurring events in her childhood, when no one realized what they were, assuming her simply to be 'chesty'. Only gradually had various conditions been recognized as triggering her attacks: the pollen of particular trees, certain kinds of fog, cats, horses, anxiety, anger. Adding mice and murder to this list, she now took care to hang the boots mouth downwards.

Her first tasks of the day were the usual ones of feeding the hens and pigs. Philip, who always rose at five, would already have milked the goats. Returning to the garden room, she picked up a trug and a pair of secateurs, laughing aloud at the picture she must present.

Cutting flowers was one of the few household tasks which a lady might perform for herself without loss of dignity. She remembered being told that twenty years earlier by her mother, who even after the birth of so many children was still slender then; golden-haired, tall and graceful as she snipped at roses.

No one would ever take Grace, in her boots and overalls, to be the lady of the house. The short layered style into which Philip trimmed her black hair was, as it happened, currently in vogue, and so was her slim, straight figure; but Grace neither knew nor cared what was 'in' or 'out' in the world of fashion. Nevertheless, she retained a sense of the ridiculous. A costume which was acceptable, even sensible, for her working hours was inappropriate for the gathering of roses.

She stepped into the garden and looked up at the clear midsummer sky. The heatwave of the past few days seemed set to continue; but that did not persuade her to change her plans and set out a picnic instead of a formal luncheon.

During the past few days she had cleaned and polished the dining room and drawing room until the mahogany shone like glass and carpets and cushions gave off a delicate perfume of rose water. It was no business of David's if the three permanent occupants of Greystones ate their meals as a rule at the scrubbed kitchen table and retired in the evenings each to a separate room. More than six years had passed since he had last been invited to visit his old home. She did not intend to give him the satisfaction of discovering the shambles which perhaps he expected.

David had never forgiven his sister for her refusal to offer Greystones as a sacrifice to The House of Hardie. Grace for her part had been slow to abandon a suspicion that without her opposition he would not merely have mortgaged it but allowed it to be sold. She had been angry, too, at what she saw as his spitefulness in cutting off funds from their mother as well as herself.

But the passing of time and a successful survival had mellowed her attitude. Since her mother appeared to feel no bitterness, why should she? What *did* upset Lucy Hardie was the coldness between two of her children. So today's family reunion represented a gesture of reconciliation – but Grace was determined that it should be seen to come from strength. That was why the table was already set with silver and crystal which shone and sparkled as if there were still a staff of eight to wash and polish. Only the great rose bowl and the six posy horns were waiting to be filled.

Breathing deeply to fill her lungs in the clear air, she set off across the terrace, over the lawn and into the serpentine garden, striding to its further boundary for the sake of the exercise. She would pick the flowers on the more meandering course of her return to the house.

The serpentine garden was Philip's self-indulgence. In the three acres of the walled garden, fruit and vegetables grew, as they had always grown, in rows of military straightness. But just as he had created a personal garden in the community from which Grace had enticed him, so too at Greystones he had felt the same need to carve out a shape from the ground – very much as Grace herself carved wood or stone.

The pattern here was not a tight spiral but a series of gentle curves which swelled and closed so that almost every step along the grass revealed a different view of the shrubberies which edged it. Grace had contributed to the design by bringing some of her larger carved shapes out of the studio to stand in alcoves framed by leaves and, indeed, had designed some of the carvings specifically for their settings.

Returning to the house with her trug basket laden, she plunged the flowers into a stone sink full of water in one of the sculleries. In the spacious days of the previous century, when Greystones was designed, separate rooms were provided for all the duties of the servants, as well as for the pleasures of their employers.

Philip came in at the same moment carrying baskets full of all the vegetables they would need. Some he had forced in a hot bed to be sure of having them ready in June; whilst several crowns of asparagus had been held back to prolong their season. He had already, earlier in the morning, brought in the milk and enough strawberries to feed the whole family. The chickens had been killed and plucked three days before, and the goat cheese had been maturing for several weeks.

Lucy Hardie, meanwhile, was preparing breakfast. Six

years earlier, when she returned from China, she was certainly startled and probably dismayed to discover what had happened to Greystones in her absence, but she accepted the situation without making more than one attempt to heal her daughter's quarrel with David. Confirming that the house had always been Grace's property, she asked with an extraordinary humility whether she might continue to live in it.

Grace had been worried about her mother at that time, and would almost have preferred her to react to the changed situation with indignation. Instead, she had seemed apathetic, making no complaint as she took on her own shoulders some of the duties which always before had been performed by servants. Her only positive action was a command to David that The House of Hardie must pay the increased fees for his brother Felix. The expense was not to be borne by Grace alone.

Under the terms of Gordon Hardie's will, his widow was entitled to a share of the business profits: but out of what he claimed to be proper caution, David had contrived that there should be no profits. Will had to be paid a better salary, and he himself was entitled to fees for the hours he had to spend on the business. Interest must be paid on the loan made necessary by Grace's intransigence. All the takings after this were spent on new stock – most of which, in the nature of a vintner's business, would not be ready for sale for several years. And now a recession was affecting sales. There was always, it seemed, some reason why his mother, who had refused to take his side, should receive not a penny from what had once provided the livelihood of the whole family.

Whether or not Lucy thought that she was being unkindly treated, she did not complain. For the first few months after returning she spent most of her time in the studio, and the walls of the boudoir which had become her

337

drawing room were now covered with the paintings she produced in this period.

There were water colours of her husband's grave in China, with a background of distant mountains. There was a large and carefully worked picture of the nurse who had cared for Gordon Hardie before his death. Grace thought this unsuccessful, because the woman somehow failed to look Chinese. A less sombre group of paintings, done from memory, depicted scenes from Lucy's honeymoon: the gorges of the Yangtse River, a mule train, a flimsy bridge over a river and, in pride of place, a sketch of Gordon Hardie as a young man, looking in amazement at a valley carpeted with gold and white lilies.

The therapy of painting had drawn Lucy at last out of her depression and into a cheerful interest in Grace's efforts to live off the Greystones estate. In those early days their only source of cash was Philip's disability pension, and there were some lean times before they mastered the arts of storing and preserving enough food to last through the winter. Right from the start, however, they had enjoyed the co-operation of the former head gardener. Rather than lose his cottage as well as his employment, Frith had agreed to an arrangement under which he found his own wages by keeping some of the food which he grew on the Greystones land and selling it in the city.

Gradually Lucy had developed her own contributions to the search for income. She painted water colours of the Oxford colleges and their gardens, and these were sold for her by the shop which supplied her materials. The farmer who rented the sloping meadow as grazing for his sheep allowed her to run two ewes of her own with his flock, and she taught herself to spin and dye and weave their wool. Neatness with the needle was one of the few practical talents encouraged in a daughter of the aristocracy, and

338

Lucy made the clothes for all three members of the household. In addition, she had learned to cook.

'How did we ever put up with overcooked meat and vegetables for so many years?' she would ask in amazement as, after a few disasters, she began to produce far tastier meals than anything that Mrs Charles had ever sent to the table. And whenever Grace expressed the hope that she was not becoming tired or overworked, she recalled the hours she had once devoted to giving instructions and sorting out the problems of the servants' hall. It might be eccentric to live without a domestic staff, but there was freedom in eccentricity.

Today, as it happened, there was to be help in the house. The inclusion of David and his family in the birthday celebration was not intended to elicit pity for their poverty but to show that they could manage comfortably without his help. The three of them had planned and prepared the menu for a feast. So in order that they could enjoy it in a gracious manner as host and hostesses, Lucy had asked Mrs Frith to serve and clear the meal.

She arrived early, accompanied by her eldest granddaughter.

'Andy's staying with us,' she explained cheerfully to Grace. 'The maddymoselle –' she had never referred to his wife as anything else – 'knows better than to show her face. But he brought his twelve-year-old, Jeanette, to meet us this time. She can't understand a word I say or say a word I can understand, but she'll be handy enough at podding the peas and broad beans and scraping the new potatoes.'

'Twelve years old!' exclaimed Grace. Was this then the child whose birth destroyed Grace's first love affair? Once upon a time she would have turned away, but time had healed the wound. 'I haven't seen Andy for years,' she said to Mrs Frith. 'Ask him to come up tomorrow and say hello?'

339

Smiling at Jeanette, she spoke to her in French and was rewarded with a smile. She was not an attractive girl, and there seemed no trace of Andy in her dark hair and sharp features. If I'd married Andy, thought Grace, what sort of daughter would I have had? She only just managed to restrain herself from asking the question out loud.

Curiously, the query failed to arouse her interest. It came as a new thought that she did not particularly like children and had no wish at all to have any of her own. There was excitement in independence. To be tied by the demands of babies and young children must be an unbearable imposition.

Had she married, she would have raised a family as a matter of course and might never have discovered the pleasures of being her own mistress. Not for the first time, she recognized how her own mother's life had been shaped by the burden of child-bearing and child-raising. What a fortunate escape she had had herself!

When everything that could be done in advance was ready, she went upstairs to dress. The frock she put on had been made by her mother out of a length of silk bought in Shanghai. Jay and Aunt Midge would recognize it as being five years old, but David and Sheila would never have seen it before. Its dropped waist flattered her slim figure, the pleated hem shimmered in the sunlight and the jewelled colours of the fabric made a dramatic contrast with her pale skin. Carefully she eased her feet into her only silk stockings and a pair of patent leather shoes borrowed from her mother.

'Fancy dress party!' she exclaimed aloud to herself and laughed with amusement. Walking with care, because she was unused to high heels, she made her way down the spiral staircase of the tower.

Her mother and Philip were still upstairs, dressing themselves for the occasion, but Mrs Frith was on duty to open the front door and announce the visitors. Grace stood for a moment in the doorway of the drawing room, stroking her silk dress with her fingers. Then she sat down to wait: the mistress of Greystones, ready to receive her guests.

2

'To Grace!'

Midge and Will Witney had brought vintage champagne as a birthday gift, and it was Will who proposed the birthday toast at the end of a magnificent meal.

Except for the youngest of David's three children, imprisoned in the high chair which had last been used by Jay, they all stood up, murmuring congratulations. Only David showed by an extra comment that the rift between them had still not quite healed. 'Not that I suppose you'll ever admit to being thirty, Grace. I've noticed that young women, especially spinsters, seem to remain twenty-nine for quite a long time.' He lifted his glass again and smiled as though this would take the sting out of his words.

Grace stared at him for a moment before tucking the remark away at the back of her mind, to be considered later. 'Shall we have coffee on the terrace?' she said. 'And then, who would like a game of croquet?'

After the game Midge and Will were happy to sit with Lucy in the sunshine and Sheila took little Peter upstairs for a rest. Grace and Jay accepted David's suggestion of a walk in the grounds, to show his elder children, John and Lilian, where he had played as a boy.

'There were no sheep in the meadow then,' he told them. 'We used to play football here, and cricket. That was when we were older, and had started school. When we were young, we were allowed to run wild in the wood and by the stream.'

He showed the way and the children ran on ahead, shouting with pleasure.

'What did you play here?' asked John as they entered the wood. It was tidier now than in the old days, because Philip chopped any fallen or dead wood to feed the log fires in the house. Even in her best silk stockings, Grace was willing to accompany them.

'All sorts of things,' David told the eight-year-old. 'Hide and seek, of course. And we had bows and arrows. Sometimes we played Robin Hood. Once, I remember, we pretended to have a tiger hunt and got a bit carried away. We killed a cat – Aunt Grace's cat.' He looked around and recognized the two pointed ears of slate which marked Pepper's grave. 'This is where it's buried. It was a very sad accident. A great pity.'

He looked straight at Grace, who was too astonished to react. Never once in the twenty-four years since Pepper's death had David made any reference to it. Was this, at long last, an attempt at an apology? But even now he had said 'We', not 'I'.

Without listening any more to the words, she watched the children questioning their father about the cat. Choosing the two pieces of slate had represented her first realization that shapes were important and could even represent ideas. At the age of six she could not have expressed her thoughts so pretentiously; but it was true, all the same, that Pepper's death had introduced her to the most important activity in her life. Perhaps she ought really to be grateful to David!

The same occasion, besides causing a still unhealed rift between herself and David, had changed the course of Kenneth's life. Or had it merely brought to the surface a side of his character which would have revealed itself sooner or later? Kenneth's compassion, like Frank's talent for leadership, Jay's love of pretence and her own feeling for form, seemed all to have sprung from a single moment of drama, but the seeds must already

343

have been sown before the accident of Pepper's death.

'Penny for your thoughts,' said Jay, handsome and self-assured as he walked beside her.

'I was thinking about you.' She smiled and took his arm, turning back towards the house. 'Tell me about your new part.'

'Not so much a part as a series of turns. Nothing in a revue lasts more than about three minutes. But I have got one recurring act as an old man of eighty. A kind of running joke. Ridiculous, isn't it? A fine upstanding youth like me, perfect material for juvenile leads, playing grandfather.' His back hunched, his hands began to tremble and an invisible walking stick supported his shuffling steps. 'But that,' he said in a quavering old man's voice, 'can't be what you were thinking about.'

'No. I was remembering – it was the day you first told me that you wanted to be an actor. That you *were* an actor, whether or not you ever got on stage to prove it. You had a great theory, I remember. Happiness comes when what you do is the expression of what you are. Or something like that.'

'I was a very perceptive little boy, though I say it myself.' Jay straightened up and the eighty-year-old disappeared. 'The theory stands the test of time. Though who'd have guessed then that what was lurking in *you* was the soul of a farmer.'

'No!' protested Grace, astonished that he should see her so wrongly.

'But you're happy. I can see it. Grace Hardie, spinster of this parish; a horny-handed daughter of toil and happy with it. Just remember, though, that it's only in fairy stories that anyone lives happily ever after. In real life, a happy ending only lasts until tomorrow.'

'For you, perhaps.' Grace had been told often enough by her brother that acting was an insecure profession. But she was in no mood to argue. She might have explained to him

344

her amazement that everything which had happened in her life seemed designed to point her in a single direction. But part of her satisfaction lay in the private nature of her work, and the fact that no one guessed how much it meant to her; so she ignored any discussion of happiness and thought about his other point instead.

'It's odd, this spinster business,' she said. 'It's a word which sounds as though everyone looks down on you. As though you've somehow failed in life. Nobody but a heartless brother would ever dare to use such a word in my hearing. Why is it so different from "bachelor", d'you think? Why are spinsters always pitied and bachelors always envied?'

'A bachelor gay am I!' Jay was never one to miss a cue and would have performed the complete song had his sister not shaken him into silence.

'I was thinking about that earlier, when Aunt Midge arrived,' she went on. 'When I was a girl – when Aunt Midge was a headmistress – I admired her enormously. To go to university and pass all those examinations and have such an important job and earn money and be in charge of her own life – if that was being a spinster, then I only wished that I had the talent to be a spinster as well. But since her marriage – well, she's somehow become just an ordinary person. Still great fun to be with and talk to; but there's nothing special about her any longer. Don't you feel that?'

'It's just that she's old now.' To Jay, anyone over forty was old, and his aunt was sixty-two. 'Just as you are, pretty well. Thirty.'

'Thank you so much for cheering me up,' said Grace, but she laughed as merrily as her brother. Jay was quite right. She was happy.

That evening, after the visitors had gone and the silver had been put back into its felt bags and locked away, Philip and his mother both went early to bed. It was not just the exertions of the day which had tired them, but the society; for they were not used to so much conversation. Grace, though, was too restless to sleep. She let herself quietly out of the house and for a second time that day made her way through Philip's garden.

This time, with no flowers to cut, she could lift her eyes to the great house higher up the hill instead of looking for the most perfect roses. No lights burned in its windows, and the rising slope behind it masked part of its outline, but there was sufficient moonlight to show the silhouette of Grace's tower.

By now she knew the reason why the tower – and, indeed, the whole house – had been built. Her mother, on returning from China, had willingly answered questions, describing the anxiety which an elderly aristocrat had once felt for a bright-eyed but asthmatic child.

'Thank you, great-grandfather,' said Grace aloud. He had wondered what would become of her, but had not lived to find out.

'A sort of farmer indeed!' she exclaimed. Had Jay never understood that all the ways in which she and Philip earned money from the land had never been more than expedients which would allow them to go on living in the house they loved? They had done well enough, although the top storey, where the servants had once slept, was now damp and the whole building needed redecoration. At least their success gave them the freedom to lead the lives they wanted to lead. Philip had inherited his father's passion for breeding new plants, whilst Grace herself . . . She smiled in contentment and began to walk back up the serpentine way, this time pausing to touch each of her carvings in turn.

Reaching the house, she groped her way towards the studio and lit one of the five lanterns which were suspended in a circle round her bench. Slipping off her silk dress and stockings, so that they should not spoil, she began to stroke the piece of polished walnut on which she had been working for the past week. Her fingers moved lightly over the parts which were already taking form, and pressed harder where the wood must be cut away.

'Just ten minutes!' she said, picking up a fluter and setting to work. Without being aware of it, she continued to talk – either to herself or to the walnut – as the shavings began to fall to the ground.

'A sort of farmer!' Jay's phrase still amused her. Still speaking aloud, she set him right. 'Grace Hardie, spinster and carver of shapes.'

Jay had been right to recognize that she was happy, but wrong to fear that tomorrow, or any of the days after tomorrow, would bring any surprises to disturb her. She was a princess in a palace, with no wish to be disturbed by any Prince Charming; and she was living happily ever after.